# IDOLMAKER

The Only In Tokyo Mysteries

NIGHTSHADE

FALLEN ANGEL

IDOLMAKER

PAINTED DOLL

Jonelle Patrick

# IDOLMAKER

An Only In Tokyo Mystery

**BANCROFT & GREENE, PUBLISHERS LLC** Published by Bancroft & Greene, Publishers LLC, 80 Santa Paula Avenue, San Francisco, CA 94127 USA

This is a work of fiction. Names, characters, places, and incidents either are the product of the author's imagination or are used fictitiously, and any resemblance to actual persons, living or dead, business establishments, events, or locales is entirely coincidental. The publisher does not have control over and does not have any responsibility for author or third-party websites or their content.

IDOLMAKER

A Bancroft & Greene book / published by arrangement with the author

PUBLISHING HISTORY Penguin/InterMix ebook edition / September 2013; Bancroft & Greene print edition / May 2016

Copyright © 2016 by Jonelle Patrick. Excerpt from *Painted Doll* copyright © 2016 by Jonelle Patrick. All images copyright © 2016 by Jonelle Patrick.

All rights reserved. No part of this book may be reproduced, scanned, or distributed in any printed or electronic form without permission. Please do not participate in or encourage piracy of copyrighted materials in violation of the author's rights. Purchase only authorized editions. For information, address: Bancroft & Greene, Publishers LLC, 80 Santa Paula Avenue, San Francisco, CA 94127 USA

Library of Congress Control Number: 2016908433

ISBN-10: 0-9975709-2-X
ISBN-13: 978-0-9975709-2-2

# Idolmaker

Thursday, November 14

•

5:30 p.m.

He picked up the top photo, and disgust with his fellow man welled up inside the priest like a cold winter tide. At least it was a Polaroid, so there were no copies.

Yano rose and surveyed the eight-mat *tatami* room that had served thirteen generations of head priests before him as living room, dining room, and study. The furnishings were spare—a floor lamp with a rice-paper shade that had been mended more than once, a stack of well-worn floor cushions, bookshelves stuffed with everything from Basho's poetry to postcards from Hokkaido. In one corner near the ceiling, an intricately pieced wooden shrine sat on a shelf, festooned with crisp zigzag paper charms and fresh offerings of sake, salt, and *sakaki* leaves. A low *kotatsu* table draped with an indigo-dyed quilt sat before the window, the black cord from its heater snaking over the grass mats to an outlet behind the bookshelves.

The cold tea in the bottom of two cups atop the table had been steaming half an hour ago when Head Priest Yano had sat looking out on the moss garden, listening to his visitor tell him a terrible secret and show him proof of something he'd have been happier not knowing about. The water in the cracked green Oribe teapot had grown cold as together they tried to peer down the many paths that led into the future.

Yano knelt and dealt the stack of Polaroids out onto the

table like a game of solitaire. Eleven pictures, eleven lives damaged. He sighed. Where should he hide the dreadful things his visitor had given him for safekeeping? It would be terrible if anyone found them, and Head Priest Yano knew it was only a matter of time before the man they'd been stolen from came looking.

It would be smart not to keep them all in the same place.

He set aside the one he'd been told would launch the biggest firestorm of scandal if it ever became public, and dropped it into the sleeve of his robe.

Gathering up the rest of the Polaroids, he slid them into the envelope that had been glued inside his visitor's photo album. The too-thick packet bulged beneath the back cover, but he pinched it shut as he carried it to the kitchen and hid it in the drawer he'd emptied, arranging a stack of dishtowels on top.

Then he returned to the main room and opened the cupboard where his vestments were kept. Even someone going through his house with a fine-toothed comb would never think to look for an unspeakable Polaroid hidden in the sleeve of the robe a head priest wore only for weddings.

Friday, December 20

•

*11:00 A.M.*

Something old: the priceless three-layered wedding kimono that had been worn by six generations of Mitsuyama brides.

Something new: the golden zori sandals that had been custom-made for Yumi Hata's size 8 feet.

Something borrowed: the elaborate Edo-style wig topped with a white silk hood to cover the horns Japanese women supposedly grew the moment they became wives.

Something blue . . . Yumi winced as she stepped up to ring the doorbell at the Mitsuyama family compound in Hiroo. Something black and blue was more like it. She'd ignored the empty seats on the train all the way across town this morning because it hurt too much to sit down.

Why, oh why, had she let herself be talked into going to the Mad Hatter last night? Even though Coco had phrased it tragically as, "your last chance to have fun before your partying days are O-V-E-R," she should have known that her best friend wouldn't let her go home before she'd abandoned all her best intentions.

When Yumi finally dragged Coco out of the Hatter at 1:00 a.m.—both of them on the wrong side of too many White Rabbits—they'd been lured into Yoyogi Park by the nearly full moon and the sound of an all-night Brazilian dance party. But after they'd sneaked past the gate, they stopped in their tracks before they got to the revelers, transfixed by the sight of lights bobbing midair between two distant trees. Drawing closer, they discovered that in fact it was two young men in Patagonia parkas, festooned with glow-rings, jumping and pirouetting on a strap stretched taut about two feet off the ground between two trees. "Come try it," called the slackliner, whose beautiful smile gleamed in the bright light of the full moon, taking a swig of Asahi Super Dry as he strolled along, a meter above the ground.

It had seemed like a good idea at the time.

Coco's eight-shot camera burst caught Yumi's expression mid-jump as it morphed from glee to horror. Her foot had strummed the line like a giant guitar string before she had landed bottom first on a knobby tree root. Coco had helped her hobble back to the Hatter, where the bartender had emptied his freezer to ice the offended region, but sitting down was not something Yumi wanted to do anytime soon.

She hoped Mrs. Mitsuyama wouldn't insist on serving her tea this morning in the *tatami*-floored room with the thin floor cushions. Yumi wasn't sure she could do it without wincing, and she couldn't let Ichiro's family guess she'd been out until all hours doing things that would be considered most unseemly for the future wife of their eldest son.

Yumi frowned at the doorbell and rang it again. Where was Mrs. Mitsuyama? Hadn't Ichiro told his mother Yumi would be stopping by this morning to pick up his *hanko* stamp so she could register their marriage at the Minato-ku Ward Office?

She called her fiancé. No answer. Scrolling to the number below it labeled "Ichiro's mother," she hesitated, gathering her courage.

He had asked her to marry him without consulting his parents. Even though they'd approved Ichiro's suggestion that she be added to the list of potential Mrs. Mitsuyamas and had been perfectly cordial at the matchmaking lunch that kicked off the *o-miai* process, they hadn't been happy when he chose her over the fifty-three more socially suitable candidates.

Since then, Mrs. Mitsuyama had been throwing up roadblocks at every stage of the wedding planning, and Yumi wouldn't have been at all surprised to discover that Ichiro had told her about the *hanko*, but she'd chosen to not be home, hoping that a miracle would permanently keep Yumi from checking this morning's chore off her to-do list. Tomorrow's wedding ceremony at the Tabata Shrine and the lavish reception planned at the Imperial Hotel afterward were really just window dressing—even without Ichiro's presence, they'd be legally married the minute their registered *hankos* were wetted with vermilion ink and stamped on the Ward Office documents this morning.

The gate behind her squeaked. She turned to see the Mitsuyamas' driver holding it open for Ichiro's mother, who was toting two bags of groceries from Meidi-ya, the ultra-premium grocery store where produce bore price tags suggesting it had been hand tended by members of the Imperial family.

"Yumi-*san*?" Ichiro's mother said, the gate squeaking again as it closed behind her.

"Let me help you with those," Yumi offered, meeting her halfway and taking the grocery bags.

"What are you doing all the way over here in Hiroo?" Mrs. Mitsuyama asked, fishing in her purse for her house keys.

"Didn't Ichiro tell you? I'm here to pick up his *hanko* so I can register our marriage at the Ward Office."

Mrs. Mitsuyama looked at her, surprised. "You're doing that this morning? Without him?"

"He said he had to work."

Displeasure flickered across her future mother-in-law's face before she fitted the key in the lock and pushed open the front door. Did she think Yumi was sneaking off to marry him behind his back? But all she said was, "Please come in."

Yumi exchanged her shoes for slippers and followed her down the hall with the groceries, setting them on the kitchen counter.

"Let me put these things away and we can have some tea before we figure out where Ichiro left his *hanko*," Mrs. Mitsuyama suggested.

She bustled around stowing her purchases, then lifted an Imari teapot from a shelf above the stove. After tossing in two scoops of loose tea, she filled it from the hot-water pot, added two cups, and arranged everything on a black lacquer tray.

"Shall we drink it in the tea room?" she asked.

Yumi managed not to groan as she lowered her bruised bottom onto the thin cushion that was the most luxurious seating tea ceremony participants were allowed. Mrs. Mitsuyama poured. They drank a few sips together and commented upon the final preparations for tomorrow's ceremony, then Ichiro's mother excused herself, asking Yumi to wait while she checked something.

Ignoring the scroll in the *tokonoma* alcove that was brushed with calligraphy so artful she couldn't read it, Yumi strained her ears to overhear the phone call her future mother-in-law was making in the next room.

"*Moshi-moshi*, this is Michiko Mitsuyama. I'm sorry to bother you suddenly like this while you're so busy, but could you tell me if today is a suitable day for my son and his bride to register their marriage? Yes, of course, I'll hold." Silence. Then, "Ah. Is that so?" More silence. "No, no, that's why I called you. It's better to know. It wouldn't do at all for them to do something so important on such an unlucky day. Thank you, Lily-san."

Ichiro's mother reappeared, apologizing for her absence, and topped up Yumi's cup.

"I'm so sorry," she said. "But as I suspected, today is *butsumetsu*, a very unlucky day for doing something as important as registering your marriage. I think you'd better wait until tomorrow, before the wedding."

"But . . . Head Priest Yano wants me to be there at ten to meet the kimono dresser, and the Ward Office isn't open before ten. Do you think Ichiro will be able to take care of it?"

"I'll call him."

Ichiro didn't pick up his mother's call, either.

"Don't worry," Yumi said, finishing her tea and shouldering her bag. "He must be in that meeting he told me about. I'll stop by his office on the way home and catch him when they break for lunch."

Twenty minutes later, Yumi rang the call button outside Mitsuyama Corporate Headquarters offices in Akasaka. The receptionist buzzed her in.

"Oh, hello again. Forget something?" she asked with a friendly smile. Then she peered at Yumi, confused. "Wait . . . perhaps I'm . . . did you just get your hair cut?"

Now it was Yumi's turn to be puzzled. "A week ago. Why?"

The receptionist colored. "Oh, I'm so sorry. You're not . . . You're Mitsuyama-san's fiancée, aren't you? Forgive me—there was a woman here earlier who . . ."

And suddenly Yumi knew who Ichiro was having his "important meeting" with. With a small forced laugh she said, "Don't worry—it happens a lot. There's a woman who works at . . . wait, you know, the meeting Ichiro had this morning . . . ?"

"The Asia Development Bank?" the receptionist supplied helpfully.

"That's right," Yumi said. "The Asia Development Bank."

Just as she feared. Why hadn't Ichiro told her his ex-girlfriend was in Tokyo?

She'd met Ami Watanabe just once, but that was all it took to discover that Ichiro's ex looked so much like Yumi, they could be sisters. Ichiro's parents had forbidden him to marry the business school girlfriend who looked Japanese but had been born and raised in America and couldn't speak Japanese well enough to order sushi, let alone move in the rarefied heights of Tokyo society that being a Mitsuyama wife required.

Ichiro had insisted he'd accepted their decision and had pursued Yumi as if he'd met her at a party instead of across the table at an *o-miai* luncheon. He'd convinced her that she was the one he'd set his heart on marrying.

But a month ago, Yumi had spotted him with Ami at a café on Omotesando Boulevard. When they met later at the wedding planner's office, he'd avoided mentioning who he'd spent the afternoon with, even though she'd asked who had helped him pick out the stylish new shirts in the fistful of shopping bags he'd been carrying. She told him she'd seen him with Ami, and he'd become angry, demanding to know what she was accusing him of. He hoped she wasn't the kind of pathetic, insecure woman who got jealous every time he had coffee with an old friend.

Since then, she'd been watching for signs he was cheating on her, that he was having second thoughts about getting married. But in the month since she'd spotted them together . . . nothing.

And now it was too late. Even if her suspicions were confirmed before their *hankos* were stamped on the registration form tomorrow, it would be impossible to stop this wedding without causing a train wreck that would leave her father's career and her family's social position in ruins.

Saturday, December 21

•

*1:00 p.m.*

Saturday morning dawned clear and cold. Even at midday, the shadows outside were still white with frost.

Yumi shivered as she took her place before the altar. The three layers of gold-embroidered silk weren't doing much to battle the chill in the Tabata Shrine sanctuary. Her fiancé adjusted the fan in the waistband of his formal silk *hakama*.

*Is Ichiro wishing it were Ami standing next to him, wearing the kimono embroidered in symbols of everlasting faithfulness?* Yumi wondered.

One of the altar candles fizzled and sent a string of sparks toward the impressive brass chandeliers that hung from the cedar beams overhead. On the altar, a length of willow-green brocade glinted with threads of pure gold, a subtle reminder that the gods of this shrine were known to favor weavers and dyers. Merchants and craftsmen—chief among them, the Tokyo branch of the Mitsuyama family—had been leaving offerings of costly fabric as well as cash for hundreds of years, keeping the shrine's gold leaf bright, the red lacquer gleaming, and the hereditary priest's family well fed.

Ichiro checked his watch and frowned, then looked back toward the sanctuary entrance.

Where was Head Priest Yano? His younger brother, Assistant Head Priest Makoto, stood near the door in green brocade vestments, head bent in urgent conversation with one of the shrine maidens. The girl slipped out in a swirl of white and scarlet robes.

The altar candles guttered as the door closed and Makoto turned toward the wedding party, hooded eyes dark above cheekbones smoothed by the candlelight, making him look younger than his forty-something years. Approaching Ichiro's father, he bowed deeply and said, "On behalf of my brother, my humblest apologies for the delay. With your permission, I'll go find out what's keeping him."

Ichiro's father's frown deepened as he nodded.

The door closed behind the priest and they were left alone with the two shrine maidens. Yumi's mother put on a nervous smile and whispered, "Now don't you worry, Yumi-*chan*. I'm sure Yano-*kannushi* be here shortly."

But the way she smoothed the chignon that didn't need smoothing and straightened the front of her kimono that didn't need straightening told Yumi that she was the one doing the worrying. Today she was clad in elegant black and gold with the crest of the Hata family freshly embroidered onto the silk in five places. The invitation to choose a kimono from the Mitsuyama Department Store's fabled collection had come from Ichiro's family. It was a gift of great generosity wrapped around a desire to minimize the vast social gulf between the Hatas and themselves. Tongues would wag in the upper reaches of Tokyo society if the bride's mother showed up wearing one of the fusty, unfashionable kimonos that had belonged to her husband's grandmother.

But Mrs. Hata wouldn't relax until the three cups of sake were safely drunk all around and the marriage registration stamped. She'd spent the better part of her married life fretting about her husband's stalled academic career and her daughter's regrettable attraction to foreign boyfriends, and was sure that defeat could be snatched from the jaws of victory even as they stood at the altar.

The fact that Yumi and Ichiro's marriage still hadn't

been registered at the Ward Office wasn't helping. Ichiro had returned Yumi's call yesterday while she was on her way home, apologizing for his mother's superstitious ways and promising to take care of the registration before the wedding. But when he'd called her at 9:30 this morning asking where her *hanko* was, she realized she'd forgotten to leave it with Mrs. Mitsuyama yesterday.

Yumi stole a glance at her fiancé, standing beside her in his stiff silk *hakama* and tasseled *haori* jacket with its five Mitsuyama crests. Ichiro wasn't tall or especially good-looking, but he was so confident of his place in the world that scores of women from very respectable families had been disappointed when his engagement to Yumi had been announced. Right now, his mind was elsewhere, a pensive look on his face. He caught her watching him and put on a smile.

Then—

He lurched at her and together they tumbled to the floor in the first shock of an earthquake. Yumi clung to Ichiro as the heavy lamps hanging from the rafters swayed overhead. The rumbling continued with occasional jolts, the thumps of shrine furnishings overturning accompanied by the sound of splintering glass. A sharp shock toppled the salt and sake offerings from the altar, spilling them across the floor. Yumi hid her face as another jolt was followed by a bang loud enough to be an explosion.

Ancient beams shrieked in protest as the quake went on and on, raining splinters and dirt on the wedding party, the altar, the *kami-sama's* wooden house.

Then, with a final lurch, it stopped. In the sudden stillness, dust swam in the air.

Yumi let go of her fiancé and cautiously raised her head. Was it really over? Or was there more to come? She looked around. The sanctuary was in shambles, debris was everywhere. How could so much be destroyed in such a short time?

"Are you all right?" Ichiro asked her, offering his hand as the two mothers and Yumi's father began to cautiously climb to their feet and brush the dust from their clothing.

"Just dirty," she said, looking down in dismay at the gold-embroidered silk, now dulled with dust. "I'm afraid we'll have to--"

A shrieking sound from above interrupted her as the bolts pinning the light fixture to the heavy wooden beams overhead began to give way.

Mrs. Mitsuyama screamed.

•

Tokyo Metropolitan Police Detective Kenji Nakamura crammed his hands into the pockets of his winter coat and hunched his shoulders against the biting December wind. Slouched on a bench across from the sanctuary at the Komagome Shrine, he regarded the thick white rope hanging over the offering box. It swayed slightly, shaken by the wind's ghostly hand, but the bell at the top remained silent. The *kami-samas'* attention wouldn't be attracted until there was a clink of a coin in the offering box and a firm tug from petitioners begging for success with exams, their job hunts, finding the girl of their dreams.

*Not that these lazy excuses for gods paid attention if they didn't feel like it,* Kenji thought bitterly. Despite the fact that he'd tossed a coin and rung the bell every time he passed, the *kami-sama* at the Komagome Shrine had ignored his pleas. Yumi Hata was getting married today. To someone else.

He swatted away the memory of how it felt to have her in his arms and pulled his phone from his pocket. 1:16. The Shinto ceremony attended only by immediate family was short. Was she already drinking the sake that would make her Mrs. Heir-To-The-Mitsuyama-Empire? Bitterness lodged in his throat. He wished he hadn't known the date and time, but

Yumi's friend Coco had texted him, flirtatiously asking if he'd be at the reception later. Needless to say, he'd disappointed her.

He would never throw a coin to these lazy gods again.

Suddenly the white rope above the offering box began to sway, shaken by a ghostly hand, the bell at the top clanging. Guiltily, he looked around. Had the powers-that-be been eavesdropping on his ungrateful thoughts?

Then he realized his bench was trembling. It wasn't the *kami-sama*, it was an earthquake.

A distant clap of thunder split the air, but it hadn't come from the sky. Somewhere nearby, glass shattered and Kenji felt a prickling of alarm as another big jolt rocked his bench. A flock of crows swirled into the sky, cawing, shocked from their roosts.

This one was bigger than usual.

Kenji glanced up, but only bare branches shivered overhead. Outside he was safe, but all around him as the shaking continued, he heard buildings groaning, alarms sounding, people shouting as they urged others to safety.

It was lasting a long time. Long enough to do real damage.

And then with a final shock, it stopped. There was a moment of silence, followed by the sound of a distant siren. Then another. And another.

Was it over? Kenji cautiously rose to his feet and pulled out his phone. In the aftermath of a quake he'd be needed, even though it was his day off. As he strode through the shrine gate, he called his father to make sure he was okay.

The conversation lasted less than a minute—as commanding officer at the Tabata neighborhood police box, Sergeant Nakamura already had his hands full with earthquake emergencies big and small.

Kenji scrolled to the Komagome Police Station number. Busy, already. Dropping his phone back in his pocket, he set off at a trot, becoming more alarmed as he saw how much broken glass was now littering the street. He detoured around clusters of residents wary of going back into their buildings. Aftershocks were sure to come.

He slowed to a fast walk and pulled out his phone again, trying to get an Internet connection to see how big the quake had been, but all he got was an endlessly circling "loading" icon. He tried the Komagome Station number again. No luck.

Crunching over broken glass and weaving between knots of worried citizens, he flattened himself against a cracked stucco wall as an ambulance crept past on the narrow street, its siren blaring. When it had passed, Kenji sped up, leaping the pile of broken teapots that had fallen from a display outside the gift store, dodging a terrier sniffing the air for its owner, past the shop filled with hand-dyed indigo goods owned by his third grade teacher and her husband.

He resumed his trot toward the Komagome Police Station, and a few minutes later pushed open the door from the stairwell to the third floor squad room, making his way to Section Chief Tanaka's desk. Today Tanaka was clad in purple golf pants and a Pebble Beach hat, no longer on his way to a tee time that the earthquake had canceled for him. The chief ended his call and said, "Ah, Nakamura-*san*, good timing. That was Tabata Station. They're short of manpower and are asking us to send someone to see about a casualty at the Tabata Shrine."

A casualty at the Tabata Shrine? Wasn't that where . . . ?
*No. Please no. Not that!*
He didn't wait for the elevator.

•

Yumi checked her phone for the time. 2:00. The shrine maidens had escorted them to relative safety in the new administration building next door to the sanctuary after the light fixture fell, narrowly missing the wedding party.

Built to the most modern earthquake standards, the admin building could have been the headquarters of any successful business. Gray industrial carpet, fluorescent lights, a thriving plant atop the glass-topped coffee table. The seating was stylish but not comfortable, designed for people who wouldn't be using it for more than five minutes while waiting to do business with shrine management.

They were still waiting for the priests to return. And Ichiro's father. After the dust had settled, they'd hurried outside before the aftershocks began to hit. But a woman with bleached, teased hair, dressed all in red, had intercepted them. She had appeared from the nearby garden, and run straight to Ichiro's father. His face had hardened into a mask of displeasure, and he'd excused himself to herd the unsuitable person away from his family.

But not before Yumi recognized her: Mami, the #1 hostess at the Queen of Hearts, the club where Coco moonlighted. Why was Mami waiting outside the sanctuary for Mr. Mitsuyama on the day of his son's wedding?

Ichiro's father reappeared, striding across the administration building lobby, talking urgently on his phone. He ended that call and made another, giving no openings for awkward questions.

Yumi turned to her mother and squeezed her cold hand. Yumi's father sat on her other side, a small smile on his face as he stared into the distance. Trivial matters like earthquakes and weddings couldn't command his attention for long. He was probably composing his next lecture on the history of Japanese trade, oblivious to the fact that his rank as full professor at Toda University had been bestowed as a favor to Ichiro's influential father, not because of his years of patient scholarship.

Across the room, Mr. Mitsuyama and Ichiro were pacing back and forth, fielding calls from Mitsuyama Department Store management and suppliers as aftershocks made the overhead lights flicker. Ichiro's mother was sitting by herself, her face closed. She'd barely uttered a word since the quake.

Ichiro's pacing paused as he drew another phone from his sleeve and checked the display. The older model was his personal phone, not the one he'd been using for Mitsuyama business.

Who was sending him a post-earthquake message that was so important he was answering it immediately, ignoring the business phone in his other hand as it began to ring again?

Yumi's own phone chimed from somewhere inside the duffel bag that held the street clothes she'd worn to the shrine that morning. She pulled it out.

Text from Coco. *Are you OK? Are you Mrs. Mitsuyama yet or not? What about the reception & afterparty?*

Yumi answered. *Not married. Everything postponed.*

Postponed, she thought. For how long? The triple-lucky date chosen by Mrs. Mitsuyama's astrologer had turn out to be triple-unlucky, but that didn't mean Ichiro's mother wouldn't insist on consulting the stars again before rescheduling. A new auspicious day would be chosen, the hotel rebooked, invitations reprinted. Who would pay for it all? Ichiro's family had generously offered to split the cost of the wedding, but Yumi's family had still gone into debt to pay for their half of the extravaganza demanded by the Mitsuyamas' social position. Even with the sympathy discounts that would surely be granted, where would the money come from?

She looked at the phone in her hand. How big had that quake been? Would the lives of everyone in Tokyo be back to normal tomorrow, or upended for months? Navigating to her favorite news site, she frowned at the "loading" icon, then gave up and dropped the phone back in her bag.

Ichiro and his father were now engaged in an intense private discussion. She wished one of the priests would return so they could go home.

Ichiro approached, phone still in hand. "Yumi, could you take care of your parents and see my mother home safely? My father and I need to get ourselves to the Nihonbashi store, and if the roads are blocked and the trains aren't running, it'll take us two hours to walk from here. Please give Yano-*kannushi* our regrets, and tell him we'll be in touch to reschedule."

"No!" Mrs. Mitsuyama leaped to her feet.

Was Mrs. Mitsuyama objecting to rescheduling the wedding? Yumi sat there, stunned. Was she finally saying out loud what she'd been thinking since her son had announced that they were engaged?

Ichiro hurried to his mother's side. "Mother, what are you saying?" He put on a tolerant smile. "I know earthquakes upset you, but it's over now. Let's not discuss this until everyone's had a chance to—" Then he looked up, realizing his mother's outburst had put them on center stage.

"*Sumimasen*," he apologized to the Hatas, bowing. He steered his mother to the seating area on the far side of the waiting room and began speaking to her in a low voice. Her shoulders hunched, shaking.

"Excuse me," came a voice from the doorway. "Did someone here call one-one-oh?"

Yumi turned, and her hand flew to her mouth. What was Kenji Nakamura doing here?

"Yumi?" he cried, belatedly recognizing her in the old-fashioned Edo-style wig. "Thank God, it's not you!"

"What?"

"The casualty. Someone from this shrine called one-one-oh."

His words ricocheted around the room. A call to 110 rather than 119 meant there had been a crime on the grounds.

"Excuse me, are you with the police?" Assistant Head Priest Makoto appeared in the doorway, breathing heavily as if he'd been running, his face ashen.

"I'm Detective Kenji Nakamura from Komagome

Station. There's been a casualty?"

Makoto opened his mouth to reply then stopped himself, not wanting to say so in front of the wedding party.

"Do we need an ambulance?" Kenji persisted.

Makoto gave an almost imperceptible shake of his head and motioned for Kenji to retreat into the privacy of the hall. But it was too late. Everyone in the room knew what a casualty that didn't require an ambulance meant.

Mrs. Mitsuyama grabbed her son's arm and cried, "What more will it take to convince you?"

•

"He was late to perform the Mitsuyama wedding," Makoto told Kenji, the words tumbling out, as if sharing the burden would lessen his own grief. "I checked his office first, but he wasn't there. The treasure house door was still padlocked, so I knew he wasn't there, either. On my way to see if he was still at his own house, the earthquake hit. When I got there, the front door was standing open."

He fell silent as they approached a fork in the path. Through the bare branches of a maple grove, Kenji spotted a plastered stone building. Its stout wooden door and lack of windows told him it must be the treasure house. Back in the days when fire regularly wiped out whole wooden cities and arson was punishable by death, anyone wealthy enough to own valuables built fireproof *kuras* to keep them in.

Makoto chose the left-hand path, and his steps slowed as they approached a modest thatch-roofed house with Head Priest Yano's name carved into a wooden plaque beside the door.

"Wait here," Kenji instructed as they stepped inside.

Leaving Makoto standing on the cold stone floor of the entryway, Kenji automatically slipped off his shoes before stepping up onto the traditional *tatami* floor.

It was no warmer in the house than it had been outside.

Kenji looked around. He didn't see the kind of space heater most old-fashioned houses used to banish the wintery chill that crept in from November through March. The priest must have spent his time at the heated *kotatsu* table that sat before the room's single window, which looked out on a jewel of a moss garden. The *kotatsu's* quilted cover was now covered in dust and littered with objects that had been shaken from the toppled shelves on the adjacent wall. Books lay helter-skelter on the floor, jumbled with reading glasses, dog-eared magazines, and the kind of cute but useless souvenirs given by friends and relatives after visiting noted sightseeing spots. In the other corner was the wreckage of a *kamidana*, a large wooden household shrine, that had fallen from a shelf near the ceiling. Beneath its splintered remains was the body of a man. The victim's snow-white wedding vestments suggested he was a Shinto priest.

Kenji picked his way through the debris and found the man's wrist, lying inert on the *tatami*. He felt for a pulse, then sat back on his heels and put his hands together in a moment of silent respect.

"Did you move anything when you discovered him?" Kenji asked Makoto, pulling on his white cotton evidence-handling gloves.

"I tried to move the *kamidana* to see if he was still alive, but it was too heavy. Then I checked for a pulse." A tear slid down Makoto's cheek. "I couldn't find it, so I called one-one-oh."

The bobble weight at the end of the light cord overhead began to swing and the floor vibrated as another quake rocked the shrine. Kenji herded Makoto outside to safety. Behind them, the framed piece of calligraphy that had been hanging askew over the kitchen door fell with a crash of shattering glass.

When the shaking stopped, Kenji pulled out his phone, scrolling to the Komagome Police Station number.

"I'm going to call my chief and ask him to send a Crime Scene Investigation team."

"Crime scene?" Makoto blurted. "Why?"

"They investigate accidents, too," he told the head priest's brother.

But after feeling the victim's cold wrist, he wasn't sure today would be one of those days.

•

After making his calls, Kenji went back inside and regarded the scene, deciding where to start.

"Excuse me for intruding," came a voice from the doorway. Even in the aftermath of a major earthquake, Assistant Detective Suzuki's impeccably polite greeting, perfectly starched shirt, and stricter-than-required haircut gave away his devotion to the finer points of police regulations. Suzuki was Kenji's *kohai*, a junior who exchanged unwavering loyalty for being taken care of as he followed his *sempai* up the career ladder.

"Suzuki-*san*, how's your family? Everybody okay after the quake?"

They exchanged reports, assuring each other that everyone was fine. Then Kenji outlined what had happened at the shrine, explaining that he was waiting for the Crime Scene Investigation unit to arrive and take a look at the victim. He led Suzuki back outside to Makoto, who was now sitting on a bench under a maple, its branches bare against the winter sky.

"This is Assistant Detective Suzuki," Kenji said. "He's going to accompany you back to the administration building to wait while our CSI team conducts their investigation. Can you ask anybody who's still here not to leave until we know if we need to speak further with any of them?"

Makoto leaped to his feet, face twisted with worry. "The Mitsuyamas are our shrine's biggest supporters, Detective. Surely there's no need to ask them to stay and be questioned?"

"We won't be questioning anyone unless we have good reason," Kenji assured him. "But can you give Assistant Detective Suzuki a list of contact information for everybody who was at the shrine today, in case we need to speak with them later?"

Makoto nodded, then he followed Suzuki back through the garden.

At the gate, they stood aside as Crime Scene Investigator Tommy Loud arrived, toting a mammoth digital camera, followed by two assistants.

"Nakamura-*san, o-hisashiburi desu.*"

As always, Kenji was surprised to hear perfect Japanese coming from the tall red-haired tech, whose wife was the Superintendent General's daughter. She'd first met the Australian crime specialist at an English conversation café, then defiantly eloped with him six months later. When a job offer had threatened to move the newlyweds to Sydney, the SG hastily arranged a job for his son-in-law at the northwest Tokyo crime lab so his unborn grandchildren wouldn't grow up to be noisy, English-speaking foreigners.

Loud said, "Lucky for you, I was in the neighborhood and the dead guy they sent me to investigate still had a pulse when I arrived."

"Well, this one doesn't," Kenji said, standing aside and nodding toward the body beneath the splintered shrine.

"Looks like today was the unluckiest day of his life, standing under that thing when the quake hit," remarked Loud, snapping surgical covers over his shoes and pulling on evidence-handling gloves. The crime tech stepped up onto the *tatami*, knelt and paid his respects to the victim, then began moving around the wreckage, his flash making shadows jump. A few minutes later he checked the display on the back of the camera, cycling through the shots to make sure he'd captured all the angles.

"Okay," Loud said, satisfied. "Let's dig him out."

They moved the loose rubble, then lifted the *kamidana* off the body, maneuvering the splintered wooden structure across the room to a corner that was relatively free of debris. Returning to the body, Loud regarded the battered corpse, sprawled face up. He crouched and gently pulled the victim's robe open to inspect the damage to the body.

"What I want to know is, where's the blood?" he said, turning to look up at Kenji.

"What do you mean?" Kenji asked peering over the tech's shoulder. The gash on the victim's temple looked plenty bloody to him.

Loud pointed to Yano's chest, which was deflated and misshapen where the heavy *kamidana* had landed. Lacerations in the skin showed red muscle beneath.

"Only his head bled like the Sumida River in monsoon season," Loud explained. "By the time that *kamidana* fell and caused the rest of this damage, his heart was long past pumping blood to these chest wounds."

Kenji's reply was interrupted by the opening chords of the VuDu Dolls' "Don't Need You." It was coming from the victim.

Tommy Loud searched the body, gingerly pulling on a red brocade charm poking out of the side pocket of the victim's robe. A phone slid out onto the *tatami*. It stopped ringing.

Kenji picked it up, but couldn't work the touch screen without taking off his evidence-handling gloves.

"Can you pull the prints now, so I can see who that call was from?" Kenji asked.

Nodding, Loud extracted a fingerprint kit from his bag. When the cloud of prints was safely transferred to tape, he handed the phone to Kenji and began to search for his thermometer.

Kenji crossed to the doorway and navigated to the list of received calls.

The final call had been from a ramen noodle shop, profusely apologizing that due to the earthquake, the priest's pre-ordered dinner couldn't be delivered. Below that, five unanswered calls from a number labeled "Makoto," starting at 1:03. Before that, a voicemail from someone called Yamamoto, left yesterday at 7:04 p.m. Kenji punched Play and held the phone to his ear.

"I'm going to pretend you didn't leave that last message, Yano-*san*. I'll bring the cash at ten o'clock tomorrow morning, and I suggest you be there."

The speaker's polite words were like a piece of tissue wrapped around a rock.

•

Kenji left Tommy Loud with the victim and moved on to inspect the rest of the house.

The kitchen was a mess. Pots and pans had toppled from open shelves above the sink and stove, and several rice bowls and cups lay in pieces on the floor. Every drawer hung open. A stack of still-folded dishtowels had been upended in front of the stove, and a heap of miscellaneous tape dispensers, paper clips, rubber bands, and outdated postage stamps mingled with a jumble of cooking utensils and chopsticks.

Kenji frowned. Earthquakes didn't reach into drawers and dump the contents. Someone had searched the kitchen.

For what? And had they found it? Perhaps the victim's brother would be able to tell him what was missing.

"Coming in," announced Detective Oki's deep voice from the entry. Kenji suspended his search and returned to the main room to find his fellow detective's considerable bulk filling the doorway.

When Kenji had called Section Chief Tanaka to inform him that the Tabata Shrine casualty had turned into a suspicious death, the chief told him he'd send Detective Oki to help decide whether it was an accident or something that warranted calling in the First Investigative Division murder unit from Chiyoda Ward headquarters. Oki was ten years ahead of Kenji, experience-wise, and although his silvering brush-cut hair and sympathetic face often lulled suspects into underestimating his brains, he'd come close to finishing a degree in psychology before transferring to the police academy.

Loud stood and pulled off his gloves. "This house is pretty cold, so I'm not going to be able to give you as narrow a window as I'd like, based only on body temp, but I can safely say he died between seven and ten this morning, long before the earthquake dropped that *kamidana* on him at one seventeen. Looks like judicial autopsy time to me."

Kenji and Oki exchanged glances.

"Rock-paper-scissors for who gets to tell the chief the bad news." Kenji said, holding out his fist.

Detective Oki smiled grimly as he extended his. A full forensic exam would have to be okayed by Section Chief Tanaka, after informing his superiors at Tokyo Metropolitan Police headquarters. Tanaka hated having his station invaded by the First Investigative Division. When the elite murder squad from headquarters took over a major crime case at Komagome Station, the local detectives were shoved to the back of the briefing room and given less-than-glamorous tasks like fetching tea, driving the commanding officer to and from the crime scene, and taking notes, while the elite career detectives talked to witnesses, gathered evidence, and questioned suspects.

Working with the headquarters team was uncomfortable for Kenji, too. He was on the same career fast track as the interlopers, even though he was currently seated among the locals, serving his time in the field before being promoted into police administration. He continued to study for the exam that would elevate him to Assistant Inspector and open the door for a transfer to the hallowed halls, but the more he worked with Detective Oki—who'd grown up in Kabukichō and didn't need a fancy rank to squeeze information from players on both sides of the law—the more he respected Oki's decision not to step onto the desk jockey escalator.

Today, though, Oki was out of luck. He grimaced and headed outside to make the call.

Kenji returned his attention to the victim's phone. Paging back through the victim's e-mail, a message caught his attention.

> From: yamamot088@docomo.ne.jp
> To: Yano15@docomo.ne.jp
> Date: March 2, 5:43 p.m.
> Sub: Re: The item we discussed
>
> My sources tell me that if I increase my bid to ¥3,000,000, it will be more than enough to outbid my competitor. I suggest it's time to end this game. My patience is wearing thin.

What had the priest been selling? Whatever it was, the same person who had left the threatening voicemail was prepared to pay an astonishing amount of money for it.

Kenji paged down and spotted another message with the subject line "The item we discussed," but this one was from the flamboyant head of the Erai Museum, an organization that had been front-page news recently when they outbid the Louvre and the Metropolitan for a coveted Renoir. A huge bequest from the founder of a distressed debt company had suddenly made them the favorite child at art auctions all over the world.

> From: Mitsubishi@eraibijutsukan.ne.jp
> To: Yano15@docomo.ne.jp
> Date: March 12, 5:30 p.m.
> Sub: Re: The item we discussed
>
> Yano-san:

I fear I'm unable to offer more than ¥2,500,000, but I beg you to look upon my bid with favor and consider factors other than price.

Matsuo Mitsubishi

Factors other than price? Was that a plea? Or another threat?

A string of four previous e-mails confirmed that the head of the Erai Museum and Yamamot088 had been bidding back and forth for a week on whatever Yano was selling.

Oki returned, pocketing his phone.

"Good news," he said, sliding out of his shoes. "The earthquake interrupted a drug sting, caught some human-trafficking gangsters with their pants down, and flushed the usual cockroaches from their hidey-holes. The major crimes teams are all too busy to deal with what Tanaka told them might still turn out to be an accidental death. We have the Superintendent General's blessing to carry on with the investigation until the post-mortem determines whether it's murder or not. You're the point man, Golden Boy, since you did such a bang-up job on the Shrine Killer." Oki refrained from mentioning Kenji's most recent murder case, after which he'd narrowly escaped being kicked back to *koban* duty in a village so remote the trains only came twice a week.

Kenji nodded and called Suzuki. The assistant detective told him that everyone but Makoto, the receptionist, and one shrine maiden had disappeared to see about their loved ones before he got there, but Makoto had given him all their contact information. Kenji asked his *kohai* to find out where everybody had been since 8:00 that morning, and who they'd seen at the shrine that day.

He ended the call, asked Tommy Loud to send a fingerprint specialist to the admin building, then handed Yano's phone to Oki.

"This belonged to the victim. What do you make of the

most recent voicemail?"

Oki listened, frowning. He handed the phone back to Kenji. "I wonder why our vic was in bed with the head of the Yamamoto-*gumi's* loser of a second son."

"Yakuza?"

"Unto the tenth generation. I'd bet my black belt that voice belongs to Koji Yamamoto—he's next in line if both daddy and Number One Son meet untimely ends. Back in middle school, he had a thriving porn racket, but when the science teacher discovered he'd been using the lab computers to store and distribute it, he reported Koji and his gang to the police. Yamamoto Jr. dodged the bullet, but three of his friends did juvie time. The day after the sentences were handed down, there was an explosion in the lab. The science teacher still walks with a cane."

Kenji grimaced. "Suspect number one," he said. "Look at this string of e-mails."

Oki scrolled through them and frowned. "What kind of merch would the head of a major museum and the son of a yak boss both want that badly? And why did Yano turn down the high bidder?"

"I was wondering the same thing."

"Well, if my old buddy Koji stopped by before ten this morning and didn't like Yano's explanation, maybe we can wrap this one up before the murder squad burns their tongues on tomorrow morning's tea."

"Huh, what have we here?" Loud exclaimed. Kneeling next to the body, he'd been systematically searching the victim's pockets. Kenji and Oki crossed the room to look over his shoulder as he pulled a Polaroid photo from the deep sleeve of the victim's ceremonial robe. An adolescent girl with downcast eyes, clad only in her Hello Kitty underpants, shivered in front of a pink-tiled bathtub filled to the brim with steaming water. A row of rubber duckies looked on with wide-eyed surprise.

In the coldest voice Kenji had ever heard, Oki said, "If this is a sample of what the priest was selling, he deserved to die."

•

"I'm sorry to ask for your help at this difficult time," Kenji said to Makoto, who'd been fetched by Oki from the administration building. He sat next to Kenji on the bench outside the head priest's house, his eyes now puffy and red, grief beginning to carve angles on his smooth face. "But as soon as the morgue team finishes, can you walk through your brother's house with me and tell me if anything is missing?"

Makoto nodded, eyes avoiding the path of cardboard the coroner's van attendants had laid for the gurney so it wouldn't destroy the garden moss as it made its journey in and out of the house. It had yet to emerge on its return trip.

"While we're waiting, would you mind looking at some messages on your brother's phone?"

Makoto accepted the phone listlessly, then his eyes widened as he read through the string of e-mails. He scrolled back to the most recent one from the Erai Museum and frowned. "This was sent last Saturday? I thought my brother told them 'no' back in January...?"

"No to what?"

"They wanted to buy a kimono from our treasure house. We didn't know how valuable it was until recently."

As Kenji took notes, Makoto explained, "The Tabata Shrine has been a favorite of weavers and dyers since the 1600s, and they often gave goods instead of money. In the early days, some of it was sold to support the shrine, but as time went by, they began to give money instead. The offerings stored in the treasure house were pretty much forgotten.

"Then last December, a professor from Tokyo University came knocking, asking if he could see our kimonos. He took one look and acted like he'd discovered King Tut's tomb. In

January, he published a piece that was circulated on the Internet, with pictures of an Edo-era kimono that had been given to us by one of the *shōgun's* concubines. The article claimed it was a rare undamaged example of a dyeing technique that had been lost over a century ago. Two days later, the Erai Museum contacted us, asking if we'd consider selling it to them. Without even asking how much they were offering, my brother turned them down. The next week, a man showed up on our doorstep, offering to buy it for half a million yen. My brother asked the professor why the guy was offering so much, and discovered the kimono was probably worth a lot more than that.

"I urged him to reconsider his decision not to sell." Makoto sighed. "My brother . . . wasn't very good with money. This place needs constant repairs, and with the economy the way it is, some of our patrons aren't able to give as generously as they have in the past.

"But he refused. I told him that at the very least we ought to make an inventory and get it appraised, because it ought to be insured." Makoto's mouth pinched into a bitter line.

"One more thing," Kenji said, pulling the evidence bag containing the Polaroid they'd found in Yano's sleeve from his pocket and showing it to the victim's brother. "Have you ever seen this before?"

Makoto's eyes widened in shock. "No! Where did you find this?"

"In your brother's sleeve," Kenji said. "Was he interested in . . . girls?"

"No! I mean yes, but not like that. He worked with kids who'd been abandoned by their parents. And runaways." He nodded at the photo. "Many of them had . . . good reason to run away."

"Do you recognize this girl?"

Makoto shook his head.

"Could she be a kid he was working with?"

"I don't know. You'll have to ask at the shelter."

The sound of a gurney bumping out the front door of the house interrupted their conversation. Makoto leaped to his feet, but Kenji was right behind him. He gently pulled Makoto back, saying, "We'll call you after the post-mortem. It would be best to wait until then to see your brother's face for the last time."

Makoto slumped, arms falling to his side. He watched as the attendants pushed the gurney over the makeshift cardboard path and through the garden gate.

Kenji gave him a few moments to collect himself, then suggested they go inside and do the walk-through.

Makoto stopped in the entry, staring at the now-bare spot amid the debris. Taking a deep breath, he slipped out of his shoes. He gazed at the jumble of belongings helplessly and shook his head. Things were too much of a mess to know if anything had been removed from the main room, he said.

Tommy Loud joined them as they moved to the kitchen.

"Did the earthquake do all this?" Makoto asked, surveying the chaos.

"We think it had a little help from an intruder."

"An intruder?" Makoto looked at him, shocked.

"Can you help us figure out what he might have been looking for?"

Brow furrowed, Makoto walked hesitantly across the room and stood looking down at a pile of unrelated miscellany. Post-its. Small change. Rubber bands. He shook his head. "I really have no idea what could be missing from the junk drawer." He looked at Kenji. "And the last time I looked through the cooking utensils was when I was in high school."

"Can you show me where they were usually stored?"

"The junk drawer is that one over there," Makoto said, pointing to a single shallow drawer above a cabinet for pots.

Kenji pulled it open. Empty, as expected.

Makoto turned and pointed to the top drawer in a column of four. "That one was for the chopsticks and chopstick rests."

Kenji pulled it open. Empty.

"The next one was for utensils."

Empty.

"And that one," Makoto said, pointing to the slightly deeper drawer that was third from the top, "is where Mother always kept the dishtowels."

Empty.

"What about this one?" Kenji said, moving on to the bottom drawer.

"Mixing bowls and measuring cups."

Kenji pulled it open. Empty. He looked around. There were no mixing bowls or measuring cups on the floor. He opened the cabinet next to the drawers and peered inside. It was crowded with stacked *nabe* pots, omelet pans, a rice cooker, a big stainless steel pot. Kenji brought out the pot, discovering there were two bowls and a set of measuring cups nested inside.

The intruder hadn't put anything else away after searching, so it was probably the victim who had relocated the bowls. To make room for something else? Something that was now missing?

He pulled the bottom drawer all the way out and shone his penlight into the back corner, where it picked up a small black triangle.

"Rowdy-san?" Kenji called, mispronouncing the tech's name in typical Japanese fashion. "Can you bring an evidence bag?"

Loud arrived, reached in with his tweezers, and drew out an old-fashioned photo corner. He slipped it into a bag and labeled it.

Was the Polaroid in the victim's sleeve from a larger collection of similar images? The corners of Kenji's mouth tightened with distaste. A whole album of exploited children? Is that what the intruder killed Yano to get?

They moved on to the small bathroom, where there was a toilet and sink, but no bath. The house must have been built in the days when people bathed at the local public *sento* rather than in the privacy of their own homes. The medicine cabinet, sink cupboard, and toilet tank held no surprises.

"What about upstairs?" Kenji asked Makoto.

The victim's brother opened a narrow wooden door adjacent to the stove, revealing steep wooden steps. Kenji climbed up first, emerging into a single six-mat room. Light filtered through a round window crisscrossed with bamboo. The wave-patterned washi paper covering the sliding doors of the futon cupboard was grimy around the finger pulls, and lifting at the seams.

An odd assortment of items was stacked in one corner. An iron. A spray bottle half filled with water. A heating pad with a neatly coiled cord. A stack of ragged towels and a foam pillow without a pillowcase.

The rest of the room was bare, except for a small triangle of red plastic lying on the *tatami* near the window. Kenji took a closer look.

"Did your brother play guitar?" he asked, as Makoto stepped up into the room.

"He used to. Why?"

Kenji pointed to the rounded plastic shape with "Fender" slashed across it.

Makoto crossed the room and crouched down to look at the guitar pick. "There hasn't been one of those here since my brother quit his band to take over the shrine."

"His band? He was a musician before he was a priest?"

"He was the guitarist for Meatsnake."

Kenji stared. "Meatsnake? The Meatsnake that's headlining Rock For Tōhoku this year?"

"Yeah. But that was over twenty years ago, before they

got famous. Back then, they were still playing small live houses in the suburbs, splitting the take with other bands trying to grab enough fans to get a major debut."

"And how did your brother feel about giving up being a rock star to become a priest?"

Makoto sighed. "He was living out of his van, and the band was still buying their own instruments and hauling their equipment themselves at every gig, but he was living the dream he'd had since he was a kid. Then Father figured out that the doctors were lying to him about having more than a year to live, and he made my brother quit his band and come back to get a crash course in being head priest. I offered to quit school and take over the shrine instead, but our family is very . . . traditional."

"So your brother wasn't happy about it?"

Makoto shook his head. "I remember that New Year's. The night I came home from school, they didn't even hear me call, '*Tadaima!*' because my dad and brother were in the middle of a shouting match. My brother stormed out of the house and disappeared for three days." He paused, face troubled. "My father made the final *hatsumōde* prayer of his life heartbroken because my brother had refused to mend their quarrels before the bells rang on New Year's Eve. But of course we were too busy that night tending the bonfire and ladling out *amazake* to look for him."

Kenji nodded. On the first three days of the new year, every shrine in Japan was mobbed.

Makoto continued, "At the end of the day on the third, my brother reappeared, right in the middle of a service, wearing his robes. And for some reason he never explained, he'd shaved off all his hair. After that, he stopped resisting Father's wishes. We never knew where he went on those three days, but nobody ever heard him play guitar again."

"When did your father die?"

"That March. My brother took over the shrine and life

went on. But even though his body was there, his spirit was . . . gone. His promoter found a new guitarist for the band, and the rest is history."

"Why didn't your father let you become head priest instead? Didn't he think you were cut out for the job?"

Makoto's face tightened. "I wasn't the eldest son."

Well, you are now, Kenji thought, as the priest moved to the window to gaze pensively at the view.

Kenji turned to the cupboard to see what it contained. The sliding door on the right concealed a folded futon with a pillow perched atop. Kenji slid the door shut and opened the other one.

The back and sides were neatly packed with the kind of miscellaneous items that silt up over a lifetime: a stack of CDs, a boxed set of Boys' Day carp streamers, childhood sports trophies. In the center, there was a clearing the same size as the pile of things in the corner of the room.

It was bare, except for a stack of ¥10,000 notes more than two and a half centimeters thick.

•

Yumi watched her mother smooth tissue over the dusty golden cranes and treasure boxes embroidered on the Mitsuyama wedding kimono before folding in the wings of its washi paper wrapper and tying them closed. It would have to be taken apart and cleaned by an antique-fabric specialist in Kyoto before being worn again.

And if Mrs. Mitsuyama had her way, the bride wearing it wouldn't be Yumi. After deciding they couldn't wait any longer for the priest to return, the wedding party had scattered to all parts of Tokyo, future plans unresolved.

Yumi glanced at her father, who was steadily putting away a bottle of Otokoyama sake at a low table that had been set before the TV, watching the nonstop news programs that were beginning to show the extent of the damage.

A scientist was solemnly pegging the quake at 7.9 on the Richter scale and reporting that the tremor had lasted a punishing two minutes and seventeen seconds. The epicenter had been on the same offshore fault that had produced the great Genroku earthquake of 1703, and the sudden displacement of water sixty kilometers from the mouth of Tokyo Bay had sent a five-meter tsunami racing toward Japan's biggest metropolis. The first land in its path as it hit Tokyo was the man-made island of Odaiba, which was barely above sea level. The water had surged over the island, destroying many buildings as it continued on its way to punish the Tokyo waterfront and send a flood crest up the Sumida River. Most of the boats that anchored at the Tsukiji fish market had been safely out to sea at the time, but the market itself had suffered considerable devastation, as had many waterfront buildings.

The news show switched to clips showing the damage to Odaiba. Workers in bright-yellow raingear battled a leak in the tunnel of the Rinkai subway line that ran beneath Tokyo Bay to the island. Another piece of footage showed a barge breaking loose from its mooring and slamming into one of the pylons supporting the monorail that looped across from Shinagawa, as a reporter solemnly intoned that at the moment, the only way on and off the disaster-struck island was by boat.

In mainland Tokyo, the quake had registered 7.2, and damage to inland areas had been moderate. The emergency system had been tested by 3/11 and disaster plans were running smoothly. Power was still out in a few neighborhoods, but some train lines were predicted to be running again as soon as tomorrow.

Yumi wondered if Ichiro and his father had made it safely to the Nihonbashi store. She checked her phone again. Ichiro still hadn't returned any of her calls. She told herself it was because he was busy taking care of the crisis, but a little peach pit of foreboding settled in her chest.

Yumi's mother knotted the last tie on the kimono wrapper and sighed. Crossing the room, she sank onto a cushion across from her husband at the low table.

"Could you move over, please?" he complained craning his neck. "I can't see."

She stayed where she was. "Hideo . . . what are we going to do if the Tabata Shrine won't give back our money?" One of the biggest expenses of the wedding had been the million yen "donation" for performing the ceremony.

Yumi's father turned his attention from the TV. "Surely they won't charge us again just because we have to choose another date."

Mrs. Hata shook her head, her mouth set in a thin line. "Yumi and Ichiro can't get married at a place that had two disasters on the same day."

"Don't tell me you're taking that astrology nonsense as seriously as Mrs. Mitsuyama!" Yumi cried.

Mrs. Hata's face pinched as she fought back tears and clutched her handkerchief. "The gods are angry that I tampered with fate! This is my punishment!"

Without consulting her daughter, Mrs. Hata had asked a local astrologer to recommend birthdates that were compatible with Ichiro's before mailing the arranged marriage questionnaire back to the Mitsuyamas. She'd replaced Yumi's real birthday with a far more auspicious date, and the wedding day had been chosen using the false information. Mrs. Hata had been doing some minor fretting about it throughout the engagement.

Yumi's mouth dropped open. "You think the *kami-sama* sent an earthquake to devastate the entire Kanto region because you changed my birthday?"

Yumi's father pointed the remote at the TV to turn up the volume and poured himself another glass of sake.

"You and Michiko Mitsuyama are both crazy," he said to

his wife, shifting sideways so he could see around her. Then he exclaimed, "Wow. Look at that!"

Yumi and her mother turned to the TV as footage taken from a vantage point above the swirling waters caught the tsunami surge uprooting a modest but futuristic-looking building, ripping it open, and relentlessly bearing the collapsing pieces inland. Elaborate antennas and broadcast dishes crumpled and tore as the building was buffeted by flotsam. The announcer intoned, "In Odaiba, studios owned by—"

The VuDu Dolls' "Heart-Shaped Hole" momentarily drowned out the broadcast. Yumi stood and dug her phone from her pocket, checking the caller ID, hoping it was Ichiro. It wasn't.

"*Moshi-moshi*? Coco?" Yumi headed for her room to escape the TV.

"Yumi!" The background murmur of a newscaster gave away that Coco's family was glued to the box, too. "Where are you? Are you okay?"

"Yeah, we're fine. We're at home. Where are you?"

"Home. Finally. It took me three hours to walk back to Komagome from your reception hotel in my high heels and I've got blisters the size of hundred-yen coins."

"Are your parents okay?" Yumi asked.

"Yeah, but my dad is complaining like he had to run a marathon because it took him four hours to walk home from the golf course. So . . . what happened?"

Yumi told her about the priest being late and how they'd been planning to register the marriage after the ceremony on the way to the reception.

"Well," her friend said, "at least that means I'll get a chance to wear my new dress again."

"Maybe."

"What do you mean?"

Yumi told her about Mrs. Mitsuyama's outburst.

"She thought the earthquake was a personal sign from the gods that her son was marrying the wrong girl?" Coco laughed. "If that's true, I guess they were telling me that buying a mattcha latte was a big no-no too, since the barista tossed mine all over the front of me when the earthquake hit."

"Well, you'll both have to do rock-paper-scissors with my mom for the blame. She thinks the whole disaster is punishment from the kami-sama for changing my birthday."

Coco groaned. "How long do you think it'll be before you have a new date?"

"I don't know. The astrologer will have to be consulted and my mother wants to find a new place for the ceremony."

"Why? In case she didn't notice, this one 'punished' every shrine in Tokyo."

Yumi sighed. "It's not just the earthquake. There was an . . . incident." She told Coco about Kenji's appearance.

Suddenly, a burst of familiar music came from the TV in the next room.

Coco shrieked. "No!"

"What?"

"It can't be true!"

"What?"

"The VuDu Dolls! They were in that studio that was washed away by the tsunami! Wait . . ." Coco was silent for a moment, the background murmur of the TV punctuated by snatches of pop music.

"Flame is dead!" Coco wailed into the phone. "They're all dead! It can't be true. It can't. I'll call you back." She hung up.

Yumi stared at her phone, stunned. The VuDu Dolls were dead? She felt like she'd been punched. The VuDu Dolls were Yumi's favorite band, too. Since middle school, she'd been to eight of their concerts, including one that had only been open to members of their fan club. Afterward, she'd been among the fifty lucky fans who had been invited backstage for a meet and greet, and although Flame hadn't spoken to her—

one of the guitarist's trademarks was that she never spoke to anyone, even on TV—the guitarist had looked into her starstruck sixteen-year-old eyes, given her a warm smile, and signed her program "To my best fan Yumi, with love, Flame."

Yumi returned to the main room in a daze as the final stanza of "Don't Need You" pounded from the TV. The screen dissolved into a still of a girl with her hair bleached platinum, playing a guitar on stage at the Nippon Budokan. Her right arm was covered to the elbow with her other trademark: a white lace fingerless glove.

•

Three hours later, Yumi leaned back against the wooden fence that bordered their neighbors' property. She hunched into her too-thin jacket as a cold breeze tumbled a handful of dried leaves past her feet.

She had lied to her mother. The third or fourth time that anxious voice had asked if Ichiro had called yet, she'd said, "Yes, what are you worrying about? We talked, and everything's going to be fine. It's just that he's got a lot on his plate right now because of the earthquake. We can't begin to think about rescheduling the wedding until he's dealt with emergencies at work."

Yumi shivered and tried to believe her own words. The truth was, every time she tried Ichiro's personal phone and got shunted to voicemail, her worry deepened. Was he not picking up because he couldn't? Or because he didn't want to?

She scrolled through her phone contacts until she landed on Ichiro, and contemplated the two numbers next to his name. She'd never called the second one. It was his work phone, and he'd given it to her to use only in case of emergency.

This wasn't an emergency. She knew it wasn't an emergency. But she wouldn't keep him long. All she wanted was to hear the words she'd already put in his mouth. Don't worry. Everything will be fine. I'll call you later.

She pushed Call. It rang, and she immediately regretted using his work number, but he picked up so fast, she couldn't hang up.

"Yumi, what is it? What happened?"

"I . . . I just wanted to see how you were," she said, hesitating. "We haven't talked since you left the shrine, and I wanted to make sure . . . I wanted to . . ."

"I thought I told you to only call this number if it was an emergency."

"But I tried your other one about ten times, and you never picked up."

"That's because the battery's dead and my charger's at home. But even if it wasn't, I don't have time for chitchat. Do you have any idea what I'm dealing with here? Supply routes are a shambles, and we've got containers of goods sitting at the dock that we won't be able to get through customs for God knows how long."

"I'm sorry, I didn't realize—"

"Well, you should have. My mother hasn't been calling and distracting my father—she knows it's a wife's job not to heap her worries on top of his at a time like this."

Yumi was silent.

"As long as you're on the line," Ichiro snapped, "is she all right? My mother?"

"She's . . . I . . . haven't you talked with her since you left the shrine?"

"No, why would I? She's with you, right?"

"No, she's not."

"What? I thought I asked you to see that she got home safely!"

"I tried! But the trains weren't running, there were no cabs, and we don't have a car, so there was no way to get her back to Hiroo. We offered to let her stay here in Komagome with us until things got back to normal, but she . . . she didn't want to. She called a friend of hers in Shinjuku and the friend's driver came to get her."

"Did the driver take her home to Hiroo?"

"I don't know."

"Which friend?"

"She didn't tell me her name."

Ichiro groaned in frustration. "Well, can you please call her and--never mind, I'll do it myself." In the background, Yumi heard Beethoven's Fifth Symphony start up. "Sorry," he said, "I have to go."

He hung up.

She stared at the dead phone in her hand and tears brimmed. She shouldn't have called. Now she felt worse. A lot worse. The combination of tears and a chilly December wind was making her nose run, but she couldn't go back to the house with her face betraying that everything was definitely not all right with Ichiro. She pulled the last tissue from the pack in her purse and swiped at her eyes, smearing mascara across her cheekbones.

Then the tissue crumpled in her fist. Beethoven's Fifth. That was the ringtone on Ichiro's personal phone, the number she usually called, the phone he'd told her had a dead battery. How come he wasn't answering her calls, but he'd hung up on her to answer that one?

•

It had been a hard day, and it was going to get harder before it got easier. Kenji turned off the main street toward Yumi's house, bracing himself to ask about every detail of this morning's wedding preparations in case she or her parents had seen anyone who might have killed Head Priest Yano.

His steps slowed as he composed the questions that would keep the interview as short and painless as possible. He'd spent the past month hoping that a miracle—or Ichiro's ex-girlfriend—would derail Yumi's plans, but seeing her this morning dressed as a bride drove a stake right through his fantasies. The quake would postpone her wedding, but he finally had to accept that it was too late to hope for more. It was time to grit his teeth and pull out the hook she'd sunk into his heart in third grade. It would hurt for a while, he told himself, but over time it would heal. The day would come when he'd be able to think of her without longing, the same way he now remembered his mother, who had died when he was in high school.

He stopped, ticking over the questions in his mind. *Okay, let's do this.* He squared his shoulders and rounded the corner near the Hatas' house, then stopped in his tracks. Someone was slumped against the neighbors' fence, staring down at the phone in her hand.

"Yumi?"

She looked up, startled. Her face was streaked with tears.

"What's the matter?" he asked, coming closer.

She shook her head, unable to answer. Knowing better than to hope that her tears meant she'd broken up with her fiancé, Kenji searched his pockets and came up with a pack of tissues. He held them out to her, and she took them, but couldn't get them open with her cold hands. He took them back and managed to extract a tissue. Handing it to her, the only thing he could think of to say that wouldn't offer comfort he couldn't give was, "You cut your hair."

She'd been wearing the wedding wig this morning, so this was the first time he'd seen her with a new chin-length razor cut.

Yumi dropped her eyes and said in a small voice, "I knew it was mistake after the first snip, but it's too late now."

She would still be beautiful to him even if she shaved her head like a Buddhist priest, but he stopped himself from saying it.

"What are you doing out here all by yourself?" he asked instead.

She shook her head and took a ragged breath. "Ichiro is . . . he's taking care of more . . . more important things."

"More important than being with you, after a major disaster and a canceled wedding?" A spark of anger replaced a little of Kenji's pain. Why was she marrying someone like that? Why couldn't she see he was a jerk who didn't deserve her?

Then her arms were around him, her wet face pressed against his shoulder.

Before he could forbid his body to do what his heart still wanted, he pulled her close. *No. Wrong. Bad idea.* But he couldn't very well push her away now. They'd been friends since third grade. And now she was sobbing in earnest against his suit coat. She'd never be his, but she was an old friend, a friend in need of comfort on a day filled with extraordinary disasters. He held her as her sobs subsided.

But then she raised her chin and looked into his eyes, stretching up on her tiptoes, her lips inches from his.

*No.* He stiffened and turned his head aside.

Stung, Yumi's eyes flew open as she recoiled and her cheeks flushed with embarrassment. She hastily let go and stepped back.

"Sorry. I . . . you must think I . . ."

"I think you made your choice," he said, hoping she couldn't tell how much it cost him to say those words. He thrust his hands into his pockets.

"Sorry, look . . . I mean . . . I'm not married yet," she said defensively. "Not officially. We were going to register at the Ward Office after the ceremony, but then the earthquake--"

"As if that changes anything."

He waited for her to tell him different, then sighed. "Why are you trying to make this hard for me?"

Yumi stared at her feet.

*Get what you came for and go home, before this gets any worse.* Kenji drew a pen and notepad from his pocket and switched to his detective voice. "I was actually on my way to ring your doorbell and ask if you or your parents saw anyone besides the wedding party at the shrine today."

Yumi took a ragged breath, wiped her nose with the ball of tissue, trying to recover some dignity. "Why do you want to know who was at the shrine today?"

"The reason the head priest didn't show up to perform your wedding is because he was dead."

Yumi gasped. "Head Priest Yano? He was the . . . the 'casualty'? Was it an accident? Because of the earthquake?"

Kenji shook his head.

"He was dead before the wedding?" Alarm. "Was he . . . ?"

"We don't have the results from the post-mortem yet."

Yumi's eyes widened. She understood what it meant when a post-mortem was ordered. Nationwide, there was such a shortage of facilities and trained professionals that only ten percent of the 150,000 unexplained deaths every year received the attentions of a medical examiner. Unless there was something suspicious about them. Then the body would be examined thoroughly, whether the family agreed to it or not.

Flipping to a fresh page in his notebook, he asked, "Can you walk me through your day, from the time you got up until the earthquake happened?"

Yumi pushed the ball of tissue into her pocket and took a shaky breath. "My mother woke me up at seven and made breakfast for me and my father. I went to her hair salon with her, then she came back home to help my father get ready, and I went to the shrine. I got there at about a quarter to ten, so I could make an offering before meeting the hair-make person and the kimono dresser."

"Where?"

"The sub-shrine near the treasure house is dedicated to happy marriages and childbirth."

"Did you see anyone who looked like they didn't

belong?"

Yumi shook her head. "The only people I saw were the pregnant woman ahead of me in line and Assistant Head Priest Makoto."

"What was Makoto-*kannushi* doing when you saw him?"

"He was carrying some odd-sized stuff wrapped in a big blue-and-white *furoshiki*. He must have been taking it somewhere other than the admin building, though, because he asked me if I knew where to go to get ready for the wedding, but didn't offer to come with me."

Was that because he had just finished killing his brother and was hurrying away with a *furoshiki* full of dirty Polaroids?

"What direction was he was coming from?"

Yumi thought for a moment, then said, "I thought he was coming from the gate on the other side of the treasure house, but I wasn't really paying attention."

The treasure house was the opposite direction from the crime scene, but Kenji made a note.

"Then what did you do?"

"I went to the administration building. They have a suite for brides to use while they get ready. The stylist and kimono dresser finished with me around eleven thirty, then they took me to another room for pictures. The only people I saw besides our families were the stylist, the wedding planner's assistant, and the photographer."

"Was there anyone in the lobby when you arrived, besides the front desk staff?"

"Just a couple waiting to meet with Assistant Head Priest Makoto."

"Anybody else? Before the wedding or after?"

Yumi hesitated. Then she said, "No. Nobody else."

Kenji slipped his pen and pad back in his pocket. "Thanks. I appreciate your help."

They stood there awkwardly for a moment.

"Can I walk you back to your house?" he offered. "It's

kind of cold out here."

She shoved her hands in her jacket pockets and shook her head. "I'll go back in a minute."

"Well, here. Take these, at least." He held out the pack of tissues.

"Thanks, Ken-*kun*."

He bowed and turned to escape the way he came. *Don't look back,* he told himself. *Don't look back like you care. Don't let her think it's hard to walk away.*

He got himself around the next corner—even though that wasn't the way home—and slumped against the wall of the nearest house. He closed his eyes.

Well, he'd done it. Ripped that hook right out of his heart. He'd never felt so alone in his life.

Sunday, December 22

•

*9:00 A.M.*

The next morning, Section Chief Tanaka was stranded at home like many of the other police station employees. The train lines were still being checked for earthquake damage. But Kenji and Oki lived close enough to walk, and Suzuki had stayed overnight on a futon at the station, saving himself a four-hour trek home to Koenji.

Kenji's green tea sat cooling on the low coffee table surrounded by easy chairs that were meant to fool suspects into thinking interview room 3 was a lounge. The bright fluorescents overhead glared on the three laptops, various writing instruments, and assorted case notes that now covered the tabletop. Someone had apparently taken pity on the struggling plant that usually lived there and removed it for rehab.

Kenji wheeled the room's whiteboard closer. He wrote Head Priest Yano's name in the middle as Oki appeared with his own cup of tea. Dark circles beneath his eyes told Kenji his colleague had also been awakened at random intervals throughout the night by the aftershocks. Assistant Detective Suzuki appeared and seated himself in front of his perfectly aligned notebook and case notes.

Kenji took a seat and said, "I talked to Rowdy-*san* this morning. He told me the money in the closet added up to three million yen, all in new ten thousand yen notes. He lifted fingerprints, and hasn't had a chance to run them through the system yet, but he compared them to the victim's and none of them matched."

"So Yano never touched that money?" Oki said. "Kind of odd, if it was handed over as payment."

"Agreed. And what do you think he was selling—art treasures or nasty Polaroids?"

"I don't believe in coincidences. Three million is exactly what Koji Yamamoto was offering. The cash had to be payment for that kimono."

Kenji uncapped the marker. Off to one side of Yano's name he wrote "Koji Yamamoto."

Then he added, "Mitsubishi (Erai Museum)" and "Makoto."

"Okay," he said, turning to Suzuki. "What did you find out about the people who were at the shrine yesterday?"

The assistant detective consulted his notes.

"Makoto is married, with one child, and lives ten minutes away by train in Komagome. He walked his daughter to Saturday school at eight thirty, then says he came to the shrine to attend to a few chores before meeting with a couple about their wedding. Figuring in train time, that would put him at the shrine at around eight forty-five. But nobody actually saw him until he arrived at the admin building around ten."

"Someone saw him at nine forty-five," Kenji said. "I talked to the bride last night, and she told me she saw him carrying a *furoshiki* full of stuff near the sub-shrine next to the treasure house. She assumed he'd just arrived through the back gate and was headed somewhere other than the admin building."

Kenji put down the black marker and picked up the red one. Under Makoto's name on the whiteboard, he noted that the younger brother had no verified alibi from 8:45 to 9:45. He nodded for Suzuki to continue.

"The shrine maidens arrived to set up for the wedding

around nine, and were seen throughout the morning as they readied the sanctuary and did their usual Saturday chores. One of the girls went home at one thirty after the earthquake, along with most of the staff. The other one stayed to help the receptionist, who was at her post from nine on.

"The receptionist told me the other three workers arrived at nine and didn't leave the building until after the earthquake."

"Anyone else?" Kenji asked.

Suzuki looked down at his notes. "The only other people spotted at the shrine that morning were the couple who came to meet with Assistant Head Priest Makoto, a handful of neighborhood dog walkers passing through, and people associated with the Mitsuyama wedding." He ticked them off. The wedding photographer and his assistant, the hair-make woman, and the kimono dresser. "None of them arrived until shortly before ten. The groom's family arrived at eleven thirty. And there was a woman calling herself Mami who appeared outside the sanctuary after the earthquake, waiting to speak with the groom's father. The shrine maiden who told me about her said she looked like a bar hostess. Nobody could tell me exactly what time she arrived."

Why hadn't Yumi mentioned seeing this person, Kenji wondered. He frowned and wrote "Mami" on the board, then said, "Someone needs to ask Mitsuyama Senior what Mami's real name is, and what it was that she wanted so badly she pushed herself on him at his son's wedding to get it." He turned to Detective Oki. "Can you handle that? Track her down and ask where she was between seven that morning and when she appeared at the Mitsuyama wedding?"

"Will do."

Kenji recapped the pen and asked Suzuki, "Did you get fingerprints from everybody who was still there yesterday?"

"Yes."

Kenji's phone buzzed. He looked at the display. Tommy

Loud.

"Good morning, Rowdy-*san*," he said. "Don't tell me you've been up all night with our priest?"

"No, I was up all night with the aftershocks. Weren't you?"

Kenji admitted he hadn't had the best night's sleep. "There must have been about fifty of them."

"Seventy-three," said Loud, "but who's counting? Anyway, I wanted to tell you that the bodies are lined up at the morgue like shrine-goers on New Year's and we won't be getting to Yano's autopsy until Thursday."

"Well, at least that means we have a few more days to investigate before the big boys from downtown step in and demote us to bag carriers. Is there any chance you could unofficially take a look at the victim's head and tell us what kind of weapon we should be looking for?"

"No problem. My team will be stuck in Sugamo all morning, but I'll try to take a look when I get back this afternoon."

"Thanks. Anything you can give us would be appreciated. Do you have anything yet from the scene?"

"Yeah, lucky for you, I decided that if I wasn't going to sleep anyway, I might as well start running the prints. The snapshot we found in the priest's sleeve had some beauties on it. One set belonged to the victim. But whose name do you think popped up when I ran the others?"

"Koji Yamamoto?"

"Nope. And I bet you'll never guess who got caught shoplifting on her eighteenth birthday." The crime tech laughed. "I'll give you a hint. You could retire on what the tabloids would pay for this name."

"Who?"

"Flame."

"Flame? The guitarist for the VuDu Dolls?" Kenji groaned. "Are you telling me we've got a celebrity suspect?"

"No," Loud said. "Because she's dead."

"What?"

"Haven't you seen the news? The VuDu Dolls were all killed when the tsunami hit Odaiba. It would have been quite a feat if Flame had been in Tabata doing away with a priest while simultaneously recording a new album at Jimmy's Top Talent Studio."

"But her prints were on that picture. That means she met with Yano sometime before the murder. Do you think she's the one who gave him that Polaroid?"

"You tell me."

"What about the stack of money? If the victim's prints weren't on it, can you tell me whose were?"

"Yep. They weren't in the system, but I found out who they belong to. I asked one of the detectives in Organized Crime if he had an unofficial set for Koji Yamamoto, and some of the prints on that stack of money matched all four fingers and the thumb of his right hand." He paused. "But that juicy tidbit is for your information only. It won't be in the forensic report. He's never been arrested, so we don't have a set that's legally in the system. You're going to have to hit him with a charge that sticks in order to get his prints and make a legitimate match."

•

Kenji ended the call and told Oki and Suzuki what Tommy Loud had discovered so far.

Oki sat back and sipped his tea thoughtfully. "So what's the connection between a dead priest and a dead idol?"

"Maybe the girl in that picture is a runaway and Flame found out that Yano works with those kind of kids. Maybe she brought the picture to Yano to find out if he knew where the girl is," Kenji suggested.

Oki nodded thoughtfully. "Maybe. That suggests Flame knew the kid in that picture."

"That's possible," Suzuki said. "Helping runaways was one of the causes she sponsored. She left home herself when she was fifteen."

Kenji and Oki turned to him, surprised.

"How do you know that?" Kenji asked.

Suzuki colored. "My little sister has been a fan since the VuDu Dolls started out. My parents wouldn't let her go to concerts alone, so I went with her. I, uh, kind of ended up liking them," he admitted. "Their music is really solid. Flame was actually a pretty decent musician. She wrote their first hit." Suzuki looked from Oki's surprised face to Kenji's. "What?" he said defensively.

Kenji's extra-straight assistant detective was a secret fan of androgynous idols like the VuDu Dolls? Kenji preferred groups in which the boys were boys and the girls were girls and it was easy to tell the difference, but because most Japanese men don't have heavy beards and aren't much bigger than Japanese women, it's easy for artists to blur the line.

"Look, I just got interested in them because of my sister," Suzuki protested.

Kenji laughed. "Knowing how you get 'interested' in things, Mr. Two-Time Kanji Champion of the Greater Kanto Region, I bet you know everything about Miss Flame, right down to what kind of toothpaste she brushes her teeth with before bed."

"Aquafresh," Suzuki supplied promptly. "But everybody knows that. The ads are all over prime-time TV. She also drives a Honda, wears a Seiko watch, and washes her hair with Super Mild."

"Where can we find out about the charities she sponsors?" Oki asked.

Suzuki typed something into his laptop, then swiveled it around so they could see the first ten of 1.9 million hits on the search term "VuDu Dolls." He clicked on the third result.

A photo of four pouting young musicians filled the

screen. They were dressed in lace and white leather, and their beautiful faces looked like dolls. Circle contacts and false eyelashes made their eyes unnaturally waif-like, and their rosebud lips could have belonged to any geisha in Gion. The vocalist wore her hair in schoolgirl bangs and pigtails, but the right half was bleached blonde. The one leaning on a sparkling pink electric bass had spiky black hair, and the drummer sported bleached ringlets. The guitarist had her ebony guitar slung low on her hips, the long braid snaking over her shoulder almost white. She was wearing one long, fingerless, white lace glove.

The words "Welcome To The Dollhouse" scrolled across the top of the website. Suzuki clicked on Bios and the page flipped to blurbs about the individual band members. He pointed to the last sentence on Flame's page, which told fans she supported A Safe Place for runaways and the abandoned animal rescue group Hope To Life.

"Why is she wearing only one glove?" Kenji asked, peering at the photo.

"It's one of her trademarks. She's never been photographed without it. There are all kinds of rumors about why she does it. Jimmy's Top Talent official fan page says it's her lucky glove. Unofficial pages say she's got scars or burns from a childhood accident. *The Dollhouse* says she's got a flame tattoo, to go with her stage name."

"Any truth to that?"

"That's the rumor I'd believe," Suzuki said. "Jimmy Harajuku is famous for creating his idols out of as much fiction as fact. He's always hiring hackers to try and take *The Dollhouse* down, because the webmaster is surprisingly good at digging up the truth and publishing it." Suzuki clicked on the Forums icon and the page filled with a list of topics like "Flame Dating Kengo?" and "Nana X Flame = Girls Love???"

"Wow, if this is all true, she's been busy." Kenji laughed, pointing to a topic further down the page titled "Flame

Secretly Married With Kids!"

"This forum is just a catch-all for the usual crazy rumors," Suzuki said. "But the guy who runs *The Dollhouse* sifts through them and somehow finds gold in the mountain of trash."

"Send me the link, will you? And can you follow up with everyone who left the shrine before you had a chance to talk to them yesterday? Oki-*san*, would you mind running down the unknown calls on the victim's phone?" Kenji checked the time. "I have to start walking to the Tabata Shrine to meet with Makoto. He left me a message that the valuable Edo-era kimono he told us about is missing from the treasure house, but he can't find any record of a sale. We sealed the head priest's office, so I warned him not to go in until I get there. He's eager to prove that his brother did a legitimate transaction with one of the two bidders, so he can claim that stack of cash we found in the upstairs room."

"Did the victim leave a will?"

"I'll ask." Kenji slipped his computer into its bag. "When I get back, let's head over to Kabuki-chō and pay a call on Koji Yamamoto."

But first he had a text to send. While they'd been looking at the fan site, it had occurred to him that if Flame had given Yano the Polaroid, whoever it belonged to must have an association with the VuDu Dolls. And he knew someone who'd been backstage, who was an even bigger fan than Suzuki. Yumi. Maybe she knew where he could get the names of the hangers-on who orbited the idols, buffing their images and catering to their needs.

•

Makoto took one file cabinet, Kenji the other. The hands on the clock over Head Priest Yano's desk ticked away the better part of an hour before Kenji got to a crisp blue folder, halfway through the third drawer. It was unlabeled, the only new-looking folder in the file. He pulled it.

"Did you find something?" asked Makoto, looking up from his own search.

"Yes," Kenji said, scanning the bound document within. "But it's not a bill of sale for an Edo-era kimono. What do you make of this?" He passed it to Makoto.

The assistant head priest's eyes widened as he flipped through the pages. "It looks like an inventory of what's stored in the treasure house." He started back at the beginning and went through it more slowly. "But . . . why did he make a list without telling me? Are there any insurance papers in the file?"

"No," Kenji said.

The priest stopped on page three, staring.

"This isn't my brother's handwriting," he said.

"Someone helped him make the inventory? Who?"

Makoto's face darkened. "The only one with enough free time would have been Taiga-*kun*."

"Who's Taiga-*kun*?"

"He's sort of an apprentice. Or—what do you call it?—an intern."

"Is he a relative?"

"No. My brother told me he was the son of an old friend. He said that Taiga was thinking about studying for the priesthood. My brother offered to let him live here for a while to see what shrine life was like. He arrived a little over a month ago, so we were still finding ways for him to be useful."

"And what kind of things were you discovering he was good at?"

Makoto looked uncomfortable. "Well, lying for one. When I asked him why he wanted to be a priest, he told me he'd been thinking about it since he was a child. But on the very first day, he faked his way through even the commonest *norito* prayers during the Rooster Day ceremony." He paused. "Also, I thought it was weird that he shaved his head, like he was considering becoming a Buddhist priest, not a Shinto *kannushi*." Makoto shook his head. "It worries me that my brother might have asked him to help with the treasure house inventory. If things went missing before they were catalogued, we'd never know."

"Has he been stealing from the shrine?"

"I don't know."

"Is he staying here on the grounds?"

"No. He spent a lot of time at my brother's house, but he doesn't live there."

"We need to talk to him about where he was yesterday," Kenji said. "When we finish here, can you find him?"

"If he shows up."

"He's not here?"

"Not when I last checked. And he's not answering his phone."

"Does he do this often?"

"He's never been a no-show, but sometimes he's late and I catch him nodding off in strange corners, like he's been up all night."

"No explanation?"

"No." Makoto hesitated, then continued, "He evades answering questions about himself, even ordinary ones like how old he is, or if he has brothers and sisters. And . . . he always wears long sleeves. I wondered if something was wrong with him. Or had been, in the past."

"Like . . . ?"

"A lot of the kids my brother works with at the runaway shelter have scars no kid should have. I wondered if Taiga-*kun* was one of those. Maybe he didn't want us to see what someone had done to him. Or what he'd done to himself."

"Meaning . . . ?"

"The suicide rate among those kids is pretty high. My brother was devastated about a year ago when one of the girls he'd been working with killed herself. I wondered if Taiga-*kun* had a history of suicide attempts. Maybe my brother invited him to work at the shrine so he could keep an eye on him, make sure he didn't try again."

"What's his first name?"

"Hikaru."

Hikaru Taiga. Kenji made a note. "Is there any way to find out where he's living? Or find out where he's from? People often run back to familiar places."

Makoto turned back to the file cabinet and opened the top drawer, drawing out a folder labeled "Employees." After paging through it, he shook his head. "Not here. Which isn't surprising, I guess, since he wasn't being paid."

They resumed their hunt through the files, but it wasn't until an hour later that Kenji discovered the last file drawer was only half full. Hidden behind the last hanging file was a battered cardboard box.

Lifting it out, Kenji removed the lid. Inside was a pile of loose photos, the colors beginning to shift with age. Snapshots of a baby's chubby face crowned with a shock of black hair matured into a toddler with red cheeks and a bowl cut, intently crouching down next to a curve-backed Martin guitar, one dimpled hand poking at the strings. The child never got older than one or two, though, the most recent shot showing the toddler laughing on the shoulders of a young man with extravagant bleached hair, who was wearing a black T-shirt with "Meatsnake" rendered across the front in elaborate gothic letters.

Stashed alongside the photos was a small blue booklet with the familiar logo of Shinsei Bank on the front. Kanji pulled it from its plastic sleeve and looked at the name on the account. Hiroshi Yano. The head priest.

He flipped it open. The victim had deposited ¥50,000 faithfully every month for twenty-six years. He showed the book to Makoto. The assistant head priest's eyes widened at the final figure. Over fifteen million yen.

"Do you have any idea why your brother opened this account?"

Makoto shook his head, but they both knew there was only one explanation.

"If he had a child," Makoto said, "nobody knew."

•

The trains were running again. Standing on the platform at Komagome Station, Yumi finished answering Kenji's text, giving him her official fan club ID and password as well as links to the biggest VuDu Dolls fan pages.

*Done.* Send.

The train arrived and she stepped aboard. Now she could return to fretting about this morning's phone conversation with Ichiro's mother.

She'd left several polite messages on Mrs. Mitsuyama's voicemail since the earthquake, asking if there was anything she could do to be of service, but there had been no return calls. Then, as she was standing in line at the Family Mart with a tuna-mayo rice ball in one hand and bottle of cold tea in the other, her phone rang. It was from the landline number at the Mitsuyama family home in Hiroo.

Yumi had quickly stowed her intended purchases next to the cello-wrapped melon bread and run outside to take the call. Standing between the hot/cold drink vending machine and the recycling bins, she exchanged pleasantries with Ichiro's mother as they politely assured each other that their families were fine and everyone had recovered considerably since the earthquake. Then Mrs. Mitsuyama had suggested that since the main streets had been cleared enough for traffic to begin flowing somewhat normally again, if Yumi wanted to pack up the clothes and personal belongings she'd moved to the rooms she'd planned to share with Ichiro after the wedding, the Mitsuyamas' driver could help her convey them back to Komagome. Would Tuesday be convenient?

Yumi bit her lip. Was Ichiro's mother just being practical, knowing that she had moved all her earthly goods to Hiroo and couldn't live for long out of the small suitcase she'd packed for the honeymoon? Or was this move intended to be more permanent?

Yumi got off the train, and a few minutes later was pushing open the door at the Mad Hatter. She was knocked back by a cloud of scotch–vodka–*shō-chū* fumes more potent than the stiffest White Rabbit.

"*Irasshaimase*, Yumi-*chan*." The owner-bartender paused with a dustpan full of broken glass. Today he was wearing a towel tied around his head like a construction worker instead of a hat from the now-dusty collection sitting on the long shelf above the bar. Boshi-*san* had never been seen without some kind of headgear; it was rumored that he was even wearing a hat in his baby pictures.

As Yumi's eyes adjusted to the grotto-like atmosphere, she saw that the earthquake had tipped Boshi-*san's* collection of Alice in Wonderland action figures helter-skelter inside the clear cases mounted on the far wall. The display had grown to include over a hundred different versions, all painted with Alice's trademark blue dress, white pinafore, and golden hair. A Godzilla Alice was lying on its side between Atom Boy Alice and the bartender's newest addition, a furry, stuffed Totoro Alice, for which someone had hand stitched a white pinafore and personally curled a yellow yarn wig.

A couple of the Lolitas had loyally turned out to help Boshi-*san* put his bar back together, pastel and Gothic Bo-Peeps wielding brooms and dust mops like a fairy tale cleaning crew. Yumi waved to Midori, whose neck bow was pristinely white against her Gothic Lolita frock coat, mopping the floor in her platform boots. A Sweet Lolita in a white ruffled pinafore and pale-yellow dress was busy unscrewing the display cases, righting the figures, and securing them with earthquake putty. She was wearing a white paper surgical mask, helping with the cleaning even though she was suffering from the cold that was rampaging through Tokyo.

Boshi-*san* dumped his dustpan in a half-full garbage bag and straightened, stretching his back. "Can I get you anything, Yumi-*chan*?"

"No thanks, Boshi-*san*. I'm looking for Coco. Is she here yet?"

"You just missed her. She got a call from the manager at the Queen of Hearts, asking her to come help clean up the club." Yumi's best friend, unbeknownst to her parents, moonlighted at a hostess club in Kabuki-chō a few nights a week, pouring drinks, flattering salarymen, and taking home ten times what she made at her day job selling tea ceremony sweets at a respectable store in Ginza.

"Thanks, I'll catch her there," Yumi said. "But as long as I'm here, can I help you clean up?"

"I can't believe she's dead!" a voice wailed as the door opened to admit a pair of Gothic Lolitas. One was hunched over, crying, and the other had an arm around her waist. Yumi recognized the weeping girl, who'd graduated from Koshikawa High School three years behind her.

"Haru-*chan*, what's wrong?" Midori dropped her brush and ran across the room to the girl whose puffy eyes and tearstained face didn't fit with her perfectly starched ruffly black dress, beribboned pigtails, and the bouncy tassel of VuDu Dolls character stuffies clipped to her purse.

"I just saw Flame live at the Budokan last month," she sobbed. "I can't believe she's gone!"

"Me neither," said Midori. "This morning on the train, I put on my earphones right in the middle of 'Don't Need You' and I nearly burst out crying."

"Haru-*chan*?" The Sweet Lolita who had been fixing the Alices emerged from the restroom. "Thank God you're safe! How did you get back?"

"Back? From where? What are you talking about?"

"Weren't you and Taku away for the weekend? It was your birthday on Saturday, right?"

Haru's eyes widened in surprise, then narrowed in anger. "Away for the weekend? He told me he had to work!"

"Wait, you didn't go . . . together?"

"How do you know he went somewhere for the weekend?" Haru demanded.

Her friend cringed. "Last Monday I was working in the trailer office at the construction site he was at, and he asked me how to find a hotel with a reasonable overnight 'stay' rate. I . . . I figured he was planning to take you away for your birthday."

Haru stamped her foot in its multi-buckled platform boot. "That cheating bastard! I knew he was lying. He's with that fangirl, I know it! The one who started stalking him after they played in Saitama!"

Haru began pouring out an aggrieved account of how Taku had promised to take her to Disneyland on Saturday for her birthday, then on Monday he'd called to ask if they could move the celebration to the next weekend because he had to work double shifts on an emergency construction job. But when Haru had gone to his construction site on Tuesday to surprise him with some homemade cupcakes, the foreman told her he wasn't there, that he'd taken the rest of the week off.

"What band is he in?" Yumi asked Midori.

"He's the guitarist for that all-boy VuDu Dolls tribute band we saw at the O-West last year."

Now Yumi remembered. Haru's boyfriend styled himself as a boy version of Flame. He didn't look much like the idol, even in stage makeup, but if you closed your eyes, his lightning-fast fingers made you think you were listening to the real thing.

". . . so Tuesday night I waited outside his building until three in the morning and when he finally came home, I asked him why he wasn't at work and wasn't returning my calls. He said he'd been at the practice studio and it's soundproofed so there's no reception, and by the time he quit and went outside for a smoke, it was too late to call me back." Haru scowled. "He had his guitar with him, so I believed him, the asshole. He promised up one side and down the other that all he'd been doing was practice. Alone. Said I could even call the rehearsal space to check if I wanted." She hung her head. "I believed him. I wanted to believe him. I stayed at his place that night and he was so sweet, said he really did have to work all weekend, that he was really sorry about my birthday, but that next weekend he'd be rolling in cash and he'd make it all up to me. He promised we'd do something way more special than going to Disneyland." She scowled. "But now that I know he's with that slut in Saitama..."

"Saitama?" Haru's friend exclaimed. "No, no, he's not in Saitama. He said he needed to find a place to stay near the Fuji TV building."

"Taku went to Odaiba on Friday?" Haru cried. "He was there during the tsunami?"

Pulling out her phone, she made a call, listening intently. Slowly, she lowered it. "Voicemail. Again. He's still not answering. He hasn't returned any of my calls since Sunday morning. Before the quake."

"His battery could be dead," Midori said. "Electricity is still out, I heard. There's probably no place to charge it."

Yumi added, "Maybe you can go to the Odaiba evacuation center home page and look for his name on the list of people who've checked in to say they're okay."

Haru nodded and began to navigate her way to the emergency pages that had been set up since the devastating Tōhoku earthquake in 2011, so people could find out quickly that their remote relatives were safe.

"Got it," she said, her eyes intently scanning the names as she scrolled down the list. She got to the end and bit her lip.

Then she jumped back to the top and scrolled again, this time more slowly. She looked up, her face stricken.

"His name's not here."

•

"We didn't find a sales receipt in Yano's office or on his computer for that kimono," Kenji told Oki as they walked toward the Yamamoto-*gumi* headquarters building in Kabuki-chō. "But we did discover that he made a full inventory of the valuables in the treasure house. Without his brother's knowledge."

"You think he was intending to get them insured?"

"Nothing suggesting that in the file. But I'm not the only one who was wondering if he was planning to sell them. The question is, why did he suddenly need the money?"

"Must have been something his younger brother wouldn't approve of."

"I'm beginning to wonder if Makoto was as surprised as he seemed to be when I found that list. What if he found out what his brother was up to? How angry would he have been to discover that the shrine's assets were being sold off and the money used for something besides urgent repairs? He makes no secret of the fact that he thought his brother was doing a bad job of being head priest, a job he wanted for himself."

"Well, if he killed his brother in order to inherit the head priest's position, that bankbook you found yesterday could put a big crimp in his plans," Oki pointed out. "We should check the succession rubrics for the priesthood at the Tabata Shrine, but if Yano has an illegitimate child and the child is a boy, it could be him who's in line to be the next head priest, not Makoto."

"If that's the case, it would be a good idea to find the kid before Makoto does."

"Agreed. But not just because he might be the next victim. I'm sure it's occurred to you that the kid might have done it."

"Suspects One-Oh-One," Kenji agreed. "Family first."

"When you think about it, how would you feel if your dad abandoned you when you were a baby? You grow up living with your mom and maybe her parents, since it's nearly impossible to raise a kid on your own and put food on the table at the same time. And whenever she's feeling like life handed her a bowl of rocks, you hear how different your lives would have been if your dad weren't such a selfish asshole. Over and over she tells you stories about how daddy was a famous musician but he threw you away before you were old enough to remember. She's none too pleased that her own life was over before it began. Every time you do something she doesn't like, she reminds you that she had to give up everything she loved—the concerts, the parties, the rich and famous—because of you."

"So you search him out and kill him?" Kenji said skeptically.

"No, but you grow up, you get curious. Is your dad really as bad as your mom says? Or is she just a bitter old wannabe, and he's actually been looking for you his whole life, eager to share the fame and fortune that are rightfully yours? So you track him down. You want to meet him, but there's a fifty-fifty chance your mom is right and the guy wants nothing to do with you. So you figure out a way to get close to him, find out."

Kenji nodded. "And in this case, Daddy turns out to be a good guy who's given up his decadent ways to become a priest and is eager to hand over the fifteen-point-six million yen he's been saving for you since you were born. So why kill him?"

"Good question," Oki conceded. "Unless you find out something about Daddy Dearest that tips you over the edge and lets out all that pent-up resentment."

Kenji nodded. "Maybe someone at the bank can help us figure out who's in line to get that savings account. And if

Yano kept a safety deposit box, there might be a copy of his will in it. Makoto told me he hadn't seen it yet because the family lawyer recently moved his office to Odaiba and everything is a shambles out there. Asking at the bank would probably be faster than waiting for the lawyer to dig his will out of the wreckage."

"And where does the missing intern Taiga fit in?"

"I'd like to ask him," Kenji replied. "What he was really doing at the shrine? Makoto thinks he might be one of the abused kids his brother worked with."

"If Yano picked up Taiga at that shelter where he volunteered, maybe the director can point us in the right direction."

They arrived at a beige tiled building crowned with a family crest of three golden tadpoles swimming in a circle. They paused before going in and Kenji said, "After we're finished here with Koji Yamamoto, I'll pay the shelter director a visit."

•

The door was locked. Oki rang the intercom button and pressed his face against the glass, peering into the lobby at the Yamamoto-*gumi chinpira* manning the lobby desk. The punk stared back, then lifted the receiver of the phone at his elbow.

"What do you want?" came his tinny voice through the intercom.

"Police. Let us in."

The door buzzed. As Oki and Kenji entered, the kid at the desk insolently lit a cigarette and regarded them through half-closed eyes.

"Ryo-*kun*! What are you doing?" Oki bellowed. "You'll never make black belt if you smoke." In a few strides, the big detective crossed the lobby and snatched the cigarette out of the kid's mouth. He ripped it in half and angrily crushed the still-burning end in the overflowing ashtray.

"Don't tell me what to do!" Ryo blazed. Then his eyes slid away and he muttered, "I quit that judo shit anyway."

"Why aren't you in school?"

He slouched back in his chair and looked at Oki defiantly. "I'm sixteen. I don't have to be in school if I don't wanna be."

"Is your brother still in jail?"

"He'll be out in seven months."

Oki sighed. "Can't you see there's no upside to getting involved with this outfit?"

The kid looked away, muttering, "Pays better than working at a *conbini*."

Oki regarded the high school dropout and sighed. "Then do your job. Call upstairs. Tell them we're here to see Koji-*kun*."

Reminded of his power as gatekeeper, the kid asked, "Do you have an appointment, Oki-*sensei*?"

"Don't push me," Oki growled.

"Well, they're gonna ask," he whined. Oki slid the phone over to him and handed him the receiver.

The kid dialed and put on his toughest voice. "Hey. There are a couple of cops here. They want to see Yamamoto-*san*. Junior." He listened for a few seconds then said, "No, they don't." He listened again. "The Hammer. And some other guy . . ." He looked questioningly at Kenji.

"Detective Nakamura."

"Some guy named Nakamura." He listened again. "Okay, I'll tell them." He dropped the phone back in its cradle. "He's coming down."

"Who?"

"Kubota-*san*."

Oki snorted. "Froggy? That guy's not in jail? I hear he liked it so much in juvie, he's been trying to get sent back ever since." The punk behind the desk frowned and reached for the cigarettes in his pocket but Oki gave him a don't-even-think-of-it look, so he pulled out his comb instead, as if that was what he'd been reaching for all along.

The elevator doors slid open, and a short, square man swaggered out in a snappy suit and dark shirt. His wide mouth told Kenji where he got his nickname.

"Well, if it isn't The Hammer," Kubota said, his jaw jutting. "I never expected to see you here. If you're thinking of quitting the cops, we can always use some dumb muscle."

"Same old Froggy—still short as a *kappa* and twice as thick. We're here to see Koji-*kun*."

He smirked. "Too bad you don't have an appointment."

Kenji stepped forward. "We don't need an appointment." He showed his badge to Kubota. "I'm Detective Nakamura and we're investigating a murder, so unless you'd like to spend the next few hours down at the station, why don't you just take us to see Mr. Yamamoto?"

Kubota squinted at Kenji's card. "Well, Detective Nakamura, Mr. Yamamoto is a very busy man. He may not be in today."

"You miss getting the shit beat out of you or something, Kubota?" said Oki. "Tell Koji we're here."

"You'll have to come back. He's really not in today."

"We'll pay him a visit at home, then."

"He's not there, either. He went to Odaiba, to deliver disaster supplies."

*Gangsters dispensing charity?*

But Oki didn't bat an eye. "Give him my regrets, then, and call Yamamoto Senior. If we can't talk to Koji, we'll talk to the *oyabun*."

"You're joking, right?"

"Call him. Unless you want a whole lot of attention to suddenly be paid to that floating mah-jongg game you're running on the sixth floor of that building in Shinjuku he asked you to find a tenant for."

Kubota blanched and reached for his phone.

Five minutes later, they stepped from the elevator into a hushed anteroom that looked like the entry to a *daimyo's* palace. Leaving their shoes on the smooth stone pavers, they stepped into the straw slippers set out on the *tatami* floor for guests.

"Wait here," Kubota growled. He crossed to the sliding door in the far wall and knocked softly. It opened and he slipped through to speak to someone on the other side. The the door whispered closed on its smooth wooden track.

While they waited, Kenji examined the sword set displayed in a spotlit showcase set into the far wall. It had to be at least five hundred years old, but the steel gleamed as brightly as the day it was made.

"Yamamoto-*oyabun* will see you now, gentlemen."

The voice belonged to a small, balding man who had appeared from beyond the sliding door. He looked like a bean counter in his plain black suit, white shirt, and dark tie.

They followed him down a hallway with shoji screens on either side. The floor was made of polished wood that chirped as they walked over it. Nobody would be sneaking up on this *oyabun* anytime soon, Kenji thought. Where had the boss of the Yamamoto crime family found an artisan who could still build a nightingale floor?

The accountant stopped at the end and knocked on the sliding door to their left.

"Enter."

The factotum slid the door aside and bowed, allowing Oki and Kenji to step up into the Yamamoto-*gumi* boss's presence.

Although the man behind the low, black lacquer table wore a modern business suit and white shirt, he sat like a samurai lord receiving petitioners. Hair too black for his years was brushed straight back from his forehead, and the thin scar angling down his cheek had aged to the same color as his bronzed skin. Behind him in the *tokonoma* alcove hung an ink scroll depicting the Battle of Sekigahara.

Oki bowed, none too deeply, and Kenji followed his cue. The man behind the desk inclined his head.

"Sit," he said, gesturing to two thin cushions on the floor opposite.

Oki offered him a business card with both hands, and Kenji did the same. Oki had explained that the Yamamoto-*gumi* went back nine generations, and if he and Kenji wanted to get anything out of them voluntarily, it paid to treat them like the businessmen they claimed to be.

The balding retainer returned, bearing a golden lacquer tray with a delicate Nabeshima teapot and three cups. Steam coiled from the spout as the lieutenant poured. He retired, shutting the door softly behind him.

The *oyabun* inhaled the steam from his cup appreciatively, admired the plum-blossom motif painted on the side, then took a sip, savoring the flavor of the tea. He set down his cup.

"It's been a long time, Oki-*kun*. You look fit. Now that you're with the police, I suppose you can assault children whenever you feel like it without fear of being punished."

"Only when they deserve it," Oki replied evenly.

Oki had told Kenji that when they were kids, he had given Koji the thin white scar that bisected his left eyebrow after he caught the *oyabun's* son tormenting a younger boy. Yamamoto Senior had apparently not forgiven or forgotten.

"How may I be of service to you today, gentlemen?" Yamamoto asked.

Oki set down his cup and said, "You can tell us why Koji-*kun* was buying himself a nice kimono from the head priest at the Tabata Shrine."

The *oyabun's* eyes narrowed. "And who told you he was doing that?"

Oki didn't answer.

"It's a pity," Yamamoto said, taking another sip of tea,

"that Yano-*kannushi* isn't more discreet. I don't think we'll be working with him again."

"I don't either," Oki said. "He's dead."

The *oyabun's* teacup stopped halfway to his lips. He stared at Oki for a moment, then said, "May he rest in peace."

He set the cup carefully in its cherry-wood saucer. Folding his hands on the table before him, he asked, "What does the priest's death have to do with me? Or my son?"

"That's what we'd like to ask him. Because the night before Yano-*san* died, Koji-*kun* left a phone message suggesting that he wasn't happy the priest had turned down his offer, and he was planning to pay a visit to the shrine to convince him otherwise. I have experience with Koji's methods, and it wouldn't surprise me if Yano ended up dead when he refused to sell."

"What do you mean? We outbid the museum. My son told me that Yano-*san* accepted our offer."

"Really?" Oki said, eyebrows raised. "Why were you buying it? I thought your taste ran more to weapons and such."

"I intend to make a present of it."

"To whom?"

The gangster smiled. "The Erai Museum."

"What?" Kenji exclaimed. "Then why were they bidding against you for it?"

Yamamoto turned to him. "Why, Mr. . . . ." He picked up Kenji's card and peered at it, as if to remind himself of Kenji's name. "Detective Nakamura, I wondered the same thing. I told them what I intended to do, and for no reason, they told me they would refuse such a gift. But they wanted it badly, I could see it in the director's eyes. I knew he wouldn't be able to resist once it was laid out in front of him."

"So why did they bid against you?"

Yamamoto shook his head sadly. "The director is a foolish man. He had the nerve to suggest that money can be dirty or clean. Money is money, Detective. Hearts may be dirty or clean, but money is just money. All I asked was that he name a museum gallery after my father, in return for a generous donation and the kimono he wanted so badly. Then he bid against me, just to drive the price up. I don't like that little man, Detective, but what could I do? In the end, I won." He took a sip of tea.

"In the end, you didn't." Oki said. "The email records show that Yano intended to accept half a million yen less than the three million Koji-*kun* offered, just so he didn't have to sell it to you."

"Three million?" Surprise, then anger flashed through Yamamoto's eyes.

"What's the matter, Yamamoto-*san*? Is that number less than what Koji told you it would cost?"

Stony silence.

"Did he deliver the goods?"

"No. Not yet. He told me he'd bring it to me along with the provenance papers when he gets back from Odaiba."

"I'd look at those papers very carefully if I were you," Oki said. "They're not worth the paper they're printed on if they're forged. Because you know what the crime scene said to me? It told me Yano refused to sell Koji that kimono, so your boy killed the priest and helped himself, leaving a stack of ten thousand yen notes in its place. When he gets back from his mission of mercy, ask him how much he paid. I'll bet my black belt the rest of the money you gave him is going into the porn biz he's running behind your back."

Yamamoto set down his cup. "I know all about his adult entertainment business. It's one of our most profitable divisions."

"What about the kiddie porn? And the snuff films?"

Yamamoto slammed his hands flat on the table. "Get out," he said, between clenched teeth.

Oki drained his cup and pointedly set it on the glossy

table instead of on its saucer. He stood.

"Thanks for the tea. And do ask Koji about that kimono deal when he gets back."

Kenji followed him out the door. Behind them, the sound of a delicate Nabeshima teacup smashing as it hit the wall.

•

Kenji and Oki skirted the pile of garbage bags outside a building that had both front windows boarded up. All along the sidewalk, boxes and bags securely taped and neatly labeled "Danger! Broken Glass Inside" were lined up, awaiting Kabuki-chō's next non-burnable trash collection day.

Kenji had felt his phone vibrate in his pocket during the meeting. He pulled it out as they returned to the police station and returned Tommy Loud's call.

"Hi Rowdy-*san*. Sorry, I was in a meeting. What have you got for me?"

"I swung by the morgue and took a look at the wound on your victim's head," Loud replied. "It's a straight gash exactly ten centimeters long. You're looking for a murder weapon with a sharp edge that thickens at about a thirty-degree angle, like a chisel. But it had to be swung with a lot of force to make a wound that deep, so it's probably got a handle, or it's heavy, or both. I was thinking maybe a vase? Or a statue?"

Kenji thought for a moment. "I didn't see anything like that at the scene."

"Me neither. Which means if the assailant took it away with him, you're also looking for a suspect who was carrying a bag or a *furoshiki* carrying cloth, something big enough to stash it in."

"Thanks. That helps a lot," Kenji said. "Any more on the fingerprints?"

"Sorry, not yet."

"Okay, thanks, Rowdy-*san*. Call me when you've got anything else." He ended the call, and as he was telling Oki about the murder weapon, he saw a man come out of the Hotel Titanic love hotel across the street.

Kenji stopped midsentence. It was Ichiro Mitsuyama.

"Nakamura-*san*?" Oki followed his gaze as a woman emerged behind him. She stopped to twist up her shoulder-length hair with a sparkly clip.

"Hey, isn't that your friend . . . ?"

Yumi. Kenji's stomach clenched. She slipped her arm through Ichiro's and then he remembered: Yumi's hair wasn't that long anymore.

The woman leaned in to give Ichiro a kiss before they parted.

Kenji held up his phone and snapped a picture.

•

Yumi pressed the bell under the backlit sign of a huge playing card emblazoned "Queen of Hearts," the hostess club where Coco moonlighted. Looking up at the security camera she knew was hidden in the crown, Yumi wiggled her fingers and blew a kiss. A few minutes later, the heavy gilded door cracked open and Coco's face appeared.

"Yu-*chan*, what took you so long?" She stood back so Yumi could enter, then led her down a hallway lined with glamour shots of the twenty-three Queen of Hearts hostesses. There was Mami, the club's top earner, leading the parade in a slinky red gown.

Yumi had hoped Mami was here today, helping clean up the club, so she could ask if Mami had seen anyone at the shrine on the morning Head Priest Yano was killed. Yumi felt guilty about withholding information from the police about Mami being there that morning, but she couldn't offer up her future father-in-law's personal peccadillos for police scrutiny without a very good reason. If the press got ahold of a juicy rumor like that, the Mitsuyama name would be splashed across tabloid headlines for days.

"What's with your nails today?" Yumi asked as Coco parted the bead curtain at the end of the hall with her extravagantly long talons.

"Like them?" Coco laughed, turning and holding her fingers together to show Yumi the red-and-gold dragon art that coiled across the tips of her fingers, the end of its tail on one pinky and its nose on the other. "Our biggest client is bringing a party of Beijing businessmen tonight."

"You're not coming to the VuDu Dolls tribute in Yoyogi Park?"

Legend had it that the famous promoter Jimmy Harajuku discovered Flame on his way to a cherry blossom drinking party in Yoyogi Park. He'd stopped to listen to four guitar-bashing teenagers because they'd managed to attract a crowd considerably larger than the loyal moms-and-boyfriends who usually cheered for the free performers. The promoter stayed to listen until the park patrolmen came by on their rounds and told the girls to pack it up, that loud music was not allowed. That was the last time anyone ever told them to stop.

Coco shook her head regretfully. "I wish I could go, but Manager-*san* needs me tonight. The last earthquake shut down all of Kabuki-chō for over a month, and the club won't survive if it happens again. Are you going?"

Yumi nodded. "With a few girls from the Hatter." She told Coco about Haru and Taku.

When she finished, Coco looked skeptical. "Well, it would be awful if Taku really is missing. But you know Haru—bit of a drama queen, even without the excuse of a major earthquake. The news is saying that only a handful of people actually died, and most of them were old. There was nearly half an hour between the quake and the tsunami, so anybody who could walk had plenty of time to scramble for higher ground. And Taku . . ." Coco wrinkled her nose. "He might not be with his latest squeeze in Saitama, but that doesn't mean he hasn't got one in Odaiba."

They emerged into the main room of the club through a columned archway glittering with crystals. The Queen of Hearts was done up in rococo gold and red, from the tasseled velvet curtains that shielded the semiprivate booths from the eyes of other customers, to the gilded sconces that threw flattering light on men whose most attractive feature was generally the thickness of their wallets. Every night except Monday, the Queen of Hearts hostesses poured drinks, lit cigarettes, and made the ordinary guys who slaved away in corporate offices feel like they were the most attractive men on the planet. For a price, of course.

Yumi followed Coco through to the crystal-spangled bar, where the woman who had appeared at the shrine the day of her wedding was helping the bartender polish earthquake dust from the liquor bottles.

"Mami-*chan*?" Coco said, pulling out two barstools. "This is my friend Yumi."

The willowy girl turned, her red sweater pulled tight by breasts she hadn't been given by Mother Nature. Long bleached hair was pulled into a messy knot atop her head, secured with a sparkly clip.

Her eyes widened in surprise. "Wait—last weekend . . . was that you? At the Tabata Shrine? In the wedding kimono?"

Yumi nodded.

Mami put down her cleaning rag and bowed low from the waist.

"*Moshiwake gozaimasen*," she apologized. "I'm so sorry for intruding. I had planned to wait until afterward and catch Mitsuyama-*san* on the way to the reception, but then the earthquake happened and everyone came out early. I . . . I hope I didn't disrupt your wedding. Did you go ahead, after everything stopped shaking?"

"No. It's been . . . postponed."

Mami cocked her head and regarded Yumi for a moment, then came around the bar and leaned against it.

"Forgive me for asking, but a few months ago, Mitsuyama-*san* told me his son was getting married to someone he met through *o-miai*. Was that . . . you?"

Yumi sighed.

"Well, if that's the case, maybe that earthquake was a gift to you from the *kami-sama*."

"What do you mean?"

"I hope I'm not shocking you," Mami continued, "but your *kon'yakusha's* father has been a client of mine for a long time, and over time we developed a . . . special relationship. He bought the apartment where I live, and he's given me many generous gifts over the years. But then about six months ago, he pretty much stopped coming to the club, except on business. He threw me a party as usual on my birthday, but when I unwrapped his present, it was just a little Louis Vuitton wallet—the kind I already have—instead of the purse I'd been hinting I wanted. I was so disappointed!"

She pulled her phone from her pocket. "Then on Tuesday, he sent me this." She navigated to an e-mail, then passed the phone to Yumi.

> To: mamichan@docomo.co.jp
> Date: March 17, 6:47 p.m.
> From:jmitsuyama@mitsuyama.co.jp
>
> It is most regrettable, but the apartment where you live is being sold and it will be necessary for you to find new accommodations by the first of next month. I will send movers to assist you with your things on the 30th. I am very sorry for the inconvenience."

"Yikes," Yumi said, handing back the phone. "Kind of . . . short notice."

"Yeah, totally unreasonable, right? I mean, it's impossible for me to find a new place that quickly, plus when I called to ask if he could at least help me with the key money and first-

and-last for a new place, he said he couldn't." Her voice rose with indignation. "'Couldn't'? More like, 'Wouldn't'! After that, he refused to pick up when I called and he didn't answer any of my messages. I couldn't go to his house because I knew they'd never let me in to talk to him, so the only thing I could think of was to come to the shrine where his son was getting married and make him talk to me there."

She apologized again. "But it didn't do any good. He said that his feelings had nothing to do with the situation, that he just couldn't afford to support me anymore." She looked at Yumi. "And this time, I think he was telling the truth. So . . ." She hesitated. "If you're marrying for love, then forget everything I just said. But if it's anything else . . . you may not be getting what you bargained for."

Was Ichiro's father really having financial problems? Or was that just something he told his mistress in order to get rid of her?

"Thanks for telling me," Yumi said. "I'll . . . think about things. But what I came here to ask you was if you saw anyone suspicious while you were at the shrine on Sunday." She explained about the head priest's death.

Mami's hand flew to her mouth. "There was a murderer there at the same time I was?"

"Maybe. But I didn't want you and Mr. Mitsuyama to be dragged into the investigation if you didn't see anything that might help Detective Nakamura. If you did, I'd be happy to tell him for you. Did you see anyone who looked like they didn't belong there? Anyone who wasn't doing what they were supposed to be doing?"

Mami's face colored and she looked away.

"What?" Yumi asked.

"Well . . . after Mitsuyama-*san* and I finished talking, I was a mess because I'd been crying. I went into the bathroom between the little wedding shrine and the treasure house to fix my makeup. One of the stalls was already occupied, so I took the other one."

She picked up the bottle of scotch she'd been polishing and started working on it again. "Earthquakes really shake me up, ever since the big one that hit Tōhoku, and I was worried about the aftershocks. So after I fixed my makeup, I decided to sit outside in the garden where it was safe, before figuring out how to get home." Mami paused, wrinkling her nose. "After about five minutes, the person who'd been in the other stall came out of the bathroom. But . . . it wasn't a woman!"

"What?"

"Even worse, it was a priest."

"What was he doing in the ladies' room?"

"What does a pervert usually do in a ladies' room?" Mami's mouth made a little moue of disgust. "I'm sure he was spying on me!"

"If he works at the shrine, he could have been checking the plumbing or cleaning up or something," Yumi objected.

Mami shook her head firmly. "I don't think so. When he came out, he sort of peeked out the door first, to see if anybody was around. Like he didn't want anybody to see him. Then he hurried back toward the treasure house."

"What did he look like?"

"I don't know—like a priest. Not young, but not old either. He was wearing those priest robes. Green ones." She shifted her weight to the other hip. "It totally creeped me out thinking there might be a peephole between the stalls, so after he was gone, I went back in to look. I figured if I found it, I'd march over to the shrine offices and tell the head priest." She paused. "I went back into the stall I'd been in, but I didn't find anything. Then an aftershock hit and when I went into the other stall to see if there was something more obvious on that side, there was a utility door behind the toilet that had popped open. I looked inside, and along with the plumbing pipes and electrical fuses were some rolls of kimono silk and a bundle of stuff wrapped in a *furoshiki*."

"A *furoshiki*?"

"Yeah, it was a big blue-and-white wrapper, with an old-fashioned waves design. The ordinary kind you use to carry odd-shaped things on the subway."

Like the one Yumi had seen Assistant Head Priest Makoto carrying from the treasure house that morning when she was standing in line to make her offering.

"What was in it?" Yumi asked.

"Just some old wooden boxes. Like the kind they store boring old tea ceremony stuff in."

"You didn't open them to see what was inside?"

"No, because then I stopped to wonder why they were there. The shrine has a treasure house, right? So there wasn't any reason to store that kind of stuff behind a toilet in the bathroom. Unless..."

"Unless what?"

"Unless he was doing something he didn't want anybody else to know about."

"Like what?"

"I don't know—maybe he was selling them?"

"Why did you think he might be doing that?"

Mami paused, biting her lip. She flicked a glance at Yumi and said, "If I... happened to see another person at the shrine that day, do the police have to know who told them?"

"Why?"

"The person I might or might not have seen is from a family that's known to collect old stuff that's stored in fancy boxes like the ones I saw. But he also... hurts people. I wouldn't want him to find out I was the one who told the police he was there."

"I understand," Yumi said. "I'll make sure Detective Nakamura doesn't tell him."

Mami nodded, twisting her cleaning rag nervously. She took a deep breath. "Okay. I didn't know what time Mitsuyama-*san* would arrive for the wedding, so I got to the shrine a little before ten. But I didn't go in right away because ahead of me, going through the torii gate, was a man I recognized from the club. He's the son of one of the big gang bosses in Kabuki-chō."

Mami looked around and lowered her voice. "Manager-*san* banned him from the Q-of-H after he recruited one of the hostesses who used to work here. She said he'd offered her an audition at his film company, that he promised she'd be a big star. Then . . . she disappeared. We tried to get the police to look for her, but they said hostesses take off all the time, that they had more important things to do than chase working girls who skipped town because they couldn't pay their rent."

Mami paused, then said, "The morning of the earthquake, I didn't go into the shrine until Koji Yamamoto was out of sight. And after I figured out he might have been there to buy the stuff hidden behind the toilet, I got out of there as fast as I could."

•

By the time Yumi made it to Yoyogi Park, the sun was nearly down, and the trees' shadows were lengthening over the cold ground.

The bright winter Sunday had coaxed record numbers of people away from their brooms and cleaning rags, eager to forget their troubles for a little while and get a breath of fresh air. Out in Tokyo Bay, the man-made island of Odaiba was a disaster zone, but the rest of Tokyo's infrastructure had been tested by the last big quake and, except for a record number of broken windows, few inland buildings had been damaged this time.

Yumi skirted the rockabillies in their leather jackets with "Strangers" written across the back. Happy hour had started earlier than usual with the Yoyogi Park Elvises, and the bottle of Four Roses they passed around their dance circle was already half empty. "Blue Suede Shoes" gave way to hip-hop as she passed three boys jiving to a Japanese artist. The balls they were contact-juggling defied gravity as they rolled over shoulders, under legs. Bounce, catch, bounce, catch, never missing a beat.

Yumi paused at a fork in the path. Left or right? The path made a big loop, and she'd eventually get to the tribute site no matter which way she went. The spot where Flame supposedly got her start was on the main route to where cherry blossom parties took place every April, so she veered left at the snack stand.

Yumi spotted Haru and Midori ahead. Apparently, the winter sniffles had caught up with Haru too—like half the people strolling in the park today, she was wearing a white flu mask.

Haru was taking a picture of Midori posing with a young man who looked like a samurai hero disguised as an itinerant monk. His shoulder-length hair was pulled back *rōnin*-style, and he wore a rustic kimono over leather sandals. His commitment to Edo-era authenticity stopped at freezing to death, however—long underwear and wool socks poked out beneath his costume. The sign penned on a flattened cardboard box leaning against his tree said, "Volunteer to help the tsunami victims on Odaiba! Talk to the Wandering Actor if you want a spot on a boat that's going on Tuesday."

"Hi," Yumi said, joining them.

Midori introduced her.

"Mansaku *to mōshimasu*," he said, with old-fashioned formality.

"Is Mansaku your real name?" Yumi asked, astounded that any parent would give their child such an old-fashioned one in this day and age.

"It's the Wandering Actor's name," he replied with a smile.

"Why are you dressed like that?" she asked.

"Usually on Sundays I perform *rakugo*, but because of

the disaster, nobody feels like they ought to enjoy themselves too much today. I'm trying to get people to come with me to help the refugees on Odaiba instead, and I wore my costume because otherwise my regular visitors might not recognize me."

"What's *rakugo*?" Yumi asked.

"Traditional Japanese storytelling. One actor plays every character while sitting on stage, changing his voice and body language as they talk to each other. I think the stories are as good today as they were two hundred years ago, but *rakugo* is kind of dying out because most young people think it's old-fashioned." He smiled. "I'm trying to change their minds." He turned to Midori and asked, "What's this tribute you're going to? Is it for the tsunami victims?"

"Four of them. The VuDu Dolls."

"Oh. I heard," Mansaku said, his face sobering. "Actually, I knew Flame. When I first started doing *rakugo*, she was performing here in the park."

"You knew her?" Midori exclaimed. "What was she like?"

"Actually, I hated her at first," he admitted. "Her band set up right next to me and they were so loud, I had to move if someone asked me to perform. On the Sunday before she was discovered, there was a freak rainstorm right in the middle of the afternoon. I helped her band haul their equipment under the trees. Afterward, we all went out for ramen together." Mansaku paused, then added, "Flame was a hell of a musician. Back then, she wrote all their songs."

"What do you mean, 'back then'?" Haru exclaimed. "She still does."

"She gets the credit, but I've got a friend who's a stylist for their label. She told me they've got a staff of composers on salary. One day they're working on the VuDu Dolls' new single, the next day they're writing bubblegum for Peachie and Baby8. Once that producer got ahold of Flame, her sound changed. And of course all the band members changed, too."

"What do you mean?" Midori objected. "They've been playing together since high school."

Mansaku shook his head. "The promoter discovered Flame's original band here in the park. But before the VuDu Dolls had their major debut, Jimmy Harajuku replaced all the other members with kids he'd discovered playing in other bands. The fairytale story about them getting their big break here in Yoyogi Park is about ninety percent bullshit."

"Well, I like the VuDu Dolls the way they are," said Haru, ever the loyal fangirl.

"So do millions of other fans," he replied with a wry smile.

Midori said, "Speaking of fans, we'd better get over to the tribute."

Mansaku bowed, handing each of them a card. "Come back when things are back to normal and watch some *rakugo*. When I'm back from Odaiba, I'll announce it on Twitter."

They promised they'd return, and headed deeper into the park.

"Are you okay, Haru-*chan*?" Yumi asked. "Why are you wearing a mask? Did you catch that cold that's going around?"

"No, I'm wearing it so I don't get it. I figure if it can keep germs in, it can keep them out, too, right?"

Yumi had never thought of it that way before.

In the gathering dusk, the never-ending drum circle was hard at work as a skateboarding beagle passed them, heading home at the heels of his trainer. At the end of the long fountain, a boy wearing a Hanshin Tigers baseball cap and shiny gold high-top sneakers sat on a bench, hunched over his guitar, picking out a haunting melody as the sky faded to black.

"There they are," Haru said, pointing past the fountains in the pond to the far shore. A flickering glow lit up the trees on the far side. As they crossed the bridge, the transporting guitar solo from "Heart-Shaped Hole" beckoned them in from speakers someone had set up. They joined the widening circle of fans who had gathered under the dark trees around thousands of candles. At the very center, a growing pile of mostly white roses made poignant reference to the chorus of "Under My Skin." The crowd was nearly all girls, many dressed as Goths or Lolitas or somewhere in between. Some wept in each other's arms, others huddled in hushed conversation, debating whether any of the rumors that the band members had been seen alive could possibly be true.

Yumi crouched and lit the candle she'd brought, then set it among the others.

"She's not dead! I'm sure I saw her yesterday in Shibuya!" insisted a girl behind her. Curious, Yumi turned.

The Gothic Lolita's face was set in stubborn lines. "I know it was Flame," she told the girl next to her. "I was standing outside the 109 Building waiting for a friend, and she walked straight past me."

"How did you know? Was she wearing her lace glove?"

"No, it was cold out, so she was wearing regular gloves just like everybody else. But it looked just like her. Her hair was the same and she was wearing an earring exactly like Flame's."

"What time?" asked a Punk Lolita in red tartan pants and a VuDu Dolls "Love's Eternal Flame" tour T-shirt.

"Around two thirty."

"You can't have seen her in Shibuya today at two thirty," the Punk Lolita objected. "Didn't you see the interview with Miyu Mika on TV? She said she spotted Flame at two thirty in Yokohama."

"You're both wrong," said a tall Goth boy, joining them, his long coat dripping with buckles and zippers. "Didn't you see the video? Anyone who was in that building when the wave hit is gone. There's no way anybody inside survived that tsunami."

Suddenly a blaze of lights raked over them and everyone

turned as a camera crew swung around and backed into the parting crowd. They were filming a young woman whose bleached hair was pulled into a curly fountain atop her head and tied with a pastel bow.

"Isn't that . . . Peachie?" gasped Haru.

Had to be, Yumi thought. Dressed like a pastel baby doll, her oversized ruby-rimmed glasses had no lenses, a look that had unfortunately become dated, but she couldn't abandon it because it was one of her trademarks.

The pop singer and budding TV actress flicked a glance at a slight man in a pink sport coat, standing on the periphery. Yumi had noticed him before, because even though he wasn't much taller than the overwhelmingly female crowd, he was wearing a fancy flu mask. It looked like it was tailored to fit his face and was fitted with a red respirator button near his mouth. Maybe he was trying to avoid the cold that was going around, too.

He nodded once at Peachie, and she began to cry.

"She's g-o-o-o-one!" the singer wailed, lace hankie clutched in one hand. The crowd parted for the camera crew, and all eyes were on the spotlit pop star as she sobbed Flame's name and fell to her knees, weeping. Picking up one white rose, she held it to the sky. "Flame, you were the best *sempai* in the whole world!" Then she collapsed in misery, shoulders heaving.

Then someone on the edge of the crowd screamed, "Nana!"

The TV lights swiveled to illuminate a young woman with one black pigtail and one blonde, holding a lit candle. With a shock, Yumi recognized the VuDu Dolls vocalist. Her left arm was in a sling and she had a white gauze patch on one cheek, but she was very much alive. The throng surged toward her, screaming, but the man in the fancy face mask stepped in front of the singer, holding up both hands to stop the fans from coming any closer. The girl murmured something in his ear, and he stepped back.

"Is it really you, Nana?" a voice cried.

"Yes," she said, holding her candle high and turning to face the crowd. "It's really me. Three of us escaped the tsunami, but . . ." She lowered the candle and bowed her head. "Flame didn't make it."

A wave of renewed wailing rippled through the crowd as she slowly made her way toward the floral mountain and Peachie, who was still collapsed gracefully atop the white roses.

The cameraman pushed past Yumi, followed by a tech with a boom mike and an assistant bearing a circular silver reflector. They assembled themselves around the celebrity duo as Nana reached out to Peachie and helped her to her feet. Nana produced another candle from her pocket and lit it before handing it to the singer. The pair bowed deeply toward the pile of roses, then turned to the crowd and held their candles high.

Slowly turning a full circle, Nana proclaimed, "Flame will never die, as long as there are fans like you to remember her!"

Mixed applause and weeping rippled out through the fans as the singers set their candles down. Nana put a comforting arm around Peachie, and led her back through the parting crowd as she wept. The camera crew filmed them, following them into the darkness of the park beyond.

Everyone was silent for a long moment, then broke out in a buzz of conversation. Yumi turned and looked into the darkness. The celebrities and their entourage had disappeared as quickly as they had come.

Next to her, Haru's phone chimed. The Gothic Lolita pulled it from her pocket and her eyes widened.

"Taku!" she cried, opening the message. Squinting at the screen, she zoomed in on the picture that had appeared.

"Is he okay?" Yumi asked.

Haru handed her the phone. No subject line, no text, just

a photo of a check for an astronomical sum, made out to Taku Shinoda from Jimmy's Top Talent.

MONDAY, DECEMBER 23

•

*9:00 A.M.*

Yumi angled her laptop so she could read it at the low kitchen table while eating her breakfast rice.

Last night, after the tribute, she'd accompanied Haru and Midori and the other Lolitas to an impromptu Flame memorial at the Mad Hatter. She'd missed the last train and had no choice but to stay, listening to the VuDu Dolls' playlist until the Yamanote Line started running again. She and Coco had reminisced about how they'd skipped school one day to speed-dial the ticket hotline for a VuDu Dolls' secret live performance. Their tickets had gotten them admitted in the first group of fans, close enough to the stage to see Flame's eyebrow piercing before her promoter made her remove it.

Yumi stirred a raw egg yolk into her rice and plopped down at the table. Through the door to the main room, she could see her mother kneeling before her ironing board in front of the TV, watching as replays of the tsunami breaching the Odaiba seawall alternated with the footage of Nana and her candle in Yoyogi Park, breaking the news that the VuDu Dolls band members had all survived except Flame.

Every online media source was wall-to-wall rumors, fueling the growing hysteria over the VuDu Dolls guitarist's death. Peachie's tearful tribute was followed by an interview with a B-list TV actor who swore that Flame's relationship with Kengo was a lie, that he'd actually seen the girl guitarist coming out of a Roppongi nightclub last week on the arm of a Korean soccer star.

A spokesman for Jimmy's Top Talent came on to say what a tragedy it was to lose such a talented artist. The band had agreed that the tracks they'd laid down on Saturday before the tsunami hit—the last tracks Flame would ever record—would be released as soon as possible, dedicated to her memory, along with a video that would benefit the tsunami victims.

Yumi clicked over to Japan's most popular video-sharing site to see if there were any teasers for it yet, where a search for "Flame video" produced a handheld camera clip of a teenage boy with bad skin wearing the uniform of a popular chain of karaoke clubs. He flipped his hair nervously out of his eyes and proclaimed the scrawled signature on the room reservation slip he was brandishing belonged to Flame, who was not only alive but had spent the night there after the earthquake.

The camera bounced after the pimply boy into a room garishly papered in glow-in-the-dark, animal-patterned wallpaper.

"This is the room where she spent the night," he proclaimed, picking up a cordless mike that had been sealed into a plastic sandwich baggie. He shoved it at the camera. "I'll be putting this up for auction tonight online." Scanning the room, he swooped down to grab a glass with an inch of melted ice and orange juice at the bottom. "This too! It actually touched Flame's lips! Follow me on Twitter for details!"

As the boy's Twitter name strobed across the screen, Yumi clicked away to a regular news site, where a shot of bare supermarket shelves accompanied a story about isolated reports of the same kind of hoarding that had followed the Tōhoku quake. The screen switched to a shot of a woman carrying a blue-and-white *furoshiki* wrapper bulging with toilet paper down a street, and Yumi was reminded of the one she'd seen Makoto carrying the morning of her wedding.

Was that the same bundle Mami had seen hidden in the bathroom? Had the assistant head priest been bringing home shopping from the supermarket, or spiriting valuables from the treasure house?

She still hadn't decided what to do with the information. She knew she should tell Kenji, but she really didn't want to involve Ichiro's father in a police investigation. Scandalous headlines about Mr. Mitsuyama's infidelity would embarrass her family as well as his.

She carried her dishes to the sink, squirted some dish soap into her bowl, and scrubbed off the egg yolk with a smiley-face scratchy sponge. As she rinsed it and balanced the bowl atop the dishes already in the drainer, she had an idea.

What if she left Mami out if it altogether and claimed she'd seen the *furoshiki*-wrapped bundle herself?

Drying her hands, she went to her room to put on some clothes. Before she talked to Kenji, she'd stop by the Tabata Shrine to check out the bathroom, so she wouldn't trip up on the details.

• 

"I've got the list of callers," Detective Oki announced, joining Kenji in interview room 3 with cups of staffroom tea in both huge paws. "Everything from the past four months."

"Anyone who might be our killer?"

Oki handed Kenji the second cup of tea and passed him a stapled list. Incoming and outgoing calls to shrine suppliers. Some familiar names: Makoto. Taiga. The director of the Erai Museum. Koji Yamamoto. Junchiro Mitsuyama. Twenty-three numbers without names attached.

"Any info on the unknowns?" Kenji asked.

Oki identified them: the Tokyo University professor who had written about the Edo-era kimono, three employees who had called in sick, one of Yano's old high school classmates, fourteen shrine-goers with various needs, three couples planning weddings, and two calls from a public phone in Odaiba.

Kenji turned to Suzuki. "What about alibis for the people who were at the shrine yesterday?"

The assistant detective opened his notebook.

"All but one shrine maiden, the receptionist, the photographer, and his assistant were vouched for by family members they live with. The shrine maiden's landlady saw her come back from walking her Chihuahua at seven ten and said she didn't go out again until she left for the train station at eight forty-five. The receptionist doesn't live with anybody, but her next-door neighbor said she was playing her exercise DVD way too loud from seven forty to eight ten, then she 'rudely, as always' slammed her door on her way out at eight forty-five. The photographer and his assistant vouched for each other. Reluctantly, on his part. It seems they're having an affair, and he doesn't want his wife to find out."

Kenji stood and erased the names of the shrine personnel and wedding support staff from their suspect list on the whiteboard. He turned to Oki.

"Did you have a chance to talk to Mr. Mitsuyama yet?"

"Yeah." The big detective grimaced. "For a guy who could only spare five minutes to meet with me, he sure took a long time trying to avoid telling me that Mameha 'Mami' Goto is his ex-mistress. She's a hostess at the Queen of Hearts in Kabuki-chō. He recently broke up with her, and she showed up outside his son's wedding to hit him up for money. When I talked to her, she told me she arrived at the sanctuary at ten, planning to wait and catch Mitsuyama Senior on his way to his car to go to the reception, but then the earthquake happened and everyone came out early. It doesn't sound like she had any reason to kill Head Priest Yano, but if her ex–sugar daddy turns up dead, she'll be my number one suspect."

Kenji nodded, erasing Mami and Junchiro Mitsuyama

from the whiteboard.

"I also talked to the director of the Erai Museum," Oki said. "He's been in America at an art fair since last Wednesday. His personal assistant sent me newspaper pictures to prove it."

Kenji erased the director's name and contemplated the remaining suspects:

Koji Yamamoto. Makoto. Taiga.

Kenji tapped his pen on his chin, thinking. He turned to Suzuki.

"Could you put together a bio of our dead idol, along with any info you can dig up about her known associates? Band members, her promoter, staff, hangers-on? I've got a username and password we can use to search the official fan club site in addition to the one you showed us, if that'll help. The owner of that Polaroid has to be someone Flame had enough contact with that she found out his dirty little secret. If he came to the shrine in search of the Polaroids and didn't kill Yano himself, maybe he saw who did."

"Yes sir."

Kenji's phone buzzed atop his Inbox.

"Nakamura *desu*." He listened. "Ten o'clock? We'll be there."

He hung up and said, "That was Makoto. He says he has something important to talk to us about."

•

Kenji and Oki approached the gate leading to the head priest's house just as a black-suited salaryman was leaving. He shifted his briefcase to his other hand and unlatched the garden gate, giving them a slight bow as they passed.

Stepping up to the front door of the head priest's house, they rang the bell.

Makoto appeared. "Ah, Detectives. Right on time. Please come in."

As Kenji exchanged his shoes for slippers, he noted that the victim's younger brother had lost no time purifying the head priest's house and taking over. New *tatami* mats gleamed from the place where Yano's body had been found. The wall plaster was patched but not yet painted, and the shelf had been rehung, its dust-free expanse awaiting the repaired *kamidana*. All the former resident's mismatched tchotchkes had been cleared away, and three freshly sealed boxes were stacked near the *kotatsu* table.

"Please have a seat."

Makoto disappeared into the kitchen and returned with a tea tray. He sank onto the cushion opposite Oki and Kenji, poured three cups, and handed them around.

"I was wondering if you could give me contact information for the two bidders on that kimono," he began. "I didn't find any record of the transaction here, but the buyer would certainly have a copy. Once we find it, how long will it be before you can return the cash that was found in the room upstairs?"

"I'll ask the prosecutor," Kenji said. "But it may be needed as trial evidence when we catch your brother's killer."

Makoto's face fell.

"Was that an insurance man we saw leaving?" Oki asked.

"Yes. I've asked him to recommend an appraiser, so we can insure the items in the treasure house."

"A wise decision," said Oki, taking a sip of his tea. "And that'll make it easier to identify valuable stuff you can sell off for the good of the shrine." He gave the assistant head priest a shrewd look and said, "You've been busy, Makoto-*kannushi*."

The acting head priest's face froze. He set his cup down on the table and met Oki's gaze. "It has been a very difficult time, Detective. But the shrine sanctuary needs a new roof and the earthquake damage will require funds we don't have. The wedding of our biggest patron's son was interrupted by the earthquake, but it will be impossible to reschedule until we attend to the repairs urgently needed in the sanctuary." He took a deep breath and continued, "I'd like to think I'm fulfilling my brother's wishes by finishing what he started when he decided to sell some of the shrine's collection. It's a pity he won't be here to see how right he was to change his mind about that."

"Why do you think he suddenly decided to sell?" Kenji asked.

"I don't know. Like I said, it was a shock to me when you discovered those e-mails bidding on the kimono and an even bigger shock that he'd done an inventory of the treasure house." Makoto shook his head sadly. "My brother was an artist, Detective. As I mentioned before, he never planned to take over the shrine, but fate decided otherwise. As long as the roof didn't actually fall on our heads, he was unwilling to consider that it might, and take measures to prevent it. In the twenty-three years he's been in charge, the buildings have steadily become shabbier, attendance at festivals has thinned, and the number of couples considering the Tabata Shrine for their weddings has dwindled. I brought it to his attention regularly, but my brother didn't care. He said that if the *kamisama* wanted him so badly that they made him give up what was most dear to him, they'd have to put up with the way he did the job. I don't know why he changed his mind."

"With your brother gone, will you take over the shrine?" Oki asked.

Makoto nodded. "The head priest position customarily passes to the eldest son. If there isn't one, it passes to the previous head priest's eldest brother." His tea stopped halfway to his lips and his eyes widened. "Unless . . . do you really think my brother has a child somewhere?"

"It's possible."

Makoto thought for a moment, then asked, "If he's mentioned in my brother's will, how can I find him? If I file a missing person report, would the police help me?"

"Maybe," Oki said. "After they finish dealing with the aftermath of the quake. But you're in luck, Makoto-*san*. Nakamura-*san* and I will be searching for that child personally." He gave the priest a cold smile. "Because most murders are committed by the victim's next of kin."

•

Kenji felt his phone vibrate in his pocket. He stepped outside to take the call.

"Yumi?"

"Are you still working on the Tabata Shrine case?"

"Yes. In fact, I'm there right now."

"Then come over to the women's bathroom near the treasure house. There's something you ought to see."

*Yumi was here? Why?*

He ended the call and asked Oki to stay with Assistant Head Priest Makoto while he checked out something a witness had just phoned in.

Out the gate, through the garden. There she was, sitting on a bench near the bathrooms, bundled up to the eyeballs in a fluffy white muffler and winter coat.

*Stop it,* he told his heart as it gave its customary leap upon seeing her. *This isn't the time or place to show her that picture of Ichiro.*

Then again, there was no longer any need to rein in his feelings and harden his heart. Since catching Yumi's fiancé kissing his ex-girlfriend, he'd allowed himself to hope again.

"What is it you want to show me?" he asked with a smile as she stood to greet him.

She pointed to the bathroom. "This morning I came to, uh, make an offering, and when I went to the ladies' room, I saw that there was a utility door behind the toilet. I looked inside and found the bundle I saw Assistant Head Priest Makoto carrying on the morning of the wedding."

What? His eyes narrowed. He'd known her long enough

to know when she was lying, and she was lying right now. Why?

"Show me," he said.

He followed her into the bathroom and, sure enough, above the toilet in one of the stalls, a door hung open and an angular bundle wrapped in a blue-and-white cloth was stashed inside. Had she put it there? No, that didn't make sense. But how had she known to open that door?

He turned and looked her in the eye. "Do you always check out utility closets in public bathrooms?"

"No, but when I saw what was in there, I wondered why Makoto-*kannushi* was storing the stuff in that bathroom instead of the treasure house."

"How did you know it was here? Who told you?"

"Nobody!" Her eyes slid away.

*She's protecting someone.*

"Yumi, do I have to remind you this is a police investigation? And you're a terrible liar. I need to talk to whoever it was and find out what else they saw."

"Look," she said, a note of desperation entering her voice. "The important thing is that I'm sure the assistant head priest put it here and I think he was planning to sell it to a gangster's son. A guy named Koji Yamamoto."

Kenji froze. Who did Yumi know who could be mixed up with Koji Yamamoto?

"How do you know all this?"

"I . . . well . . . I saw him. Arriving at the shrine."

"What does he look like?"

"I don't know, average."

"No distinguishing features? Scars? Moles? Tattoos?"

"I didn't get that good of a look. I just knew it was him," she insisted.

Now he was getting annoyed. Time to put a stop to this charade and make her tell him who had actually witnessed their favorite suspect arriving to kill the head priest.

"Yumi. Look at me. Who told you they saw Koji Yamamoto? And what time did they see him? This is important."

"It was around ten. He came in the front gate around ten."

"This is a murder investigation, not a game. Who saw him?"

"I . . . I can't tell you."

She looked at her feet to avoid his disapproving stare, but that wasn't going to work, not with so much at stake. She was protecting someone close to her, and Kenji had a very good idea who that might be. Last spring Ichiro and his family had forbidden her to testify against a man who assaulted her, and their actions had nearly allowed a killer to go free. Kenji wasn't about to let that happen again.

"Who are you protecting, Yu-*chan*?" he snapped. "Your fiancé's so-rich-they-think-they're-above-the-law family? Is that why you also 'forgot' to tell me about your father-in-law's mistress, the hostess who interrupted your wedding?"

Yumi's head jerked up. Now he had her attention.

"What kind of incompetents do you think we are? You think we didn't interview the shrine maiden who saw a woman who looked like a hostess waiting for your philandering father-in-law?" He snorted. "Like father, like son."

"What are you talking about? How dare you!"

Pulling out his phone, Kenji stabbed at the keys. She wouldn't want to protect that cheating bastard after she saw *this*.

He handed her the phone.

•

Yumi peered at the picture on the display, then zoomed in. The bottom fell out of her stomach. She looked at Kenji, stricken.

"Where did you get this?"
"I took it in Kabuki-chō."
"When?"
"Yesterday."

*Ichiro is cheating on me. Here's the proof.*

Yumi had considered the possibility so many times since seeing him with Ami a month ago, she'd begun to hope it was true. She'd let herself dream about what it would be like to be free, to be with Kenji. But she hadn't thought about what it would be like to be faced with hard proof that Ichiro had never loved her, and he never would. There would be no deepening of their relationship over time. She felt like a fool. Had everyone known it but her? Had they held their tongues, seeing how eager she'd been to believe he cared for her, even though they'd met through *o-miai*? Was she the only one who didn't realize he was only turning on the charm long enough to reel in the Japanese-speaking daughter-in-law his parents demanded, before going back to the woman he really loved?

And to make matters worse, it was Kenji who had caught him, Kenji who was witnessing her humiliation. Kenji, who had been right about Ichiro all along. How did he just happen to be there at exactly the right moment to catch Ichiro with Ami, anyway?

Her hurt erupted as anger. "What were you doing—stalking him? I thought you were supposed to be investigating a murder!"

"I was! Don't blame me if your fiancé is having a rendezvous with his girlfriend at a love hotel across from Yamamoto-*gumi* headquarters," Kenji shot back.

Furious, Yumi threw his phone on the ground and flung out her arm to push him out of her way, but he caught her wrist before she connected. His expression hardened and his eyes were cold. He dropped her arm and stepped back.

"You can go now," he said. "Thanks for your help, but we won't be needing any more of it. We'll take the investigation from here."

His cold words were like a slap in the face. Yumi backed away, then turned and ran, the greens of the garden blurring together, swimming in tears. She got through the gate before a sob escaped and she began to choke on the knowledge that her life had turned into one big mistake.

And Kenji would no longer be around to help her fix it.

•

Kenji went into the stall with the utility door and leaned his forehead against the cold metal, a huge lump in his throat. How had that gone so wrong, so fast?

That wasn't at all what he'd intended to do with the photo he'd taken of Ichiro. Staring up at the ceiling over his bed last night, he'd imagined himself and Yumi sitting together at a cozy café. She'd look at the picture and be horrified and hurt, but he'd patiently show her it was the key that would release her and her family from the commitment she now regretted. After he pointed out that a gross indiscretion on the part of the groom might be grounds for negotiating with the Mitsuyamas for damages, she'd be grateful that he'd caught Ichiro in the wrong. If they played their cards right, Yumi's father would keep his professorship and the Hatas wouldn't have to move away from Tokyo in disgrace. And Yumi would finally be his.

But instead of using the picture to draw her closer, he'd hit her over the head with it to punish her for caring about that cheating asshole. He groaned. She might break off her engagement now, but she'd forever resent the part he'd played. And if she went ahead with the marriage, she'd never forgive Kenji for knowing that her glittering new life was so empty inside.

The utility door still hung open, reminding him he had a job to do. Oki was waiting. Turning wearily, he snapped a few cell-phone shots of the cloth-wrapped bundle and the rolls of kimono silk that were hidden behind it, then called his partner, asking him to bring Makoto. Stationing himself outside the bathroom door to wait for them, he pushed aside thoughts of Yumi to concentrate on the business at hand.

Makoto and Oki arrived. Kenji stepped aside and invited the priest to take a look at what was behind the utility door.

Makoto stopped in his tracks.

"Do you recognize this *furoshiki*, Makoto-*kannushi*?"

"I . . . it's . . ."

"Shall we unwrap it and see what's inside?"

A few minutes later, back at the priest's house, Makoto removed the tea things from the low table and Kenji laid out the items in the bundle one by one. Two tea bowls, made by long-dead masters whose work graced many a museum showcase. A set of five red lacquer soup bowls, with pine needles delicately painted on the lids. A bamboo basket, its random-looking weave an intricate exercise in mastery. A set of five teacups, their rims shaped to resemble plum blossoms.

The priest looked at the items silently, his face a mask.

"Can you explain what these items were doing in the women's bathroom utility closet, Makoto-*kannushi*?"

"I . . . I don't know. Maybe Taiga took them when he and my brother did the inventory. Maybe he decided to hide them until he found a buyer."

"Are they on the treasure house inventory list?"

Makoto rose and fetched it, then handed it to Kenji. The items were all there.

"I don't think it was Taiga who was intending to sell these, Mr. Assistant Head Priest," Oki said.

"What do you mean?"

"I'm thinking maybe the sanctuary will get a new roof this spring after all."

"What are you suggesting, Detective?"

"I'm saying that a priest desperate for money to repair his family's legacy might have discovered that his brother was liquidating the shrine's assets and grabbed some of the loot before it was all gone."

"That's . . . insulting!" Makoto drew himself upright. "Impossible!"

"I'm afraid not," Kenji said. "Because Miss Hata saw you on the morning of her wedding, carrying this bundle."

Makoto's eyes jumped to Oki, who was seated across from him. The big detective raised his eyebrows, waiting for an answer.

The priest's eyes darted back to Kenji.

"What did you do with the missing kimono, Makoto-*kannushi*? Where is it now?"

"I don't know."

Oki slammed his hands on the low table and Makoto jumped. Oki leaned toward him and said, "Now is the time for damage control, Mr. Assistant Head Priest. If you don't tell us what really happened to it, we're going to have to take you down to the station and ask you some very serious questions about how badly you wanted your brother dead. Who did you sell it to?"

"Nobody!" Then he seemed to deflate. "But . . . you're right. I did take these things from the treasure house on the morning of the earthquake. In fact, I've been selling off small items for three months." He looked at the detectives, a spark of defiance returning. "Last year, I went to my brother and showed him the books. I pointed out that if the shrine's income continued to slip, within a year it wouldn't even cover our expenses. He brushed me off and said the *kami-sama* would provide, but it was less an expression of faith than a hope that the shrine would have to close and he'd finally be released from his obligation to run it. I decided that it would be better to sell off our collection than let that happen. Nobody had paid attention to what was in the treasure house for years, nobody would miss a few kimonos and tea bowls. One by one, I started selling things to buyers I found on the

Internet and using the money for the most urgent repairs.

"But last Saturday morning, my brother called me in and told me he'd decided to sell the Edo-era kimono and give the money to Taiga." Outrage tinged his voice as he relived the scene. "I demanded to know why he was doing that when the shrine had so many urgent needs, but he refused to tell me. I asked him if Taiga was blackmailing him, but he just clammed up.

"I was afraid that wouldn't be the end of it, that Taiga would keep coming back for more. So I decided I would spirit away some of the most valuable stuff and hide it so my brother couldn't get to it first. On Saturday morning before I met with that couple about their wedding, I took out the first load. I hid it in the women's bathroom, because I knew nobody would be in there to use the cleaning supplies for another week. I took the rolls of kimono silk right after the earthquake, before I found my brother."

"How did you know which stuff to take?"

Makoto sighed. "The first time I sold something from the treasure house was after that professor told me how valuable the Edo-era kimono was. He showed me a few Internet sites where collectors search for acquisitions. While we were looking for comparable kimono values, I saw how much Rikyu water jars were worth. I remembered that my father once showed me the one that was in our collection, so I found it and took some pictures and listed it on the site. It was bought by a museum in Aomori and I used the proceeds to renew the gold leaf in the sanctuary before the Mitsuyama wedding and fix the plumbing in the bathrooms near the treasure house. After that, I studied the site and found out what kind of things were in highest demand. Then I searched the treasure house and made a list of things to sell in the future."

"And you never found out why your brother suddenly decided to sell the kimono and give the money to Taiga?" Oki probed.

Makoto hesitated. Then he said, "After we found those baby pictures yesterday, I wondered if Taiga was the son he hadn't told me about. But why would my brother need to sell part of the collection when he's been saving for the kid since he was born?"

"Good question," Kenji agreed. "We'll be looking into that. When we track him down, we'll ask him."

"And we'd better find him alive," Oki added. "Because it hasn't escaped our attention that if your brother had a son, he's next in line for the head priest's job. If anything unfortunate happens to him, you'll be our first suspect."

•

As Oki unlatched the gate and held it for Kenji, his pocket buzzed. He fished out his phone and stepped away to take the call.

When he rejoined Kenji, he said, "Koji's back. That was Yamamoto Senior calling to tell me that Junior has returned from aiding the suffering citizens of Odaiba, and we can contact him anytime at his office." He paused. "He also told me Koji delivered the missing kimono, as promised."

"Does that mean he did the deal with Yano before Yano was killed?"

"Or tried to make it look that way. I'd say it's just as likely he killed Yano and did the deal after the fact. But why waste time guessing, when we can ask him?"

They passed under the big *torii* gate at the entrance to the shrine and turned toward the Tabata train station. It would be much faster than returning to the Komagome Police Station and checking out a car.

Twenty minutes later, they stood across the street from a fancy office building in West Shinjuku. Koji Yamamoto apparently ran his branch of the family enterprise as far from Kabuki-chō as he could get, while still remaining within the protective sphere of the various "understandings" the Yamamoto-*gumi* had worked out with the Shinjuku powers-that-be.

"Looks like he does pretty well for himself," Kenji noted, looking up at the forty-two-story steel-and-glass tower.

"Crime pays," Oki said. "And look, the Prince of Porn is going to save us an elevator ride."

Three men emerged from the revolving glass door and walked away together toward Shin-Okubo. Kenji began to cross the street to intercept them, but Oki pulled him back.

"I don't think we want to discuss our business out here on the street," he warned. "It's nearly lunchtime. Let's see where they're going."

They fell in behind the trio half a block back, keeping to the opposite side of the street.

"I see Koji's still got his loyal pet Tiny at his heels," Oki observed.

"You mean the big guy?"

"Yeah. We've all called him Tiny since first grade, because even then, he wasn't."

Their quarry entered a Korean barbecue restaurant on a quiet backstreet.

"Excellent choice." Oki grinned. "Looks like Koji-*kun* is going to buy us some topnotch *yakiniku* for lunch today."

They waited outside the restaurant for a few minutes, allowing Koji's party to get their coats off and settled, so they couldn't make a quick exit.

While Oki checked his messages, Kenji stretched the pitching shoulder that always ached in cold weather. The earthquake had disrupted his judo practice schedule. He had to get back on the mats. Kenji had played baseball all the way through high school and hadn't started studying martial arts until he needed to pass the physical for the police academy. He was dreading his first night back. Missed practices always meant he'd get thrown again and again, by the most humiliating of sparring partners. Children. Girls. Old men. He sighed.

The tantalizing aroma of grilling meat wafted from the restaurant as two customers opened the door and went in. Kenji's stomach growled.

"*Oi*," Oki grunted, stowing his phone and catching the door before it swung shut. "After you."

Inside, gas fires glowed under the small hibachis set into the center of each table. Most patrons had arrived at the stroke of noon and were already grilling their fresh meat and vegetables, conjuring up mouthwatering curls of smoke that made Kenji's knees weak with hunger.

A handsome middle-aged Korean man bustled from the kitchen, his face brightening when he saw who was loosening his muffler and pulling off his gloves.

"Well if it isn't Oki-*sama*!" he said. Despite his use of the extreme honorific reserved for heads of state and potential in-laws, the man grabbed Oki's arm like an old buddy and clapped him on the back. "Long time no see!"

Then he leaned in and said in a confidential voice, "Never had any trouble with that *chinpira* again after you, uh, 'talked' to him." He bowed. "In fact—you won't believe this—he and his boss have become regular customers."

He pulled two menus from the slot next to the cash register, but Oki grimaced and stopped him.

"You won't be thanking me after you hear why we're here today. I need to talk to those customers of yours. Where are they? In the private room?"

The man's smile faded. "Oki-*san*, you know I can't . . . I mean, if you disturb them while they're eating, they'll . . ."

"Don't worry, Kim-*san*. Show me where they are, and let's play it the usual way."

The owner led them through the restaurant to a closed door near the kitchen. They all removed their shoes, then Mr. Kim obediently turned his back to Oki. The detective deftly twisted his left arm behind him and grabbed him around the neck. He nodded to Kenji. "Open the door for us, will you? Quickly, okay?"

Kenji whipped it open and Oki marched Kim through it. Three startled faces looked up from their menus as Oki released the proprietor with a shove and growled, "Thank you for your, uh, 'cooperation,' Mr. Kim. Next time I trust you'll give us a warmer welcome?"

Kim cringed and bowed, rubbing his arm as if Oki had hurt him, as a huge man in the seat nearest the door shot to his feet. His head was shaved except for a long piece on top that he'd pulled into a greasy ponytail. His pouty mouth was framed by a neatly trimmed goatee.

"Who invited you, Chubbs?" he squeaked at Oki in a surprisingly high voice.

Anger flickered across Oki's face before being replaced with an expression of tolerant pity. "Why, Tiny, you surprise me. I thought you had a better memory. The last time you called me that, I seem to recall you regretted it."

The muscle-mountain bristled, but the man in the corner waved him back into his seat. "What are you doing here, Oki?"

"Me and my colleague," he nodded at Kenji, "happened to be in the mood for some good *yakiniku* and since we have a little business to discuss with you, we thought we could kill two birds with one stone."

Kenji stared at the little man in the corner. For someone who'd been a serious criminal since he was in middle school, Koji Yamamoto was, well, forgettable was the word that came to mind. Despite the thin white scar that angled through his eyebrow, his neatly combed black hair and three-button suit would render him invisible among the salarymen packed into the morning trains. The third man in the group looked more like the son of a yakuza boss, in his aggressively pinstriped suit and gold jewelry.

Oki turned to Mr. Kim. "Bring us a double order of your house special marinated short ribs, a couple plates of tongue, an order of liver, and some miso-lettuce wrappers. And to drink . . ." Oki picked up the large-size bottle of Ichiban Shibori beer that was already on the table and eyed the level. He waggled it at Kim. "Another one of these. And two more glasses."

The proprietor looked back and forth anxiously between Oki and the man seated in the corner, who frowned, but nodded.

The restaurant owner bowed low, apologizing profusely for allowing the intrusion, but Koji stopped him, saying, "I understand, Kim-*san*. Detective Oki is good at talking with his fists, and you're not the only one who can't beat him at that game."

Bowing deeply, Kim replied, "Mr. Yamamoto, I—"

"Bring us an avocado-tuna salad, too, will you?" Koji said. "For one."

Kim bowed himself out the door, closing it carefully behind him.

Oki took off his coat and folded it neatly, then asked for Kenji's, suggesting he introduce himself to their hosts while he found a place for their things. He moved to the corner where the gangsters had already piled their outerwear.

Kenji bowed and offered them cards, remembering what Oki had taught him about treating them like businessmen if they wanted cooperation. Like the *oyabun*, however, they offered no cards in return.

"Don't mind if I do," Oki said, seating himself.

With a discreet knock, Kim returned, bearing two hot hand towels, another large bottle of beer, and two small glasses. He set them before Oki and Kenji, apologizing as he stooped to ignite the table grill.

Oki wiped his hands and face with the hot towel, then picked up the bottle of beer and poured for Kenji. After Kenji returned the favor, he raised his glass and drank off half of it. Setting it down, he sat back with a sigh of satisfaction.

"What business do you imagine you have with me?" Koji said.

"I doubt it's the kind you want to discuss in front of your, er, colleagues."

The *oyabun's* son stared at Oki for a long moment, then said, "Tiny stays."

He turned to the other man. "Gen-*kun*, I'm afraid we'll have to celebrate signing your new talent on a day when my old friend Oki isn't here to spoil the party."

"But—"

"Go."

Scowling, the flashy gangster got up and found his coat.

As the door shut behind him, Koji snapped, "State your business, Oki."

The detective gave him a pleasant smile and took a sip of beer. "I was just wondering how Daddy liked his kimono?"

"What kimono?"

Oki shook his head. "Koji-*kun*, you disappoint me. Let's not waste time pretending you weren't trying to buy an Edo-era kimono from the Tabata Shrine."

"Why are the police investigating a perfectly legal business transaction between two consenting parties?"

"Oh, I think you know why, Koji-*kun*. The head priest turned down your offer, didn't he? I bet that pissed you off." When Koji didn't answer, Oki continued, "So you paid him a little visit, didn't you? To have a heart-to-heart talk about doing the right thing. Before he had a chance to hand over the goods to the Erai Museum."

"What are you talking about? We outbid the Erai Museum."

"But that doesn't mean Yano decided to sell it to you. That message you left Friday night makes me think you stopped by the next morning to try and change his mind."

The door opened, and Mr. Kim reappeared, bearing a tray loaded with a tub of white rice, platters of thin-sliced raw meat, and a basket of lettuce leaves, accompanied by a small dish of savory miso paste. Leaving them on the table, he bowed and asked them to push the bell if they needed anything else.

As the door closed, Oki said, "What were you doing Saturday morning, between eight and when the earthquake happened?"

Koji sighed and peered at the plate of tongue. Selecting a slice with his chopsticks, he laid it carefully on the grill.

"I woke up at seven thirty and made an offering to my ancestors. Then I ate a bowl of miso soup, a nice little piece of grilled salmon, and a bowl of rice with fermented soybeans and pickles on top. I'm afraid nobody can verify that, though, because both your sisters were too busy hooking in Kabuki-chō to spend the night with me."

Kenji saw Oki's jaw tense, but he didn't rise to the bait.

"I went to the shrine with the provenance papers around ten because Yano-*kannushi* forgot to put his seal on them before he gave them to me." Koji picked up his beer glass and frowned, contemplating the beads of water slipping down the side. "You see, after I left that message on his phone, Yano-*kannushi* changed his mind. I met with him Friday night. He gave me the kimono and I gave him the cash. I hope you found it in his home, detective, and entered the full amount into evidence. It would be a pity if any of the five million disappeared before being returned to Yano-*kannushi's* family."

"Is that how much Daddy gave you to buy the goods? Because it would be a pity if you lied about the amount you left after killing the head priest and stealing the kimono. I might have to mention to your esteemed father that we only found three mil and you pocketed the rest."

Koji's hand hesitated for a split second, then he flipped

his meat. "After making an offering Saturday morning, I took the papers to Yano-*san's* house and knocked. He didn't answer his door, so I went home." He dunked the meat in his sauce and ate it.

"You went home? Without getting that paper signed?" Oki laughed. "That's a good one. I can just picture you telling Daddy, 'So sorry, that kimono I bought for you is worthless because I forgot to get the provenance papers signed and the guy I bought it from didn't answer his door when I knocked.'" Oki's smile disappeared. "Cut the bullshit. You expect me to believe you gave up without even calling to find out why the fuck Yano wasn't answering his door when the son of the most powerful crime boss in Tokyo told him to be there at ten? That's some serious disrespect."

Koji lowered his eyes, but not before Kenji glimpsed the anger that had flashed into them at the mention of Yano's persistent failure to give Koji and his family the deference they were used to commanding.

"The Koji Yamamoto I know wouldn't have taken no for an answer," Oki goaded. "The Koji I know would have tried the door to see if it was unlocked. And he would have kicked it in if it wasn't."

"Sorry to disappoint you, Detective."

"That's not the right answer, Koji-*kun*." Laying a slice of grilled steak on a miso-smeared lettuce leaf and folding it, Oki continued, "You'd have been stupid to leave without doing everything you could to get those papers signed, and the Koji Yamamoto I know has never been stupid. You went in. You confronted Yano, and when he refused to sell you the kimono, you hit him over the head."

Koji shook his head. "You were always lousy at writing fiction, Oki. There's nothing in that house that puts me inside with a dead priest."

"Oh really?" Oki swallowed a bite of short ribs. "Tell me, Koji-*kun*—have you seen your Yamamoto-*gumi* badge lately?"

Koji glanced down at his lapel. A gold pin with three tadpoles circling a red stone glinted from the place it should be.

"What do you mean? It's right here."

"I mean the one on your coat," Oki said with a feral smile. "The coat you wore to visit Head Priest Yano on Saturday."

Koji gave him a hard stare, then jerked his chin at Tiny. The giant lumbered to the corner where jackets and bags had been stacked and picked up a black overcoat. He unfolded it and held it up for Koji to see. There was no gold pin winking from this lapel.

"That pin fell off in the main room of Yano's house," Oki said, biting off a piece of grilled tongue wrapped in lettuce. "And don't even think of trying to tell me the one we found isn't yours, unless you want to drop your older brother in a steaming pile of shit. We both know only two Yamamoto-*gumi* members wear badges with red stones in the center." Oki used the last of his lettuce roll to wipe a drip of sauce from his plate.

"It doesn't prove I was there."

"We've got a witness who says otherwise. So if you don't have a really good story about what you were doing inside the priest's house Saturday morning at just about the time he was being murdered, I'm going to have to cut this party short and haul you down to the station in handcuffs."

Koji frowned and stared at his plate. Then he pushed it away, folding his hands in front of him on the table. "That would be a big mistake, Oki-*kun*."

"Why?"

"Because then I might not show you the picture of who really killed him."

•

Oki sat back and crossed his arms over his chest, his face

skeptical.

"Show me."

Koji jerked his chin at Tiny, who reached into the briefcase sitting between them and handed a phone to his boss. Koji navigated to a photo, and handed the phone to Oki.

Kenji got up and looked over his shoulder. A slight figure with a shaved head, wearing faded jeans and a dark hoodie was emerging from the doorway of the head priest's house, carrying a guitar. As Oki flicked through the next two shots, the figure looked back toward the camera, then turned toward the treasure house. Oki paged back to the middle shot and zoomed in. Even wearing a troubled look, the boy's face was beautiful. His lack of hair drew attention to long narrow eyes fringed with dark lashes over high cheekbones and a mouth caught between cherubic softness and chiseled bow. They'd have to confirm with Makoto, but this had to be Taiga, the missing intern.

Oki looked at Koji. "How did you get this?"

"I rang the bell at the priest's house, then I noticed that it was open, so I went in. At the same time I saw the body, I heard someone coming down the stairs in the kitchen. I backed out the door and waited around the corner of the house with my phone camera ready. When he came out, I took those pictures."

"I'm going to mail them to myself, okay?" Oki said.

The gangster didn't object.

Oki handed the phone back to its owner. He drank off his beer and placed his hands flat on the table to lever himself up.

"Thanks for lunch," Oki said, crossing the room and tossing Kenji his coat from the corner. He hunched into his own and said, "We'll be in touch."

Outside, the first warning splats of rain began to dot the sidewalk as they walked back to Shinjuku Station.

"The time stamp on that photo Koji showed us of Taiga

was ten-oh-eight a.m.," Oki said. "Which puts both him and Taiga there during the time-of-death window. Either of them could have done it."

Kenji hesitated, then said, "That pin. I don't remember seeing it entered into evidence. Why didn't you tell anybody you found it?"

"Because I didn't." Oki reached into his pocket. He opened his hand to reveal a small gold pin with three tadpoles. A red stone winked in the center. "I took it off his coat while you were introducing yourself. Koji-*kun* is so oblivious to what he's wearing that he used to come to school with one brown sock and one blue one."

"So . . . it's not really evidence?"

"No, but it convinced him to give us what we wanted, didn't it?"

●

"I can't leave until six, when I find out if I'm the high bidder or not," Coco said, the clickety-click of keys telling Yumi that her friend was upping the ante at the net café where she'd parked herself. "Why don't you come here? I had to rent a double cubicle anyway, because all the singles were taken."

"Okay," Yumi said, "Where?"

Coco gave her directions to the deluxe Bagus Gran Cyber Café near Shibuya Station.

Yumi ended the call and wondered what Coco wanted so badly that she'd called in sick to work and was camping at a net café for five hours to get it. A limited-edition Prada handbag? A "barely worn" pair of red-soled Louboutin high heels? Since Coco had been working at the Queen of Hearts, she'd been sporting the kind of accessories no shopgirl could afford.

A Yamanote Line train eased to a stop, and Yumi stepped aboard. There was one seat left. She grabbed it, across from a tall man who reminded her of Kenji.

Hurt and sorrow swamped her again as she remembered the photo he had shoved in her face. It had blasted a big empty hole inside of her, and all kinds of feelings were trying to fill it.

Had Ichiro ever intended to be faithful? Was everything he'd said to her a lie? She should be relieved fate had stepped in before she stamped her *hanko* at the Ward Office, but she couldn't help but mourn the death of the dream that she and Ichiro would learn to love each other, that their life together would be built on something more solid than mere attraction.

If she confronted Ichiro with the picture, would he try to deny it? Or would he tell her she'd been naive to think that having an arranged marriage meant he'd be faithful unto death? If he refused to call off the marriage and she was the one to break the engagement, what would happen to her father's professorship? Would Ichiro's father stop funding the chair the minute there was no longer a connection between the two families?

And then there was the shame. Yumi cheeks burned, remembering how Kenji had watched as she recognized the lovers in the photo. Then she'd made it even worse by accusing him of stalking, and she'd thrown his phone on the ground. What if she'd broken it?

The train came to a stop at Ikebukuro Station a little abruptly and the standing passengers staggered. She looked up, noticing that the woman in front of her had a cane and was clutching the commuter strap with white knuckles. Quickly, Yumi offered her seat, ashamed she hadn't noticed the woman earlier. She made her way closer to the doors as the train eased away.

Tomorrow she had to go to the Mitsuyamas' house to get her things. What would she say to Ichiro's mother? Her Americanized side wanted to have a frank conversation, tell her about Ichiro and Ami, find out whether the Mitsuyamas would let her out of the engagement without endangering her father's job.

But her Japanese side recognized that for the impossible fantasy it was. If Yumi asked the kind of straightforward questions that were perfectly acceptable in America, they'd be met with polite sidestepping that hid what Mrs. Mitsuyama would really be feeling. She'd be shocked and offended that her intended daughter-in-law had committed the double sin of telling her something unpleasant she didn't know, and asking her to respond to it without discussing it first with her husband and son.

No, Yumi told herself, it was better to be patient and see which way the wind was blowing, then decide what to do.

The doors eased open at Shibuya and she streamed off with the other passengers, flowing toward the Hachiko exit. Down the stairs, through the ticket gate, out into the plaza crowded with the young and beautiful, all waiting on the shore of the giant five-way intersection. The light changed, and over a thousand people flowed across in all directions. Yumi veered left toward the 109 Building, looking for the plate-glass window featuring the trendy fake-fur miniskirts that Coco had described. The Bagus Gran Cyber Café was upstairs. Entering the elevator, she punched 7.

The doors opened on a sleek reception desk that was all gray Formica curves. Spotlights beamed down on three cashiers. A pair of *otakus* stood at the first one, their backpacks dripping with One Piece keychains. Next to them, three high school boys with untucked white shirts hanging out over their gray-flannel uniform pants, cutting cram school. On the far end, a salaryman, probably planning to job hunt from a computer that didn't belong to his company.

She knew the line would be considerably longer after midnight, when commuters who'd failed to make the last train showed up to rent cubicles where they could cheaply pass out in semiprivacy after a night of work-related drinking. For less than ¥2,000, they could park their disheveled bodies until the first trains left the station at 5:00 a.m.

She called Coco to let her know she'd arrived, and a minute later her friend emerged from a corridor lined floor to ceiling with Japanese comic books. Coco told the pigtailed girl behind the counter that Yumi was going to share her "pair."

"*Kashiko-marimashita*," the cashier sang. Your wish is my command. She handed Yumi a slip of paper clamped to a narrow clipboard, imprinted with a time stamp and the number of Coco's cubicle. It was going to cost Yumi ¥500 to pour out her heart today.

Today Coco was wearing over-the-knee suede boots with her cutoffs and tights, the wide neck of her fluffy purple sweater falling off one shoulder to reveal the black tank top she wore beneath.

Yumi followed as she clicked down the hall past a rank of vending machines that promised to deliver everything from French fries to hot ramen.

"Want some ice cream?" Coco pointed to a machine dispensing vanilla on one side and chocolate on the other. "Or a soft drink? It's free, comes with the cubicle . . . ?"

Yumi shook her head, and they continued their zigzag through comic-book-lined corridors, deep into the net café. The hallway ended at a vast room without windows, painted a vague brownish-grayish color, the shadowy pipes and wiring above concealed in murky shadow. The only light was the blue TV-like flicker that escaped from the warren of cubicles.

Near the end of the farthest aisle, Coco ushered Yumi through a chin-height door labeled I-5. Slipping off her shoes, Yumi stepped into a tight cubicle with a computer shelf running the width of it. Two padded "executive-style" brown leatherette desk chairs sat before the shelf, matching footstools crouching beneath. Headphones hung on pegs to either side. She moved Coco's voluminous Gucci bag onto the shelf next to the computer and settled herself into the chair it had been occupying.

On the cubicle's monitor, an auction site's familiar logo

presided over a photograph of a photograph. In the picture, a figure bent over a guitar sat in front of a microphone, spiky black hair falling in the musician's closed eyes. It looked like the snapshot was mounted in an album, old-fashioned black triangles holding it in place against a heathery-gray page. One photo corner was missing.

"Wasn't she adorable?" Coco gushed, sliding into her own chair.

"Who?"

"Flame!"

"That's Flame?"

Yumi zoomed in on the photo. The guitarist was wearing long sleeves, but sure enough, her teenage hand was sheathed in a dark fingerless glove.

"Who's the seller?"

"They're using the name FlameFan," Coco said. "But it must be a relative or a close family friend, don't you think? I mean, look at the other pictures in the set." Coco paged through the seller's offering, twelve pictures in all. The final four were different from the family snapshots. They were recording session blowups of a young Flame without her stage makeup, bleached hair bundled atop her head in a clip. The series caught her wearing giant headphones, fingers blurry on the guitar strings in a white lace glove, her eyes locked on Nana as the vocalist made love to a microphone.

Coco said, "Whoever the seller is, they probably saw how much that kid who works at Big Echo was getting for the dirty glass Flame supposedly used, and realized the baby pix would be worth a bundle."

"That's awful. What kind of person would do that?"

"I bet it's her mom," Coco speculated. "Flame ran away from home when she was fifteen. Don't you think that the kind of mom who was so bad she made you run away might be the kind who'd have no problem cashing in on your tragic death?" Coco picked up her soft-drink cup and pulled a sip through the striped pink straw.

"How much are you bidding?" Yumi asked. She peered at the screen. "Fifty thousand yen?" she gasped, turning to her friend, openmouthed.

"I can always resell it if I need the money," Coco said defensively. "I mean, it's a collector's item, right?"

"How do you even know it's legit?" Yumi asked.

"Because of this," Coco said, clicking through to the Q&A section.

Q. Who are you?

A. A relative.

Q. How did you get these photos?

A. They were in the family.

Q. Do her parents know you're selling these?

A. They're fine with it.

Q. How do I know these are real pictures of Flame?

A. Would I have this if they weren't?

The seller had uploaded a picture. It was date stamped the day after the earthquake, and showed a photo album open to two of the photos being offered for sale, sitting next to an angular Lucite trophy with Flame's name on it. The items were arranged on a kitchen table. In the background, a sink under a window.

"These have gotta be the real thing," Coco said. "Because that's the Oricon Award the VuDu Dolls won for 'Don't Need You.'"

Yumi peered at the photo. "Hey, where was this was taken?" She pointed to the window above the sink in the background. "Can you zoom in?"

Coco zoomed.

"See that tiled roof through the trees?" Yumi said. "Doesn't that look like it could be the storehouse at the Tabata Shrine?"

"The place you were supposed to get hitched?" Coco asked.

"Yeah. The weird thing is, Flame apparently knew the head priest there. Kenji Nakamura texted me, asking for background on the VuDu Dolls. He said they found her fingerprints in the house where the head priest was killed."

"Really? Why?"

"They don't know. But if a relative of hers lives nearby, maybe that's the connection."

"So . . . speaking of you getting hitched, what's happening with that?" Coco asked.

Yumi was silent.

"Uh-oh, trouble in paradise," her friend said, hanging up her headphones and pushing back her chair. She picked up her empty drink cup. "Let me run to the ladies', then you can give me all the gory details."

•

Yumi put her headphones on and shifted over to Coco's chair, clicking on the window half hidden behind the auction site bid screen.

The flashing words *Look!Look!* zoomed into view. It was the streaming Internet talk show hosted by a woman who had rocketed to stardom by posting videos of herself ambushing celebrities. The graphics gave way to a studio "lounge" and zoomed in on a miniskirted woman, seated in an armchair.

"Welcome to *Look!Look!* You've all seen the tragic footage of the Jimmy's Top Talent Studio being washed away by the tsunami with megastar band VuDu Dolls inside . . ." she narrated as the now-familiar video began to play on a screen behind her head, ". . . only to be whiplashed by the revelation that all the members had survived but Flame." Nana and her lighted candle appeared with the dark trees of Yoyogi Park in the background.

The camera zoomed in for a close-up of the celebrity ambusher as she leaned toward the lens and announced, "But today I have a guest in studio who has even more shocking news. In order to protect him from powerful entertainment industry figures who have their own reasons for wanting you to believe Flame is dead, we'll alter his voice and obscure his identity. But what he's going to tell you will rock the entertainment world."

The camera zoomed out to a wider view that included a man seated in an adjacent chair, his face electronically blurred.

"Welcome to *Look!Look!*" she said. "May I call you Mr. X?"

"Yeah, sure," he replied in an artificially deep robotic voice. "Thank you for not showing my face or using my real name. I promised not to tell anybody what I know, but I'm a huge VuDu Dolls fan, and I can't stand the way Flame's fans are suffering. A piece of paper isn't enough to keep me from telling the world the truth."

"Which is . . . ?"

"Flame is alive."

The studio audience gasped on cue.

"How do you know?"

"Because I was there, in the recording studio, when the earthquake hit."

Excited audience buzz.

"Tell us what happened."

"We'd just finished recording the VuDu Dolls' new single 'Kiss Me, Kill Me' when everything started shaking. We all ran out of the building as soon as it stopped. By the time the tsunami hit, we were safely at the Disaster Prevention Park."

"And Flame was with you then, alive?"

"No."

"But I thought you said she got out safely?"

"She wasn't at the studio at all that day."

A gasp from the audience.

"But . . . didn't you say the VuDu Dolls were recording

their new single?"

"They were doing it without her. I'm a guitarist. I was playing her part."

The show host paused to let the audience reaction reach the viewers.

"Why were you standing in for her?"

"Because she quit the band a month ago, and her promoter didn't want anybody to know. Jimmy Harajuku hired me to fill in because he heard my tribute band play in Shibuya last year and he knew I could handle the guitar parts."

*Guitarist. Tribute band. Shibuya. Was the guy with the fuzzed-out face Haru's boyfriend, Taku?*

"So they contacted me on Monday, and on Thursday I went to Odaiba for an audition, along with four other guitarists. After the promoter told me I'd made the cut and the contract was signed, I practiced with the band. At first I could barely play, I was so excited, but . . ."

It *was* Taku. Was Haru watching this? She should call. Or better yet, tweet. Calling was still unreliable, as towers continued to be checked and repaired.

"So where do you think Flame is now?" the interviewer was asking.

"I don't know. But there are plenty of rumors to choose from—one of them has to be true."

"Thank you, Mr. X."

"Thank you for helping me get the truth out."

Yumi fumbled in her purse for her phone, her attention glued to the "Flame Sightings" map of Japan that had appeared on the screen. It was peppered with dots from the southernmost tip of Kyushu to the northern reaches of Hokkaido, attesting to fans' desperate desire to believe their idol was still alive. Tokyo looked like a solid red blob until the camera zoomed in to show that the sightings were predictably clustered in the entertainment districts of Shinjuku and Shibuya.

The celebrity ambusher's face filled the screen again. "We don't know how or why Flame has disappeared, but we're going to find out! Our team has analyzed the data and concluded that she must be staying at one of the three big net cafés, where anonymous overnighters are a way of life. Follow me as we take a camera crew to hunt her down!"

The map was replaced with three building photos, captioned, "Is Flame staying here?"

Yumi's mouth dropped open. In the third photo, she recognized the cheaply made miniskirts in the window of the fashion outlet downstairs. She stood and spun around, peering over the wall of her cubicle, scanning the dark room.

Phone in hand, Yumi pulled off her headphones, then grabbed her purse and the narrow clipboard with her time stamp. If Flame was here, she was in one of the other rooms. If she'd seen the *Look!Look!* webcast and wanted to get out before the camera team arrived, she'd have to leave the same way she came in, stopping to settle her bill at the cashier's desk before going. Yumi trotted through the cubicles, through the hallway lined with manga, and got in line with the customers waiting to pay.

There were only four. Two boys whose rumpled clothes gave away that they'd probably been playing an online role-playing game for days, living on Cup Noodles. An older man who probably stayed here more or less permanently, but had to go out occasionally to buy whatever wasn't sold in the vending machines. A boy with close-cropped hair dancing from one foot to the other, in a yellow-and-black Hanshin Tigers baseball cap. A guitar and duffel bag sat at his feet.

None of the waiting customers were girls. If Flame was here, she was still inside. Yumi heard footsteps behind her and glanced back, but they belonged to a boy just passing by the cashier station to feed coins into one of the vending machines.

The pair of gamers finished paying and slouched over to wait for the elevator. The boy in the Tigers cap shoved his bag forward with his foot as the man ahead of him stepped up to pay. The man pocketed his receipt, and the boy in the baseball cap picked up his guitar. Something fell out of his hoodie pocket as he pulled out his wallet, but he didn't notice as he stepped up to the desk.

Yumi stared at it, then scooped it up. It was a long, white lace, fingerless glove.

•

Yumi looked at the glove in her hand, then at the back of the Hanshin Tigers hat. Shaving your head was the easiest disguise in the world. Was the guitarist who was right now crumpling his receipt into his pants pocket and shrugging his duffel onto his shoulder really an idol on the run? He turned toward the elevator and Yumi recognized the profile she'd seen eight times on stage and countless times in music videos. It was Flame.

"Next customer, please."

Yumi leaped to the counter and shoved her slip at the girl along with . . . damn, what had happened to all her money? She groaned, remembering she'd spent her last ¥1,000 note on lunch, then forgotten to stop by the ATM. Wadding the lace glove into a side pocket, she fished out her coin purse and found a ¥500 coin. Thrusting it at the cashier, she didn't wait for a receipt. She dashed to the elevator, but she was too late. The numbers above were already counting down 6 . . . 5 . . . 4 . . .

Yumi stabbed at the call button, vibrating with impatience. The other elevator arrived and she jumped in, but it descended with what seemed like glacial slowness. Come on, come on!

Out on the sidewalk, Yumi looked up and down the crowded Shibuya street. Tigers hat, where are you?

Guessing her quarry would be trying to get out of Shibuya fast, Yumi turned toward the train station and wove through the crowd, looking for the telltale yellow-and-black cap. There! Ahead of her, waiting to cross the big intersection. She followed the guitar-and-duffel-toting figure across the street and into the maw of the station, eyes fixed on the hat that finally turned at the gate to the Yamanote Line.

Digging in her purse for her train pass, Yumi beeped her way through and leaped up the stairs, just in time to spot the guitarist boarding a train stopped at the platform. Yumi dashed for the car and just managed to squeeze on, then followed the guitarist off again at the next stop. Down the escalator, out the ticket gate, underground to the Hibiya Line. Yumi slipped onto an inbound train behind the disguised Flame and squinted at the stops on the map above the door, mystified. The guitarist seemed to have a plan, but the Hibiya Line didn't stop in any entertainment districts with big, anonymous net cafés.

Now wearing sunglasses as well as the baseball cap, the missing idol turned to face the dark window as the train eased away from the platform.

Yumi studied the guitarist's reflection. Since abandoning her assumption that buzzed hair and baggy boyish clothes meant the guitarist was male, she couldn't believe she hadn't recognized Flame right away. Would Coco have . . . Coco. She'd run out of the net café without telling Coco. Yumi pulled out her phone and typed, *Sorry had to go, Flame was at net café!* Then she stopped. How secure were cell-phone texts? She'd heard they could be intercepted. Deleting all but *Sorry had to go* she added, *Will explain later!* and sent it as the train paused to disgorge a few passengers and allow a few others to board in their place.

The fugitive stuck to the spot by the door, averting her face as a train station security team boarded, doing a routine anti-terror check. They glanced at the back of the guitarist's head and moved on as the doors slid shut, but Yumi was reminded that fans weren't the only ones who wanted to talk to Flame.

Should she tell Kenji? No. He'd told her to butt out. A lump rose in her throat as this morning's painful scene at the shrine bathroom looped through her head again. Kenji's badgering questions, catching her lying, telling her he didn't need her help, not now, not ever. In one day, she'd lost Kenji, she'd lost Ichiro, she'd gone from being caught between two men to being utterly alone. Her eyes brimmed.

And then Flame was pulling her duffel off the overhead rack, hoisting her guitar, stepping out onto the platform. Jolted back to reality, Yumi pushed past the standing commuters, followed her toward the ticket gate.

She dashed away her tears. What station was this? Tsukiji? The place with the big fish market? Why Tsukiji?

Yumi hustled to the gate and waved her train pass over the sensor. Bong. Oh no. She didn't have enough money on her card to exit. Dashing back to the Add Fare machine, she opened her coin purse and dug through the remaining coins. She managed to scrape together enough to get her out of Tsukiji Station, but now she'd lost Flame. Taking a chance, Yumi ran up the Exit 1 steps. She looked up and down the street. Yes, there was the yellow hat, crossing the intersection at the end of the block, passing the shuttered ramen stands on the fringes of the wholesale fish market.

Yumi followed Flame as she worked her way through the narrow deserted alleyways that were a bedlam of buying and selling every morning before the sun came up, each stall brimming with seafood so fresh, most of it was still moving.

But by early afternoon, it was eerily deserted, and as she got closer to the water she saw that the tsunami had damaged many of the huge auction buildings next to the river, and only a handful of boats were anchored offshore.

Ahead, she saw Flame approach a young man in wellies hosing down a spot where pallets of fish had sat earlier. Folding money changed hands and the fisherman pointed farther down the quay, then got out his phone to make a call as Flame bowed and trotted off.

Yumi followed the guitarist, and watched as a rubber dinghy from one of the boats swung around to pick up the fleeing idol. Where was she going?

Yumi spun around and ran back to the man in the wellies.

"Excuse me!" she called. He shut off his hose and frowned at her.

"That boat," she said, pointing to the one the rubber dinghy was heading for. "Where's it going?"

"Odaiba. Taking emergency supplies to the tsunami victims."

"I want to help, too. Can you ask them to wait for me?"

He regarded her impassively.

"How much?" she asked.

"Five thousand yen."

Yumi's heart sank. She was down to small change, with no ATM in sight. She thanked the man and turned back toward the station.

She couldn't follow Flame today, but she wouldn't give up until she found out why the idol was on the run. After picking up her things at the Mitsuyamas' tomorrow, she'd find a way to get herself to the heart of the disaster zone. She bet she could pick up Flame's trail at one of the refugee centers.

•

Yumi checked her phone as she walked slowly back toward Tsukiji Station. Three tweets from Coco.

> @yumihata what happened? why did you leave? #needweddingnooz

> omg looklook camera crew is here! @yumihata @midori328 @harugothic

they're saying flame is alive! @yumihata @midori328 @harugothic

The guitarist had barely gotten out in time. Yumi bit her lip. Coco would never forgive her for not tweeting instantly, but this was the kind of secret Coco would find impossible to keep, and Yumi didn't want to be the one who pointed the media bloodhounds at the idol she'd adored since middle school. Yumi remembered all too well what it was like to live in fear that her private life was about to be sacrificed on the chopping block for public entertainment, because last fall, she and Kenji had risked everything trying to catch a criminal who nearly slipped through their grasp. It was only by sheer luck that the details hadn't become public and ruined both of their lives.

She started down the steps to the station, puzzling over why Flame wasn't coming forward to say she was alive. Why was she on the run, masquerading as a boy?

In his *Look!Look!* video, Taku had said Flame quit the VuDu Dolls a month ago. That wasn't a huge shock; there had been rumors of discord in the group for over a year. According to what Yumi had read on *The Dollhouse*, Flame wanted to take the VuDu Dolls in a new direction, artistically. The rest of the band, their promoter, and most of the fans were against it. They wanted the VuDu Dolls to keep recording the kind of music they'd become famous for.

But if Flame had left for artistic reasons, why had the manager hired Taku to play on the new single, pretending to be her? If what Taku had said on *Look!Look!* was true, Flame had disappeared long before the earthquake and tsunami.

But how could she find out the truth? Yumi didn't know anybody in the music industry. Then she remembered. She knew someone who did. Waking her phone, she searched for @rakugoactor, the guy who performed in Yoyogi Park and knew the VuDu Dolls' stylist.

How could she convince him to introduce her to the

stylist without giving away why she was suddenly making such a strange request? Then a tweet from @rakugoactor in the column to the right caught her eye.

> Going to Odaiba Tuesday to help earthquake victims. If you want to join, let me know. Fishing boat fare ¥3000 #earthquakehelp

Yumi thought for a moment, then sent a private message.

> @rakugoactor saw your #earthquakehelp tweet. what time are you leaving?

•

Yumi perched on the edge of the hard vinyl sofa in the lobby of the Komagome Police Station.

Every time the scene with Kenji had replayed in her head today, she'd cringed a little more at her reaction to seeing the picture of Ichiro and Ami together. Why had she aimed all the anger that Ichiro deserved at Kenji? And what if she'd broken his phone? The more she thought about it, the guiltier she felt. Smartphones weren't cheap. If she'd killed it, she should offer to pay.

So when she stepped off the train in Komagome, she turned toward the police station instead of home. But Kenji wasn't in, and they didn't know when he'd be back. She gazed at the bulletin board on the wall opposite, where a pencil sketch of a fugitive scowled down at her. Small drawings to the side detailed his few remaining snaggle teeth. It shouldn't be too hard to identify that guy, Yumi thought. He really ought to have been more diligent about his dental hygiene if he wanted to get away with cutting up a body and leaving it in Lake Biwa.

She looked at her watch.

"Hata-*san*?"

She jumped. Oh. It was Detective Oki.

"Are you waiting to see Detective Nakamura?" he asked,

the front door easing closed behind him.

"Uh, yes, but he's not here and—"

"Why don't you come upstairs? It'll be warmer."

Relief. If she waited upstairs, she wouldn't have to make her apology in the lobby. She followed Oki to the elevator and up to the squad room. The big detective pulled out the visitor chair in front of Kenji's desk, then moved around to his own, shedding his jacket and opening his laptop. He bent down and typed a password, then picked up his teacup and peered at the cold dregs in the bottom.

"I'm going to get myself a cup of tea," he said. "Want some?"

"Yes, please."

Kenji's desk was so neat, there wasn't much to entertain her while she waited. His powered-down police laptop sat to one side, Inbox stacked with paperwork on the other. She read the title of the notice on top: "Tokyo Metropolitan Police Examination Schedule." But what was that, in the clear plastic bag sticking out beneath it? Curious, she pulled it out and flipped it over, then was sorry she had. Yumi quickly put it back and covered it with the exam notice. She could no longer see the Polaroid of an unhappy-looking teenager shivering in front of a pink-tiled bathtub in her underwear, but she couldn't scrub away the knowledge that someone Kenji was investigating was exploiting underage girls.

Oki reappeared and handed her a cup of tea as the landline on his desk rang.

"Oki *desu*." He listened. "Okay, I'll tell her."

He hung up and said, "Sorry, but the front desk says Nakamura-*san* just called, and he's going straight home. Do you want to leave him a message?"

She hesitated, then thanked Oki and said she'd stop by Kenji's house on her way home.

●

Wearily, Kenji gave a little shove to the front door to get it past the warped spot on its wooden track. The house was dark. And cold. With a pang of disappointment, Kenji remembered tonight was his father's poker night and he wouldn't be home until the last train.

Kenji pulled off his muffler and shrugged out of his coat, then his jacket, hanging them on the entryway wall pegs. Then he kicked off his shoes, too tired to put them in the shoe cupboard, and stepped up onto the *tatami* floor, scuffing into his slippers. Unbuttoning his top button and whipping off his tie as he headed for the deep wooden tub in the bathroom, he paused to switch on the heater so the kitchen would be warm by the time he came back to eat his lonely dinner there.

Ten minutes later, with the grime of the day scrubbed away and up to his neck in water hot enough to chase the chill from his bones, he felt better. Now he could think about what Suzuki had called to tell him on the way home.

The assistant detective's mother was in the hospital, and he was taking emergency leave, starting tomorrow. He'd promised to meet Kenji early, to brief him on today's research, but after that, they'd be one man down on the Tabata Shrine case.

*Bzzzzzzt.*

No. Kenji groaned. Not the doorbell. Why did it always ring when he was in the bath? He considered pretending nobody was home, but whoever it was had certainly seen the light glowing through the bathroom window.

Sighing, he climbed out of the tub and fitted on the wooden cover to keep the water hot. Wrapping himself in a cotton yukata and toweling his hair, he made his way to the front door. He hoped it was just a deliveryman who could be dealt with in thirty seconds and sent on his way.

He slid the front door open. Brr, it was freezing, and nobody was there. Had he gotten out of the bath for nothing? Irritated, he glanced left and right, then started to shut the door.

"Ken-*kun* . . . ?"

Yumi. She was across the street in the deepening twilight, wearing a funny droopy knit hat and looking like a small woodland animal that was about to bolt. She took a few tentative steps toward him, clutching her purse nervously.

"I . . . you didn't answer the door right away, so I thought you weren't home. I know you told me to get lost, but I was worried that I broke your phone and—"

"Huh? My phone?"

"Yeah, I was afraid that, you know, when I . . . I mean, is it broken? Is it all right?"

What was she talking about?

"Why don't you come inside?" he said, shivering in his yukata. "It's too cold out here."

She bobbed her head apologetically and said, "*O-jamaa shimasu*" as she stepped through the door.

After sliding the door closed, she stood in the entry, biting her lip and looking up at him uncertainly. Her body was a shapeless bundle in her winter coat and muffler, but her cheeks were pink and her lips were red after walking through the cold streets.

He busied himself digging in the slipper bin and setting out a pair, noticing too late that he'd picked two that didn't match. She put them on and glanced past him toward the kitchen.

"He's out tonight," Kenji said. "Playing poker."

"Ah." She stared down at the two different plaids on her feet and took a deep breath. "Is your phone really okay? Because I . . . I . . ." Then she bowed deeply from the waist and said, "I'm so sorry. About what I said this morning. Of course you weren't stalking Ichiro. Please forgive me. I—"

"No," he said, embarrassed. "Stop bowing like that. There's nothing to forgive. I'm sorry, too. I didn't mean to hurt you. I—"

"I can't marry him," she said. She looked into his eyes and said, "I'm not going to marry Ichiro. Not after . . . what you showed me."

Kenji froze. Had she really said the words he'd been waiting so long to hear? He searched her face, looking for any sign that she didn't mean it.

But this time she didn't look away. "I'm sorry it took me so long. I know I've been an idiot. I wouldn't blame you if . . . I mean, I know it's probably too late, but . . ."

He didn't need to hear any more. He reached out and pulled her to him.

"Aah!" he yelped, jumping back. "Your buttons are cold!"

She laughed and shed her coat, letting it fall to the floor. Her hat fell off as their lips met, but neither of them noticed. He buried his hands in her hair, devouring the lips he thought he'd never taste again. She let go of him long enough to pull a strand of hair from her mouth and tug at her muffler as his hands clasped themselves behind her back and pulled her to him with a fierceness that gave away the longing he'd felt ever since she stood up in front of his third grade class, the new girl from across the wide Pacific.

Finally, dizzy and a little bruised, they came up for air and just held each other, rocking back and forth. When their breathing slowed, he bent down to kiss her again, but she stopped him, laying a finger gently against his lips. She stepped back, keeping one hand in hers.

She looked into his eyes and said, "I know what I have to do, but I don't know how. Ichiro's the one who's in the wrong, but if I show him that picture, he'll want to know where I got it."

Kenji nodded. She was right. It had to be done carefully. Backing out of an arranged marriage with a family like the Mitsuyamas wouldn't be easy. If Yumi and her family wanted to walk away undamaged, it had to be the Mitsuyamas who called things off, it had to be Ichiro who apologized. He pulled Yumi into the kitchen and switched on the light. Time to think like a detective. He sat Yumi down at the low kitchen table and made two cups of tea. Handing one to her, he dropped into the seat across the table.

"Okay," he said. "Let's figure this out. You want to make sure that you end things with them owing you damages, not the other way around."

"Damages? What do you mean?"

"You and Ichiro met through *o-miai*, right? So you have a contract."

Yumi looked at him, puzzled. "A contract? No, we didn't sign anything."

"Did you have an engagement ceremony?"

"Well, yes. At the Tokyo Club."

"That's a formal agreement, and it can be argued that the party that breaks it is liable for damages."

"But . . . I don't want money. I just want out."

"What about your dad's professorship?"

Yumi was silent. It was the single biggest reason she hadn't been able to escape the decision she'd made.

"You want him to be able to keep his job until he retires, right? For that you'll need more proof than the picture I took. There has to be evidence. Is there any way you can search Ichiro's office? Or his home?"

"I'm going to their house tomorrow to take back the things I moved into his rooms before the wedding. If I find something, what should I do?"

"Take a picture of it with your phone, but leave it where it is. E-mail the picture to . . ." No, she shouldn't send it to him. From now on, they had to be careful nobody guessed they had any kind of relationship besides their childhood friendship. "Just send me an e-mail saying you found something to do with the Tabata Shrine case."

Yumi nodded. Then she said, "Actually, I did see

something today that has to do with your case."

She pulled out her phone and keyed something in. He came around the table and looked over her shoulder. It was a page on an auction website.

"The pictures in that album sitting on the table in front of that Oricon Award are childhood pictures of Flame," Yumi explained. "But look at the roof you can see through that window above the sink. Don't you think that looks like the treasure house at the Tabata Shrine?"

But Kenji wasn't looking at the window. He snatched the phone from her and zoomed in on the Oricon Award. Its base was made of beveled Lucite.

He'd bet his MVP baseball trophy that when they found it, it would turn out to be exactly the width of the deadly gash on Head Priest Yano's head.

•

Kenji and Oki made their way along the row of houses on the narrow street behind the Tabata Shrine.

After Kenji had said a private good-bye to Yumi in the kitchen and a carefully proper one at the front door, he'd called Oki and asked if he had time this evening to go door to door, helping Kenji search for Flame's Oricon Award.

The sixth door they knocked on opened to reveal the suspicious face of a lanky teenage boy. His conservative haircut and wire-rimmed glasses were at odds with the black T-shirt boasting an elaborate pattern of skulls, barbed wire, and white roses. Gothic lettering woven into the design spelled "VuDu Dolls." The boy's mouth made an "O" of surprise when Kenji displayed his police badge and asked if they could come in.

"Uh, my parents aren't home yet."

"We're not looking for your parents," Oki said, stepping up to the door. "We're looking for whoever put some childhood photos of the VuDu Dolls' guitarist up for sale online."

The boy's eyes darted right, then left. "Um, I don't think . . . I mean, I don't know . . ."

"I think you do," Oki said. "May we come in, or would you like us to wait on the doorstep for your mother and father to come home?"

The boy's Adam's apple bobbed in his skinny neck and he opened the door.

Oki and Kenji stepped inside.

"What's your name?" Oki asked.

"Shota," he muttered.

"Okay, Shota-*kun*," Oki said, his bulk filling the narrow entry, "let's see the things you put up for sale the day after the earthquake."

"Wait," the boy said, scowling. "Why do you think it's me?"

"Because you're no good at hiding your electronic tracks," Oki said. "The pictures?"

"They're not here," he replied, a little too quickly.

"Really?" Oki said. "Look at me."

Shota's eyes flicked up to Oki's, then slid away.

"Where are they?"

The boy didn't answer.

"Selling things that don't belong to you is a crime, you know. Once we trace them to your computer, you'll be in serious trouble."

Alarm. "My computer?"

"Yes, the one you used to upload photos of the stuff you're trying to sell."

Shota's face drained of color.

"Where is it?"

"I . . . don't have one."

"Then how did you get the pix up on eBay?"

Silence.

"Shota-*kun*?"

His shoulders slumped. "It's my dad's," he admitted. "I . . . used it while he was asleep." He looked at Oki, all bravado suddenly gone. "But don't tell him," he pleaded. "He'll kill me if he finds out."

"Then don't waste any more of our time. Show us what you're selling."

Defeated, the boy led them to an open door on the way to the kitchen.

Covers were heaped in a pile at the end of an unmade futon. The boy quickly scooped up a magazine lying face down next to it and shoved it underneath, then slung a shiny vinyl athletic bag emblazoned "Kaisei High School Baseball" into the far corner and kicked a pile of discarded clothes over it. The wall over his bed was papered with VuDu Dolls posters.

Oki cleared his throat. "The photos?" he reminded the boy.

Shota flicked a resentful glance at him, then picked his way over to the futon cupboard. He slid the door all the way open and carefully pushed aside a tower of comic books. Pulling out a plastic Tokyu Store grocery bag with something square inside, he shut the door.

Oki and Kenji put on their evidence-handling gloves. Oki held out his hand and the boy reluctantly gave him the bag.

The big detective looked inside and removed a cheap photo album with a water stain on the cover. He paged through it. A baby with a shock of black hair peeked out from a white Hello Kitty blanket, in the arms of a smiling girl, her makeup-free face a model of flawless youth except for the dark circles beneath her eyes. In the next picture, arms thrown wide, the toddler took a wobbly step away from the corner of a green sofa. In the next one, he rode on the shoulders of a young man in a Meatsnake T-shirt with bleached platinum hair.

Kenji and Oki exchanged surprised glances. It was the

same photo that was in the box Kenji had found in Yano's office.

They looked through the rest of the shots, as the toddler turned into a teenager bent over a Martin guitar at a microphone. By the time they reached the photo of the VuDu Dolls guitarist gazing at the teenage Nana, they knew that Head Priest Yano didn't have an illegitimate son who called himself Taiga. He had an illegitimate daughter who called herself Flame.

Oki flipped through the blank pages to the end and found an empty white envelope pasted inside the back cover. It looked like it had been stuffed at one time with something a lot thicker than a single photograph, and the creases were approximately the size of the Polaroid they'd found in Yano's sleeve.

He looked at Shota. "What was in here?"

"It was empty when I got the album," the boy insisted. "I swear. I wondered, too."

Oki gave him a hard look and said, "When we track these pictures down, if I find anything that tells me you're lying, I'll be back here with a warrant and zero sympathy. Do you understand? Now's the time to tell me if you sold them."

"I didn't. The envelope really was empty when I found it."

"When you found it? What do you mean, found it?"

"It was in the garbage. Right outside in the street. Honest. I'm not lying. I can show you. Someone threw it out and I found it."

Silence.

"Don't ask me why, but they did," the boy insisted. "There was no trash collection the day after the earthquake, but my mom made me take out the garbage anyway. Crows were tearing apart a bag of burnable trash from the day before and I was afraid it was ours because two of them were fighting over a seafood instant ramen cup. So I shooed them away and checked. I found the album in a bag someone had tried to hide under the one the crows got."

"And the music award? Where's the music award?"

The boy sighed and returned to the cupboard.

He reached in, but Oki stopped him. "Wait a second. Let me."

He peered past the stacks of comic books and his gloved hand emerged clutching a Lucite trophy. The clear prism was about half a meter tall, with a golden emblem embedded in the center. Flame's name and "VuDu Dolls" were engraved near the bottom. Oki passed it to Kenji, who measured the beveled edge of the base against his index finger.

Ten centimeters wide.

•

Yumi checked the tweet she'd received from @rakugoactor and copied his address into her phone. The actor rented a room in one of the buildings where students and unmarried people who came to Tokyo from other parts of Japan stayed until they found a more permanent toehold.

Ah, there it was, on the next block. From the sidewalk outside, Yumi sent Mansaku a message she'd arrived, and a few minutes later he appeared at the door, looking like an Edo-era monk in modern clothing. His hair was pulled into the same Edo-style knot he'd worn while performing, but now he was wearing a Banksy T-shirt of an anarchist throwing a bouquet, along with baggy pants and a pair of brown vinyl slippers. She left her shoes on the shelves by the door, slid into the too-large pair of slippers he set out for her, and followed him to a common room. Floor pillows were strewn about on the *tatami* and a large TV in the corner was tuned to earthquake news. He found the remote and turned it off.

They exchanged pleasantries, then Yumi said, "So, about tomorrow. Is it okay for me to come along?"

Mansaku nodded. "There's plenty of room on the boat.

It's a trawler heading out to deep ocean. They'll drop us at Odaiba on the way. Three thou apiece, to help pay for the extra fuel."

"How did you find it?"

"My brother's the pilot."

"You come from a Tsukiji family? How did you end up performing *rakugo*?"

"My parents ask me the same question. Repeatedly." He grimaced. "In fact, the earthquake postponed another 'important talk' scheduled for next week."

Yumi winced in sympathy. Men who waded too deep into their thirties without getting married and/or landing the kind of career that set them on a corporate promotion escalator were often taken aside by their parents to have a *daijina hanashi*. Inevitably, this talk included exhortations to find a bride who would take care of the negligent son's parents in their old age, which they claimed was fast approaching. It went without saying that supporting such a woman would also require giving up whatever frivolous pursuits the son had been indulging in and buckle down to a real job.

"So are you going to do it? Trade in your kimono for some wellies?"

He groaned.

Yumi asked, "What kind of volunteer work are you planning to do on Odaiba?"

"I want to join an animal recue team," he said. "Looking for survivors. After the Tōhoku earthquake, nobody realized how many pets had survived the tsunami. Cats and some breeds of dogs did okay until someone got around to bringing them in a month later, but dachshunds, Pomeranians, Chihuahuas . . . dogs like that just aren't bred for survival in the wild. I saw some really sad cases." Then he brightened. "I also might do a few performances at the refugee centers at night. I've been talking to a woman there who's in charge of entertainment." Mansaku shifted on his cushion. "What are you planning to do?"

"I . . . I just want to help," she said. And search for a missing idol.

He nodded. "Why don't you come with me to the refugee center? I'm sure they'll be able to tell you where volunteers are needed."

"Sounds good. How long are you planning to stay?"

"Don't know exactly. I'll stay until the restaurant where I work reopens."

"How will you get back?"

"If the trains aren't up and running yet, I'll ask my brother if he can pick me up on his way back in."

Yumi nodded. "Do you have somewhere to stay?"

"The Oedo Onsen got turned into one of the refugee centers, and I'm hoping they have some futons set aside for volunteers, too. That's what I'm planning to do, unless . . ." His pocket started buzzing. He reached in and checked the number on his phone display. "Unless the friend who's returning my call right now knows of something better." He pressed Answer and said, "Chiho-*san*, long time. How are you?"

He listened, nodding and saying "*hai*" occasionally.

"Whoa, that would be great," he said finally, a smile spreading across his face. He glanced at Yumi. "Is there room for another person, too? There's a volunteer coming with me who doesn't have anywhere . . ." He listened. "Woman." He nodded. "Great. Perfect. So how much stuff does this stylist have . . . ? Okay, okay, sorry, 'image consultant.'" He listened, then answered, "Could he meet us at Tsukiji Station, Exit 3 at three o'clock? Great. Ja, ne." He ended the call.

"Good news," he said. "I don't know if you remember, but I have a friend who's a stylist for one of the big promoters. Chiho-*san* was in Odaiba at his studio last week working on a new promo for some band, and got stuck there after the earthquake. But some other guy she works with—he's an 'image consultant,' whatever that is—sneaked back into town for a hot date Friday night and couldn't get back on Sunday after the earthquake. Now she's in a pinch because the promoter guy just told her he's returning with the band to reshoot some of the video to make it into an earthquake memorial, and he'll be pissed as hell if he finds out the image consultant guy isn't there. She says if we can bring him and some stuff she needs, we can stay at the promoter's place until the celebs arrive."

"Which band?" she asked.

"Dunno. Those idol bands – they're all the same, aren't they?"

Tuesday, December 24

•

*8:45 A.M.*

Kenji tossed a scoop of green tea leaves into the staffroom pot and filled it from the hot-water dispenser.

As he returned to his desk, two cups of tea in hand, Assistant Detective Suzuki stepped out of the elevator, pulling a wheelie bag behind him. He'd be heading straight to Tokyo Station to catch the train back to his hometown after he briefed Kenji. Even though he was on leave, he was wearing a starched white shirt and black suit.

"Sorry I'm late, sir," he apologized, stopping in front of Kenji's desk to bow. It was 8:42, but like most Japanese, Suzuki believed 8:40 was the correct time to arrive for an 8:45 meeting.

"Thanks for coming in," Kenji said. He inquired about Suzuki's mom as his *kohai* parked his bag. Handing him one of the cups of tea, Kenji suggested they set up in an interview room.

"So what have you got for me?" he asked, once they were settled.

"Here's what I was able to put together about Flame, sir."

The guitarist had been born twenty-six years ago on December 18, the child of a single mother. Rumors about her real name were legion, because she hadn't used it since she ran away from home at age fifteen. She was already using the stage name Flame when Jimmy Harajuku discovered her playing in

Yoyogi Park.

In the early days, the promoter was still discovering talent rather than training his idols from scratch, but he already had an eye for what would sell. He signed Flame's band, but replaced the other members within a month. The only things he kept were the name VuDu Dolls and Flame. His "image consultant" Shiro and head stylist Chiho dreamed up a doll-like makeup and costume design, and a month after Flame turned sixteen, the VuDu Dolls had their major debut. After that, it was hard to pass a newsstand without seeing Flame's face on magazine covers, hard to flip the TV channel without hearing the band members making small talk on variety shows, and impossible to turn on the radio without hearing their latest song. They were the first of Jimmy Harajuku's blockbuster girl bands. Over the years, fans had linked Flame romantically with a parade of celebrities, the most recent rumors fed by paparazzi-like shots that caught Flame and actor Kentaro Goto—or Kengo, as he was known to his fans—coming out of nightclubs and restaurants. Suzuki had attached images.

"Thanks, Suzuki-*san*," Kenji said when he'd finished reading. He sat back in his chair. "Which of Flame's associates do you think is most likely to have a thing for underage girls?"

"Well, I'd probably rule out the female stylist," Suzuki said. "And it's probably not that actor, Kengo. He's got a different celebrity girlfriend every month, but he never gets married. Must be gay."

"Speaking of that, how about this guy?" Kenji frowned at the flamboyant image consultant's picture.

Suzuki agreed that Shiro was an unlikely candidate.

Kenji sat back in his chair. "What do you know about the promoter, Jimmy Harajuku?"

"He's one of the most powerful figures in the entertainment business," Suzuki replied. "I've heard that if a TV producer refuses to cast his latest up-and-comers in a new drama, Jimmy pulls all his talent from the station and its affiliates. Since his idols are known ratings-makers, none of the stations want to risk getting on his bad side. And--" Suzuki paused. "He's a weird guy. He's apparently got a thing about germs. Always wears one of those white masks and gloves, even when he does TV appearances. Never eats at restaurants if he hasn't inspected the kitchen first."

"Huh. Maybe he's got a thing about taking pictures of underage girls, too."

Suzuki clicked on another file and said, "I also scanned the photos you found in that box in the treasure house and blew them up. I couldn't tell where they were taken, but I did find something interesting."

He opened the picture of the toddler with the guitar and zoomed in. Angling his laptop so they could both see the screen, he pointed to the child's half-hidden right arm, the one that wasn't poking at the strings. It was mottled with red. "See this? Doesn't that look like a birthmark to you?"

"Or a burn," Kenji said. "Good work. Could you send me those scans?"

His *kohai* attached the pictures to an e-mail and pushed Send, then slid his laptop into its carrying case. They stood.

"Thank you," Kenji said. "I hope your mom will be okay."

"She's tough," Suzuki said, trying to keep the worry from his voice. "But maybe next time they're without power for a day in the middle of winter, she'll go stay somewhere they have heat instead of putting on a sweater and catching pneumonia."

After the elevator doors closed on Suzuki, Kenji returned to his desk to study the photo of the toddler.

Oki appeared, his hand dwarfing a cup of tea.

"What are you looking at?" he asked, peering over Kenji's shoulder.

"One of Flame's baby pictures. See this here?" Kenji said,

pointing to the arm. "Do you think that's a birthmark or a burn?"

"Could be either. If it's a birthmark, it could explain why she always wears that weird glove."

"If it's a burn, I wonder how she got it."

"Maybe the mother had good reason to run away and raise the girl without a dad."

"Or maybe the mom did it."

Oki nodded. "Could be why Yano volunteered at the shelter. If it was the mom who was abusive, maybe he felt guilty that he couldn't rescue his own kid."

"I'm going to head over there after I stop in at the bank. I'd like to ask the director about Yano's volunteer work and show him the Polaroid we found in Yano's sleeve. Maybe someone at the shelter will recognize the girl."

The door from the stairwell opened and Section Chief Tanaka strode into the squad room, talking on his phone. ". . . right, I'll get someone over there right away." He ended the call and scanned the squad room.

"Oki!" he barked, detouring to collect the big detective on the way to his desk. "I need you to look into a suspicious death."

•

Kenji arrived at the bank just in time to see a balding man in a conservative suit bidding farewell to a couple who looked like they'd just been granted a loan.

"Excuse me," said Kenji, after the couple had been bowed out the door. He introduced himself and asked, "Are you the manager?"

The man inspected Kenji's card, then warily admitted he was. He nodded toward an open door across the lobby, with the character for his name on a plaque outside. "Please step into my office, Detective."

On the way, he stopped to ask a woman who was

working at her computer to fetch them some coffee. She agreed with outward meekness, but as the manager turned away, she pulled off her glasses and shot an annoyed frown at his back, pausing to add a few more keystrokes to the document she was working on before complying.

"Please," the manager said to Kenji, indicating the chair in front of his desk. He glanced at the stack of paperwork in his Inbox as he pulled out his own chair and sat. He picked up the top document, frowned at it, and checked his watch. Message sent, he placed it back on the stack, folded his hands in front of him and asked how he could be of service.

Kenji produced the bankbook and slid it across the desk. "Do you recognize this?"

The manager picked it up and read the name of the account holder, then checked the balance. "Yes," he said, handing it back. "The head priest at the Tabata Shrine is a regular customer."

"Was."

The manager expressed polite shock as Kenji explained.

"Do you have any idea why he opened this account?" Kenji asked.

"That was before my time. All I can tell you is what you already know—he added to it faithfully every month."

"Is there anybody who might know? Someone who was here when he opened it?"

"I'm sorry, but that was a long time ago. Anybody who was working here back then would be retired by now."

"Could you give me some names and last known contact information," Kenji persisted, "so we can try to track them down?"

Taking back the bankbook, the manager checked the opening date, then pulled a thick ledger from his bottom drawer. Running his finger down a page near the front, he stopped at a name, then closed the book. "Unfortunately, the gentleman who was manager at that time passed away several years ago."

"What about a safety deposit box? Did Yano-*kannushi* keep one here?"

The manager turned to his computer to check. A few keystrokes later he said, "Yes, he did."

"Excellent. If I could just have a quick look inside..."

Frown. "I'm afraid I can't allow that without a court order."

"We'll get the information anyway," Kenji pointed out. "As soon as Yano-*kannushi's* lawyer reopens his office. Unfortunately, he's on Odaiba, so you could help us get a head start on reuniting the heir with his inheritance if you just take a peek in the box yourself and happen to mention what's inside while I'm within earshot..."

The manager pursed his lips primly. "If you return with a court order, Detective, I'll be delighted to assist you. But until then, I'm afraid..."

Thwarted, Kenji closed his notebook. He stood and bowed, thanking the manager somewhat ironically for his help.

*Now what?* He pushed open the front door and stepped out to the sidewalk. All he could do was leave another message for the lawyer.

"Ken-*kun*?"

He turned. It was the woman who had been sent for coffee, holding a paper bag from Doutor. She took a step closer to Kenji and her face brightened.

"I knew it! It *is* you."

The moment she smiled he recognized the crossed front teeth of the girl who'd sat behind him in class for four years at Koshikawa High School. She'd grown even plumper, and wore her hair in a chin-length bob now, but she was definitely the same girl who once passed him the answers to a quiz on the Battle of Sekigahara.

"Kana-*chan*?" Kenji ventured.

She nodded, beaming. "I almost didn't recognize you! You got your mole fixed!"

He nodded. Until he had taken his Coming-Of-Age Day money to the dermatologist when he was twenty, the most noteworthy feature on his face had been a giant mole next to his nose. Afterward, he'd suddenly become a lot more visible to girls who'd previously looked right through him.

"Are you already finished meeting with Manager-*san*?" Kana asked.

"Unfortunately."

She laughed. "A short meeting with him is far better than a long one, believe me. Did he tell you what you wanted to know?"

"No," Kenji said. He explained that he was trying to track down a missing heir.

Kana thought for a moment, then stepped over to peer through the window into the bank lobby. "Good," she said. "His door's shut."

She turned a smile on Kenji. "Let's not waste the coffee I had to go all the way to Doutor to get. Come back in and tell me what you've been doing since high school. And," she added in a slightly conspiratorial voice, "let's talk about those questions you need answered."

Ten minutes later, Kenji had learned that Kana had been engaged to the first baseman from his high school team, and although that hadn't worked out, she had a memento in the form of a three-year-old daughter. Kana remembered that Kenji had gotten into Tokyo University and learned he was on the career-public-servant fast track to a position downtown at Tokyo Metropolitan Police headquarters. When she'd coyly asked why he wasn't wearing a wedding ring, he smiled and told her he just hadn't found the right girl yet. Then he brought out the bankbook and told her why he was there.

She flicked a glance at the manager's still-closed door. Leaning closer to Kenji, she said in a low voice, "Although some people here treat me like an office lady, I'm actually the loan officer. What can I do for you?"

"Can you let me take a look inside Yano-*san's* safety deposit box?"

Kana bit her lip. "I'd like to help you, but in order to do that, I'd have to sign you into the privacy room. Manager-*san* would have my head next time he checks the ledger."

"What if you took a peek and just told me what was in there?"

"That would work," Kana said with a sly smile.

"What I'm looking for is a will, photos, anything that would tell me where to start looking for Yano's kid."

Kana nodded. "Can do. And if you happen to be sitting in Matsumoto's about half an hour from now when I take my tea break..." She raised her eyebrows at him and smiled.

He bowed to her over the desk.

"It was great to catch up with you, Kana-*chan*. I hope I see you again." He smiled. "Soon."

•

The bell at Matsumoto's coffee shop jangled its familiar welcome, and Mrs. Matsumoto called out an Okinawa-flavored "*Irasshaimase!*" as Kenji pushed his way through the front door. His favorite table in the far corner was empty, the pattern on its pink Formica surface faded by countless scrubbings since the day he and Yumi had first sat there in third grade, assigned to build a model of the Ise Shrine together. Matsumoto's hadn't changed a bit—same flaking gold letters on the big plate-glass windows, same hand-lettered menu—except . . . where was the clock that usually hung over the register? The one with plastic pieces of sushi instead of numbers?

"Good morning, Ken-*kun*, what can I bring you today?"

Mrs. Matsumoto set a steaming cup of green tea before him. She'd worn the same indigo-dyed apron and kerchief ever since he'd know her. The only thing that had changed was her waistline, which had expanded a bit over the years.

"How about an order of *o-hagi*?" Kenji said.

"You want three or five?" Mrs. Matsumoto asked.

Kenji thought for a moment. He ought to offer some to Kana-*chan* when she arrived. "Five, please."

She looked at him speculatively. "Expecting company?"

"Yeah, do you remember Kana from my class at Koshikawa High School?"

Mrs. Matsumoto gave him a questioning look, and Kenji reddened. Not much escaped her watchful eye. She knew how he felt about Yumi Hata.

"She's helping me with a case," he explained.

"Ah," Mrs. Matsumoto said, flipping her order book closed without commenting on his love life. "Were you and your father both okay after the earthquake? Any damage to your house?"

"No, everything is fine. You?"

"Lost a few glasses. And the sushi clock. It fell off the wall in the earthquake," Mrs. Matsumoto explained. "But I talked to Akiyama-*san*, and he said if I brought him a plate of *o-hagi*, he'd fix it for me as soon as he gets his shop cleaned up."

"Sounds to me like he's getting the better end of that deal."

She laughed and went to fetch the rice cakes as the bell above the door jangled again and Kana appeared. She looked around and spotted Kenji, breaking into a big smile. As she made her way to his table, he wondered if it was it his imagination, or if her skirt was now considerably shorter than it had been at the bank. No, there was definitely a lot more thigh showing. She'd also spent most of the past half hour in the bathroom putting on makeup. Her lips were now dark red, and without her glasses, he could see her eyelashes poking up at a weird angle where she'd crimped them.

"Ooo, *o-hagi*! My favorite!" She clapped her hands in

delight as Mrs. Matsumoto arrived with the sweets and her tea. Kenji pushed the plate closer to her.

"I really shouldn't, but . . ." Her hand fluttered over the sweets, dithering over her selection, before settling on the smallest one. After a polite "*Itadakimasu*," she took a ladylike nibble from one end.

Kenji echoed her "*Itadakimasu*," then wolfed his down in two bites. He reached for another.

"Did you find anything?" he asked, taking a bite.

Her lips twitched into a cat-that-ate-the-canary smile and she cocked her head. "May-y-be. What will you give me if I tell you?"

Uh-oh, this information was going to be more expensive than he thought.

"How about my undying gratitude?" he countered, tossing the rest of the *o-hagi* in his mouth.

"How about a drink after work today?"

"Um . . ." Think fast. "I'd love to, but—"

"Good, what time do you get off? How about seven at that new wine bar near the station? I noticed they opened up again right after the earthquake."

"Uh, sorry," he waffled. "Today's kind of crazy. I'll be working late. On this case," he added, hoping details would disguise the lie a little better.

"How about Friday?" she persisted. "Give me your phone number. I'll call you. Maybe we can have dinner, too."

Worse and worse. Reluctantly, he keyed in the number she rattled off and dialed it so she could capture his.

Time to get the goods he was paying so dearly for. "So . . . what did you find in the safety deposit box? Was there a copy of Yano's will?"

"No." She sat back, cradling her tea in both hands. "The only papers were old car insurance policies, boring stuff like that. And a bunch of old newspaper clippings in a folder."

"What were they about?"

"Music artists."

"Such as . . . ?"

"Most of them I'd never heard of. Maybe half of the articles had that famous picture of the Meatsnake drummer playing with his sticks on fire. I recognized it because the papers printed it over and over when he died. The priest must have been a big fan "

That was interesting. Yano had renounced his musical life, but he still followed his old band from afar. It must have been torture to watch his mates make it big, then, one by one, suffer the side effects of too much success, too young. The drummer had committed suicide when he was twenty-eight. The vocalist had just divorced his third wife. The bass player had made front-page news for drunkenly taking off all his clothes and shouting up at the sky in the middle of Roppongi Midtown park. The band could still fill a stadium and their promoter still raked in a king's ransom every time a new version of one of their hit singles was reissued, but they hadn't recorded anything new in years.

"There were also a few photos," Kana continued.

"Photos? Can you describe them?"

"There were three or four taken at a beach that looked like Shimoda. The guy in them was superskinny, wearing a black leather jacket. And the girl was about six months pregnant."

"Any identifying features? Hair? Tattoos?"

"He had long, superbleached hair."

Just like the young Yano in the picture with the kid on his shoulders.

"What about the girl?"

"She was pretty, in a no-makeup granola-y sort of way. Long hair, black. And she was wearing a T-shirt that said 'No Nukes Now' on the front." Kana paused. "There was one more picture. It was of a chubby older priest with a strawberry birthmark on his face, holding a baby that had the same sticking-out ears. The blond guy and the long-haired girl were standing next to him. On the back it said, 'Hikaru Ohkawa, one month old.' The name was written like this." She penned four characters on her napkin, then turned it so Kenji could see.

Kenji stared. The most common way to read the characters in the baby's last name was Ohkawa. But it could also be pronounced . . . Taiga. The baby's name was Hikaru Taiga. Why did Yano have a baby picture of the missing intern in his safety deposit box? Was it possible he had two illegitimate children?

"Could you tell where the picture was taken?"

"I can't be sure, since I've only been there once," Kana said. "But it looked like the Zeniarai Benten Shrine, in Kamakura."

•

Yumi rang the bell at the Mitsuyama family compound in Hiroo, listening to it echo though the rooms beyond. Huddling into her coat, she shifted from one foot to the other nervously. She felt like a spy, crossing over into enemy territory.

The door opened. Mrs. Mitsuyama stood there, in a dark skirt and twin set.

"Please come in, she said, setting out a pair of slippers.

Yumi stepped out of her shoes and stowed them in the spacious shoe cupboard near the door. It was full of expensive ladylike pumps; hers looked shabby in comparison.

Following Mrs. Mitsuyama down the hallway, they arrived at the sitting room that had been tastefully redecorated when Ichiro's part of the house had been renovated into a newlywed suite. Filled with splendid neutral furniture and elegant throw pillows, the effect was marred only by a large garbage bag in the process of being stuffed with papers and miscellaneous trash.

"Oh dear, I'm sorry, Yumi-*san*—I can't believe Ichiro left that garbage bag here," Mrs. Mitsuyama apologized, shoving it behind the sofa. "I made him start his *ōsōji* cleaning early, He's been so busy, I worried it might not get done by New Year's."

Year-end cleaning was a ritual all Japanese observed, not only taking scouring powder to nooks and crannies that didn't get scrubbed all year, but also weeding out memorabilia that had silted up since last New Year's *ōsōji*.

"Would you like some tea?"

Yumi bowed her appreciation and replied, "Yes, please."

Mrs. Mitsuyama disappeared to fetch the tea and Yumi went to the bedroom to begin packing. Ichiro's mother had already laid out her open suitcases on the bed. Was she being thoughtful, or hoping all traces of Yumi would be cleared away before the new year began?

Yumi sighed and decided she'd start packing the drawers first. Underwear, socks, T-shirts, sweaters, shorts.

Shorts. It was winter now. She didn't need her shorts. If Mrs. Mitsuyama believed the wedding would be rescheduled, Yumi would be living in these rooms by next summer.

Ichiro's mother returned with a tea tray, and the roasted fragrance of *genmai-cha* filled the room as she poured a cup for Yumi.

"Thank you," Yumi said, taking a sip from the delicate rim of the celadon Arita-ware. "This is delicious." It was now or never. "Uh, Mitsuyama-*san*?"

"Yes?"

"I was wondering . . . do you think I should pack this drawer of shorts or not?"

Mrs. Mitsuyama regarded the open drawer thoughtfully, then raised her eyes to Yumi's. "I think it might be best to pack everything. Until you're more clear in your mind about what you want to do."

"Until . . . what?"

"Ichiro told us. That you've been having second thoughts. Since the earthquake." She paused. "We've all been thinking about our lives lately, haven't we?"

Without waiting for a reply, she bowed slightly and disappeared down the stairs.

Yumi stared after her. *Ichiro told them I'm having second thoughts?* She hadn't even spoken to him since that terrible call when he'd scolded her for using his work number! What had he been telling his family? Was Ichiro planning to back out of the wedding and say it was her idea?

She set down her teacup and surveyed the room. Crossing to Ichiro's drawers, she opened them one by one. His drawers gave nothing away. No half-empty box of condoms, no love letters.

The trash bag. She returned to the sitting room and pulled it from behind the sofa. Through the semi-clear plastic, she recognized the program from the benefit concert where she'd heard Ichiro's quartet perform for the Empress. He was throwing it away? She pulled it from the bag and knelt, smoothing it out on the carpet. They'd played Schubert's Death and the Maiden. Afterward, at a party high atop the Grand Hyatt, she'd looked out over Tokyo and for the first time seriously considered spending her life with Ichiro.

What else was he throwing away? She rooted through the bag. Was that the menu from the night they got engaged? She grabbed it by the corner and pulled out the crumpled paper. Then she spotted something red down at the bottom. It was the funny socks she'd bought for him as a joke at the Big Red Underwear store in Sugamo. She'd liked the grinning monkey on them, and because Ichiro had been born in the Year of the Monkey, she'd given them to him for good luck.

Her eyes brimmed as she looked at the hopeful little figure on the cuff. The thought of Ichiro tossing her gift in the trash hurt more than seeing the picture of him with Ami. They were cheap little socks, not the fine quality he was used to, but didn't it mean anything to him that they'd been a gift from her? Tears spilled down her cheeks as she hugged the pair of socks to her chest. Even though she didn't love Ichiro, the loss of everything she'd hoped for was suddenly too much. A sob escaped and she couldn't stop. It was only when she swiped at her eyes with her sweater and looked around for some tissues to wipe her streaming nose that she saw Mrs. Mitsuyama standing in the doorway, a stricken expression on her face.

"Yumi, what's wrong?"

"I ... Ichiro ..." she couldn't explain, so she held out the unworn pair of socks with the little metal clip still holding them together.

Mrs. Mitsuyama looked at them puzzled, then at the crumpled pieces of paper on the carpet around Yumi. She crossed the room and knelt, first picking up the smoothed-out concert program, then uncrumpling the menu from Tofuya-Ukai.

"That was ... that was what we ate, the night we ... we got engaged."

Mrs. Mitsuyama shook her head, her eyes puzzled.

"It's—it's not me," Yumi said, her chest heaving. "It's not me who's having second thoughts. It's Ichiro. I—I saw him with her."

"Her?"

"Ami. Ami Watanabe. His ex-girlfriend."

Ichiro's mother closed her eyes, as if in pain.

"I know," she whispered, her face a mask of sorrow. "I'm so sorry, Yumi-*san*. He's a Mitsuyama. Just like his father."

And suddenly Yumi realized that Mrs. Mitsuyama wasn't her adversary. They were just two women, with something terrible in common.

Ichiro's mother rose, and seated herself on the edge of the beige sofa, staring at her hands, clenched in her lap. "Two weeks ago, he used my connections to make a last-minute reservation at Serenya, and the owner called to tell me how much he enjoyed meeting Ichiro's fiancé. But . . . I knew you were in Hakone with your parents that weekend."

She raised her eyes to Yumi's. "I don't think he ever gave up on her, even though he agreed to meet more suitable girls through *o-miai*. His father and I picked the first five and he rejected them all after the first date. Then he asked us if you could be next. I had high hopes until we met you. You looked so much like Ami, I was afraid he was pursuing you for all the wrong reasons. When he rushed into asking you to marry him, I knew, but I didn't know what to do. I felt you really cared for him, so I couldn't tell you, but I knew what your life would be like if she ever reappeared. I did everything I could to derail the wedding, but I only delayed it." She looked at Yumi with eyes that had suffered in silence for most of her married life. "If you decide to go through with the marriage, I won't stop you. But if you want to walk away, I'll make sure Ichiro understands that the piper must be paid."

•

Setting off toward the address Makoto had given him for the shelter, Kenji thought about the tangle of suspects who might have murdered the head priest.

Koji Yamamoto was still on the list, but unless they discovered some hard evidence tying him to the scene, they couldn't get near him.

The missing intern, Taiga. What was the real relationship between him and the victim? Why had Yano sold the kimono in order to give him ¥3,000,000?

And how did Flame fit in, besides being Yano's daughter? She had been in a recording studio out on Odaiba at the time Yano was killed, but the fact that her fingerprints were on the Polaroid they found in his sleeve irritated Kenji like a burr in his sock.

Kenji slowed, searching for the shelter's address. This

part of East Shinjuku was a warren of tiny alleyways, a mishmash of businesses catering to customers with all kinds of appetites. Ramen shops, a capsule hotel, tobacco shops, a liquor store, clothing stores offering cheap slinky gowns for girls who worked at hostess bars. It was a good location for a runaway shelter, because kids who ran out of money often ended up a few streets over in Kabuki-chō, selling the only thing they had left.

Kenji pulled out his phone to check the map and tapped his GPS.

"Damn, already passed it," he muttered.

Retracing his steps, he discovered an unassuming five-story building sandwiched between a karaoke box and a ramen shop. The only entrance was an unmarked glass door with a call button next to it. Nothing on the outside of the building gave away that it was a runaway shelter.

"To enter, dial two oh one followed by the pound sign." He did. The sound of a phone ringing crackled from the speaker, and when a woman's voice asked who was there, Kenji introduced himself and told her he wanted to speak with the shelter's director. The voice told him to wait with his ID out. She'd come down.

A few moments later, a boyish girl with spiky black hair and complicated ear piercings appeared. Black leather pants scrunched around the ankles of her multi-buckled boots, and a tribal armband tattoo was visible through the loose black mesh of her sweater. She motioned for Kenji to hold his badge up to the glass. She studied it, compared the picture to his face, then released the lock and invited him in. Apologizing for her suspicion, she explained that sometimes people came looking for the kids who came there for refuge, and it was easier to keep them out than throw them out.

"Takki-*san* is waiting for you upstairs in his office," she said.

Kenji followed her up the stairs and through a waiting

room, where she used the magnetic stripe on the ID hanging around her neck to buzz her way past the next door. They entered a dim hallway that reeked of cigarette smoke. Stopping at a door near the end, she poked her head in and said, "Takki-*san*, there's a detective here to see you." She stood aside so Kenji could enter.

The man seated behind the scratched wooden desk crushed out his cigarette as he stood. Skinny black jeans, silver-studded belt, black T-shirt and leather vest, silver jewelry threaded through piercings in his ears, lip, and eyebrow. His hair was rock-star long, but the lines around his eyes told Kenji he had aged out of that game.

Kenji introduced himself, and showed his badge. The man bowed in return and said his name was Takeshi Kimura, but everybody still called him Takki.

"I'm sorry to bother you in the middle of work," Kenji began, as soon as they were seated. "But I have a few questions about one of the people who volunteered here." He explained about Yano's death, and after the shelter director said he'd heard, and expressed his shock, Kenji asked, "How did Head Priest Yano come to volunteer at your shelter?"

"We knew each other from way back," Takki said. "Did you know he used to be the guitarist for Meatsnake?"

"Yes," Kenji replied.

"Well, I was the drummer for Moth."

"Moth?" Kenji asked.

Takki made a face. "Yeah, we weren't quite in Meatsnake's league." He shook a cigarette from the pack of Larks on his desk. "Do you mind?"

Kenji did, but there was already so much smoke in the office, one more cigarette wouldn't make any difference.

Takki lit it with a tarnished silver lighter, took a drag, and settled back in his chair. "I knew Yano back when both of our bands had made it to the almost-bigtime. We had the same promoter and were making the same round of live houses. We'd be loading out just as they were loading in, or vice versa." He took another puff and tapped his ash. "For every band like Meatsnake that makes it, there are a hundred like Moth fighting to get noticed. Our promoter would sign bands, toss them into the fray, and watch to see which artists filled a house, which members got the fan mail. The popular kids would get pulled, advanced to salary status, and shuffled into new groups until the promoter hit on a winning combo. My band fell apart when he swiped our guitarist."

He took another drag on his cigarette. "For every kid whose dream comes true, there are hundreds who don't make the cut. Some can't do anything else, and they just become lost souls. I was one of those until I met up with the guy who started this shelter. He got me back on my feet. Straightened me out. I stayed on working here because all I knew how to do was bang on the drums and fight. When the guy who saved me died, I took over."

"And how did Head Priest Yano find you?"

Takki pulled in another lungful of smoke and blew it toward the ceiling. "People in the business know about us, send us kids who have nowhere else to go when their band bites the dust. About ten, eleven years ago, Yano showed up at the door with a photo, asking if I'd seen the boy in the picture. Said he'd disappeared. Yano had heard the kid had been talking about going to Tokyo, starting a band. He never found the boy, as far as I know, but he came back month after month, looking for him. Over time, he got to know a few of our kids, started giving them advice about their music." Takki snuffed his cigarette. "He liked them. Connected with them."

"How much did he like them?" Kenji asked.

"What do you mean?"

Kenji handed him the Polaroid they'd found in Yano's sleeve.

Takki's face pinched in disgust. "Where did you get this?"

"Yano-*san* had it on him when he was killed."

Takki gave Kenji a hard look. "Don't even think what you're thinking. I don't know why he had this, but I know one thing for sure: He would have been trying to help this girl, not hurt her. He hated the people who took advantage of the kids who came through our doors." Takki pushed the photo across the desk.

Kenji pushed it back. "At least take a second look and tell me if you recognize her."

Takki studied her face, then he switched on his desk light and held the Polaroid under it. His eyes widened.

"Isn't this Nana, the vocalist from the VuDu Dolls?"

Nana. From the VuDu Dolls. Flame *had* known the girl in the picture.

"Are you sure?"

Takki nodded, handing the photo back. "Not many people would recognize her from the days before she bleached half her hair blonde, but I remember her mouth always turned down at the corners like that when someone asked her a question she didn't want to answer."

Kenji put the photo back in his pocket. "The only fingerprints we found on that picture besides Yano's belonged to the VuDu Dolls guitarist, Flame," Kenji said. "We think she gave it to Yano. I was wondering if she came through here years ago, back before she was a famous idol?"

Takki sat back in his chair and smoked in silence. Kenji waited.

"I guess I'm not breaking any confidences, since she's dead," he said, finally. "Ten years ago, Flame lived here for a couple of months, until she got discovered by Jimmy Harajuku. This is where she met the other kids in her band—her original band, the one she played with in the park. Yano showed up, looking for that runaway boy, heard them playing. He stayed to listen, talked to them about the business."

"Do you have any idea why Flame might have given

Yano that picture? Any idea where she might have gotten it? Or who might have taken it?"

"I can guess," Takki said, his voice dripping with disgust. "Jimmy Harajuku. Her promoter. He's got something funny going on with the girls whose parents hand them over to be made into stars, but nobody's ever been able to make the charges stick." He took a last puff and stubbed out his cigarette. "The ones who tried ended up ruined, so don't get your hopes up you can nail him, just because you've got that Polaroid. Nana would have to stand up in court and connect that picture to him, but even though she's the victim, publicity like that would kill her career. Plus, chances are Jimmy would still weasel out of it."

Kenji made a note to check into Jimmy Harajuku's history, then asked, "Do you know where Flame was from? Where she grew up?"

Takki thought for a moment. "She was a runaway. They almost never tell us where they're from, not the truth, anyway. But I remember her talking about going inside the giant Buddha when she was little. Could be she grew up in Kamakura."

Kamakura—home of the Zeniarai Benten Shrine, where the picture of the priest holding Yano's baby had been taken.

Kenji thanked him, gave him a card, and asked him to call if he remembered anything else.

Standing outside on the sidewalk, he thought about what Takki had told him.

If that Polaroid belonged to Jimmy Harajuku, he'd be crazy if he wasn't doing everything in his power to get it back. Did he know that Flame had given it to Head Priest Yano? Had he killed Yano to get it?

But if that were true, he wouldn't have left it at the scene. Still, Kenji added him to the list of suspects.

•

A plastic bag crackled as Mansaku pulled it from his backpack. He and Yumi and the "image consultant" Shiro were huddled together in the meager warmth of the pilot's cabin as the fishing trawler plowed through the cold green waves of Tokyo Bay. Yumi hugged her jacket tighter. The short trip to Odaiba was taking forever. Mansaku's brother could only run the boat at half speed because there was so much debris in the water.

"Anyone ready for a squid snack?" Mansaku asked, waving the clear bag of purple-and-white tentacles.

"No!" Yumi yelped. "Don't open that in here!"

"What? Why?"

"Because I didn't bring a gas mask," she said, not wanting to admit how queasy she felt from the up and down, up and down, as the boat sliced through the swells. In the small enclosed space, the smell of squid snacks would send her running for the boat rail for sure.

"You'd better butch up, little missy," Shiro advised. "If you think squid snacks smell bad, wait till you get a whiff of the tsunami zone. If it's anything like Tōhoku, the dead fish and the food left in the wrecked buildings will be getting pretty ripe by now. Not to mention the—" He broke off. None of them needed to be reminded that there could be bodies buried in the wreckage as well.

In his canary-colored pants, pointy yellow boots, and Anpanman-patterned Hawaiian shirt, Shiro was a cheerful presence. He'd refused to don a rain slicker over his fur-trimmed jacket, explaining that being seen in a yellow jacket that failed to match his yellow pants would be the death of his career. The fishing crew was giving him a wide berth.

"I brought some NoseMint," Mansaku offered. "It's even better than menthol jelly, I heard."

"I may have to borrow some," Shiro said.

"For what?" Mansaku snorted. "I thought you were going to be working on a rock video, not searching for survivors."

"Yeah, well, working for Jimmy Harajuku, there's sure to be all kinds of stuff going on that smells."

"What do you mean?" Yumi asked.

He raised his eyebrows at her. "Don't worry, girlfriend, he won't be interested in you."

Did he mean Jimmy Harajuku wasn't interested in . . . women? No, that wasn't right. She remembered something she'd heard.

"Wasn't he taken to court a few years ago for, uh, improper advances? Toward one of his artists?"

"Yeah. Remember KiriKiri?"

"Actually . . . no."

"Exactly." Shiro said. "That's what happens to anybody who tries to cross the almighty Jimmy. KiriKiri was the star vocalist of the second group he trained from scratch. After launching the VuDu Dolls, he figured out how inefficient it is to scout kids who are already showing potential, then mix and match them until he gets a winning combination. So he started signing them up when they were eleven or twelve, brought them to live in his 'idol palace' in Shibuya, and trotted them around from singing to dancing to acting lessons until they were ready to debut at fourteen or fifteen.

"His first group never made it big, but KiriKiri's band hit the Oricon charts with their first single. Pretty soon they were playing all the arenas, swanning around in limos. But behind the scenes, KiriKiri started drinking. Their third year out, the band won two Oricon awards, and even though she was still too young to drive, Kiri-*chan* celebrated by getting a DUI. It was all hushed up at the time," Shiro said, dropping his voice to a confidential whisper, "but that wasn't the worst of it. She stole the keys to Jimmy's limo and had Top Talent's next star girl band in the back. She narrowly missed piling them all into a tree, and that gave her a big enough scare that she sobered up and started wondering how everything had gone so wrong with her life.

"Some shrink convinced her that it was her 'special relationship' with Jimmy that was the cause of everything, and Kiri-*chan* thought she had enough star power to out him." Shiro shook his head sadly. "Big mistake. There was a trial, but all it did was turn her career into a giant smoking crater, along with her band. People started calling her 'HaraKiri' because bringing charges against Jimmy turned out to be such total professional suicide. The band's CDs were pulled from the shelves, concert dates canceled, sponsorships dropped. They disappeared as if they'd never existed. KiriKiri was found dead of a sleeping pill overdose a few weeks later, and her bandmates sank without a trace."

"Yikes," Yumi said. "Why do you work for this guy Jimmy if he's such a slimebucket?"

Shiro sighed. "He may be a creep, but at least he pays. You have any idea what kind of sharks become successful enough to hire consultants like me? You don't want to take any of them home to mummy."

"Actually, I've been wondering," Mansaku said. "What exactly does an image consultant do, anyway?"

Shiro rolled his eyes. "I have to explain to people all the time how essential it is to manage your image. I mean, do you have any idea how kiss-of-death it is to pick an unlucky stage name? Or get an uncool piercing? Or—heaven forbid!—be caught by someone's camera phone wearing something so lame, it goes viral? Jimmy hires me to come up with 'concept looks' for his artists, and make sure they make personal style decisions that don't hurt their careers."

He glanced around as though tabloid reporters might be hiding behind the nautical charts, adding, "And let me tell you: Sometimes that ain't easy. One of my clients texted me just last night, to tell me Burnable Trash's drummer is going through another tedious beard stage." He pursed his lips. "How many times do I have to tell him: Crimson hair plus scraggly black chin whiskers equals Not Cute." He waggled his finger back and forth. "Not, not, not. Why can't he remember that even though he's pushing twenty-seven, his fans never get any older and thirteen-year-olds think any beard is icky." He sighed. "And that's not the worst of it. Chiho told me that Nana went and got herself a tattoo! If Jimmy sees it, he'll hit the roof. What was the girl thinking? My first job when we hit Odaiba is to talk her into getting it lasered off."

Mansaku's brother, who'd been silently steering the boat, turned around and gave his brother a look that said, Mom and dad were right about the unsavory career you've chosen for yourself.

The actor ignored his brother's stare and asked Shiro, "What's this video you're rushing back for?"

The image consultant grimaced. "One that I thought was already in the can. But after the tsunami, Jimmy decided to turn the one we shot for 'Kiss Me, Kill Me' into a tribute to Flame and give five hundred yen of every DVD sale to the earthquake victims." Shiro shook his head. "He hasn't kept a death grip on the music business for ten years by failing to land on his little cat feet, even in a Class A disaster. If any other producer lost the star guitarist of his biggest moneymaker, he'd be cursing the gods, but Jimmy figured out how to turn it into the biggest ka-ching of his career. Half a million hits on the VuDu Dolls website since Sunday, over a hundred thousand downloads of Flame's last song."

"But was it Flame's last song?" Yumi asked. "Did you see that video on *Look!Look!*?"

"Who hasn't?" Shiro rolled his eyes." But sweet pea, don't tell me you took that bullshit seriously? I mean, fuzzed-out face? Robot voice? That guy was just a wannabe trying to grab his fifteen minutes of fame." He gave a derisive laugh. "If he was for real, would he have decided to tell all on *Look!Look!*, the Internet's most talent-free zone?"

The pilot turned and asked Mansaku, "Where do you want me to put you in?"

"Uh, I don't know. Are the trains running yet?" Mansaku asked Yumi.

She pulled out her phone and frowned. "No signal."

"No signal?" Shiro yelped, pulling his own phone out to check.

"The towers are probably still down after the tsunami," Mansaku said. He turned back toward his brother. "I'm supposed to perform at the Oedo Onsen refugee center tonight. Are there any docks near there?"

His brother grunted and turned the wheel to skirt the island that was now dominating their view through the salt-spray-frosted windshield. He throttled the boat back even further as flotsam and jetsam began bumping against the hull.

They all peered at the shoreline, curious to see with their own eyes the damage wreaked by the tsunami, but the side of the island facing Tokyo Bay had been sheltered from the punishing wave. As they continued around, though, they began to see buildings that had been uprooted, toppled on their sides, broken in half.

Rounding the shore to the ocean side, they all gasped. They'd seen countless videos of the destruction as the wave ripped through the architectural marvels that had been built on the new modern island, but nothing prepared them for the sight of the untouched buildings that stood in shocking contrast to the flat field of rubble that stretched up to their doorsteps.

Mansaku's brother raised a pair of binoculars and focused on a boat that had been left high and dry on its side, about two hundred meters inland. He shook his head and passed the glasses to Mansaku.

"Oh no!" the *rakugo* artist cried. "That's not Sayaka's family's boat, is it?"

His brother shifted his toothpick to the other corner of his mouth.

Mansaku lowered the binoculars. "Insurance will pay,

won't it?"

"Eventually." He didn't have to spell out that the lost income from every day the boat wasn't out on the water fishing might mean the family went bankrupt anyway.

Mansaku handed the binoculars back to his brother and said, "I'll text Sayaka right now."

"It would be better if you gave up that acting shit, got a real job and married her instead," his brother muttered, turning the wheel.

Mansaku didn't answer. He ducked out of the pilot house and walked to the back of the boat, where he stared out over the trawler's wake, hunched into his jacket.

The boat started a slow carve toward what used to be a marina. Stalwart concrete docks still stood against the swirling sea, but the tsunami had heaped so much debris against them, the boat couldn't get close.

Mansaku's brother throttled the engine back to idle. "One of the crew will take you ashore in the dinghy. This is as close as I can get."

Yumi went to tell Mansaku. He sighed and rejoined them to thank his brother as Yumi and Shiro offered the cash they'd agreed to pay for fuel.

The pilot took the money with a bow and thanked them. Then he hollered through the door at one of the fishing crew, who got up and tossed his cigarette butt overboard, then began to take the canvas cover off a rubber dinghy lashed inside the aft rail. As Yumi and Mansaku shouldered their backpacks, Shiro appeared, dragging his bulging duffel bag.

The fisherman launched the boat and they climbed down the ladder. A crew member lowered Shiro's duffel on a line and they maneuvered it into the dinghy.

"What's in this thing, anyway?" Mansaku asked, wedging the heavy bag between them.

"Tools of the trade," Shiro said, "and stuff Chiho asked me to bring. Jimmy wants the band to look like tattered refugees, but he insisted on new costumes being 'distressed.' I'm charging him boatloads of overtime, because I didn't finish until three this morning. I went through an entire box of X-Acto blades!"

The crewman at the back of the dinghy swung the boat around and cranked the engine up to full speed. The rubber boat's nose lifted, and spray was flung into their faces as it bounced from wave to wave toward the shore.

"Sorry, it might get a bit wet," the crewman shouted, too late.

The slicker-less Shiro hid behind his bag, letting the duffel take the punishment instead of his fur-trimmed jacket. Yumi pulled her hood up, but her bangs were soon dripping, sending periodic tears down her cheeks from the tips of the curls that sprang to life anytime her hair got wet.

They were making for the closest patch of buildings left standing, and Yumi recognized the old-fashioned tiled roof of the Oedo Onsen, the hot-spring theme park that many refugees now temporarily called home.

•

A few hours later, Mansaku knelt on a low stage at the Oedo Onsen, holding his expression for a well-timed beat as the final punch line of the *rakugo* story "Scary Bean Buns" hit the audience and sent a wave of laughter rippling through the "town square." The entire indoor attraction was built to look like a Japanese village from bygone days, complete with wooden storefronts, a watchtower, and stars sparkling overhead.

It was a popular place for city dwellers to experience the pleasures of visiting a hot-spring resort without the expense of traveling. Leaving their modern street clothes behind in favor of colorful cotton kimonos, visitors could take a dip in the mineral baths, then eat and drink to their heart's content while being entertained in the perpetual twilight of an old-fashioned town.

But two days ago, the Oedo Onsen had been spared by the tsunami and transformed into an impromptu refugee center. Most Odaiba residents had congregated at the official Disaster Park on the other side of the island, built to dispense food, medical care, and bandwidth in case of emergency. But several hundred convention-goers had been stranded at the nearby Big Sight, and a number of locals too elderly or injured to make it across the island had ended up here.

The rows of shoe lockers near the front door now held valuables that fleeing locals had salvaged before the tsunami flattened their buildings. The colorful Edo-style *yukatas* visitors usually wore while eating, drinking, and enjoying the mineral baths had become sleeping robes for those who had escaped with only the clothes on their backs. The restaurants ringing the quaint town square now prepared three meals a day with whatever food made its way to the island by boat. And the vast *tatami*-floored party rooms were now filled with meal tables by day and bedding by night. Colorful New Year's decorations were still hanging in the central performing area, but the charming effect was spoiled somewhat by worktables that had been set up to dispense medical advice, toiletries, hot tea, and phone charging. As a refugee center, the Onsen was given priority for restored mobile phone service as the carriers set about putting temporary fixes in place before rebuilding the ravaged network.

Yumi, Shiro, and Mansaku's friend Chiho, the stylist, clapped enthusiastically from the back of the hall as the *rakugo* punch line brought smiles to faces that had become careworn in the past forty-eight hours. Chiho's shaggy cropped hair was bleached and dyed silver, tipped with lavender. She wore her usual uniform of black leggings, short skirt, two belts slung around her hips, black dancer's leotard, and a voluminous loose-necked sweater. Her earrings were fully articulated silver skeletons that nearly brushed her shoulders.

"I didn't expect to enjoy that as much as I did," she admitted. "Want to stay for the next part of the show? One of Jimmy's up-and-coming idol bands is playing."

Mansaku was making his way toward them now, stopping every few steps to bow and exchange a few words with audience members, who were congratulating him on his performance. His face still had a wide grin on it when he finally arrived in their midst with an energetic-looking forty-ish woman in tow.

"Great show," Yumi said.

"It could have been better. But thank you," he said modestly, bowing. Then he introduced the woman at his side as Beni, who'd taken it upon herself to arrange nightly entertainment at the refugee centers. True to her name, her hair was highlighted in *benibana* crimson.

Chiho apparently already knew her, because she called her "Red-*chan*" and asked when Baby8 would start performing.

The woman grimaced and said, "Never. The lead vocalist threw a hissy fit when I told her they'd have to perform acoustic. Said it would ruin her voice." She snorted. "As if she has one." She and Chiho both laughed.

Chiho said, "She probably didn't want to reveal that they can't actually sing and dance at the same time. They lip-sync all their live performances, you know."

"I should have guessed," Beni said, shaking her head. "Their fans will be disappointed, but anyone who loves music won't. If you've got time, you should come with me over to the other refugee center and hear the group I found to play there. They're local talent, been playing cafés around Odaiba for about six months, but they just picked up a new guitarist. I don't know where he came from, but he's smokin' hot."

A hot new "boy" guitarist? Yumi was all ears.

"You're telling me this 'smokin' hot' guy wasn't on your

radar? Be careful," Chiho joked. "You're slipping. Jimmy'll give you the ax!"

"Wrong-o, missy. That guitarist could be Hide reincarnated but since he's not a girl, Jimmy couldn't give a shit."

"No idea where he came from?"

"Nope. Never seen him before." Noting that Yumi had joined them, she explained, "I sometimes scout new kids for Jimmy's Top Talent. He says anybody with raw ability is okay, but the truth is, the last time he signed a boy was more than ten years ago." Beni checked the time on her phone and said, "We should go now if we're going to catch their set. It takes about a half hour to walk from here."

The band had already started to play when they squeezed into the back of a dark high school cafeteria with an atmosphere that crackled like a live house. The audience was jumping, fists pumping to the beat. Cafeteria tables had been pushed together to make a stage, and the chairs had all been stowed. It was standing room only, and the plastic signs prohibiting smoking were being universally ignored. The band had apparently brought their own generator—Yumi heard it chugging away in the alleyway outside—because a spotlight beam cut through the haze to illuminate a female vocalist throwing the microphone stand from hand to hand as she belted out a song. Her long hair was bleached and dyed orange, ragged bangs falling in her eyes as she headbanged, then stepped back into the shadows as the guitarist took her place, fingers flying.

The volunteer tech sitting atop a stack of toilet paper cartons behind the spotlight angled its beam to highlight the guitarist's hands as they ranged up and down the neck of his guitar and blurred over the strings.

Was this the same "boy" Yumi had seen fleeing from the net café? No glove, but a loose, black T-shirt with too-long sleeves hid his arm, so Yumi couldn't tell if it was covered in a red flame tattoo or not. She stood on her tiptoes and craned her neck. His curly rainbow wig bobbed over his guitar, finishing off a frenzy of final chords with a flourish. He stepped aside to give the spotlight back to the vocalist. Wild applause.

Pulling the mike from the stand, the singer stepped to the front of the stage.

Chest heaving, she shouted, "Thank you, Odaiba Earthquake Babies!" The crowd cheered. "Tomorrow we're all gonna to get out there and help each start putting our lives back together again, but tonight . . . tonight we're gonna party!" Another roar as the band launched into what must have been a local favorite, because all over the room hands were raised in a *para-para* hand jive as she belted out the song.

Three tunes later, they took a breather. The singer grabbed the mike from the stand again and announced, "Most of you know us as Revenant, but after the earthquake, we decided to rename ourselves Tinderbox. Our homes, our schools, our lives have all been reduced to matchsticks, but instead of giving up, let's build a new world, a better one!" She turned and pointed, "Kenichi on drums!" The crowd clapped and whistled.

"Jin on bass!" More acclaim.

"Me, I'm Risa." She paused for a moment until the cheers subsided. "And our newest member, all the way from the other side of Tokyo Bay, Hikaru on guitar!"

General pandemonium, which turned into jumping and shouting as the guitarist launched into some very familiar-sounding solo chords.

Yumi stood, rooted to the floor. Was he going to play "Don't Need You"? No, it was changing now. The song had just started out the same. This one had a similar heavy guitar beat, but the melody was less upbeat, more edgy. As the vocalist began belting out the words, Yumi guessed they had been rewritten in the last two days, because they were a commentary on the tsunami. The bassist came forward to join the guitarist in a classic battle, trading riffs, then finishing in unison as the crowd roared.

They wound things up in a blaze of glory, and as the musicians took their bows, Mansaku turned to her, his face puzzled.

"You're going to think I'm crazy," he said. "But I swear I recognized that last song. The singer said it was written after the earthquake, but . . . I think they stole it. Flame used to play that one in the park, before she was discovered. The words are new, but every weekend I used to hear her band blasting that one right next to where I performed *rakugo*." He frowned. "But . . . where did they get it? Do you think one of them knew Flame, before she got famous?"

Yumi didn't think one of them knew Flame, she thought one of them *was* Flame. But she had to find out for sure. Maybe Beni would introduce her. She looked around, searching for the crimson-haired organizer. Ah, there she was, at the side of the stage, waiting with hand towels so the band members could mop the sweat that was running down their faces despite the fact that the building was unheated and many of their fans were bundled into jackets and mufflers.

"Thank you," the singer breathed into the microphone, tendrils of hair stuck to her forehead. "Remember, we're Tinderbox and when this town gets back on its feet, you can catch us every Wednesday at the Crokodile Rock Café, which . . . Crok-*san*, are you here?" She shaded her eyes from the spotlight and spotted the owner standing along the wall and asked, "When are you reopening?"

He said something to her over the heads of the crowd and she repeated, "Crok-*san* says Thursday! But BYO glasses—the tsunami stopped a block away, so the building's still standing, but he's down to about ten mugs that don't have cracks. The kitchen won't be open, but draft beer will be flowing until the three kegs in the back room run out."

The crowd applauded and whistled.

Crok shouted something else over the heads of the crowd. The vocalist grinned and said, "Absolutely!" Off-mike, she said something to the rest of the band. They all nodded their heads and gave thumbs-up.

She turned back to the crowd and announced, "Tinderbox will be playing at the CrokRock for Thursday's reopen, five hundred yen at the door, and all proceeds will go to the Disaster Relief Fund. So come support a good cause and get some of that good *nama*-beer before it's all gone." The band members picked up their instruments again as she shouted, "You're a great audience. Let's rebuild this town together!"

The drummer hit his sticks together 1-2-3-4 and they launched into their final song.

When they finished, the crowd clamored for an encore, and the band returned to play until the spotlight began to dim, signaling the end of the diesel that was powering the generator. They took a final bow and left the stage.

Yumi turned to ask if the others would wait while she went to ask Beni if she'd introduce her to the band, but Mansaku was already halfway to the door and the others were following him as he melted into the exiting crowd.

There would be no way to find the producer's house where they were supposed to be staying if she didn't follow Chiho and Mansaku now.

Shrugging on her coat, she ran to catch up with the others. If she didn't manage to track down the guitarist on her own, she'd catch him at the CrokRock on Thursday night.

## Wednesday, December 25

•

*8:00 A.M.*

The next morning, Kenji walked blindly down the sidewalk toward work, texting a reply to Yumi's message. He told her he'd grinned ear to ear when he read about her conversation with Mrs. Mitsuyama, and he was proud of her for heading to Odaiba to help the refugees. Good luck, come back soon, he wrote. *Send.*

He looked up as he turned onto the walkway that cut through the parking lot in front of Komagome Police Station and frowned. In front of the big glass doors, two men loomed over a girl wearing a dark-blue skirt and jacket. Her back was turned, shoulders hunched. What was that pair of idiots thinking? Were they so stupid they didn't realize they were threatening her on the doorstep of a police station?

"*Oi*! What's going on here?" Kenji demanded, trotting toward the trio.

The men looked up, scowling. Black hair slicked back over tanned faces, sharp black suits, matching gold pins glinting in their lapels.

"Are these men bothering you, miss?"

"No," she said, her back still turned.

"Because if they are . . ." Kenji reached for his police ID. "I'd be happy to detain them and help you file a report." He held up his badge so the men could see he was a detective.

The shorter man's lip curled into a cruel smile. Leaning

toward the woman, he said, "Want to file a complaint, Aya-chan? We'd be happy to explain to Mr. Detective why we stopped by this morning to have a friendly chat with you . . ."

"No," she said, her hands clenching into fists at her side. "That won't be necessary."

"See you around, then." He leaned close to her ear and whispered, "Soon."

Jerking his head toward the street, he said to his buddy, "Let's go."

As they swaggered off, some of the tension went out of the girl's shoulders. She turned. Her navy-blue suit was a little big, as if she'd borrowed it from her mother after being told that was what one wore to a police station. She looked barely out of her teens. Unfashionably long black hair was scraped back and bundled into a tortoiseshell clip, and tilted almond eyes regarded him unblinkingly over broad cheekbones. No makeup hid the sprinkling of freckles across her nose.

"I'm Detective Kenji Nakamura," he said. "Pardon me for intruding, but it sounds like you have some history with those men. If you file a complaint, we'll do everything we can to protect you from further harassment."

"Really?" she said. "Thank you, but no. I can take care of myself."

There was something familiar about her. Did she work nearby, maybe at a restaurant he'd been to recently?

She was returning his puzzled look. "Don't I know you from somewhere?"

Then he remembered, and his cheeks burned. A few months ago he was working out at the Bunkyo Ward Sports Center, and he'd encountered her on the judo mats. He'd been feeling good, like he was really making some progress, then she'd smacked him down in record time. Oki had laughed so hard at the sight of him being trounced by a slip of a girl that everyone in the entire gym turned to stare. It had been humiliatingly memorable.

"No," he lied quickly. "I don't think so."

She stared at him for a long moment, then dropped her gaze and said, "Sorry, I must have been mistaken."

She knew. His face got redder.

"Well, if there's nothing else I can help you with . . ." he said stiffly.

"Actually," she said, "I was waiting for Detective Oki. Is he . . . ?"

Kenji peered through the glass at the clock in the lobby. 8:20. "You're a little early."

"Is there somewhere I could sit and wait for him?" she asked.

Did she hope he'd invite her up to the squad room? No way.

"You can sit in the lobby, if you like."

He held the door for her and escaped to the elevator. Upstairs, he scooped some loose tea into the staffroom pot and filled it from the hot-water dispenser.

Why was she waiting for Oki? Those two guys had something on her, and they looked like gangsters. Kenji groaned. What had possessed him to lie to her? It had just slipped out. What if Oki brought her with him up to the squad room? Kenji expected him any minute. His colleague had sent a text late last night, saying that he thought the suspicious death he'd been sent to investigate yesterday was tied to Kenji's Tabata Shrine case. He'd offered to come in at 8:30 to give Kenji the lowdown.

Kenji carried his laptop to interview room 3, shut the door, and twirled the blinds shut. He started up his computer and opened his notebook to yesterday's interview with Takki. Returning to the window, he parted the blinds a sliver just in time to see Oki emerging from the elevator. Alone. Whew.

Kenji opened the door and called, "Oki-*san*! I'm set up in here."

His colleague scooped his teacup from his desk and said

he'd be there in a minute.

"Looks like you covered some ground last night," Kenji observed when Oki returned, his face sagging with fatigue. "Still working on the suspicious death?"

"Yeah. And I've gotta go back to fetch and carry for the First Investigative Division boys in half an hour."

"Does that mean it turned out to be homicide?"

"Yeah. There was no excuse not to call them in once I saw how impossible it would have been for the victim to shoot himself in the back of the head."

"It was a shooting?" Kenji asked, surprised. It was illegal to use a gun in Japan outside of the police or military, and the penalties for firing one—even if you didn't hit anything—were so severe, even gangsters didn't often chance it.

"Who was the victim?" Kenji asked.

"Takuya Shinoda. Local boy, from Hon-Komagome. Twenty-three years old, found on the roof of his building. Practicing his guitar, apparently, when he met his doom. Inspector Kobayashi is making the troops scramble twenty-four seven to get a handle on this one because the media is going to be on us like a pack of wolves when they discover that the vic is in a *Look!Look!* video that's going viral on the Internet." Oki drank a slug of tea. "That's what I came in early to tell you about. Our vic Taku went on some Internet talk show claiming Flame quit the VuDu Dolls a month ago and disappeared, that she wasn't at the Top Talent studio on the day of the earthquake. Says Jimmy Harajuku hired him to fill in for Flame on the recording."

"So she could have been at the shrine the day her father was killed. Was this guy Taku telling the truth?"

"Jimmy Harajuku is all over the Internet, denying it, says the check made out to Taku from Jimmy's Top Talent was for some session work with a band he was trying to put together, that the kid went on *Look!Look!* because he was paid a million yen to lie."

"A million yen? Damn."

"What's new on your Tabata Shrine thing?"

Kenji told him what he'd learned from Takki, the shelter director.

"So that Polaroid we think Flame gave to Yano was of his bandmate, and it might belong to Jimmy Harajuku? Inspector Kobayashi would be very interested to hear that." Oki put both hands on his knees to lever himself to his feet. "I'd better get moving. What's your plan for today?"

Kenji told him what he'd learned at the bank, and that he intended to visit the Zeniarai Benten Shrine in Kamakura today to try and find out more about Taiga's relationship with Head Priest Yano. If he was lucky, he'd discover whether Taiga had a motive to kill the head priest, and/or where the missing intern had run to after the earthquake.

Oki nodded and wished him luck. As the big detective opened the door to leave, Kenji heard someone shout an enthusiastic, "*Yoroshiku onegaishimasu!*" begging the assembled company out in the squad room for their ongoing support.

Kenji hastily retreated. Must be a new officer joining the squad. Right about now, the chief would be scanning the room, picking a victim to show the newbie around, walk him through the paperwork and explain about the malfunctioning staffroom hot pot. Kenji peeked through the blinds. Everyone was standing, facing Tanaka's desk. The new guy must be up front, bowing. Kenji let the blinds fall shut, wondering about the weird timing. Usually officers were promoted from *koban* duty on the first of April.

Kenji returned to his chair and killed some time cleaning out old e-mail messages. When he got to the bottom of his tea, he parted the blinds again. Everyone was back to work. Good. Safe to come out.

Kenji dropped into his chair as Oki reappeared, his hands dwarfing two fresh cups of tea.

"You're still here?" Kenji said.

"Yeah. I was wondering if you wanted some company in Kamakura?"

"I thought you had to bird-dog for the murder squad on that shooting?"

"I do. But I thought since Suzuki's on leave, our new assistant detective could give you a hand."

He moved aside and a small figure in a slightly-too-large blue suit appeared at Oki's elbow.

"Detective Nakamura, meet Assistant Detective Aya Kurosawa."

•

Yumi smiled at the next foreigner stepping up to the information table. Her English skills had been pressed into service communicating with the surprisingly large number of non-Japanese who'd been stranded on the island when their day at the Miraikan Science Museum or the International Chiropractors' Convention had turned into a nightmare.

There had been a steady stream of *gaijin* in various degrees of desperation since eight this morning. This one began telling Yumi his tale of woe, but broke off when a stooped woman with thin gray hair stepped in front of him. Yumi recognized her as the elderly tsunami refugee who stationed herself in a folding chair next to the garbage cans, making sure everyone sorted their trash into the proper recycling bins.

The woman held out a gnarled hand with a bandage around the palm. "*Sumimasen*, I need another bag."

"Uh, just a minute," Yumi apologized to the foreigner, ducking under the table. She pulled out a handful of trash bags.

"Here, take a few," Yumi said, handing them to the woman. "To save you a trip next time."

The woman's mouth pulled down at the corners. She

separated one from the bunch and handed the rest back.

"Waste not, want not," she sniffed, and walked away.

The stocky foreigner with the curly blond beard and X Japan T-shirt watched her go and laughed. "Who was that, the Queen of Trash?"

Yumi stuffed the extra bags back in the box and looked at him. "That's Mrs. Soto. Sorting the trash is the only thing she's got left of her old life. She lost everything in the tsunami—her house, her garden, her dog, and the man she'd been married to for sixty-three years."

The foreigner's ruddy cheeks got a little redder, and he had the decency to say, "Hey, sorry, more power to her, then."

Unzipping his backpack, he fished around for his phone. "So, like I was saying, could you talk to my mom? Tell her everything's A-OK? The English-language media is going apeshit just like it did after the Tōhoku quake, but there's no way I'm going back to Kansas when all the excitement is right here in Japan."

"Excitement?" Yumi said. What did he think this was, a TV reality show?

"Sorry, bad choice of words," he backpedaled. "But c'mon, help me out. Tell her you're the director of the refugee center or something. You're the only one for miles around who can speak English."

"No she's not, mate," said a man with a Liverpool accent, stepping up to the table with a wild-haired guy in sunglasses wearing a faded Uniqlo T-shirt. "But I'm afraid the director wants us to hijack this young lady to help my man Blade here get where he needs to go."

The bearded foreigner shifted his gaze and his jaw dropped. "Whoa, no way! Are you really . . . ?"

The second man had a two-day growth of beard and was hiding behind a pair of Ray Bans, but with his crooked nose and untamed hair, he was unmistakably Blade Running, guitarist for the British band Exit Strategy.

As the bearded foreigner was digging for a pen to ask for the artist's autograph, the woman he was with pulled him away. Yumi could hear him arguing with her in imperfect textbook Japanese as the refugee center's director hurried up to the table.

"Miss Hata, I was wondering if you could help Mr. Running and Mr. Ace find their way to Mr. Harajuku's studio?" he said in Japanese. "They've got a driver, but they need directions and someone to explain to Harajuku-*san's* staff who they are and why they're here. I'm afraid my English isn't good enough to help them."

"Yes—of course, I, uh, I'd be happy to" Yumi stammered. She looked at the man from Liverpool, bowed, and said in English, "My name is Yumi Hata. I can help you get to the studio and explain things to the people there. Mr. . . . Ace, is it?"

The man gave a bark of laughter. "No 'Mister,' just Ace. And this is Blade."

"I know. I mean—" Yumi's cheeks flamed. "Everybody knows. You'd have to be from Mars not to know who Blade is." Yumi had never been a huge fan, but you really would have to be from another planet not to know Exit Strategy filled stadiums from New York to Istanbul.

The guitarist's mouth quirked in a half smile and he said, "Nice to meet you. But I'm for out of here before anyone besides that beardy bloke cottons on, you know what I mean?" He nodded toward the foreigner fan, who was now surrounded by a knot of Japanese girls who had all turned to stare.

"Right. Car's out front," Ace said. "Follow me."

A green taxi from a Tokyo cab company waited in the cracked parking lot outside the front entrance to the Oedo Onsen. Leaning against the door was a man wearing a white wifebeater under a black leather jacket with "Strangers" in white script across the back, his hair waxed and combed into the most exaggerated rockabilly pompadour Yumi had ever seen. It swooped out a good four inches from his forehead, then doubled back, parking itself in a meticulous ducktail behind. The only nod the driver gave to his chosen profession was the pair of white cotton gloves all cabbies wore while driving.

As Yumi and Blade slid into the backseat, Ace explained that they'd been crossing the Rainbow Bridge for an interview at Fuji TV when the quake hit, so they'd decided they'd just keep paying Stranger to drive them around, as long as they were all stuck on Odaiba. The rockabilly didn't speak English and they didn't speak Japanese, but somehow they got along by waving and pointing.

"Hey, Stranger, let's go," said Ace. The door they'd just come through now framed the foreigner and six excited fangirls. The driver nodded and started the engine, spinning around in a spray of gravel and shooting toward the exit.

He rounded a corner and stopped at the end of the first block. Turning in his seat, the unlit cigarette in the corner of his mouth waggled as he asked Yumi in Japanese, "Which way?"

"Just a second." She consulted the map on her phone, where she'd stored the location of Jimmy Harajuku's penthouse-studio. Good, they were still close enough to the refugee center to take advantage of the restored cell tower. She passed the phone to the driver. He looked at it and handed it back.

As they bumped over streets that had begun to be cleared of rubble and threaded their way between carcasses of cars and trucks awaiting the overworked tow trucks, Yumi asked Blade why they were still on Odaiba four days after the quake. Surely they had the cash and connections to leave if they wanted to.

"Decided to stay and help, since we were already here, you know?" he said, picking out a riff on the guitar he'd taken out of its case as soon as they were rolling. "Played Tokyo Dome on Friday and were supposed to be in Osaka Saturday, but the rest of the tour took a walk after the shaker. The other guys hightailed it out on the jet Saturday night, but I wanted to stay, see what I could do to lend a hand. Ace here—" He did a little bada-boom slap on his guitar and pointed at the man in the front seat. "—is our manager. He made some calls and found out one of the biggest promoters in Japan had a concert scheduled with all of his artists, and he decided to turn it into some kinda benefit for the victims. Invited me to join, for you know, like, international brotherhood and shit. Plus, the top band needed a guitarist." Blade's fingers paused over the strings. "Really sad story, that. Promoter said she died in the tsunami. Concert's gonna to be a sort of memorial for her." Blade resumed picking, shifting into a minor key.

"Are you talking about . . . the VuDu Dolls?" Yumi asked.

"Yeah, that's them. Never heard of 'em, myself, but I checked 'em out and I like their sound." He segued into a slightly bluesy version of Flame's solo from "Don't Need You."

•

*Goddamn newbie.* It didn't help that Assistant Detective Aya Kurosawa was no better at hiding her disappointment at being paired with Kenji than he was at hiding his lack of enthusiasm about getting stuck with her.

So far, all he'd been able to pry out of her on their hour-long train ride to the Zeniarai Benten Shrine in Kamakura was that her previous posting had been in Asakusa. When he asked why she'd been transferred at such an odd time of year, she clammed up like a *chinpira* caught with his hand in the boss's pocket.

Had she blown an operation? Dropped her partner in the shit? Crippled her superior at judo practice? Whatever it was, he had to get rid of her before this arrangement settled into permanence.

It was sunny, but a bitter December wind blew against them as they climbed the steep hill to the Zeniarai Benten Shrine. Despite the buffeting, Aya was steadily pulling ahead of him like some kind of fitness robot.

"*Oi*," he called, catching his breath outside a weathered wooden *torii* gate that framed a dark opening in the sheer rock wall bordering the road. "The entrance is back here."

Aya stopped, long strands of hair pulling loose from her clip and blowing into her face as she turned to retrace her steps.

"Sorry," she said. "Sir."

Kenji gritted his teeth. Her tardy honorifics were also beginning to get on his nerves. He didn't know if she was doing it on purpose to show her contempt for him or whether it was a general lack of respect for the chain of command. But mentioning it would make him feel petty, so he kept his mouth shut and ducked into the dark passageway, which was blessedly out of the wind.

At the other end, they made their way through a tunnel of unpainted wooden *torii* gates, bright sunlight striping the ground between them. Emerging into the grotto beyond, Kenji stopped in his tracks. What a beautiful place. All around, waterfalls poured into deep pools, shimmering against rock walls cloaked in ferns.

They stopped to purify their hands and mouths at the stone basin before going any farther. Drying his mouth with his handkerchief, Kenji looked around, trying to figure out where they might find someone who could help them locate the priest who'd been holding the baby in the snapshot from Yano's safety deposit box.

"There's the *o-mamori* stand." Kenji nodded toward a weathered building where charms, wooden prayer plaques, and bundles of incense were sold. "Let's ask the guy at the window where to find someone who can help us."

They waited their turn behind a pair of businessmen emptying their wallets into the damp baskets stacked beneath the window. Seeing Kenji's puzzled expression, the priest behind the counter asked Kenji if he wanted to double his money.

"What?"

The priest gestured toward a low, wide, cave guarded by a giant incense urn. "If you wash your money in the stream that flows through that cave, the goddess Benten will double it within a year," he explained.

"Thank you, but we're actually here to look at your employee records," Kenji said, introducing himself, showing his police ID. "We were told that someone who could help us would be here today."

"Ah, that would be Iida-*kannushi*. Go around to the side of this building and you'll find the shrine office entrance."

Thirty minutes later, Kenji's and Aya's necks were getting stiff from looking over the shoulder of a balding priest as he flipped slowly through a ledger penned with old employee records. Occasionally he'd stop to reminisce about a name he chanced across, remembering that this priest secretly swiped eggs left in the offering bins for the snake-goddess Benten, and that one hated scrubbing the money-washing baskets. He proudly pointed to the page where his name appeared for the first time, then continued flipping back in time until he reached the year Yano opened the bank account.

"Ah," he said. "Here we are. Let's see, there were four priests working here then." He took out a pen and meticulously copied their names onto a paper bag from the store. "How old did you say that man you're looking for was at the time the photo was taken?"

"Old enough to be a grandfather," Kenji replied. "In the picture my colleague saw, he was holding a baby who resembled him, but he looked too old to be the father. And he had a strawberry birthmark on his face, if that helps."

"Well, why didn't you say so? That would have been Ohkawa-*kannushi*. Ask the young man at the *o-mamori* stand. His grandfather played go at the Ohkawas' house every Sunday."

•

The salt-and-pepper-haired woman looked up from the dog mannequin she was dressing in a cowboy costume. All around, fluffy little outfits on doll-sized hangers tempted dog owners to dress their pets in canine kimonos, overalls, and panda costumes.

Kenji pulled out the plastic sleeve with the sales documents the new owner of Ohkawa-*kannushi's* Kamakura house had copied for them.

"Excuse me, ma'am, we're looking for someone who works here." Kenji pointed to a typed name sealed with a *hanko* stamp near the bottom. "Is this you?"

She looked at the papers and said, "Yes . . . ?"

"We're actually looking for information about your son."

"Son?" Confusion. "I'm afraid I never had children."

"What about your sister?"

She turned her back to Kenji, fluffing the pink curly wig on another mannequin. "I don't have a sister."

"I think you do," he said, producing a letter renouncing any claim to the parents' house. A vermilion *hanko* stamp sealed the name Mariko Ohkawa typed at the bottom.

The woman scowled. "Don't tell me she's gone through all her money and wants more!"

"Is Mariko your sister?" Kenji asked. "The one you don't have?"

"Yes. I mean no." Her frown lines deepened. "She's not my real sister."

"If she's not your sister, then what's the relationship?" Kenji persisted.

The woman's hands stilled, but she didn't turn around. "Half sister," she grudgingly admitted. "My father married my mother after Mariko's mom passed away. Mariko was ten when I was born. She quit school and left home when I was six." She turned and crossed her arms over her chest. "After that, I only saw her once that I can remember, when she showed up pregnant on my ninth birthday. After Daddy died, I found the present she brought me that day. It was still wrapped, in pink paper with birthday candles on it. My parents never told me."

"They didn't want you to have a relationship with her?" Kenji asked.

"In middle school she started getting mixed up in political causes, dumb stuff that could get you arrested. My mother tried to help her, told her that the system could only be changed by people working peacefully together from inside. Mom meant well, but Mariko didn't want to hear it. They fought like two cats in a sack. The more my mother clamped down, the more rebellious Mariko got, until finally one day she emptied my mother's purse and took off. Mom was so worried she'd end up in jail and the scandal would ruin my life, she insisted my father cut off all contact with Mariko."

"So you don't know where we can find her child?"

"No. I never saw the baby."

"Your father did. We found a picture of him with a baby in his arms at the Zeniarai Benten Shrine."

"I knew it," she muttered. "After Daddy died, I found out that he sneaked out to see Mariko, gave her money. A lot of money. That's why she didn't get half of the house." She began to straighten the bottles of Pet Sweat electrolyte water. "He was asking for her, at the end. Not me. Her. Even though I took care of him every day and she hadn't darkened the door for twenty years. When was Mariko coming? Why didn't Mariko call?" Her face closed tight as a fist.

"So after she left home, you never talked to her again?

She never tried to contact you?"

"No. Like I told you, I can't help you find her. Or the child."

Kenji sighed. He tried for a while longer, but no matter how he asked the questions, she had nothing to give. Flipping his notebook shut, he put it away and thanked her for her time. Aya followed him as they took their leave, but Kenji was halfway down the block before he realized she was no longer behind him. She was standing a few paces from the store they'd just left, staring back at the closed door. She looked at him, then back at the door.

"What?" He returned.

"Why didn't you ask what was in the birthday present? Sir."

"How could that possibly help us find Taiga?"

"I was thinking that if the gift was from a store that they only have in Kamakura or Mito or somewhere, that would at least help us narrow down where to start looking for a birth certificate."

Damn it, she was right.

"Why didn't you say something when we were inside?"

"You told me not to. Sir."

He'd told her to let him do the talking, but he hadn't meant to hold back whispering a little something in his ear if she thought of something useful. Why did she have to be so difficult? Suzuki would never have . . . Turning on his heel, he pushed back through the door.

"*Irassh* . . ." Then the woman saw who it was and her smile faded. "Oh, it's you. Now what?"

"I'm sorry to bother you again, but there's something I ought to have asked. What was in the birthday present your half sister brought you the last time you saw her? After you found it among your father's things, did you open it?"

"Yes. I was curious."

"What was it?"

"A souvenir."

"What kind of souvenir?"

"A dog. A stuffed dog."

"You know where it was from?"

"No."

"Do you still have it?"

She sighed. "Yes. It was cute, and I was born in the Year of the Dog, so I didn't give it away with the rest of Daddy's things. I brought it into the store. Wait a minute."

She disappeared through a door behind the register and returned with a small stuffed figure of what looked like a beagle, sitting on a cushion. She set it on the counter. Kenji picked it up and turned it over. No identifying marks.

He handed it back and thanked her. Dead end.

Aya followed him back out the door and they trudged back to Kamakura station in silence. Waiting for the train, she asked, "Are we going straight to Ningyo-chō when we get back, sir, or waiting until tomorrow?"

"Ningyo-chō? Why Ningyo-chō?"

She looked at him strangely. "That souvenir. Didn't you recognize it? It's the famous dog from the Suitengu pregnancy shrine. In Ningyo-cho."

•

Kenji and Aya struck out at Ningyo-cho's St. Luke's Hospital, where they'd gone to find out when Mariko Ohkawa had her baby. Files over twenty years old hadn't been computerized, and were organized by date, not by the mother's name. Without knowing the year and day of birth, it would be nearly impossible to find the record among the hundreds of boxes stored in the archives. The registrar suggested they might have better luck searching for a patient named Mariko Ohkawa at the local women's clinics where the ob-gyns had their offices. She gave them a list.

Kenji checked his GPS and turned the corner into the

narrow street that led to the closest clinic.

Aya's steps slowed, then she stopped, fifteen feet shy of the entrance.

Kenji followed her gaze to the car that was parked illegally across from the clinic. White sedan, blue number plates, the windows tinted so dark it must be perpetual twilight inside.

"I can't go into that clinic. Sir." Her face was set in stubborn refusal.

"What?" he replied, not believing what he'd just heard. Lack of respect was one thing, but refusing to do her job? He couldn't let her get away with that.

"Not only will you go in, Assistant Detective, you'll sit quietly and take notes while I find out if they know when that baby was delivered and where his mother was living at the time. That's an order."

Across the street, the driver's door opened and a brick wall of a man in a dark suit and open-collared floral shirt got out. A jagged white scar interrupted his buzz-cut hair above his cauliflowered right ear, and his nose had two bumps on it, as if it had been broken more than once.

The man regarded them for a moment from behind his dark glasses before lighting a cigarette and sauntering around to the trunk, pulling out a long lamb's-wool wand and idly running it over the already spotless car.

Aya turned and walked away as fast as she could.

*What the hell?* Kenji stared after her.

"Hey!" he called. She didn't stop. *Goddamit.* He ran after her and grabbed her elbow, spinning her around. "What's your problem?"

"I can't go in there."

"Why not? You scared of doctors or something?"

Aya's face was tense, her hands clenched at her sides.

"Come on, we're wasting time."

"No." A note of desperation crept into her voice. "Can't

you ask about those records without me?"

The clinic door opened and a nurse emerged, pushing a wheelchair across the street toward the white car. The young woman in the chair wore Chanel sunglasses and had tied an Hermes scarf over her hair. The driver plucked his cigarette from his lips, flinging it to the gutter before solicitously opening the back door to help the patient in. The woman moved awkwardly; she was perilously close to her due date. As the driver closed the door behind her, the nurse bowed and returned to the clinic with the empty wheelchair. The driver tossed his duster in the trunk and, with a last glance at Kenji and Aya, fitted himself in behind the wheel.

Kenji pulled out his phone and held it up in front of Aya. "Are you coming with me, or am I calling Section Chief Tanaka to request a new partner?"

She stood there a moment, her face like a thundercloud, then abruptly about-faced and stalked back toward the clinic, yanking open the front door as the white car rolled slowly past. Kenji followed her in.

After showing his police ID, Kenji explained to the receptionist that they were trying to track down a missing person who was about to come into an inheritance and they needed to speak with someone who could access patient records from twenty-six years before.

Twenty minutes later, they were seated in a cramped and cluttered back office lined with metal filing cabinets, the silent and stony-faced Aya taking notes.

Mariko Ohkawa had indeed been a patient there. She'd given birth to a baby boy twenty-six years ago on December 18. She'd given her address as a nearby weekly mansion rental that the clinic nurse told them had been torn down five years ago to make way for luxury condos.

•

Kenji stared at Flame's bio page on *The Dollhouse* website, his head spinning.

Just as he'd thought: The reason December 18 had given him a shot of déjà vu was that Flame had been born on the exact same day that Mariko Ohkawa had given birth to a boy named Hikaru Taiga.

So who was the baby in the picture? Was it Flame, or the missing intern? Or . . . were Flame and Taiga the same person?

What if one of the most famous girl idols in the Japanese music industry was actually . . . a boy? Kenji clicked over to the VuDu Dolls' photo and zoomed in. The truth was, every one of the beautifully androgynous artists could go either way. He pulled out his phone and looked up the shot Koji Yamamoto had taken of the fleeing intern on the morning Head Priest Yano was killed. His shaved head automatically made him think "boy," but his build was slight enough to be a girl. Could Taiga be the missing-and-presumed-dead Flame? If Flame was Taiga, that meant the guitarist definitely hadn't died in the tsunami, and Oki's shooting victim had been telling the truth.

Kenji did a search and found the *LookLook!* segment. He watched it all the way through, then went back and watched it again.

Kenji sat back in his chair. What if Flame had left the VuDu Dolls a month ago, just as Taku had claimed? Had the girl who was really a boy shaved off his hair and reinvented himself as the male intern Taiga at his father's shrine?

But . . . why?

He had to find that missing intern. The Ningyocho weekly mansion where Mariko Ohkawa had been living when Taiga was born was a dead end, but maybe his anti-nuke–T-shirt-wearing mother had left a trail of activism that could be traced on the Internet.

Kenji typed her name into his browser and hit the jackpot on the ninth page of results. In an article that had appeared over ten years ago, Mariko Ohkawa was identified as one of the founding members of the protest group No Nukes Now, currently known as NoNNo. He refined his search and found newspaper articles quoting her and mentioning her picketing presence as a nuisance at various nuclear plants around Japan. But back then, anti-nuclear activism was a long way from being the flavor of the month. Flame's mother and her small group of firebrands had a hard time recruiting support when most of the activists in Japan were up in arms about saving the whales and recycling trash.

Then a radiation scare had catapulted her cause into the spotlight. An accident at the troubled Mihama Nuclear Power Plant had killed four workers and brought the facility's history of hushed-up radiation leaks to public attention. Mariko's name was mentioned more frequently for a while, then it suddenly dropped out of the news. What had happened to Mariko Ohkawa ten years ago? Had she died?

Searching death records was a long and tedious process, and without a location to narrow it down, would take longer than he wanted to spend. He thought for a moment. If she'd been the victim of a crime, perhaps there was a record of it in the police database.

Bingo.

But she hadn't been a victim, she'd been the perp. Mariko Ohkawa had gone to prison ten years ago as a member of a conspiracy to sabotage the Hamaoka Nuclear Power Plant. She and another radical member of NoNNo had been caught posing as employees in a restricted zone deep inside the sensitive control center of the plant, and subsequent investigation had shown they intended to create a radiation scare that would fan the growing public uneasiness about the aging plant into a raging bonfire. Fearing copycats, the arrest and trial had been kept out of the media.

Kenji sat back in his chair. Ten years ago, Mariko Ohkawa's child would have been fifteen. The same age as Flame when the soon-to-be idol left home and ended up at

Takki's shelter. It all fit.

But where had they been living before Flame ran away? He went back to reread the arrest record.

He groaned. When asked for her address, Mariko Ohkawa had told the arresting officer she was a citizen of the world.

•

Kenji pushed through the heavy wooden door to the old-fashioned soba shop on the Shimofuri shopping street. He spotted Oki sitting at a scarred wooden table in the corner, unrolling his hot hand towel. The big detective wiped his hands, then scrubbed his weary face. He hoisted his mug and downed a long draft of lager.

"So, how was your day with the big boys from downtown?" Kenji asked, seating himself in the chair across from the big detective and ordering a beer for himself.

"About what you'd expect. Inspector Kobayashi wisely used my ten years' experience investigating crime in this neighborhood to tell him where the best ramen shop was." Oki sighed and drank a slug of beer. "But I don't envy him being lead investigator on this one. Taku Shinoda was shot while he was practicing his guitar on the roof, and the trajectory shows that the only place the shooter could have been when he pulled the trigger was on top of a building half a block away. That wouldn't be news if he'd been using a rifle, but the guy would have to be a real sharpshooter to do that with a nine-millimeter handgun. Nobody wants the media to get ahold of the news that there's a sniper loose in Tokyo, gunning people down with a concealable weapon. Kobayashi is so worried about them finding out before we catch the guy, he tossed them the *Look!Look!* video to chew on while we try to trace the handgun."

"You sure it's your victim in the video? I watched it, and it'd be pretty hard to identify him from that."

"Yeah, but he deposited a check from *Look!Look!* for a mil on Monday. The so-called journalist who runs the *Look!Look!* site tried to hide behind all kinds of 'I protect my sources' crap until Inspector Kobayashi slapped some cuffs on her and said he was going to charge her with causing the boy's death. She couldn't talk fast enough after that. Seems the kid was no fool, had the tabloids bidding against each other for the scoop. Taku apparently showed Miss LookLook a signed nondisclosure agreement from Jimmy's Top Talent, told her she'd have to make it worth his while because he'd be banned from working in the music industry ever again if he talked."

"Jimmy Harajuku can't be too happy about that. You think he was mad enough to kill the guitarist?"

"If he was, he hides it well. When Kobayashi interviewed him, he kind of laughed it off, said stuff like that happened in his world every day. Called the victim a publicity ghoul. Told Kobayashi 'the price of being famous is all the little people want a piece of you.' Arrogant bastard."

"Well, I think your vic was telling the truth." Kenji told Oki what he and Aya had learned, ending with his new theory of the missing intern's identity.

Oki was shaking his head in amazement by the time he finished.

"So let me get this straight—you think the missing intern Taiga might be Yano's illegitimate son, who's been posing as a girl idol for years and is supposedly dead?"

Kenji grimaced. "When you put it like that . . ."

"How are you going to go about finding him?"

"I don't know yet."

"Well, keep me in the loop," Oki said.

The waitress brought their bowls of *chikara* soba and Oki traded his empty glass for another beer. They broke apart their chopsticks, muttered "*itadakimasu*," and began slurping up their noodles.

When the edge was off their hunger, Oki said, "Sounds

like Aya did okay on her first day."

Kenji looked uncomfortable, and set down the tempura prawn that was halfway to his mouth. "Actually, I wanted to talk to you about that."

Oki frowned.

"She's got some . . . issues. I had trouble with her this afternoon."

"What kind of trouble?"

Kenji explained about her refusal to go into the women's clinic. "I'd say it was just lack of experience," he concluded, "but it seemed like she was actually afraid to go in. I wonder if she's going to have a hard time working criminal investigation because she's had some bad experiences."

"With doctors?" Oki laughed.

"Or with yakuza."

Oki's face froze. "Yakuza? What yakuza?"

Kenji explained about the guy in the white car with the twice-broken nose.

"Aw, fuck."

"What aren't you telling me? You know her from the Sports Center, right? Did she have some bad experience with gangsters that's going to affect the way she does her job?"

"I didn't think she'd let it."

"Did they hassle her when she was a kid or something? Rough up someone in her family?"

Oki didn't answer.

Then Kenji put women's clinic and gangsters together. "Was she raped?"

"No, that's not it." Oki sighed. "Actually, me and Aya-*chan* go way back. I've known her since she was a skinny eleven-year-old—she was one of my judo students back when I taught at my *sensei's* dojo in Kabuki-chō. Her brothers were in my class and she just kept pestering me until I let her join, too. She was tiny, but every time she got smacked down, she'd just come back for more. She was one of the best students I ever had."

"So you recruited her?"

"God forbid. I actually tried to talk her out of it. It was the only time she refused to listen to me. Her family was so against it they disowned her the day she graduated from the police academy." He sighed. "But I'll have a little talk with her. Aya-*chan*'s always had a bit of a problem giving people respect before she's decided they deserve it. Give her a chance. She's got her strengths. She could be a great detective if anybody lets her stay long enough in one place to find out."

•

Yumi looked longingly at the big double bed in Jimmy Harajuku's private master suite, but it was sealed in a custom-made plastic dust sheet that protected the white linen coverlet from mites, germs, and uninvited guests who might otherwise lie down just for a moment because they'd been standing all day volunteering at an unheated refugee center.

Mansaku, Shiro, and the two Brits were all sharing the bathroom down the hall, because Chiho had firmly designated Jimmy's private lavatory Ladies Only. But even so, Yumi wasn't looking forward to hauling herself into the bathroom to wash off the grime of the day with cold water. So for just a moment she lowered herself into one of the equally hermetically sealed armchairs that flanked the bed.

The rockabilly driver had taken her back to the refugee center after she turned Ace and Blade over to Chiho to get them settled. There hadn't been any more foreigners who needed help, so the refugee center director had put her to work cleaning up the bits and pieces of peoples' lives.

As volunteers searched the wreckage for survivors, more often what they found were memories. Photo albums, sports trophies, diplomas; thousands of little milestones in thousands of lives were dug from the mud and debris and brought to the refugee center. Tables had been set up, the items cleaned and carefully displayed. Some were snatched up with shouts of joy and tears; others sat there silently unclaimed, memories that lived on after the ones who'd treasured them were gone.

Yumi looked up at the crystal chandelier hanging from Jimmy's ceiling and sighed. It was so strange to come back to a place like this after spending the day among people whose belongings had been reduced to the clothes on their backs.

The power was still off, so they were lucky that Jimmy's penthouse was at the top of a ten-story building, not a forty-story one. They didn't have electricity, but Jimmy's place was stocked with dozens and dozens of candles from a previous photo shoot, so they weren't living in complete darkness. And otherwise, the building was fine. The island had been developed after earthquake engineering had become an advanced science, so everything at Jimmy's was still in one piece except for a few vases and statues.

More's the pity, Yumi thought, because Jimmy had remarkably similar taste to whoever had decorated one of the love hotels she'd been to with Ichiro in the early days of their engagement. Fewer life-sized marble statues would be a big improvement to the decor, in her opinion. Cold stone figures lurked in every room. She hated rounding a corner and being startled by a hand reaching toward her or a pair of loinclothed warriors locked in combat. And Jimmy's black marble floors were painfully chilly without the radiant heating that usually warmed them.

They still didn't have cell-phone service on this part of the island, though, which meant she hadn't been able to answer the e-mail from Ichiro's mother she'd found on her phone at the end of her shift at the refugee center.

Mrs. Mitsuyama had followed up yesterday's conversation with a kind message asking Yumi to let her know when she'd decided what to do about her future. She offered to either reschedule the wedding or set the wheels in motion to dissolve the engagement.

In the shuttle bus on the way to Jimmy's penthouse, Yumi had crafted the reply that would free her from her engagement. She really ought to tell her parents before making such a huge move, but that didn't seen like the kind of thing she could do over the phone. She'd send the message to Mitsuyama-*san* tomorrow morning as soon as she was in range of the signal at the refugee center, then start thinking about the right words to break the news to her mother and father.

As she held up her candle, the shadows of a life-sized Venus de Milo's wings beat silently on the walls in the flickering glow. Yumi wondered if Jimmy ever used it as a coatrack. Climbing to her feet with a sigh, she padded to the bathroom.

Wow. It was huge. Her single candle didn't even begin to illuminate all four walls. Far bigger than the four-mat room she slept in at her parents' house, every surface but the ceiling was tiled. She put her candle on the floor, ran some cold water into the sink, and set about taking a chilly and unsatisfying sponge bath. Without heat, it was too cold to do anything but remove one piece of clothing at a time, wash, then quickly put it back on. Finally dressed again and feeling somewhat cleaner, she peered at her ghostly-looking face in the dark mirror. How long before her hair got so dirty that washing it in cold water would be preferable to going another day with it stuck to her head?

She wrung out the washcloth and looked for a place to hang it. All the towel racks were full, so she draped it over the edge of the sink to dry.

Carrying the candle, she retraced her steps down the hall, heading back toward the kitchen. Hearing voices in the entry, she detoured, wondering if Mansaku had come back from his day of pet searching.

"No, no, I was asking if you had a generator somewhere

around here?" asked a Liverpool-flavored voice. A beat of silence while he waited for an answer, then he enunciated, "Gen-er-a-tor," loudly and slowly, as if by some miracle that would get the meaning across.

"Je-na-re-ta?" echoed a Japanese man's voice.

Yumi rounded the corner. Ace and Chiho were standing in the entry with a small man in a pink sport coat who must have just arrived, judging by the luggage now clogging the entry. With a start, she recognized the man who had stepped between Nana and her fans in Yoyogi Park, the night of the Flame tribute. A fancy surgical mask with a red respirator button still covered the lower half of his face.

Chiho glanced at her, looking like a dog caught sleeping on the sofa. If this was Jimmy Harajuku, they were in trouble. He wasn't supposed to be here until tomorrow, and Yumi and Mansaku were supposed to be gone by then.

As if reading her mind, Jimmy turned, looked Yumi up and down, and snapped, "Who's this?"

Before Chiho could answer, Ace exclaimed, "Thank God, I was wondering where you were. None of these people speak a word of English. Now we can get somewhere!"

Yumi bowed and spoke in Japanese to the man in the pink jacket. "I'm Yumi Hata. And Ace was just asking if you have a *hatsudenki*."

"What? A generator?" Then understanding filled his eyes as he realized Yumi was the key to communicating with Ace. Then a line appeared between his brows. He rounded on Chiho. "Are you telling me we don't have any power yet?"

He looked around, noticing the candles burning everywhere. "Why hasn't anyone dealt with this situation? Chi-*chan*, get the mayor or whoever deals with these things on the line for me, then find us some generators. But before you do that, get me something to eat. And a drink. I do hope we have ice?"

Then he turned to Yumi. "Forgive me. I'm Jimmy

Harajuku. If you're Ace-*san's* translator, I have a feeling you'll be working overtime this week."

"*Yoroshiku onegaishimasu*," Yumi replied, bowing.

But Jimmy's attention had darted elsewhere, as he looked around for the pair of slippers he'd expected to be greeted with. Chiho sighed and opened the shoe cupboard, fetching a lordly blue-velvet pair with gold crests on the toes.

Then he turned to the young man who'd silently appeared behind him in the doorway, breathing hard from carrying two bulging suitcases up twenty flights of stairs.

"Ninjaboy. Take my luggage to my room, then you're released."

*Ninjaboy?* Yumi looked at him and wondered how he got that nickname. He was even shorter than Jimmy, but his beaky face looked like a younger version of the promoter's. A relative?

As Jimmy's bag carrier picked up the suitcases and turned toward the stairs, she remembered she'd left her washcloth draped on Jimmy's private sink. Not good, especially after what she'd heard about Jimmy's germ fetish.

"I've got a candle," she offered. "Why don't I go first and light the way?"

Ninjaboy followed her down the hall, and Yumi realized her translating skills had just saved her from having to find another place to stay. Shouldering open the door to Jimmy's bedroom, she quickly crossed to the bathroom and grabbed her wet washcloth.

Suddenly, all the lights blazed on. Power had been restored.

She blinked in the sudden glare and looked around, surprised to find herself in a room where everything but the ceiling was a shocking shade of pink. All except the row of rubber duckies that stared at her from the far side of the tub.

Yumi recoiled, instantly remembering where she'd seen them before. They'd been looking into the camera with that same unblinking stare from behind the downcast girl in the Polaroid she seen in Kenji's Inbox.

She backed out of the bathroom, stunned, and nearly tripped over Ninjaboy, who was crouched down by the nightstand, feeling around in one of the drawers. He scrambled to his feet and said, "What?"

Wiping the guilty look off his face, he replaced it with a smirk. "I was looking for a flashlight, but I guess we don't need it now, do we?"

Yumi didn't care what he'd been snooping around for, she just wanted out of there. She bowed and excused herself, feeling the unblinking stare of the rubber ducks on her back all the way down the hall.

•

Indigo twilight deepened to black. Kenji and Oki bowed and parted ways outside the restaurant. Oki headed off to teach a self-defense class at the Bunkyo Ward Sports Center, and Kenji headed home.

Trudging up the shopping street toward the small wooden house he shared with his father, Kenji pulled his jacket tighter as a chilly breeze stirred the curtain hanging across the door of the corner *izakaya*. A few dead leaves tumbled down the lane toward him.

*Ching, ching.* A beam brightened the pavement as the tofu shop owner passed him, bicycling home for dinner. He disappeared up the dark street. The girl who cashiered at the noodle restaurant bowed briefly to Kenji as she hurried past with a green plume of daikon radish bobbing from the top of her grocery bag.

Most of the businesses were already shuttered, but ahead Kenji spotted the fish store owner's youngest son sluicing down the sidewalk in front of their shop. All the ice-filled bins had been pulled inside except one displaying the leftovers being offered at half price. The awning behind him squeaked as the son cranked it down for the night.

Past the real estate rental office, Kenji turned into the street where he lived. No gruff bark greeted him as he passed the Ikedas' fence—must be too cold for them to leave their dog outside.

A loose corner of the tarp concealing the scaffolding on their neighbor's partly framed house flapped in the breeze, and he wondered how he was going to get rid of that new assistant detective.

And then someone grabbed him around the neck from behind.

*Choking. Couldn't breathe.*

Struggling to pull the beefy arm off his windpipe, he was dragged off the street into the shrouded construction site. Kenji twisted to try and break the hold, but his assailant was too strong. The next thing he knew, he was on the ground, a heavy knee planted hard between his shoulder blades, pinning him to the rubble-strewn dirt.

"Hey!" he gasped, thrashing, "What are you—"

"Shut up." He heard the unmistakable snick of a butterfly knife and felt a prick behind his right ear.

Kenji froze, but his mind raced. Who was this guy? A thief? Why wasn't he asking for money?

A pair of gleaming, pointy-toed shoes approached. They stopped, crushing a little weed growing up from the broken concrete in front of Kenji's nose.

"Up," a voice commanded.

Kenji was hauled to his feet, his arms pinned from behind.

A young businessman regarded him without expression. Black suit, white shirt, Windsor-knotted tie the color of blood. Expensive clothes. And he must be older than he looked—a distinctive, circular, gold pin set with diamonds winked in his lapel. This guy was a player, and he was management, not muscle. What was he doing in Komagome?

His almond eyes and elegant, straight brows were set above chiseled cheekbones, hollowed by the moonlight. Collar-brushing jet-black hair was waxed up from his smooth forehead, a few strands falling back in a movie-idol curl, his meticulously trimmed goatee framing lips almost too beautiful to belong to a man. Lifting his hand, he curled his fingers as if to inspect his manicure, then, quick as lightning, hardened them into a fist and punched Kenji in the face, then in the gut. Kenji doubled over, the wind knocked out of him, pain radiating from his nose as blood began to flow. He couldn't even cry out as he struggled to breathe, diaphragm paralyzed by the blow.

"That's just for starters if we can't come to an agreement."

Agreement? Huh? Through his haze of pain, Kenji tried to think. Yakuza didn't pick fights with detectives. Especially yakuza exalted enough to wear diamond pins in their lapels. Had be been sent by Koji Yamamoto?

Pulling in a ragged breath, Kenji gasped, "I don't know who you are—but you're making—a big mistake. I'm—"

"Car," said the owner of the shoes, turning on his heel and pushing out past the loose corner of tarp as if he were exiting a sushi bar.

Kenji was marched behind him, his face throbbing, blood dripping steadily onto his shirt and tie. "Look," he said, hoping the bearish guy behind him was a better listener than his boss. "Tell him he's got the wrong guy. I'm—"

"Shut it." Kenji felt a businesslike jab from the knife point that had been hovering like a hornet behind his right kidney.

A white luxury sedan was parked right around the corner, the passenger side hard up against an old-fashioned tile and plaster wall. The goateed man in the black suit opened the back door.

"Get in," he said.

His companion let go of Kenji's arm, but stayed too close for him to run. Kenji's phone rang. He automatically reached for it, but the bodyguard stopped him.

"The boss doesn't like interruptions."

He relieved Kenji of his phone and swiftly patted him down for weapons.

The goateed man held out a white handkerchief. "Don't get blood on my seats."

Kenji accepted the cloth and pressed it to his face. As he turned to get in the car, he stole a glance at the one who had taken him down. It was the driver he and Aya Kurosawa had seen outside the Ningyo-cho women's clinic.

The yakuza lieutenant slid in next to Kenji. His bodyguard closed the door and stood watch outside. The Mercedes was new, probably filled with the fragrance of fine leather, but Kenji's nose was in no shape to smell it.

The goateed man turned to him, his voice cold with fury. "You probably thought if you took care of things out in Ningyo-cho, nobody would ever find out. Well, I've got news for you, asshole—we keep closer tabs on her than that."

What was he talking about?

"I want you to listen very carefully to my next question, and I'd better hear the right answer. Are you planning to marry her?"

Huh?

"She told you she doesn't have any family, didn't she? You thought she was alone, that nobody would make you man up and take responsibility. I'm here to tell you you're dead wrong about that."

Now Kenji was thoroughly confused. "What are you talking about?"

"Cut the crap, you're just making me angry."

"You must be confusing me with someone else," Kenji said, taking the hankie away from his face. Still bleeding. "I'm nowhere close to getting married to anybody."

The lieutenant grabbed the front of Kenji's shirt, pulling him close. "Well you'd better get there quick then," he said through clenched teeth. "My driver saw you two arguing outside the women's clinic, then she tried to walk away and you ran after her and grabbed her arm and dragged her inside." He let go of Kenji's shirt with a shove that rocked him back against the door.

"Wait—are you talking about . . . Kurosawa-*san*?"

"I'm talking about my sister, asshole. I don't know what she sees in a prick like you, but if you knocked her up and aren't planning to marry her and take responsibility for the kid, I promise you: you'll wish you'd never been born. She might be estranged from our father, but blood is blood and my brother and I still look out for her."

Realization hit Kenji upside the head. A whole string of things suddenly made horrifying sense: Oki taught judo in Kabuki-chō. Aya Kurosawa was his student. Her brother was a high-ranking yakuza lieutenant. She joined the police and her father disowned her.

She was the Kurosawa-*gumi oyabun's* daughter.

"Wait, I can explain," Kenji said. He reached for the police ID inside his jacket.

A knife was under his chin with a casual flick of the brother's wrist.

"Don't."

Kenji froze, blood trickling anew from one nostril. Slowly he raised his hands. "In my pocket. My police ID. I'm not your sister's boyfriend, I'm her partner."

Aya's brother stared at him, then lowered the knife. Using the tip to push Kenji's jacket aside, he reached into the breast pocket. His eyes flicked down to the ID and he pressed his lips together.

He tossed it back. Kenji returned the leather wallet to his pocket and dabbed at his nose with the handkerchief. "If you don't believe me, why don't you ask her?"

The brother frowned, didn't answer. After a moment, he put his knife away.

Kenji tentatively lowered the handkerchief and inspected it to see if the blood has stopped yet. Maybe. He looked at Aya's brother. "You got any aspirin?"

The yakuza lieutenant sighed and rolled down the window. Pulling a new ¥10,000 note from his wallet, he handed it through the gap to his bodyguard. "Go get us some Bufferin." He glanced at Kenji. "And some *shō-chū* to wash it down with. Barley, not sweet potato. Rice, if they don't have barley."

"Yes, boss."

He rolled the window up and leaned back in his seat, regarding Kenji with a slight frown. "Just because you're a cop doesn't mean you're off the hook. What were you and Aya doing at that place?"

"We're trying to track down the illegitimate child of a murder victim."

Aya's brother fitted a cigarette between his lips. "You guys always go for the family first, don't you?"

"Not always. We also like a guy named Koji Yamamoto."

The lighter froze halfway to his cigarette.

"You know him?" Kenji asked.

He lit his cigarette and inhaled. Cracking the window, he blew his smoke toward it. "You could say that." He looked at Kenji speculatively. "You trying to put him away?"

"Trying. You know anything that'll help us?"

Aya's brother took another puff and tapped his ashes into a stylish personal ashtray. "Depends on what you've got already."

Was it was ethical to divulge information from their investigation to a gangster? No. But Kenji knew what Oki would say: There's breaking the rules, and there's bending them.

Kenji told him about the photo corner, the Polaroid of

one of Jimmy Harajuku's idols in the sleeve of the victim's jacket, their theory that Koji killed the priest, came across a stash of more Polaroids while searching for the kimono and took them as a bonus, leaving cash in exchange for the kimono he found upstairs to make it look like a legitimate transaction.

The goateed man smoked in silence while he considered what Kenji had just told him. "Sounds to me like you've got a nice little story, but all you can really prove is that Koji left a stack of money. Which wasn't a crime, last time I checked."

"Yeah. That's the problem."

"It's always the problem with him." Aya's brother contemplated the burning end of his cigarette. "What about Jimmy Harajuku? Seems like he might have more than a little skin in this game."

Kenji looked up sharply. "You know something about him that'll help us?"

"Maybe. Last week I heard he was trying to recruit a shooter to do a hit on someone who was already dead."

"What?"

"I overheard a guy telling his buddy about the wacko who wanted him to do a hit. Harajuku was trying to convince him he couldn't be sent away for it, because they couldn't convict him of killing someone who was already pronounced dead. You ever heard of anything so crazy?"

"No," Kenji said. But there was only one person Jimmy Harajuku could have been talking about. Flame. If Jimmy was looking for someone to kill Flame, that meant he knew Flame was alive. And everything he'd told the press was a lie.

"Did he find anyone to do it for him?"

The gangster shook his head. "Got laughed out of town. Apparently he gave up and decided to do it himself. Bought a gun."

"What kind?"

"Handgun. Nine mil."

The kind of gun that had just killed Oki's victim, Taku Shinoda.

"Brand?"

"Dunno. Give me your card. If I hear any more, I'll call you."

There was a knock on the window and the bodyguard passed a brown paper bag to his boss. Aya's brother drew out a bottle of Iichiko barley *shō-chū* and a pair of cheap tumblers with price tags still stuck to the sides. He poked his head back out the window and said, "No ice?"

"Sorry, boss."

The gangster sighed, set the glasses into the cupholders between the seats, and poured a couple of fingers of clear liquor into each, then turned to face Kenji. Hands flat on his knees and bowing stiffly from the waist, he lowered his head and said with old-fashioned formality, "Please accept my apologies for my hasty behavior."

What? Surprised, Kenji awkwardly returned the bow and muttered, "Accepted."

Aya's brother handed him one of the tumblers. They raised their glasses to each other and drank it off.

Delving back into the bag, the gangster tossed a bottle of Bufferin to Kenji, who stripped off the safety seal and shook a couple into his hand. Glass refilled with *shō-chū*, he washed them down, the distilled spirits chasing the painkillers with a blaze of heat.

"You going to tell me your name?" Kenji asked presently, the glow radiating.

Aya's brother drank, then replied, "Tetsu."

"Why didn't you just ask your sister about the clinic?"

"Can't." He turned his gaze out the window. "Father forbids it."

"Because she joined the police?"

"That . . . and other things."

Kenji waited.

Aya's brother shook his head and finished his *shō-chū*. He glanced at Kenji and one corner of his mouth twitched into a smile. "She still a handful?"

Kenji snorted, "What do you think?"

Tetsu filled their glasses again, this time to the brim.

•

Kenji moved the icepack away from his lip long enough to slurp up a bite of instant ramen. *Ow.* He stared down at the steaming noodles longingly, then sighed and smoothed the paper cover back down before moving the cup to the refrigerator. Surveying the contents of the fridge, he spotted half a package of grilled eel at the back. He removed it and heated the fillets in the microwave, along with a packet of pre-made rice, then settled himself back at the scarred kitchen table in front of the TV.

". . . and in the quiet neighborhood of Hon-Komagome yesterday," the newscaster intoned as the screen switched to an aerial shot of police swarming around a cordoned-off section of houses, "police were investigating the shooting death of Takuya Shinoda, twenty-three, who recently claimed during an anonymous interview on the site *Look!Look!* that VuDu Dolls guitarist Flame was not only still alive, but had quit the band and been quietly replaced on the band's just-released single 'Kiss Me, Kill Me.'"

The screen cut to the video featuring Taku's fuzzed-out face. This was the third time Kenji had watched it, and this time he noticed that the interviewer constantly tried to goad Taku into embellishing on his story, but he stubbornly refused to budge from his account.

He said that Jimmy told him that Flame had walked away from the band, and promised that if things worked out with the recording, Taku would become the VuDu Dolls' new guitarist.

He'd happily signed away all his rights to the recording,

and promised never to tell anyone that it wasn't Flame playing guitar on the "Kiss Me, Kill Me" single. He thought he'd finally gotten his big break. But then the earthquake and tsunami happened. Jimmy changed his mind and decided to spread the news that Flame was dead. Taku was put on a boat back home two days later, told "don't call us, we'll call you," and given a parting warning that he had signed a nondisclosure agreement, and if he ever wanted to work in the music industry again, it would be best to keep his mouth shut.

Kenji carried his plate to the sink, then returned to the table and put the ice pack back on his lip. Now the TV was showing Jimmy Harajuku being asked for his reaction to the frenzy of Flame rumors. It was the first time Kenji had seen him without his anti-germ face mask. His pointy chin and sharp little teeth reminded Kenji of a fox, and not a cuddly one.

The pink-jacketed promoter lounged back in a studio armchair, loafered ankle resting casually across his other knee. The station's anchorman sat opposite, firing questions at the impresario, who was answering with an air of patient humor.

Harajuku: ". . . you forget I was Flame's biggest fan, that I mourn her more than all the other fans put together. I'd do anything to bring her back from the dead to star in the video we're shooting as a tribute to all the victims of the earthquake and tsunami."

Anchorman: "If you weren't trying to cover up Flame's departure from the VuDu Dolls, why did you make Taku Shinoda sign an agreement that he wouldn't divulge what he'd been hired to do for Jimmy's Top Talent?"

Harajuku (sighing): "Mr. Shinoda signed our boilerplate nondisclosure agreement. He was auditioning for another band I was putting together. Naturally, we can't have details about new artists leaked before they've had their debut. Shinoda-*san* was a talented musician, but his statements are pure fabrication."

Anchorman: "But his video does raise questions, since the VuDu Dolls guitarist hasn't actually appeared in public since before Rooster Day. Only three band members showed up to pose with lucky rakes at Senso-ji Temple on December ninth, and since then, Flame has been a no-show on two variety programs, Nana stood in for her as a presenter at the Junior Music Awards, and candid shots of her with the singer Kengo stopped showing up on the Internet. It suggests there's some truth behind Taku Shinoda's story that Flame left the band over a month ago."

Harajuku: "As I explained before, Flame came down with a cold that turned into pneumonia. I made the decision to put her in a private hospital so she could recover fully before resuming her challenging schedule of appearances. The welfare of my artists is my highest priority. She was fully recovered by the time we recorded 'Kiss Me, Kill Me' on Saturday and was planning to return to the spotlight for the band's New Year's Eve appearance on the countdown variety show. Then the tsunami tragically canceled all those plans."

Anchorman: "So is there any truth to Taku Shinoda's allegations?"

The camera zoomed in on Harajuku's face. "Taku Shinoda's death was a tragedy. I mourn the loss of fine session guitarist, even though he broke his agreement with me and hurt Flame's true fans by giving them false hope. It hurts me unbearably that some fans believe his accusations, but I didn't want Taku Shinoda dead."

Kenji sat up straight in his chair. Had he just seen what he thought he'd seen? He looked around for the remote, then remembered this was live TV and he couldn't replay that segment. Maybe a recording of the interview would be up on the station's website by tomorrow.

He'd take another look at it with Oki. The detective who'd nearly completed his psychology degree would be able to confirm whether the fact that Jimmy Harajuku's eyes had flicked up and to the right while he was denying that he wanted Taku Shinoda dead meant he was lying through his teeth.

THURSDAY, DECEMBER 26

•

*9:00 A.M.*

"Tea?" Kenji offered, turning to Detective Oki in the lunchroom after filling his own mug from the first pot of the day.

Oki's eyebrows shot up as he took in Kenji's split lip. "What happened to you?"

"I met Kurosawa-*san's* brother."

Oki leaned in closer to inspect the damage and frowned. "Which brother?"

"There's more than one?"

"Yeah. Was it the big one or the little one?"

"I don't know. Tetsu."

"Bish did that to you?"

"Huh?"

"He's the little one. Her younger brother. They call him 'Bish,' short for '*bishōnen*.' He hated being called 'Pretty Boy' so much he quit judo when he was thirteen and took up boxing—thought if he went around for a while with a black eye and a split lip, he'd lose the 'Pretty Boy' nickname. It totally backfired on him—even his boxing buddies started calling him 'Bish.'" Oki shook his head. "You're lucky it's only a split lip. He turned out to be a lot better at boxing than judo."

"Why didn't you warn me?"

The big detective had the grace to look uncomfortable. "I

thought the *oyabun* didn't allow them to have anything to do with her anymore. I'm sorry you got blindsided. I guess I should have told you, but..." He leaned back against the counter and sighed. "You have any idea what happens the minute her colleagues find out who she is? Three transfers in four years."

"Why, because they're afraid she might side with the wrong guys in a fight?"

"Or worse, that she wouldn't. What if something happened to her and papa decided her partner did a bad job of watching her back?" Oki took a slurp of tea.

"And you didn't think I needed to know that?"

"I didn't think you'd run across any Kurosawa-*gumi* at a pregnancy clinic or a shrine."

Aya arrived, empty tea mug in hand.

"What happened to you?" she said.

"Bish."

She closed her eyes and groaned. "Oh no. I was afraid of this."

Oki said, "I think you'd better explain things to Nakamura-*san*."

"It was because of the women's clinic, right? Goro-*niisan* was standing right outside! I tried to tell him I couldn't be seen going into that place," she protested.

Oki glared at her. "Yeah, well, it looks like your powers of persuasion could use some work, missy."

She dropped her gaze. "Yes, *sensei*."

"Sir," Oki corrected. "I'm not your judo teacher anymore, I'm your senior officer. And I'm ordering you to sit down with Detective Nakamura and explain this to him. I want you to explain everything to him. After you apologize."

Aya bit her lip and glanced at Kenji.

"You're going to have to trust him if you want to work here."

"Yes, *sensei*. I mean, sir."

He looked at his watch. "Do it now."

Oki left, and Aya stared at the floor. Then she took a deep breath and bowed, holding it at a maximally penitent ninety degrees.

"I am very sorry my brother did that to you." She held the bow, waiting for his acknowledgment.

He couldn't very well refuse. Bowing slightly in return, he muttered, "Accepted."

A pair of Traffic Section policewomen appeared in the doorway, stopped in their tracks by the strange tableau. Kenji hustled Aya out the lunchroom door.

"There's not that much to tell," she said, when they were both seated in interview room 2. This one was, appropriately enough, furnished with the standard interrogation setup: a small table with two chairs facing each other, and a computer station in the far corner for the note-taker. Kenji closed the blinds to shut out curious passers-by.

"I guess you know now that I'm one of *those* Kurosawas." She picked at a hangnail. "Did you also hear that my father doesn't consider me a member of the family anymore?"

Kenji nodded. "Because you joined the police?"

She was silent.

"He wants you to fail, doesn't he? Those two guys who were hassling you in front of the station Monday morning—they work for your father?"

She shook her head. "No. They're Yamamoto-*gumi*. They work for Koji Yamamoto, the Yamamoto boss's number two son." She studied her hangnail.

"Koji Yamamoto? The same Koji Yamamoto we're investigating?"

"Yes." Aya sighed. "His boys show up to harass me wherever I go. There's some bad blood between us because of something that happened when I was in high school. My father had to send me to his brother's in Osaka while he dealt with the fallout, but his solution was to demand I return and apologize on my knees. Mine was to apply to the police academy. My father said he'd disown me if I went, and he kept his word. I haven't seen him or my mother or my brothers since the day I graduated."

Kenji drank his tea as he digested what he'd just heard. Setting down his cup, he said, "They might not be quite as distant as you think—according to your brother, there's not much you do that gets past them. Including the fact that you just earned your third-degree black belt. He and I, uh, bonded over that. Apparently, you used to smack him down, too." Kenji paused. "He also told me that Jimmy Harajuku bought a gun last week. Right before that guitarist was killed." He drained his cup and stood. "But Oki should hear this, too. I'm going to get some more tea. You want a refill?"

•

Standing in the staffroom, waiting for a fresh pot to brew, Kenji checked his messages. The text from Yumi made his eyes widen. Jimmy Harajuku *had* taken that Polaroid of Nana. Yumi had seen the scene of the crime.

Kenji returned to the interview room and told them about Yumi's text, confirming that the promoter was the one who'd taken the Polaroid they'd found in Head Priest Yano's sleeve. That moved him to the top of their suspect list.

Kenji and Aya looked over Oki's shoulder as they all watched Jimmy Harajuku's video interview again on the network's streaming site.

"There!" Oki said, stopping the recording as Jimmy's eyes gave away his lie. They watched the clip again and discovered that not only had the promoter been lying when he said that he didn't want Taku Shinoda dead, the classic psychological tell also confirmed he'd lied when he claimed Flame had failed to appear at Senso-ji Temple due to illness, and that Taku hadn't been in the same studio as the VuDu Dolls on Saturday.

Aya asked for the video to be frozen on the final close-up and zoomed in on Jimmy's nose. She pointed out that he'd inserted a "nose mask" into his nostrils, little cups that supposedly trapped ninety-nine percent of germs and pollen.

"He's got a germ fetish," she explained. "Washes his hands obsessively, never goes anywhere in public without a mask. If he agreed to be interviewed without his mask, he must really be desperate to get his side of the story out."

"I'm going to show this to Inspector Kobayashi," Oki said, pushing back his chair. "Jimmy Harajuku had a pretty good reason to shut up Taku Shinoda, and I think the profilers will agree with me that he's lying when he claims he didn't. How are you going to pursue him on Yano's murder?"

"I've been thinking about that," Kenji said. "Let's assume that Flame decided to run away, start a new life and go back to being a boy. He goes to his dad and tells Yano about the abuse young idols-to-be are suffering at the hands of Jimmy Harajuku and shows him the Polaroids to prove it. He begs Yano to help him disappear, shaves off his long blond hair, reinvents himself as the intern Taiga. Meanwhile, Jimmy discovers the Polaroids are missing and he knows who took them. So what does he do?"

"Hires a private eye?" Aya suggested.

"Maybe. Or picks someone he trusts completely, someone who owes him, someone who can sniff around without anybody recognizing him." Kenji said. "Harajuku's one of the most connected guys in the music biz, and there must be plenty of people who fit the bill." He paused, then added, "Takki didn't say anybody had been asking about Flame at the shelter recently, but Jimmy knows about Flame's connections there. It had to have been one of the first places he sent someone to snoop around."

Oki nodded. "So let's say Jimmy tracks Flame down, only to discover Flame no longer has the Polaroids. But if Flame gave them to someone for safekeeping, Yano is the obvious choice. So maybe Jimmy sets up a meeting with Yano to bribe or threaten him, or maybe Yano surprises Jimmy breaking and entering, but whatever happened, Jimmy ends up bashing Yano over the head with the music award. Jimmy searches the house for the Polaroids, and finds them in the kitchen. He takes the photos, then ditches the music award and the photo album in the burnable trash outside Shota's house."

"But when he gets home," Kenji said, picking up the story, "he discovers he doesn't have all the Polaroids after all. He's missing the one hidden in Yano's sleeve. He doesn't know we have it—he thinks Flame kept it for insurance. And that puts Flame right in the crosshairs, because Flame could destroy him with it."

"So how are you going to find Flame before Jimmy does?" Oki asked.

Kenji thought for a moment. "First, I'll go back to the shelter and ask Takki if he has any idea where to start looking." He turned to Aya. "Can you do a net search, check the latest fan sightings?"

She nodded.

He paused, then asked Oki, "Did Kobayashi put a tail on Jimmy Harajuku?"

"No."

"Well, if Takki can't help me figure out where to look for Flame, I'll tail Jimmy myself. At least I can try to stop him from using that gun again if he gets to Flame before we do."

•

Takki's eyes flicked between the blown-up face in Koji Yamamoto's photo of the fleeing Taiga to a signed poster of the VuDu Dolls he had on the back of his door. He handed the phone back to Kenji and returned to his chair. "You're right. It is Flame. Or a damn good look-alike."

"But . . . why would anyone throw away fame and fortune like that?"

Takki lit another cigarette and tossed his lighter on his desk.

"Celebrity life." He shook his head. "You don't know what it's like. From the outside it looks like you've got it made, but the truth is, it's lonely at the top. After ten years, some idols start to want to have a life, want to eat something besides room service."

"What are you talking about? Flame is friends with everybody who's anybody, goes to all the exclusive clubs, eats at the best restaurants. What's wrong with that?"

"You think any of it's real?" Takki tapped his ash and laughed. "You must not have seen how big a crew it takes to get such flatteringly lit 'candid' shots in restaurants and bars. If you think Flame and Mr. Hottie-of-the-Week were enjoying their drinks in romantic privacy, you're dead wrong. Of course, Flame probably didn't mind the crowd, because it's unlikely she knows her 'dates' well enough to even call them by their first names. It's all part of the publicity machine. Jimmy's contracts forbid his idols to have relationships. Real ones, anyway."

"You're kidding me. Is that even legal?"

"Yep. When twelve- and thirteen-year-olds sign up for his idol factory—or when their parents do it for them—they think it's a small price to pay for stardom. Idols' popularity drops like a stone – along with merchandise, concert ticket, and CD sales – the moment any real relationship shows its un-Photoshopped face. But if Jimmy has the right to control every part of his stars' lives, the fangirls can live vicariously and the fanboys can still imagine themselves as Prince Charming. Jimmy even makes money off of doing deals with other promoters who've got a fading star who could use a shot of publicity by being seen with one of Jimmy's golden geese."

"You mean he . . . rents them out?"

"Now you're catching on. But if what you're telling me about Flame quitting the band and disappearing is true, that tsunami really saved Jimmy's bacon." He took another drag on his cigarette and frowned. "Of course, he needs Flame to stay dead in order for his bacon to stay saved."

"Explain."

"If Flame leaves the VuDu Dolls to do her own thing, no matter how hot a guitarist Jimmy finds to replace her, a lot of the fans will follow Flame. That's what happened when Gackt left Malice Mizer and went solo. But if Flame dies tragically in the tsunami, not only does her 'last recording' become a runaway hit, but VuDu Dolls fans sympathy-buy every piece of merchandise on the shelves. When Jimmy finds a new guitarist, fans stay loyal to the band, even though they wave little Flame dolls in tribute at every concert. Look at X Japan— their most popular tour souvenir to this day is a figure of their original guitarist Hide, and he's been dead for over fifteen years." He tapped his ash. "If Flame isn't dead, I wouldn't be at all surprised if Jimmy is trying to figure out a way to fix that. Especially if he thinks she has that Polaroid of Nana."

"So, where would you start looking?"

"The Internet. A musician like Flame can't live without playing. I never saw her without her guitar, and she was always noodling around on it, even when she wasn't rehearsing. If she really disappeared a month ago, you can be sure someone's uploaded a video of her playing somewhere by now."

He pulled his laptop closer to him and thought for a moment. Navigating to a video-sharing site, he tried a search, clicked through several videos, watching each for a few seconds, then tried a new search. Five minutes and two cigarettes later, what sounded like the first haunting chords of "Don't Need You" wafted from the laptop's tiny built-in speakers. Kenji came around behind Takki to take a look. On the screen was a shaky handheld phone video, taken over the heads of a standing-room crowd. A guitarist in a rainbow wig with the fastest fingers Kenji had ever seen launched into a soaring riff.

"It's her," Takki said. "I'd know her style anywhere. The words have changed, but this tune is one she used to play before she got famous. She worked out the kinks here at the shelter with the kids she was originally discovered with."

"Can you tell where this video was shot? And when?" Kenji asked.

"Modern technology, at your service," Takki said, hitting a few keys. He read off the embedded information. "Two days ago. Odaiba. She's playing with a band calling themselves Tinderbox."

•

The rockabilly taxi driver stood over a head taller than the elderly men and women who were waiting patiently with their teacups as Yumi ran back and forth to the kitchen of the nearest Oedo Onsen restaurant, refilling the collection of assorted hot-water pots that stood on the tea table like a platoon of volunteer soldiers. She topped up the last one, settling it back in the lineup. Whipping off the apron and headscarf that were required serving wear, even in conditions of emergency, she handed them to the motherly woman who had volunteered to replace her, bowing and thanking her for stepping in before Yumi's shift was over.

Asking Ace's driver to wait while she fetched her phone, Yumi ran to the tangle of power strips that had been set up for refugees. Good, it was back to a hundred percent. This morning it had died as soon as she took advantage of the Wi-Fi bars at the refugee center to send a reply to Ichiro's mother and a text to Kenji, apologizing for peeking at the evidence bag in his Inbox, but telling him she'd found the place where that Polaroid of the half-naked girl was taken.

When she emerged, Stranger was leaning against his cab in his sunglasses, arms crossed, chewing on a toothpick. He boosted himself off the car and got in the driver's seat to operate the lever that would open the door for her.

"Ace-*san* is going to be mighty happy to see you," he confided as she scooted into the backseat. "This morning nobody knew what he was going on about, until somebody finally figured out he wanted sugar for his green tea—" The taxi driver shuddered. "—and eggs for breakfast, cooked until they were hard." He shifted the toothpick to the other side of his mouth and turned the key.

"He eventually got fed without me, though, right? So, why did Harajuku-*san* ask you to fetch me from the refugee center?"

"Dunno. I expect he'll tell you when we get there." Stranger swung the car onto the deserted boulevard. They drove in companionable silence, and few minutes later bumped into the semicircular drive in front of Jimmy's building.

After spending the morning at a place where everybody was acutely aware of the need to conserve power and behave with utmost courtesy to their fellow suffering human beings, she wasn't prepared for the scene at Jimmy's penthouse. In her absence, the VuDu Dolls had arrived.

She walked in on a blaze of lights, speakers blasting competing tunes from different rooms, and a heated fight between Shiro and Nana.

"I'm keeping it," Nana said. "And nothing you can say will change my mind."

She turned away from the pamphlet the image consultant was showing her, on which was printed before and after pictures of laser tattoo removal. Catching a glimpse of Yumi, the vocalist's face brightened and she said, "Hey, let's ask her. You're a fan, right? What do you think? Is this cool with you?"

She turned and pulled up her T-shirt to reveal fresh ink on her lower back, still slightly puffy and red around the edges. It was a black rose entwined with barbed wire. Encircling it were the words, "Only One Life To Live."

Yumi hesitated, then said, "It's very . . . edgy."

"See?" Nana said, turning to Shiro, triumphant. "Edgy. I like that." She shot a look of appreciation and a thumbs-up in Yumi's direction.

Shiro rolled his eyes and said, "Nana. Sweetheart. Edgy is not one of VuDu Dolls' keywords. We do 'thrilling.' We do 'cool.' We don't do 'edgy.' Not right now. Think of your fans. They're already reeling from Flame passing away—may the poor girl rest in peace. Right now you need to reassure them, remind them that the rest of you are still alive and making the music they adore. Really, Nana, darling, I'm shocked you don't have more respect for Flame's memory."

Nana rounded on him, furious. "Don't tell me how to respect Flame's memory. I got this in memory of Flame. Flame's the one who—"

She shoved aside the magazines on the top of the coffee table, blinking back tears, searching for a lighter. She found one and flicked it, igniting the end of the cigarette she'd fitted between her babydoll lips. She took in a deep lungful of smoke, then exhaled, calming herself. A few puffs later, she turned to Shiro and said, "I'm still there for the fans, I'm just there for them with a tattoo, that's all. What does it matter, anyway? They're never going to see it. It's on my back, not my arm. It's the music that's important."

"It is, I know it is, but babycakes, it's not just the music, it's the look, it's the feel, it's the package. Of course your music is important, sweetie, but—"

"But nothing." Nana pulled an ashtray closer and tapped her ash. "Look," she said, her voice carefully neutral. "If nobody takes any pictures of me in the bathtub, the fans will never know." She scooped up her cigarettes and lighter, and walked out.

The bathtub. Jolted by the reminder, she looked at Shiro, but he just sighed, gave her an 'I tried' look, and tossed the tattoo removal brochure at the wastebasket.

In the next room, Jimmy Harajuku ended the call he was on by saying he didn't care how tapped out they were because of emergency earthquake demand, he needed four generators delivered immediately to where his studio had stood before the tsunami had washed six stories out from under it. He strode into the room, dialing his next call.

Spotting Yumi, he said, "Ah, Miss Hata, there you are. Please don't run off again—we need you here to help Mr. Blade work with the band this afternoon. Hello? Is this the Pro Camera rental department? Hang on a sec." He covered the mouthpiece and finished saying, "Before I go out to make sure these idiots don't set things up wrong at tomorrow's shoot location, can you help me explain the schedule to Ace-*san*?"

"*Hai*," Yumi agreed, following him back to the kitchen as he badgered the person on the other end of the line to find a truck—he didn't care how—and drive a carload of lighting equipment to the video shoot site immediately if not sooner.

"Yo," said Blade, shooting her a mock salute from behind his guitar and a cup of coffee, sitting at a table with the remains of breakfast still stuck to plates that had been stacked but not cleared.

"Good morning," Yumi said, bowing to the guitarist and his manager, who looked up from checking his phone messages and grinned with relief.

"Miss Hata! Am I ever happy to see you! Can you explain to these nice people that Blade needs to start checking out the equipment and tuning up and having a go with the band before they even think of videoing anything? I can't seem to . . ."

Yumi smiled and held up a hand. "Don't worry Ace-*san*, you're all on the same page. Mr. Harajuku has asked me to help Blade work with the band this afternoon. And I think he wants Blade to talk to the stylist about his costume for the music video."

"Costume?" Blade frowned and looked down at the faded

Sex Pistols T-shirt he was wearing and said, "This in't good enough?"

"Uh . . ." Yumi looked to Jimmy for help.

The promoter punched a new number into his phone and barked at it, "Chiho! Kitchen." A minute later, the stylist appeared.

"I was just down the hall," she said, annoyed. "You didn't have to phone me on speaker."

Jimmy ignored her complaint and donned a fresh set of white gloves, directing her to use Yumi to talk to Blade about his costume, clear up the breakfast dishes, and be sure to have all the props ready for review by the time he returned from the shooting location at four.

The stylist muttered, "Your wish is my command," and made an ironic namaste at Jimmy's receding back.

He strode to the front door, cocking a gun-finger at Shiro by way of farewell and yelling down the hall for Ninjaboy on his way out.

When he'd gone, Blade and Yumi helped Chiho clear up the dishes. After they'd wiped the counters and helped themselves to fresh cups of coffee, Chiho beckoned them down the hall to a bedroom with a mountain of wardrobe heaped on the bed. Wedged into the corner, a silent girl in huge black glasses sat before a desktop computer, her hair pulled into a spiky fountain atop her head and her fingers flying over the keyboard as screens of code scrolled past. Chiho introduced her to Blade as Eva—short for Evangelion, her favorite anime—the video artist who was throwing together the promo video that would play behind the VuDu Dolls and Blade when they were on stage at what had turned into Jimmy's Top Talent Tsunami Benefit Concert at Zepp Tokyo.

"Benefit concert?" Yumi said.

"Hasn't Jimmy told you about it?" Chiho began sorting through the tattered black and silver clothing on the bed, frowning as she considered this item or that. "Originally, it was scheduled as a Jimmy's Top Talent Showcase, but it got postponed by the tsunami. Then they announced that the Rinkai Line will be back in service by tomorrow and people will be able to come and go from Odaiba as usual. So it's back on again. And Jimmy's turning it into a sort of memorial for Flame. It's sold out, and scalped tickets are going for over twenty thousand yen."

Suddenly, in the corner, the computer screen burst into flames as Eva played back a piece she'd just composed, dancing fire morphing into a stream of hearts that took over the screen, then formed themselves into silhouettes of the VuDu Dolls. After scrutinizing the effect, she hit a key and went back to her screens of scrolling code.

"Now," Chiho said, turning her attention to Blade and holding up a fistful of tattered garments. "About your costume..."

•

Nana might act like an overgrown teenager, but she had a voice like an angel. She drew out the last note of "Kiss Me, Kill Me," the song the VuDu Dolls had recorded last weekend before the tsunami hit, and stood there, eyes closed, face upturned, one Sennheiser headphone held to her ear as the chords faded.

This version would be released after the memorial concert, with words that had been changed to pay tribute to Flame and the other victims of the earthquake. The band and Blade stood there, frozen, for a moment, then pulled off their headphones and grinned, exchanging high fives all around for a take they knew they'd nailed.

Yumi was pinned to her seat, stunned, her ears still echoing with the haunting melody that was already going platinum. Fans were downloading the version they'd recorded on the day of the earthquake at a rate of one a second.

Blade had stopped needing her services as soon as he picked up his guitar; music was a language they all spoke fluently. Although the VuDu Dolls sounded a little different with his bluesy influence, Yumi predicted that the crowd would go wild when he took the stage with them Saturday night.

Jimmy must have thought so, too, because he turned to the tech at the mixing board with two thumbs up. They were recording at the studio that occupied half the floor below his penthouse, connected by a private elevator.

He strode through the door to the recording room.

"Splendid!" he pronounced, throwing his arms wide. "You'll kill them on Saturday. If you play half this well at Zepp Tokyo, I'll have director-boy cut some live clips into the promo video." He bowed to Blade, saying in honorific Japanese, "Thank you for your contribution."

Apparently, this had been said to the British guitarist often enough in the past twelve hours that he didn't look to Yumi for a translation before nodding and saying, "You too, mate," letting loose a short riff from his guitar.

Jimmy looked around the room and said, "Okay, that's it for today, kids. The Rinkai Line is up and running ahead of schedule, so as a little bonus, I sent Chiho into Roppongi for a boatload of sushi." The musicians cheered, except for Blade, who raised his eyebrows questioningly at Yumi. Jimmy slapped his forehead and turned to her. "I forgot foreigners don't eat raw fish. Can you ask him if he wants me to have Chiho bring him a, I don't know, what do foreigners eat? Hamburgers?"

Yumi crossed the room to Blade and said, "Jimmy says he's sent Chiho over to Roppongi for sushi, but if you'd prefer something else . . ."

"Sushi?" Blade said.

"Yeah. If you can't eat raw fish, he says—"

"What are you talking about, 'can't eat raw fish'?" Blade

exclaimed, disgusted. "Everybody eats raw fish! Can you ask him to order some *engawa*—it's really hard to get in the U.K. except at über-expensive places and..."

Yumi relayed the request to Jimmy, whose look of surprise mixed with slight displeasure told her that Blade had just destroyed one of his more cherished stereotypes about foreigners. Jimmy told her he'd ask Chiho to see to the *engawa* order, then instructed the band to meet them upstairs in an hour.

He disappeared, and the bass player crossed to Blade, asking something about the chord progression the guitarist had improvised in the "Kiss Me, Kill Me" bridge section. Yumi moved closer in case Blade needed her. The British guitarist looked up at the ceiling, fingers ghosting over the strings, recalling what he'd played. Then he angled the neck of his guitar so the bass player could see it clearly as he went through the passage in slow motion. She nodded and echoed it as a bass line, then the drummer, who'd been watching the exchange, hit her sticks together 1-2-3-4, and they did it together. Grins all around when they got it right in one, then Blade asked the bass player to give him some advice about the opening guitar solo in "Don't Need You."

By the time they were called up to the kitchen to get some sushi before it was all gone, Blade had mastered Flame's unconventional fingering, the VuDu Dolls' bassist had learned the tricky finale to Exit Strategy's "Hell Is Other People," and they'd gotten lost in an improvised guitar–bass jam that started with X Japan's "Rose of Pain" and ended with Zeromancer's "Need You Like A Drug."

Yumi had never heard anything like it. She could have sat there listening to them all night, but eventually hunger got the better of them, and they put down their instruments to head upstairs to join the group in the penthouse kitchen.

Rain mixed with sleet was now streaking the big window that looked down on the darkened landscape far below. Yumi spotted Beni and waved, then her jaw dropped in amazement at the spread on the table. Platters of all the usual selections—dark red tuna, translucent ama-ebi shrimp, glistening orange salmon eggs, flounder sliced so thin you could see the smear of green wasabi through it—were joined by bowls of purple-and-white firefly squid, cone-shaped hand rolls sprouting salmon strips and radish shoots. A rainbow of sliced *maki* rolls paved a tray the size of a large pizza like a slice of Italian millefiore glass. The centerpiece was a magnificent spread of tuna that made a smooth gradation from red to pale pink as lean *maguro* gave way to the extra-fatty *toro* prized by aficionados. Surrounding it was the frilly "skirt" of flounder Blade had requested.

Jimmy clapped his hands for attention.

"Now that everyone's here, I've got an announcement to make. The VuDu Dolls are going to bat cleanup at the concert on Saturday night, in honor of Flame. Let's give it all we've got and make her proud."

Everyone clapped.

"Tonight and tomorrow night I want you all to get a good night's sleep. Everyone stays in. Bed check at midnight."

Groans.

"God, Jimmy, we're not teenagers anymore," Nana glowered. "You don't have to—"

"Hair-make call at five a.m., we're shooting on location by six," the promoter continued. "No mercy. Midnight, boys and girls. No later, no exceptions. You can party after the show on Saturday. There's beer in the fridge, but remember you'll get a wet washcloth in the face if you're still in bed tomorrow at five oh five."

Yumi crossed to Blade to fill him on what had just been said in a language he didn't understand, apologizing to the thirty-something international star when she told him about the curfew.

But Blade just shrugged and said, "If we were in Berlin,

I'd be out the window the minute he had me tucked up, even if I had to make a bedsheet rope ten stories tall." He gave her a lopsided grin. "But a disaster zone's not much of a hot spot, innit? Can't see sneakin' out for bingo at the refugee center, you know?"

Actually, there *was* one thing worth sneaking out for tonight. Yumi needed to ask Beni where the Crokodile Rock Café was, so she could find out whether the rainbow-wigged guitarist was Flame or not.

She excused herself, saying, "I'm going to sit down and eat now. Call me if you need me to explain anything, okay?"

She looked around, then carried her laden plate down the wide stairs to the corner of the sunken living room where Chiho and Beni were sitting.

"Just ask him," Beni was begging Chiho. "Please? If it's not me pushing, maybe he'll say yes. They know Jimmy's the wrong promoter to rep them, but he knows everyone in the business. If he says no, play some of that video I uploaded last night. He'd be an ass not to go listen to Tinderbox's guitarist after hearing him play 'Hot Rain.'"

Chiho grimaced. "Being an ass is what he does best. But I'll ask him. Wait here." She took her plate back to the kitchen for seconds, and Yumi saw her sidle up to Jimmy, who was sitting apart, guarding his plate from germs. He was systematically eating his way through an order of nothing but high-grade tuna.

Yumi asked Beni. "You think Jimmy might be interested in Tinderbox?"

The red-haired talent scout nodded, her mouth full of salmon egg sushi. She pointed to her bulging cheek with a wait-a-second look, swallowed, and said, "I've been trying to get Jimmy to take a look at them, but he can be such a narrow-minded jerk sometimes. I know he likes girls, but that guitarist is really something special."

If only she knew how special. If Jimmy Harajuku heard

the Tinderbox guitarist play, would he recognize Flame, even with no hair and dressed as a boy?

"Are you going to their gig tonight?" Yumi asked.

"Yeah. You coming?"

"Wouldn't miss it. Do you have a ride?"

"Don't need one. I've got some stuff to do first so I might miss the first half of their set, but the CrokRock is walking distance. I'll give you the address." She asked for Yumi's phone and keyed in the bar's location. "You can't miss it. But get there early—it'll be SRO tonight with Tinderbox playing and Crok-*san* emptying his kegs."

"Thanks," said Yumi.

Beni's eyes strayed to the kitchen, where Chiho was pitching Tinderbox to Jimmy. He was shaking his head with a pained look on his face. The stylist set down her plate and pulled out her phone. As Jimmy waited, he plucked another piece of high-end tuna from the covered box next to him on the counter, quickly closing the lid to shield his personal sushi stash from germs. He crammed the entire piece in his mouth, his eyes flicking from Nana—who had moodily eaten all the fish off the top of a pile of wasabi-smeared rice pillows—to the drummer, who was helping herself to her third beer. Now Chiho was plugging one earbud into her own ear and handing the other to Jimmy as she stared at her tiny screen and waited for the video to load.

Jimmy took the earbud between gloved thumb and forefinger, looked at it with disgust, then cleaned it thoroughly with an antiseptic wipe he pulled from a packet in his pocket. He gingerly placed it in his ear, turning a bored face to the video.

Suddenly his eyes widened and he snatched the other earbud from Chiho, cramming it into his other ear without thinking twice, riveted to the screen.

•

By the time Kenji stepped out into the Komagome Police Station parking lot, the cold rain that had been falling since he'd returned to the station had turned to sleet. He groaned. Although he'd checked the weather report this morning and brought along an umbrella, it wasn't wide enough to keep the slanting rain off his legs as well as his head. The last time he'd left his seventy-centimeter model in the rack outside the soba restaurant, someone had taken it, leaving this pitiful smaller one in its place.

He pulled out his phone to check his calls. Maybe there would be something to cheer him up after spending the afternoon in the company of Yano's cold body.

Attending post-mortems was a necessary part of detective work, but it always depressed him. The medical examiner told him he ought to see the procedure as giving the victim a voice, a chance to tell them what happened in the last moments of life, but Kenji had a hard time believing anybody wanted to utter their last words from a slab in the morgue.

As always, though, the autopsy had produced some useful information. The medical examiner had done an angle-of-attack calculation on the whiteboard, and suggested that Kenji look for a suspect who was much shorter than the 179-centimeter victim, probably around 160–165 centimeters.

That let Koji Yamamoto off the hook. Who did it leave? Jimmy Harajuku. And Taiga/Flame.

"*Oi*. Nakamura." A big man under an extra-wide black silk umbrella stepped out from the shadows of the neighbors' half-finished construction project.

Startled, Kenji jumped. Oh. Bish's driver.

"Boss wants a word with you."

"Can't you guys call or text like normal people?" Kenji grumbled, following the driver to the now-familiar white sedan. A clean towel was fetched from the trunk and spread on the leather seat before Kenji was allowed to fold his cheap umbrella and seat himself in the back beside Aya's brother.

"*Konban wa*," Bish said, wishing him a good evening as if they were meeting at the Kabuki theater. Which is where he looked like he was going, his black-and-brown houndstooth muffler expertly tucked inside the collar of a black cashmere overcoat. He'd removed one calfskin glove to check his messages while he was waiting.

"Nice coat," Kenji said.

"I've got something for you." Bish navigated to his stored photos and passed the phone. The picture on the display was of a black handgun, serial number filed.

"This is the piece Jimmy Harajuku bought last week from my . . . acquaintance. It's a Beretta. Nine mil. And enough ammo to take out fifty idols who are singing off-key, if he's a really good shot. Which he is," Bish added, "if what the dealer told me is right. He watched Jimmy load the magazine like a pro, like he could do it in his sleep."

Oki would be interested to hear that, Kenji thought, remembering that Taku had been killed by someone who had sniper-level skill.

"Can you mail me this picture?" Kenji asked.

Bish took his phone back. "I'll ask my acquaintance to send you your very own copy, if you can give him the usual assurances."

"Such as . . . ?"

"He'll sign a statement as long as it doesn't land him in jail for pursuing his, er, profession."

"Oh. Right. Of course," Kenji said, hoping "the usual assurances" were, in fact, usual.

"And in return, when you take down Jimmy Harajuku, you'll give my sister some of the credit, right?"

Kenji nodded.

"One more thing," Bish smiled. "Could you give her a message for me? Tell her she just became an auntie."

•

At the Crokodile Rock Café, amps weren't necessary for Tinderbox to have the fans on their feet, hand jiving to "Hot Rain."

Battered tables and chairs had been stacked outside the CrokRock to make room for the standing-room-only crowd. Although it was close enough to the refugee center to catch a few bars of cell-phone service, there was no electricity yet on this part of Odaiba. A miniature skyline of mismatched flashlights had been lined up along the baseboards, throwing beams of varying strengths up the walls. The same guy who'd manned the spotlight last night perched on a stack of bottle crates, training a pair of industrial-strength flashlight beams on the performers.

The stuffed crocodile that gave the shop its name was suspended above the bar as it had always been, although tonight its gaping jaws held a sign that read, "Draft Beer ¥500 Until the Kegs Run Dry." Earlier, one of the bar's regulars had climbed up on a chair to settle a battered cowboy hat he'd rescued from the tsunami zone on its head, because the bartender told him that even though the giant reptile had turned into a bucking bronco during the quake, it rode out the disaster like a champ.

Yumi's pocket buzzed. She sneaked a peek at the caller ID. Kenji.

It stopped buzzing as she pushed her way out the front door. She pressed the Callback button.

It was cold enough to see her breath. Clumps of wet snow plummeted from the dark sky, spotting the pavement with splats of white as it began to stick. The door eased shut behind her, and in the sudden silence, she heard Kenji pick up.

"Thanks for calling me right back," he said. "Are you still on Odaiba?"

"Yes, why?"

"Because the Rinkai Line started running again twelve hours ahead of schedule, and I just arrived at Tokyo Teleport

Station. I'm looking for one of the suspects in Head Priest Yano's murder and I could use your help."

Kenji explained how a shrine intern named Hikaru Taiga had been missing since the day Yano had been found dead.

"He was last seen fleeing the shrine, carrying a guitar, the morning of the earthquake," Kenji concluded. "I think he's here on Odaiba, because someone put a video up online a few nights ago, of him performing at one of the refugee centers with a band calling themselves Tinderbox."

Tinderbox? An intern who'd been working at the Tabata Shrine was playing guitar for Tinderbox? Did that meant the guy Kenji was looking for was actually...Flame?

"So, have you heard of this band?" Kenji asked. "Do you have any idea where I might start looking for them?"

The window behind her vibrated with the finale of "Hot Rain." Should she tell him that Tinderbox was playing right here, right now? Then she remembered he'd called Taiga a "suspect."

"Why exactly are you looking for this . . . Taiga?" Yumi asked.

"Well, technically he's a suspect. When I find him, I'll bring him in for questioning. But what I'm really hoping is that he's a witness. I think he can help us nail Jimmy Harajuku for Head Priest Yano's murder."

"What? Jimmy Harajuku killed Head Priest Yano?"

Kenji made her promise to keep what he was about to tell her confidential, then told her his theory that Yano had been killed by the promoter for a set of Polaroids like the one she'd seen with the rubber ducks in it. He believed Jimmy had traced the collection to Head Priest Yano and killed him when he refused to hand it over.

"But . . . where did the head priest get them?"

"We think Taiga is actually--" Kenji hesitated. "We think he has ties to the girl in the picture you saw. We think the Polaroid collection was stolen from Jimmy Harajuku and the intern gave them to Head Priest Yano for safekeeping."

So Kenji didn't know the guy he was looking for was actually the famous female idol, Flame. Or did he? Did that pause before he told her about the missing Polaroids mean he knew, but he'd decided she couldn't be trusted?

Kenji continued, "I think that after Jimmy killed the head priest, he took the Polaroid collection, but he didn't realize they weren't all there. The one you saw on my desk was hidden in Head Priest Yano's sleeve, and Jimmy doesn't know we found it. When he discovers that he's short one picture, he's going to think that Taiga still has it. He'll be desperate to get it back, because if we find Taiga first, Taiga can connect that picture to Jimmy and Jimmy will go to jail. So, to get back to your question, Taiga is technically still a suspect, but what I'm really trying to do is keep him from becoming the next victim. Jimmy Harajuku is dangerous, and he has a gun."

"A gun?"

"A gun he's not afraid to use. He bought a nine-millimeter Beretta from a black-market dealer in Kabuki-chō, and we think he used it to kill a session guitarist named Taku Shinoda--"

"What? Taku is dead?" Yumi had been too busy to watch the news since the power had been restored. Weak-kneed, she leaned back against the cold stucco wall of the CrokRock, snow whitening her boots, shaking her head as Kenji told her how Haru's boyfriend had been gunned down.

"So I'm in a race with Jimmy Harajuku to track down Taiga. If I find him first, we'll finally be able to put Jimmy Harajuku in jail. But if he finds him first . . ."

Flame was in danger. Yumi spun around and peered through the CrokRock's window at the hopping crowd as the band hammered out its final chord.

Chiho had convinced Jimmy Harajuku to come hear Tinderbox play tonight. Was he here? She scanned the crowd. Yes. Jimmy was standing in the corner, not dancing, not clapping, just staring at the guitarist.

She had to warn Flame. By the time Kenji got here from Teleport Station, it would be too late.

"I'll ask around," she told him hastily." But I've got to go now. I'll call you back."

She pushed back through the door and wriggled her way toward the band, as the vocalist Risa announced, "We're Tinderbox, and we're going to take a short break now to get some of that good beer before you guys drink it all!"

The clapping and cheering died down as a large part of the audience joined the line for the kegs.

The guitarist followed Risa toward the bathrooms, upstream against the keg crowd.

Yumi altered her course, aiming at the bathroom sign that pointed down the hallway in back. She glanced over her shoulder. Jimmy was trapped on the wrong side of the keg line, trying to shoulder his way through the crush and not making much progress. With luck, she'd get to the guitarist first.

The Tinderbox musicians had disappeared by the time Yumi got to the hall and discovered that male relief was to the left, female to the right, and the kitchen was at the end. The guy who'd been manning the "spotlights" came out of the men's room and she stopped him to ask if the guitarist was in there. He shook his head.

Yumi thanked him and headed into the ladies' room. Maybe Risa could tell her where the guitarist had gone.

•

There was a line, but Risa wasn't in it. Yumi crouched down and checked the stalls. High-heeled ankle boots, brown Uggs, platform Mary Janes with striped black-and-white socks, dirty red Puma sneakers. Which ones belonged to the vocalist?

She pretended to fix her makeup, using the mirror to keep an eye on the stalls.

After the first flush, the Uggs emerged. Pigtailed girl in a knit cap with earflaps and long pom-pom ties.

The platform Mary Janes belonged to a Punk Goth girl bundled into several layers of SEX POT ReVeNGe hoodies.

The high-heeled ankle boots walked out on the feet of the vocalist.

As the singer flicked water off her hands, looking around for the hand dryer, Yumi apologized and introduced herself, saying, "Hey, you guys were great. I came to see Hikaru-*kun* because I know a friend he went to middle school with. You know where he went?"

"Probably where I'm headed now," she replied. "Out for a smoke. Back door's through the kitchen."

Yumi and the singer flattened themselves against the wall as Crok burst through the swinging door at the end of the hall, rolling a fresh keg. They waited for him to pass, then ducked into the kitchen. Flashlights had been propped to shine down onto two workstations. The kitchen staff was dressed in hats and mufflers, one turning a dead keg on its side to roll it toward the back door for collection.

"Did Hikaru come through here?" Risa asked the guy washing the motley collection of glasses that had been pressed into service as beer mugs.

He straightened and pointed to the back door.

Outside, Risa lit a cigarette, then peered into the pack and frowned. "Damn, is that my last one? Wonder if Hikaru's got some." She stuffed the crumpled pack back in her pocket and looked around for the guitarist.

Yumi's breath was a pale fog, echoing the cigarette smoke. She took a peek back through the window and saw that Jimmy had finally made it to the hall leading to the bathrooms, and was pushing toward the men's room.

"There he is." Risa nodded at the store across the street.

Yumi turned. The top of a head in a rainbow wig was visible through the big plate-glass windows of a nearly dark convenience store.

They crossed the street, the singer pausing for one last hit of nicotine outside the entrance as her cigarette burned down into the filter. Dropping it, she crushed it with her boot, then stepped over the broom handle that had been used to prop the automatic door open.

"*Irasshaimase*," called the wizened man behind the counter, bundled to his eyeballs in overcoat, muffler, and some obviously borrowed pink fur earmuffs.

Flashlights illuminated shelves that had been stripped bare in random-looking sections, some items completely sold out, others still arrayed in neat rows, untouched. The dark refrigerator cases still held full inventories of milk drinks—now well past their sell-by date—but the water, soft drinks, and beer were long gone. The dried-squid snack pegs were empty, but not many people had done a panic buy on *umeboshi* salty pickled plums.

The guitarist looked up.

"I can't believe how expensive tissues are!" he said.

"Only for guys," laughed Risa. "I get mine for free!"

Yumi never bought tissues, either—all winter long, outside every train station, packs of tissues with ads exhorting women to try a lucrative new career in the sex chat business were pressed on female commuters.

Yumi followed the pair to the cash register, waiting for a chance to take Flame aside and warn her. Risa stopped to pluck the last bag of ginger-lemon throat drops from the peg as they passed. The cash registers were dark, but the cashier picked up a calculator as they approached.

Risa ventured, "I suppose it's too much to hope you have any cigarettes left . . . ?"

"Sorry," the man replied, shaking his head. "They were the first thing to sell out."

"Just these, then." The singer plucked the tissues from Flame's hand and put them on the counter with her throat drops.

The old man punched a button on the calculator with a wool-gloved finger, then frowned as it failed to light up. He set it down, then ducked behind the register to rummage around.

"*Ara!* Look what we have here!" he exclaimed, reappearing triumphantly with a wooden abacus and a pack of Hopes. "They must have fallen in the earthquake. If you don't mind menthol..."

"No problem," Risa said. "I'd smoke an old sock, I'm that desperate."

The old man laughed and pulled off his glove. He flicked his fingers over the abacus's wooden beads. "Eight hundred forty-four yen."

The band's drummer appeared at the door, shivering in his T-shirt and leather pants. He hadn't bothered to put on a coat just to run across the street. "Crok says it's time for our second set."

Yumi's anxiety kicked up a notch. Time was running out.

"I've got a date with one of these Hopes," said Risa. "Tell him we'll be there in a minute."

The drummer nodded and scurried back across the street, hugging his arms.

"You need a smoke before we go back in?" Risa asked the guitarist, offering the open pack as they ambled back toward the club.

"I need the bathroom more. Catch you inside."

Oh no, not the bathroom. That's where—

The guitarist froze.

Silhouetted in the door of the club, Jimmy Harajuku.

Flame spun around and bumped into Yumi, not even apologizing before taking off down the alley next to the convenience store.

As Jimmy's sinister masked face turned in her direction, Yumi slipped behind Risa, then took off after the guitarist, punching another set of black footprints into the fresh snow.

FRIDAY, DECEMBER 27

•

*10:30 A.M.*

"Just drop me off here," Yumi groaned to Stranger the next morning as they pulled up in front of the Oedo Onsen. "I don't think they're going need me to help with Blade until this afternoon. If anyone asks, tell them I'll be back by lunchtime."

She dragged herself to the entry, every muscle aching, thinking about last night's utter fail. She'd followed Flame's footsteps through the snow to a corner where the narrow alley intersected a main street. There, the trail joined a path that had been trampled by so many feet that picking out a single set of marks left by the fleeing idol had been impossible. The snow had been falling thick and fast by the time she made it back to the CrokRock. Her hat, coat, pants, and even her purse were caked with white, which melted as soon as she stepped through the door.

She'd been so soaked that the yen notes inside her purse were still damp this morning when Chiho's alarm went off at five a.m. No surprise, her throat hurt like hell.

But Jimmy had been serious about the "no mercy" rule. Yumi had been shuttling between Ace and Blade since six a.m. on the video set, helping them understand what the director and Jimmy wanted from them.

By nine thirty, when she took a break and dragged herself to the car trunk that had been set up as a tea station, her teeth were aching with the beginnings of a sinus headache. She told

Chiho, who bullied Jimmy into allowing Yumi to go off with Stranger in search of some cold pills that would get her through the day.

They'd gone from drugstore to drugstore, but the cold/flu section was stripped bare at every single one. Then Yumi remembered the emergency supply table at the Oedo Onsen refugee shelter. She'd been there when a handsome man in a cashmere overcoat with a gold pin shining in his lapel had arrived, followed by a burly guy wheeling a hand truck stacked with boxes of diapers, infant formula, cold remedies, over-the-counter drugs, feminine hygiene products, and other necessities that were in short supply.

The elderly man in charge of dispensing supplies had run out from behind the table and faced up to the pair like a bantam rooster. He'd gotten as far as telling the man in the cashmere overcoat that he could turn around and take those boxes right back where they came from, when the refugee center director had trotted up and pulled him away. They'd held a hushed but heated conversation, which resulted in the elderly man stalking away in disgust and the director returning to bow and apologize and thank the man in the overcoat for his generous and desperately needed donations. Later she'd found out that this happened after every disaster—yakuza gangsters were often on the spot with relief supplies before anyone else, demonstrating how well they took care of the citizens in their territory.

Head throbbing, teeth aching, she nodded to the desk volunteers and scurried through the changing area to the town square.

Yumi felt terrible asking for supplies donated to help the refugees, but she was desperate. She got in line. A young mother with a baby in a sling stepped up to the table and requested disposable diapers. The next man in line said he was out of toothpaste. Six more people, then it would be her turn. Infant formula . . . batteries . . . diapers again . . . laundry detergent . . . headache pills . . .

Yumi looked up as the boy in the Hanshin Tigers cap thanked the volunteer and accepted a handful of Bufferin packets, hurrying toward the nearby bathrooms. Wait, wasn't that *Flame*?

"What do you need, dear?"

"Oh, uh, sorry," Yumi stammered, tearing her eyes away. "I—I'm coming down with a cold and I have a terrible sinus headache. Do you have anything that might help?"

The woman looked at her with sympathy and said, "I'm sure we do. Let me check." She turned and shifted a few of the boxes stacked behind the table, then triumphantly came up with a handful of single-dosage packets.

"How many do you need?"

Keenly aware she wasn't a refugee, she said "Three should do it. I'll come again tomorrow if I need more. Thank you."

She pocketed them and crossed to the tea station nearest the bathrooms to pour herself a glass of water. Dry-swallowing the pills, she chased them with the water, keeping an eye on the entrance to the men's room.

The "boy" in the Tigers hat came out and looked around, then headed straight toward her, checking phone messages.

He'd ditched the rainbow afro. Buzzed hair, shiny gold high-tops, and . . . yes, red showing at the edge of the dark hoodie sleeve as the guitarist chose a cup and splashed hot green tea into it.

He carried the cup to a nearby table and sat down, watching something on his phone.

Yumi got herself a cup of tea. The idol didn't look up as she settled herself across the table.

"Hi. My name is Yumi Hata. I know who you are." She paused, then added, "Flame."

The guitarist froze, then pasted on a smile and said, "Flame? Hey, thanks for the compliment. I wish I could play like her. Weren't you with Risa at the Tinderbox 'live' last night?"

"Yeah. But I was also at the Bagus net café in Shibuya when that *Look!Look!* video aired and you ran for your life. I've been following you ever since."

A hunted look appeared in Flame's eyes.

"But not because I'm a fan," Yumi said quickly. "I mean, I am, but that's not why I was following you. I think you're in danger. The detective who's in charge of the Tabata Shrine investigation thinks Jimmy Harajuku killed Head Priest Yano, then he killed Taku. He thinks you're next."

The guitarist stared. "Who's Taku?"

"The guitarist who stood in for you on the 'Kiss Me, Kill Me' single. He was the fuzzed out guy on *LookLook!* who was responsible for putting that camera team on your trail. Jimmy couldn't let Taku do any more to sabotage the moneymaking machine he set up to profit from your 'death,' so he killed him." Yumi paused. "But you're an even bigger danger to his plans than Taku was."

Flame stared. "What are you, a cop?"

"No. But the detective in charge of investigating Head Priest Yano's murder is a childhood friend of mine. He says—"

"Let me guess," Flame interrupted. "Your friend the detective wants me to turn myself in, right? And you're chasing me because you 'just want to help'?"

"I . . ."

Flame leaned into the table. "Well, let me tell you something, sister. If I really am who you think I am, you'll realize that the only way you can really help me is by walking away and forgetting what you think you know. Flame is dead. Dead. And you're wrong about Jimmy. He's not after me. Not anymore. I'm not going to explain, but believe me when I tell you he got what he wanted, and as long as Flame stays dead, I've got nothing to fear from him."

Yumi shook her head. "You'll never be safe as long as Jimmy Harajuku thinks you have that Polaroid."

Flame went deadly still. "What Polaroid?"

"The one of a half-naked girl standing in front of a bathtub in that creepy penthouse bathroom of Jimmy's. It was hidden in Head Priest Yano's sleeve when he died."

"It wasn't with the rest?"

"No the police have it."

Flame digested that, frowning. "How do you know where it was taken?"

"I'm staying there right now."

Flame's eyes narrowed. "You don't look like one of his idols. And the only crew he allows into his penthouse are people whose careers would be destroyed if they crossed him. Who are you? Whose side are you on?"

"Yours," Yumi insisted. "The reason I'm staying at Jimmy's penthouse is that I'm interpreting for Blade, the Exit Strategy guitarist who's joining the VuDu Dolls on stage tomorrow night for the benefit concert."

"So you're in Blade's entourage, not Jimmy's?" Flame frowned, wheels turning. "And you're staying at Jimmy's Odaiba place? Right now?"

A ball bounced off Flame's back, kicked by a small boy who ran up, apologized breathlessly, then continued chasing it through the eating area.

"Maybe there *is* something you can do to help me," Flame said. "But let's go somewhere we won't be interrupted."

Yumi thought for a moment, then said, "How about the baths? This time of day, only a few old grannies will be using the ones on the women's side."

"The baths? You're kidding, right? They'd kick me out of the women's locker room faster than you can say 'upskirt photo.'"

"Look," Yumi said, "you don't have to pretend with me. I know you're a girl."

Flame threw his head back and laughed. "No. I'm not."

•

When Flame appeared in one of the cotton kimonos everybody wore while taking a sand bath, he caught Yumi looking at his bare arm, which was mottled with a strawberry birthmark.

"Not many people have seen me without my glove," he said. "Now you know why."

They lay down in the trenches that had been prepared for them and allowed the burly attendant to shovel hot sand onto them up to their necks. When he'd tamped it around them to his satisfaction, he told them he'd return in fifteen minutes unless they called for him sooner.

"So . . . how did you pretend to be a girl all those years?" Yumi asked. "And why?"

Flame sighed and let his head fall back on his sand "pillow."

"The 'how' wasn't that hard—I never had much of a beard, so a few laser treatments took care of that. And learning to shave my legs wasn't any harder for me than it was for you. But why? That's another story."

He closed his eyes.

"I never knew my dad. My mom raised me alone, but she wasn't a very traditional Japanese mother. I pretty much raised myself while she was off protesting her *cause*." The edge on that last word made Yumi glance at the guitarist's face, but Flame looked more sad then resentful.

"While I was growing up, we lived here and there, never in one place for long. Then Mom was arrested for sabotaging a nuclear plant when I was fifteen, so I decided to try and find my father.

"I didn't know anything about him except that he'd been a musician, but had quit his band to become a priest. My mother refused to tell me his name, said the past was dead, that he had no place for me in his life and I should to stay in school and live with her friend's family until I graduated. But I thought that if I was going to have a future playing in a band, there was no point wasting time learning math and studying *kanji*. I left a note for the family I was staying with, telling them not to worry, that I'd decided to go live with my father. I didn't tell them I had no idea how to find him.

"A month later, I'd made five thousand yen playing my guitar in Yoyogi Park, but spent nearly all my savings on food and a cheap room. I learned pretty quickly that girls made better tips than boys and the park patrolmen were a lot nicer about letting them perform without a permit, so I got myself a pigtailed wig and some skirts from a secondhand store. By the time my money ran low, everybody at the park knew me as a girl, and so did the woman who took me to the shelter for runaways. Good thing, too, because the boys' rooms were all filled up, but they had a couple of beds free on the girls' side. I found a public bath in another neighborhood to go to instead of using the one at the shelter, so all the time I stayed there, nobody ever saw me without my clothes on. And lucky for me, the shelter attracted a lot of girls who'd washed out of the music biz, some of them pretty decent musicians.

"I hooked up with a drummer and a bass player and a singer who wanted to start over and give it another go. We played in Yoyogi Park on weekends, and got our big break when Jimmy heard us and offered us a debut."

He paused, then said, "But if I was going to play for his label, I had to keep pretending to be a girl. So I had to decide.

"By then I'd found my father. Or rather, he'd found me, he just didn't know it. I guess my mother broke down and wrote to him from jail after I left that note, because he came to the shelter with a picture, looking for me. I knew right away who he was, because even though he was old, if you imagined him with long bleached hair, he still looked like the picture my mother kept at the very back of her underwear drawer. I decided to get to know him and find out what kind of person he was before telling him that the girl in the band he was helping was really his son.

"Then we got the offer from Jimmy's Top Talent and I had to choose: live at a shrine with my dad and go back to being a boy, or get a major debut as a girl." He shook his head and laughed bitterly. "Took me about thirty seconds, especially once my father tried to talk us out of accepting the offer, calling Jimmy a bad guy."

"But he was right, wasn't he?"

Flame snorted. "In spades. Ironically, I might have been the only kid he ever made famous who was safe from his . . . attentions. Fortunately for me, he was so busy with our major debut that he didn't find out I was a boy until it was too late and our faces were all over the newsstands."

"How did he find out?"

"Well, you know he changed all the members of the VuDu Dolls but me before we had our debut, right? Back then, Nana was Jimmy's flavor of the month. I knew because we shared a room and Jimmy was always bringing her little presents, letting her choose where we ate, taking her side when she picked a fight with one of us. And . . ." He flicked a glance at Yumi. ". . . when we went to the Top Talent studio to record, we stayed at the Odaiba penthouse. Nana got to use the big bath in Jimmy's private bathroom instead of taking showers like the rest of us. So I had the bathroom we shared to myself, mostly. Until we went on the road for our first big tour. The first night after our concert, Nana walked in on me just as I was getting out of the shower. She was totally shocked, but she didn't scream or anything. She just stood there, staring, then she said, 'You're so lucky. You'll never be his favorite, looking like that.'"

Flame fell silent, then he sighed. "Instead of asking what she meant, I just begged her not to tell Jimmy. She sort of laughed and said not to worry, that she wasn't about to throw away all her hard work just when it was finally starting to pay off. She was the one who let the others in on the secret and talked them into helping me hide the fact I was a boy. Once we had this big shared secret, I stopped hating them for replacing the girls from the shelter. They became my new best friends." He laughed. "We actually started playing a lot better together after that. And Jimmy might never have found out if he hadn't taken a temporary fancy to me when Nana went back to her family one weekend for her grandmother's funeral."

Flame grimaced. "The first night Nana was gone, Jimmy invited me to take a bath in his suite upstairs and wouldn't take no for an answer. I discovered too late that there was no lock on the door, and as soon as I was undressed and had finished washing before getting into the tub, Jimmy appeared with his Polaroid camera."

Flame gave a grim laugh. "The look on his face! But at the time, of course, it wasn't funny. I was scared shitless that he'd toss me out of the band.

"But we were the first artists Jimmy was making real money off of, so after he calmed down, he didn't cut bait like he did later when Kiri-*chan* crossed him. He told me not to make my mother sorry she'd signed the contract, and threatened to kill me if I ever let anybody outside the band find out I wasn't a girl.

"After that, he came up with the idea that one of my 'trademarks' would be that I never spoke, so when my voice changed, it wouldn't give away my secret. From that day on, even when the band was interviewed or appeared on a variety show, Nana did my talking for me. Weirdly, when it became known that I never spoke, talk show hosts started competing with each other, trying to be the first to trick me into saying something.

"It wasn't until much later that I really thought about Jimmy and that Polaroid camera and realized what Nana meant when she said I was lucky I'd never be Jimmy's favorite. I tried to talk to her, but she refused. I think she was so ashamed, she couldn't even admit to herself what was going on. But after that, I always looked out for her, covered for her when she sneaked out to meet boys she wasn't supposed to be meeting, took care of her when she was sick as a dog after drinking too much, told Jimmy she had a fever when actually she was just sleeping in after being out all night."

"So why did you suddenly decide to call it quits?"

"It wasn't sudden. I'd been thinking about it for a long time. But Jimmy told us a month ago that our fan base wasn't growing anymore, so it was time to go on a world tour and boost our sales outside Japan. We were scheduled to be on the road for almost a year and I just . . . I just couldn't take it anymore."

He sighed. "For ten years I played the music the Top Talent hacks churned out. Jimmy would never let us try anything new, even though I kept giving him the music I was writing in my spare time. Not that we needed much new material anyway—we were recording less and less, and Jimmy couldn't have been happier. He pays our salaries, but keeps the rights to all our songs and gets all the money from our sponsorships. The less time we spent playing music and the more time we spent selling toothpaste, the richer he got.

"I woke up on my twenty-sixth birthday, dreading the party scheduled for that night. I knew I'd have to wear my sponsor's watch, pull up to the event in my sponsor's car, and pretend that self-absorbed, has-been Kengo was the love of my life. I was twenty-six years old, but I'd never had a girlfriend, never been on a real date. The only time I'd ever been kissed was when I was seventeen. I covered my long hair with a boy-style wig and sneaked out to a club in Osaka. I ended up making out with a girl who didn't recognize me, who probably regretted it the rest of her life because someone shot a picture of us and it got reposted all over the Internet along with rumors that Flame from the VuDu Dolls was a lesbian.

"So I decided to get out. But I knew it wouldn't be easy. Partly because Jimmy wouldn't let me out of my contract as long as he was making money off me, but mostly because I'd be killing the VuDu Dolls if I left. I tried to talk to them about it, suggested we all quit together and start fresh, use my new songs and start our own label, but they said Jimmy would kill us. I thought they just meant professionally, but I guess I was wrong about that."

"You mean he tried?"

Flame nodded. "A month after I walked out, taking Jimmy's collection of bathtime Polaroids with me for insurance, he tracked me down. I was working with my father at the shrine, and I'd never been happier in my life. I should have known it couldn't last."

"So Head Priest Yano knew you were his son?"

Flame nodded, then blinked rapidly as tears filled his eyes. "He was so happy when I told him. He said he'd followed my career, ever since we met at the shelter. That knowing just one homeless kid's dream had come true was what kept him coming back to help, even on the days when it seemed hopeless. He knew all our songs. He wasn't mad that I'd chosen Jimmy over him all those years ago, admitted he'd have done the same thing in my place.

"He's the one who came up with the idea of shaving my head and becoming an 'intern' at his shrine until Jimmy stopped looking for me. Said it had worked for him years ago, that nobody had recognized him without his hair.

"So I did it. Started working at the shrine, learning what it was like to live a normal life." Flame looked off into the distance. "But I didn't really know my dad until the night he played a riff on my old Martin guitar, and suddenly I felt closer to him than to anyone in my whole life. We were practically strangers, but we played the same way! I'd taught myself to play when I was a kid because my mom had that old Martin just sitting around. She never told me it had belonged to him, never told me he used to play for Meatsnake. I never met anybody else who used the same weird fingering, and both of us came up with it on our own!

"But that's not all we had in common. My dad totally understood why I wanted to start over. He knew what the life was like, said he'd watched his old bandmates destroy themselves and the only people who ever ended up happy were the ones with their own labels who controlled their own destinies. He offered to help me."

Flame shifted slightly, making cracks in the sand packed on top of him. "When I left Jimmy, I couldn't take my savings out of the bank because it would tip him off that I was up to something. I'd hidden some cash to get myself safely away to somewhere Jimmy couldn't find me, but I didn't have anywhere near enough to set up my own label. I thought I'd have to start from scratch, get myself discovered again by a different promoter, using a different name.

"Then my father showed me a bankbook, told me he'd been saving money for me ever since I was born. It wasn't quite enough to start a recording studio, but he said that as head priest, he could sell off some of the dusty old stuff in that treasure house and use the cash to start something that would pay off a lot better for our family than making endless repairs to an old shrine that barely broke even.

"I helped him make a list of the stuff that was stored in the treasure house, and he got in touch with some people who were falling all over themselves to pay tons of money for it. Then . . . Jimmy found me."

"How?"

"He's got this nephew. When the little creep dropped out of school, Jimmy's sister badgered Jimmy into letting him be his driver. Everybody started calling him Ninjaboy when it turned out his real talent was sneaking around and spying on people. Made a lot of coin off of Jimmy's latest girl band by threatening to tell Jimmy that the vocalist has a boyfriend in Shibuya she's been calling allergy treatments, and Baby8's star dancer can't get out of bed in the morning before she has a handful of pills to make facing the world bearable.

"So Jimmy sicced him on me. I managed to fly under his radar until two Sundays ago in Yoyogi Park. It was getting dark and pretty much everybody had gone home, so I was just fooling around on my guitar. Without thinking, I ended up goofing on the intro to 'Don't Need You.' The next day, someone blogged that they'd heard a guitarist in Yoyogi Park who played just like Flame."

He grimaced. "Jimmy's errand boy read it, and the next Sunday he started lurking around the park. He followed me to the *manga* café where I was crashing. Jimmy was on the road with Baby8, but he told Ninjacreep not to let me out of his sight. That Friday, I played an all-night club thing, and when I finally dragged myself back to the *manga* café the next morning, Jimmy was waiting for me."

Another bead of sweat rolled down Yumi's forehead into her hair. The attendant returned. It was time to get out of the hot sand.

"Tea?" Yumi suggested.

After showering and dressing, they met up at tables near the restaurant area that Yumi knew would remain deserted until the stroke of twelve. The refugees clung to small vestiges of their former lives—including a lunch hour that spanned from exactly twelve to exactly one—even though the reasons for it had been cast adrift along with all their worldly possessions.

Yumi set down her teacup and the glass of water she'd poured for herself, popping open her second packet of painkillers. The headache was beginning to return. She washed down the tablet, then turned to Flame and asked, "So what did you do when you saw Jimmy at the *manga* café, waiting for you?"

Wrapping his hands around his warm cup, Flame hunched into his hoodie. "I backed away, hoping he hadn't seen me, but Jimmy said, 'Don't even think of it. I'll just find you again, and next time I might not be in such a reasonable mood. Sit down. Let's talk about this. I'm sure we can come to an agreement.'"

Flame took a sip of tea. "So I sat down. That's when I noticed that none of my stuff was lying around the way I'd left it. He'd gone through everything in the cubicle, then packed it into my duffel bag. I told him he'd wasted his time, because I wasn't coming back. He said that was a pity, because he'd decided that in addition to the world tour he was planning to send the VuDu Dolls on, he'd looked into booking solo dates for me in the same cities we were visiting.

"For a minute I was tempted. Then I reminded myself there was nothing he could offer me that was better than setting up my own label. I told him his offer was too little, too late, that he'd have to find another guitarist for the VuDu Dolls."

Flame laughed bitterly. "I can't believe I was so naive. I even told him I wanted my songs back. All except the one they'd just recorded, 'Kiss Me, Kill Me.' I told him the VuDu Dolls could have that one as a good-bye gift."

"I thought you said Jimmy never used any of the songs you wrote."

"I know, right? I was shocked when I heard it playing at a café. He'd never recorded anything I'd given him. It's kind of ironic Jimmy didn't produce anything of mine until after I was 'dead,' but when he saw it was selling faster than anything the VuDu Dolls had ever released, he realized what a goldmine he was sitting on. The fans were voting with their pocketbooks, and me being 'dead' meant he could serve up this new sound with a new guitarist. The old fans would stay out of loyalty to my memory and new fans would be attracted because of the music.

"So when I asked for my songs back, he laughed. Then he said, 'Tell you what—I'll give you the rights to the songs you wrote while you were on my payroll if you give me the things you stole from me before you left.'"

"Did he mean . . . the Polaroids?"

"Yeah. I told him I had no intention of giving them back, that they were my insurance. I told him that I knew he could get me blackballed from the music industry, but if he ever interfered with the label my father and I were setting up, he'd find himself back in court, and this time there would be evidence he couldn't talk his way out of."

"What did he say to that?"

"He just sat there for a minute, then he . . . he pulled out a gun.

"I was scared shitless. I've seen guns on TV plenty of times, but it's different when the thing is pointed right at you. He asked me where I'd hidden the pictures. And then . . . then I made a terrible mistake."

He closed his eyes and swallowed. "I told him they were somewhere safe. That if anything happened to me, the person who had them would take him down. I told him to leave us alone, that I wouldn't hurt him as long as he didn't get in my way."

Flame hung his head.

"I didn't realize I'd just signed my father's death warrant. Jimmy put away his gun and said, 'I'll be waiting for you outside. When you come out, I'm going to follow you. From now on, someone will always be following you. Eventually you are going to lead me to whoever has those pictures, and unless you want something very bad to happen to that person, you'll give them back.' Then he put the gun away and left."

Flame took a ragged breath. "I sat there shaking, afraid to go to work, afraid Jimmy would follow me to the shrine, wondering how I was ever going out get out from under his thumb. I'd been up all night, so I wasn't thinking very clearly. It took me nearly half an hour to realize that even if Jimmy was waiting for me outside, he couldn't watch the front and back exits at the same time. I took the elevator down to the parking garage, and sure enough, no Jimmy. I ran to the train station and caught the next one to Tabata, planning to get the pictures back from my dad and hide them somewhere else, somewhere they wouldn't put him in danger. I got to the shrine around eight thirty, knowing my dad would be awake by then, but nobody else would be at work yet."

He swallowed. "That's why I was surprised when I saw a priest letting himself out the gate at my father's house. He was carrying a trash bag. Then I noticed he was wearing summer robes and I saw my Oricon Award in the bag with the trash, and I knew. Even before he was close enough for me to see his face, I knew. I hid behind the little shrine by the treasure house and took a picture of him with my phone as he passed on his way to the back entrance. Then I ran to my father's house, praying that he'd handed over my stuff without resisting.

"When I got to his house, the front door was unlocked. I went in and--" Flame swiped at his eyes. "He was dead. My dad was dead." He took a ragged breath. "I knew right away because there was a big . . . his head was all bloody. I ran to the kitchen to look for the stuff I'd given him for safekeeping, but Jimmy had dumped out all the drawers. My Oricon Award and my photo album with the envelope of Polaroids taped in the back weren't there. I ran upstairs, hoping dad had moved them to his room. But they weren't there either, so I grabbed my old guitar and ran."

He stared down into his teacup. "I didn't know what to do or where to go. I just ran. I hadn't had any sleep for twenty-four hours, so the first night I crashed at a karaoke box in Shinjuku. The next morning I woke up and it really hit me: I'd killed my father. It was all my fault. The minute I told

Jimmy that I'd left those pictures with someone I trusted, Jimmy knew exactly who it was. He didn't need to wait outside the café to follow me to the shrine. He already knew where it was. He just wanted to make me afraid of going out, to give himself a head start. He must have gone straight to the shrine and demanded my father give him the pictures back." Flame buried his head in his hands. "And when he wouldn't, Jimmy killed him."

"But he didn't get them all," Yumi said. "How long will it take for Jimmy to realize one is missing?"

"There were only eleven. He'd know right away. Which one do the police have?"

"I didn't get a good look at her face, but she was wearing pink Hello Kitty underpants."

Flame groaned. "It's the one of Nana. If the media get ahold of that . . . Are you sure Jimmy doesn't know that the police have it?"

Yumi thought for a moment, trying to recall what Kenji had said. "I don't know."

"Can you find out? I need to know how much danger I'm in. If Jimmy thinks I have it, he won't be trying to kill me, he'll be trying to get it back. But if he knows the police have it, he'll be trying to get rid of me before they catch me and put me on the witness stand."

Yumi nodded and pulled out her phone. "I'll call Detective Nakamura." She found his number. It rang.

"Nakamura *desu*."

"Ken-*kun*, it's Yumi. I'm working on the thing we talked about last night, but I've got a question. Are you sure Jimmy thinks Taiga has that picture? There's no way he could know it's on your desk in an evidence bag?"

"Not unless he has sources I don't know about."

"You haven't questioned Jimmy yet?"

"On what grounds? We don't have any hard evidence connecting him to that Polaroid or to Head Priest Yano's death. The only fingerprints on the picture belonged to the guitarist and the victim. Which is why," he reminded her, "we're chasing Taiga. So if you hear anything..."

"I'll call you right away," Yumi lied, feeling a pang of guilt that she was breaking her word before it was even out of her mouth.

"So Jimmy doesn't know the police have it," Flame confirmed as she ended the call.

Yumi nodded.

"I have to get it back," he said. "The only way I'll ever be safe is if I get that Polaroid back from the police and give it to Jimmy, then convince him that I don't want Flame brought back to life any more than he does."

Yumi shook her head. "The only way you'll ever be safe is if Jimmy's in jail. You've got to tell Detective Nakamura you saw Jimmy at the shrine that morning and give him the picture you took."

Flame laughed bitterly. "And after he says 'thank you very much' and calls Jimmy in for 'voluntary questioning,' Jimmy will know the police have the Polaroid and they're going to make me testify against him. Then while they prance around trying to sell their case to the prosecutor, Jimmy hires someone to hunt me down with his new black gun, and *bam bam*—no witness, case closed."

"No, listen to me," Yumi said. "If you turn yourself in, the police will protect you. They wouldn't let anything happen to a star witness."

"Tell that to the DJ at the Million Club. Don't you read the papers? He was going to testify against Koji Yamamoto a couple of months ago, until they found him face down in an alley."

Yumi's phone buzzed in her pocket. This was the third time in the past twenty minutes. She sighed and pulled it out, checking the caller ID. Chiho, Chiho, Chiho.

"Excuse me a minute." She returned the call, listened,

then said, "*Hai*," and hung up.

"They need me back on set," she said reluctantly. "Stranger is going to be out in the parking lot in five minutes, and if I'm not waiting for him, he'll come looking."

Flame grabbed her arm. "You're not going to tell anybody about me, are you?"

"No." She looked him in the eye. "If anything happened to you, I'd never forgive myself. Let me think this through. There has to be a way we can take Jimmy down without putting you in danger. How can I contact you?"

"I've got this prepaid." Flame showed her his phone. "Here's the number."

•

Kenji and Aya stood at the information counter at the Wangan Police Station with their IDs out, waiting for someone to direct them to the detective section so they could pay a courtesy call on their counterparts in Odaiba. Although they all worked for the Tokyo Metropolitan Police, it would be a big mistake to conduct any sort of investigation on another station's turf without their knowledge.

Besides, Kenji thought, he and Aya might need their help. It wasn't going to be easy to find a celebrity guitarist who so far had eluded capture by the police, the media, and thousands of fans.

He and Aya had pored over fan sites on the Internet after studying the video Takki had discovered. Pictures tagged "Flame" numbered in the thousands, from cosplay look-alikes to photos of peoples' dogs wearing platinum wigs and a lace glove. None of the so-called memorabilia was authentic enough to help them track down where the guitarist might be holed up.

"Can I help you?" A harried-looking female officer repinned a loose strand of hair as she stepped up to the counter.

Kenji introduced himself and Aya, and told her they were there to check in with whoever was in charge of the Major Crimes Section. Her eyebrows shot up and she asked what kind of major crime he'd come all the way out to Odaiba to investigate, and when he told her, her nose wrinkled as if he'd just dropped a week-old fish on the counter.

"You'll be wanting Section Chief Honda, then. Fourth floor. Don't tell him I sent you."

"Why?" Aya asked.

"In case you hadn't noticed, we've had a bit of a natural disaster out here. But that didn't stop some idiot from deciding to stage a big benefit concert tomorrow night at Zepp Tokyo, with God knows how many celebrities and their entourages who'll need security both coming and going. Honda's had a full plate just trying to get on top of the crimes people thought they could get away with under cover of the earthquake, then today it was announced that every warm body in every department is being diverted to deal with this event. He's not in what I'd call a good mood."

Aya nodded. "Understood. We'll buckle on our body armor."

The woman gave her a tired smile and wished them luck.

The elevator doors opened on the fourth floor, and the squad room they stepped into looked disconcertingly familiar. The home of the Wangan detective team was laid out the same as the one in Komagome, and the only difference between Section Chief Honda's desk and Section Chief Tanaka's was that Honda had a judo figure on his trophy instead of a golfer.

Kenji and Aya waited a respectful distance from the section chief's desk until he finished conducting a heated phone conversation with someone about why there would be no patrol cars available at all after four o'clock tomorrow. He ended the call angrily, but jabbing at a touch screen hadn't been nearly as satisfying as slamming a receiver into its cradle, so now he was looking around for a new target. He settled on

Kenji and Aya.

"Who are you and what do you want?"

Kenji stepped up and offered his name, rank, and ID. The section chief's scowl deepened when he heard the name Jimmy Harajuku.

"Can't this wait until next week? Or next year? Or never?" he barked, warming to his subject. "Sato!" he called to a beefy detective who was just returning to his desk. "Tell these detectives from Komagome how successful everybody's been in the past, trying to pin something on Jimmy Harajuku."

"Don't waste your time," Detective Sato said, joining them. "And don't waste ours."

"We know he's escaped prosecution any number of times, and that he got off the last time he was taken to court. But this time we've got proof."

"I'll believe that when I see it," scoffed Sato.

Kenji drew the evidence bag with the picture of Nana from his pocket and set it on Honda's desk. Sato's eyebrows shot up and he said, "Where did you get this and how do you know it's his?"

Kenji told them it had been found on the body of a murder victim in Tabata, and the kid in the picture was the vocalist from Jimmy's most famous band, the VuDu Dolls.

"And who's going to stand up in court and testify to that, since it's unlikely you can call your witness back from the dead?"

"That's why we're looking for Flame."

"Isn't she dead, too?"

"We intend to find out."

Honda and Sato looked at each other, then Honda said, "I'd like to help you, but you're catching us at a bad time. I can't give you any backup until we get rid of the plague of VIPs that's about to descend on us like a swarm of locusts. If you could delay any fireworks until Sunday, it would be greatly appreciated."

"We'll do our best," Kenji said.

Honda and Sato both handed him their cards. Honda said, "Keep me informed."

"Will do." They exchanged bows, then Kenji and Aya retreated to the elevators.

"Looks like we're on our own," Kenji said as they descended to the first floor and made for the revolving glass doors.

"Which could be a good thing," Aya said. "Did you notice the picture on Sato's desk as we left? It was of him and his son posing at some music awards thing with a 'The Kid's Got Talent' banner hanging over their heads. Guess who was handing the kid first prize? Jimmy Harajuku."

•

"Kiss me. Or kill me. Without you, I'm better off dead," sang Nana, pulling a black gun. The holster was strapped over her artfully slashed black leather pants, and featured an unnecessary number of silver buckles. Straight-arming it with a twist she'd learned from watching American hip-hop videos, she pointed it at the audience.

"Cut, cut, cut!" the director cried. "Nana, that was *chō-primo*. But Blade, man, how many times do I have to tell you? Can't you play without making that face?" He turned to Yumi, exasperated. "Didn't you explain it to him last time I asked? Every time he gets to that part, he looks like he's about to howl at the moon."

"I tried!" Yumi shot back. "He can't help it. He said he gets lost in the music, stops thinking about what he looks like and just plays."

"Yeah, well, tell him to just fake the guitar shit on this next take and think about looking like Nana's hotshot backup posse instead. We can put the guitar track back in later."

Yumi picked her way through the pile of rubble the band

was standing on. It was all that was left of Jimmy's studio. Chiho and her assistants had scoured the wreckage, picking up mangled mike stands, disemboweled speakers, a twisted sound board with wires hanging out, and other muddy, smashed equipment that had once been state of the art. They'd half buried the junk in an artful postapocalyptic way among the band members, who'd been furnished with instruments that worked just fine but had been "distressed" to match the artifacts rescued from the wreckage.

"I know, I know, my face," Blade grimaced as Yumi approached.

"Can you fake the guitar on this next take?" Yumi asked. "The director says he can lay the music back in later."

Blade shook his head. "The fingering won't match. I play it a little different each time."

Yumi returned to the director and explained. He cursed under his breath, and shouted for Blade and the bass player to switch places, so the guitarist would be less distracting during Nana's big gun finale.

"I want your best 'don't eff with me' face," he directed the bass player. "Let's get it right in one." She nodded and tugged some slack cord over to her new position.

"Okay, one more time, from the top," the director called. He bent over the cameraman's shoulder, peering into the digital display. Then he straightened and called to a tech guy on the sidelines. "Hey, fix the corner of the damn blue screen, will you?"

The tech scurried on set and retied the corner of the special blue tarp that had been stretched between supports behind the band. Chiho took advantage of the break to flit between the musicians, touching up the powder on their shiny noses and tweaking Nana's hair, fixing it with a mist of superhard hairspray.

When she returned to the sidelines, Yumi asked why they'd blocked the destruction behind the band for this take and Chiho explained that Eva would use this one to make the video that would play behind the band on stage tomorrow night. She'd lay in the digital effects she'd been working on yesterday over the blue screen, so it looked like the band playing in the video was backed by a wall of flames. When Nana pulled the trigger, fire would explode from the gun on screen and morph into hearts that would fly toward the audience.

"That should be memorable," Yumi said.

"Yeah, well, it better be, for all the trouble it's caused me. Jimmy liked Eva's demo so much yesterday, it gave him an idea for a crazy stunt to pull at the concert tomorrow night. I owe favors all over Tokyo now, trying to get my hands on four snow-white suits, including one that will fit a foreigner. Jimmy is in the process of bullying the concert producer into installing a bank of pyrotechnics. He wants to shoot a wall of flames in front of the band as they play the final chord. While they're hidden behind the fire, they'll rip off their 'refugee' duds and be standing there dressed in pure white when the pyro shuts off for the curtain call. Poor Shiro has been working his fingers to the bone, altering all the costumes so they have tearaway backs."

The director shouted, "Okay, everybody ready now? Let's try this one more time."

Nana tucked the gun back into her holster and the VuDu Dolls launched into their latest hit single.

"Is that a real gun?" Yumi asked.

"Are you kidding? It's an air gun. I bought it at a toy store in Ueno. But it looks real, doesn't it?"

"Fooled me. Of course, I've never seen a real one."

"Yeah, well, neither have the fans. But that didn't keep Jimmy from being a real asshole about it. He tore me a new one because the store didn't have the brand he asked for, so even though I brought back three others for him to choose from, he made me call the store and do a special order, rush. I have to be waiting at the front door when they open tomorrow, then hand carry it back here so Nana can use it at the concert."

In front of the blue tarp, Nana raised one of the rejected air guns as she sang the last lines of "Kiss Me, Kill Me." The last chord faded and the director yelled, "Cut, cut, cut!" but Jimmy was already climbing the rubble toward Nana, telling her she needed to pull up after firing so it looked real. He took the gun from her and pointed it at the audience, showing her how to fake a recoil. He made her do it a few times until she got it right, then rejoined the director behind the cameraman.

The band began to play "Kiss Me, Kill Me" one more time, and Yumi felt her phone buzz in her pocket. She snatched it out to look at the caller ID, thinking it might be Kenji. But it wasn't. The call was from the Mitsuyama house in Hiroo. She'd have to call back later when she had more privacy.

This time Nana pulled the gun like a pro, the final chord faded, and Jimmy smiled when he watched the replay. He straightened and clapped his hands.

"Okay! Everybody! This time you nailed it. That's it for this afternoon. *O-tsukare-sama deshita*. Dinner at my place on the tenth floor at seven."

Everybody relaxed, high-fived, and began to pack up.

Yumi walked away to listen to Mrs. Mitsuyama's voicemail.

"I hope this call finds you well, Yumi-*san*. It's so kind of you to help the suffering people in the tsunami zone. Speaking of the tsunami zone, I heard this morning that the Rinkai Line is running again, and I was wondering when you might be returning from Odaiba? My husband and son and I would like to fix a time to sit down with you and your family for our important discussion. Please call me when you have a chance."

Yumi slowly lowered the phone. The wheels were in motion. She was about to become officially unengaged.

She'd been so caught up in the hunt for Flame, she hadn't had time to think about Ichiro or her own future very much in the past few days. She knew she'd be happier after it was all over, but getting through the actual breakup was going to be painful. Would Ichiro take responsibility and apologize for ending their relationship, or would he say, "It is regrettable that . . ."? Would Mr. Mitsuyama fund her father's history chair until he found another sponsor, or would he try to walk away the minute Ichiro's connection to Yumi was broken?

"Hey, Yumi, there's room for one more in the van!" Chiho called.

"Coming."

Squeezing into the white van between Chiho and Shiro, she sent e-mail to Mrs. Mitsuyama, promising to call when she returned from Odaiba the day after tomorrow.

•

Privacy was in short supply that night at Jimmy's penthouse, crowded now with the VuDu Dolls, the video crew, and the support staff who'd arrived to work tomorrow's event.

Yumi turned the lock on the bathroom door and returned Flame's call.

"Can you get me into the concert tomorrow?" the guitarist asked without preamble. "Jimmy gave you a pair of comp tickets and backstage passes, didn't he?"

"No. Not yet, anyway."

"Well, he will. If you give one to me and one to that detective friend of yours, after the concert I'll give him the picture of Jimmy at the shrine and tell him what I know." Flame paused. "But I want something in return. If I help him put Jimmy away for killing my father, he has to give me the Polaroid of Nana. I'll give it to Jimmy to get him off my back. Otherwise, I might not be alive to testify. And don't try to tell me the police will protect me—I can't take that chance. Tell your friend the detective: No picture, no deal."

"Okay, I'll try. But . . ." Yumi bit her lip. "The police don't really work that way, you know. They don't cut deals with evidence."

Flame laughed. "You haven't spent much time on the streets of Kabuki-chō have you? The police cut deals all the time. They'll do anything to up their solve rate."

"But that's why they won't give you that Polaroid," Yumi argued. "They'll need it if they're ever going to put Jimmy in jail for taking pictures of underage girls."

"Can't they be satisfied with putting him away for murder?" Flame countered. "I left the VuDu Dolls to start over, but Nana stayed. I can't let my decision put her in danger. As long as the police have that picture, she's in the crosshairs, too—either Jimmy will get rid of her so she can't testify against him, or the police will put her on the stand and ruin her life. Tell your detective friend he has to choose: Put Jimmy away for murder, or try to prosecute for abuse without me."

"Okay," Yumi said. "I'll talk to him. But the minute I tell him you want to make a deal, he'll know I'm in touch with you. He'll want to meet you face to face. What do you want me to say?"

Flame thought for moment, then said, "Tell him I'll meet him outside Zepp Tokyo before the concert to get the Polaroid, then afterward I'll give him everything he needs. But I want that Polaroid first. During the concert it'll be crazy backstage. Everyone will be too busy to pay attention to an extra stagehand. I'll pull Jimmy aside, give him the Polaroid, and convince him Flame is going to stay dead."

"Okay. I'll call you back after I talk to Detective Nakamura."

•

Kenji said goodbye to Yumi and lowered his phone. Then he remembered guiltily that he still hadn't answered the text that had arrived that morning from Kana, flirtatiously suggesting that they meet at the wine bar near Komagome Station so he could pay up for her snooping into Yano's safetly deposit box. He keyed in a reply, explaining he was out on Odaiba and unable to get back. When this case was over, he'd have to figure out how he was going to back away without hurting her feelings.

Switching his attention back to the case, he pushed back through the coffee shop door and returned to the table where Aya was staring out the window, two cups of coffee cooling on the table.

"The good news is, we've found Taiga-slash-Flame," Kenji told her, sliding into his chair. "Or, rather, my friend Yumi did. She says he's got a time-stamped picture on his phone that shows Jimmy Harajuku leaving the scene of Head Priest Yano's murder with a trash bag. She says you can see the music award through the plastic. The bad news is, Flame wants to trade it for that Polaroid we found in the victim's sleeve."

"Why?"

Kenji told her what Yumi had explained about Flame and Nana and the perverse world of music idols.

"So are you going to give it to him?"

"Do you think we should?"

"I think we should ask Detective Oki."

Good idea. Kenji excused himself to go outside and make the call.

When Kenji got to the part of Flame's story where Jimmy threatened him at the *manga* café, Oki said, "Wait, wait, wait. This gun he pulled—what kind was it?"

"I don't know. Yumi didn't say."

"Because if it's a Beretta, it means he hasn't ditched the one he used to kill Taku Shinoda yet. Go on."

Kenji finished telling him about the picture Flame had snapped at the Tabata Shrine the morning Head Priest Yano was killed, and the deal the guitarist had proposed.

"So, what do you think we ought to do?" Kenji asked.

"Fork over that Polaroid, of course," Oki replied without hesitation. "Or, rather, fork over *a* Polaroid."

"What do you mean?"

"Give him a copy."

"There aren't any copies. That's the thing with Polaroids: no negatives. They're one of a kind."

"Not if you take a Polaroid of a Polaroid. The squad doesn't have a camera, but I know there's one in a cold-case box down in the evidence room. I think Inspector Kobayashi is going to be interested enough in connecting Jimmy to that Beretta he'll cut me loose to bring it out to Odaiba. We'll snap a picture of the picture, then you can give it to our new star witness and set the whole trap in motion. As long as what you give Flame fools him and he fools Jimmy, everybody wins."

"Okay," Kenji agreed. "When can you be here?"

"I'll run over to Bic Camera and pick up a pack of film before they close. If I come first thing tomorrow morning, will that be soon enough?"

The concert didn't start until seven at night. Kenji looked up the Rinkai Line schedule on his phone, and said he'd be at Tokyo Teleport Station to meet the 9:07 a.m. train.

Returning to the café, he brought Aya up to speed.

"Now," he concluded, "how are we going to get you and Oki into that concert?"

"We could volunteer to help the Wangan Station detectives with security duty," Aya suggested. "Seems like they might welcome the extra bodies."

Saturday, December 28

•

*11:00 a.m.*

A curtain of fire leaped up in front of the band, cutting off Yumi's view of the Zepp Tokyo arena from her perch next to Blade. The flames abruptly shut off, then leaped up higher, then shut off again.

"We're getting there," Jimmy Harajuku called from his seat in the center of the first-row balcony. "But higher. The wall of fire has to be higher. I can still see the top of Blade's head from up here."

The VuDu Dolls and the Exit Strategy guitarist were standing in position on stage, holding their instruments, but not playing. Because the finale required fine-tuning of the live pyro effects, Jimmy had arranged for them to come in before any of the other bands showed up for sound checks at noon.

"Blade!" Jimmy called to the guitarist. "Move in closer to Nana. I don't want to see the neck of your guitar after that fire turns on."

Yumi explained what Jimmy wanted, then returned to her perch, trying to stay out of the way of the roadies and techs who were laying cables and deciding where the equipment would be staged so the VuDu Dolls could get on as quickly as possible after the artists performing before them.

"'Scuse me, but I gotta put the guitar stands here, so could you scoot over a little?"

"Yeah, sorry," she said to the stagehand who'd appeared,

toting a piece of battered chrome equipment. He must have been on Jimmy's payroll for a long time, because his Jimmy's Top Talent jacket was one of the nice high-end windbreakers from the Love's Eternal Flame tour. Yumi had asked Chiho how she could get one of those instead of the cheap new one she'd been issued, but Chiho said too bad, she'd have to pry one out of the cold dead hands of one of the four crew members who had been on staff eight years ago.

The chief stylist appeared in one of those collector's-item windbreakers now, toting a Yamashiro-ya shopping bag. She looked so cranky Yumi guessed she probably hadn't had time for her morning coffee before making her run to the far side of Tokyo to fetch the special air gun Jimmy had insisted upon.

"Want me to get you a latte?" Yumi offered.

"I'd kiss your feet if you did," Chiho said. "But first can you take care of this while I look for something to open it with? The damn thing is sealed inside one of those plastic packages you need a machete to get into."

She handed the bag to Yumi and disappeared backstage toward the dressing rooms. The toy inside felt heavy enough to be a real gun. Yumi pulled it out. "Beretta M92FS Air Pistol," it said on the front. The detailed metal gun looked deadly real.

Beretta. Yumi glanced up at Jimmy Harajuku, sitting in the balcony. Chiho had said he'd been a real pisser about the make. Why had he been so insistent that the prop gun be a Beretta? Wasn't that the same kind of gun Kenji said the pink-jacketed promoter had bought from a real gun dealer in Kabuki-chō? The kind of gun Taku had been killed with?

She looked at the toy in her hand, then took out her phone and snapped a picture.

"Let's see if this does the trick," Chiho said, reappearing with a wicked-looking utility knife.

Yumi handed her the package and went in search of coffee. She returned with a pair of lattes just in time to see the stylist triumphantly hold up the air gun and stuff the vanquished packaging into the toy shop bag.

Chiho delivered the toy Beretta to Nana, accepted one of the lattes from Yumi with thanks, then said she was going down to the dressing room to help Shiro get the costumes unpacked and steamed. Jimmy could call her cell if he needed her.

"No, no, no, you're aiming too low," Jimmy called to Nana from the balcony as she practiced with the new gun. "Aim up here. In fact, aim straight at me."

The vocalist shaded her eyes against the spotlights. "I can't see you."

Jimmy called for the lighting designer. A tall man wearing a headset appeared and walked to the front of the stage.

"You're going to be raking the audience with spots during 'Kiss Me, Kill Me,' right?" Jimmy confirmed. "Can one of them swing around and hold steady on my seat while Nana sings her last line?"

The lighting designer spoke into his mike and a single spot traced an oval track around the auditorium then stopped on Jimmy. The promoter asked Nana to run through the last stanza a couple of times so they could get the timing right. She did.

"Okay. Now try it with the gun," Jimmy said. "Yeah, much better. That looks like the angle in the video. When you see my pink jacket, take aim, then pull the trigger. Okay, good. Now try that entire last stanza again, and don't forget to fake the recoil this time."

•

Kenji shifted from one foot to the other and his hand strayed to his breast pocket, making sure the original of Nana's Polaroid was still there. He couldn't risk storing it anywhere it could get into the wrong hands.

Resisting the urge to pull the fresh evidence bag with the Polaroid-of-a-Polaroid from his other pocket to reassure himself that the copy he and Oki had shot that morning looked good enough, he took a deep breath instead.

5:50. Where was Yumi? She was late to the rendezvous she'd suggested on the walkway beneath the Ferris wheel.

"Kenji, hi, sorry." Yumi arrived, breathless. "Jimmy grabbed me on my way out and asked me to explain something to Blade."

"Where's Flame?" Kenji asked.

"Coming in ten minutes," Yumi replied." I asked him to meet us in the little courtyard behind Zepp Tokyo, but I wanted to talk to you alone first. Jimmy made the stylist go all the way to Ueno this morning to pick up a Beretta air gun for the VuDu Dolls vocalist to use on stage during the concert. He insisted it be a certain model. Isn't that the kind of gun you told me Jimmy bought in Kabuki-chō?"

"Yes." Kenji frowned. "Why does the singer need an air gun?"

Yumi described the video and the grand finale, how Nana would point the gun at the same time the figure in the video behind shot flaming hearts at the audience.

"How good a replica is it?" Kenji asked.

Yumi showed him the photo of the prop she'd snapped with her phone. Kenji navigated to the one Oki had forwarded to him from the dealer who had sold the real gun to Jimmy.

"Damn close," he muttered, glancing back and forth between them. "The trigger guard on the air gun isn't rounded at the front like the real one, and it looks like the air gun has some extra diagonal chamfering on the barrel, but otherwise . . ."

"You think Jimmy plans to switch the prop for the real one during the concert?" Yumi asked. "But why would he want Nana to fire a real gun into the audience?"

"Who will she be aiming at?"

"That's the weird thing. He told her to aim at where he's sitting," Yumi said. "Up in the balcony. He said he wants it to match the video. So unless he's planning to commit suicide in front of almost three thousand fans . . ."

Her phone rang. She answered it and listened, then said, "Okay" and described where they were standing.

"That was Flame," she said, ending the call. "He says too many people who might recognize him use that courtyard to take tobacco breaks. He'll come find us up here."

A figure with shaggy black hair emerged from the double glass doors of the giant Toyota showroom, and at first Kenji didn't recognize the beautiful androgynous face he'd expected to see with a buzz cut.

He fought the urge to grab him now instead of taking a chance he'd disappear later, but it would be a disaster if the idol made good on his threat to come down with a bad case of memory loss. With Kenji's blessing, Oki had told Inspector Kobayashi that they were going to be taking a statement from a witness who could tie Jimmy Harajuku to the gun that killed Taku Shinoda. Kobayashi had decided to be here for the interview, and was already on his way to Odaiba with his entourage. It would hurt Kenji's career worse than Oki's if he failed to produce the informative witness they'd promised.

Flame stopped in front of them and nodded as Kenji introduced himself, but didn't take the card Kenji offered.

"All I want is that picture," he said.

Kenji reached into his jacket pocket and brought out the evidence bag with the copy in it. He handed it to Flame.

The black-wigged boy looked at it through the plastic, then unzipped the bag and fished it out. But he didn't even glance at the picture of Nana before flipping it over and looking at the back. He scowled.

"Where's the real photo?" he demanded, shaking it in Kenji's face. "This film isn't from Yodabashi Camera! Why are you trying to scam me with a fake!"

He rounded on Yumi. "Did you know about this? I thought you said I could trust this guy! I thought you said he was your friend!"

"Hey," Kenji blurted. "I'm sorry, okay? If my superiors found out I'd given a piece of evidence in a murder case to someone who's still technically a suspect, my career would be over."

"So you're not really in charge of the investigation. You don't have the power to make a deal with me. Who does? Tell me who can give me the picture that'll keep me alive long enough to help them catch my father's killer!"

Kenji's heart sank. Nobody had that power. Not legally. But if Flame didn't give them the photo he'd snapped of Jimmy Harajuku leaving the scene of Yano's murder, the head priest's killer would go free, Inspector Kobayashi would be furious with him for wasting a day of his time coming out to Odaiba for nothing, and Yumi would never trust him again.

What should he do? What would Oki do?

Kenji took a deep breath, then he reached into the breast pocket of his jacket and put his job on the line.

•

Apparently, comp ticket holders were let in last, after all the paying customers. The crowd waiting outside Zepp Tokyo had dwindled to a few hundred hard-core fans, whose devotion had won them free entrance and backstage passes.

Kenji kept a sharp eye on the figure who held his future in his pocket. Flame was standing a few feet away with Yumi's other ticket in hand, pretending they'd never met.

After stowing the genuine Polaroid of Nana in a zippered pants pocket, the idol had been annoyed to discover that Kenji intended to stick to him like glue, even while he was in the nearest men's room, transforming himself into a roadie. He emerged from the stall wearing a black sweatshirt over his black jeans, then stepped up to the mirror, adjusting the spiky, shoulder-length black wig he'd used to hide his buzz cut. He pulled it into a short ponytail in back. Shaking out a black knit cap, he yanked it down over his ears. Finally, he exchanged his gold lamé high-tops for a pair of black Pumas.

Hoisting his duffel onto his shoulder, he'd turned to Kenji. "If you're going to follow me, do a better job than you've been doing so far. A guy dressed like me would have absolutely nothing to do with a guy dressed like you, and if it looks like we're together, every fangirl in that arena is going to wonder why. I need to blend in with the backstage crew and get close to Jimmy without anyone recognizing me, but with you sticking to me like my most unlikely best friend, I'm going to stand out like an eel in a *koi* pond."

"B one hundred through B two hundred," announced the man in the Zepp Tokyo Staff jacket, flipping over a new card on the sign he held. "Ticket numbers B one hundred through two hundred."

Kenji joined the scrum, keeping an eye on Flame's head bobbing amid the fangirls ahead. Kenji handed the door staff ticket B126, and then paused to peel the paper off his backstage pass sticker and slap it on the front of his jacket. Flame was standing amid the crush of fans waiting to show their tickets to the usher at the top of the aisle leading down to the stage. Inside, fans were excusing themselves along the rows as they found their seats, but Flame continued toward a discreet door beside the stage labeled, "Private, Staff Only."

Kenji followed him through it, two fans behind, and had a moment of panic before he spotted Flame among the other roadies and techs, the only man in black standing around empty-handed.

Jimmy Harajuku appeared, his pink jacket and red-trimmed face mask a beacon. He'd just come up the stairs from the dressing rooms with Yumi and a wild-haired foreigner. Flame hovered behind a nearby bank of speakers, awaiting his chance.

Jimmy turned to go, and Flame scrambled to catch up to the promoter as he disappeared back down the stairs.

Kenji followed them into the bowels of the building. The stairway led to a hallway lined with dressing room doors, each with a paper sign taped alongside, bearing the names of the Top Talent artists assigned to share the crowded quarters. Stylists, musicians, and their entourages were going in and out of the rooms and crowding the hallway like it was Shinagawa Station at rush hour.

Suddenly everything backed up like a train wreck as Jimmy Harajuku reached the end of the hall and turned, openmouthed, to stare at the tech behind him. Before the crowd could change course and flow around the pair, Jimmy pulled the disguised guitarist around the corner. By the time Kenji got there, they were gone. Had they disappeared into one of the rooms beyond, or out the exit?

"Excuse me! Excuse me! You can't be down here."

A woman in a blue suit with a clipboard pushed through the crowd from behind and pointed her pen at Kenji's backstage pass. "Access to this area is restricted to artists and members of their support staff. Fan passes allow you access to upstairs only."

Kenji pulled out his police badge.

Miss Clipboard looked it and frowned. "Kenji Nakamura? Komagome Station?" She consulted her list. "You're not on my security roster. Who should I call to check that you've got clearance?"

"Never mind," Kenji said, giving her a sketchy bow, remembering that the Wangan Station section chief had specifically asked him not to conduct his investigation during the concert madness.

The security officer escorted him back to the foot of the stairs and watched to make sure he climbed them.

Kenji emerged into the maelstrom of techs. Now what? He'd have to wait for Flame to reemerge. But this couldn't be the only exit from the dressing rooms. Kenji grabbed the sleeve of a passing stagehand and flashed his badge, asking her about the layout of the floor below. The harried woman told him there were three exits, this one, a matching set of stairs on the other side of the stage, and a corridor leading to a side door that allowed artists to escape to their limos without running a gauntlet of fans.

Kenji thanked her and let her go, his anxiety kicking up a notch. He had to get all three exits covered before Flame finished doing his deal with Jimmy Harajuku, in case the idol decided to do a runner and not keep his half of the bargain. How long did he have? Five minutes? Ten?

Skirting the projection scrim that hung behind where the artists would perform, he discovered that both stairwells from the dressing rooms could be watched from a vantage point between them. But he'd have to find someone to watch the side door, someone with official security clearance.

He called Aya.

"Where are you?" he asked.

"At the entrance. Once the section chief discovered I was a third-degree black belt, he stuck me with the goons. Why?"

After Kenji explained, she replied, "The guy who's in charge of these muscleheads thinks I'm just window dressing. I'm sure he won't cry if I tell him my superior officer is asking for me to be reassigned."

"Great. Let me talk to him."

Kenji spoke to the Wangan Station detective, keeping an eye on the stairwells. Stylists, staff, and famous artists ran up and down to the dressing rooms, with coffee, costumes, and the occasional VIP in tow.

When he'd finished getting Aya released to watch the back door, he rang Oki, who reported that Inspector Kobayashi had pulled rank on the Wangan Station section chief and gotten Oki assigned to balcony security.

Kobayashi had held the rank of Inspector in the First

Investigative Division for twenty years, his career stalled because his approach to solving crimes was a lot like Oki's—his success was built on calculating how much he could bend the rules without breaking them.

He'd told the Wangan officer in charge of balcony security that a witness in one of his cases was going to be sitting in the first row, and because there was danger of an assassination attempt, everybody arriving to sit in the first three rows needed to be searched for weapons before they could be allowed to take their seats. He got Oki and one of his assistant inspectors assigned to pat-down duty, with the orders that if they were lucky enough to catch Jimmy carrying the illegal Beretta, they were to arrest him on the spot. They could charge him with possession and detain him for up to ten days while they sent the gun through Ballistics.

Kenji had to admire the plan, even though a hit from Ballistics tying the gun to Taku's murder would mean he would have to wait until the First Investigative Division was done with Jimmy to charge him with Yano's killing.

Aya appeared at the door from the auditorium and flashed her security clearance. After Kenji described what Flame was wearing, she asked Kenji to send a photo of him to her phone so she'd recognize him if he tried to bolt. She trotted down the stairs. A minute later, Kenji's phone buzzed. Aya hadn't seen any sign of the idol on her way to the side door, but she was in position.

Traffic on the stairs increased. Stylist. Gofer. Tech. VIP. Stylist. Hair-make. Yumi.

Emerging from the far stairwell carrying Blade's red electric guitar, she looked around for a moment, then waved to attract the attention of someone Kenji couldn't see.

Then right behind her, a short man in a pink jacket. The red respirator button in the middle of his face mask bobbed as he nodded to the stage manager before striding to the door that led to the auditorium.

•

Yumi settled into a backstage niche where she'd be out of the way, but still have a good view of the concert. From her vantage point against the back wall, she could watch everything that was invisible to the audience. Lights, sound, equipment, props—it took an army of specialists working like demons behind the scenes to make the magic on stage happen.

After delivering Blade's guitar to the tech who'd be in charge of tuning it before he performed, she'd been told her only job was to enjoy herself until after the concert, when Blade would be called upon to answer media questions.

Squinting at the balcony through the video projection scrim, she noticed that the two seats belonging to Kenji and Flame were still empty. And so was Jimmy's.

Then she saw the promoter come up the stairs from the dressing rooms. He gave a nod to the stage manager, opened the door to the auditorium, and strode up the aisle. A few minutes later, he appeared at the top of one of the balcony aisles. Halfway to his seat in the front row, he was stopped by . . . was that Detective Oki? Jimmy spread his arms wide in response to whatever question had accompanied the big detective's apologetic bow, and allowed himself to be patted down.

The apologetic bow Oki gave him afterward told Yumi that Jimmy Harajuku didn't have the Beretta. If he didn't, who did?

•

Kenji watched Oki fail to find either the gun or the Polaroid when he searched the pink-jacketed promoter up in the balcony. Had Flame given him the picture? If so, what had he done with it?

The guitarist must still be down in the dressing rooms. There had been no call from Aya, so Kenji knew he hadn't tried to escape out the back. He had a moment of worry that

Jimmy had rid himself of Flame once he had the Polaroid back, but Kenji reminded himself of the madhouse he'd seen downstairs. Any activities involving gunshots, blood, or hiding a dead body would be discovered within minutes.

The stairs were still crazy busy. Stylist. Musician. Hair-make. VIP. Kenji had seen so many people come and go by the time a hard-core Gilrugamesh fanboy with a familiar-looking duffel bag plodded up the stairs, he almost didn't recognize the idol in his altered disguise.

Flame had taken off the black sweatshirt to reveal a faded Stupid Tour T-shirt with his backstage pass sticker prominently pasted on the front. He'd removed the rubber band from his wig and raked his fingers through it, so now lank black hair hung over a pair of black-rimmed glasses. Fake piercings now adorned his nose and lip, and he still wore the black Pumas. Kenji hoped that wasn't because he intended to make a run for it. Without glancing at Kenji, he aimed for the door to the auditorium. Kenji allowed him a slight head start, then followed him up the aisle, through the lobby, and outside.

He readied himself for a chase, but Flame stopped next to the bank of coin lockers, fishing in his pocket. Pulling out a fistful of change, he selected three coins, then opened one of the last doors with a key dangling from the lock. He stowed the duffel bag, fed in the coins, then about-faced and showed his ticket at the door, heading for his comped seat in the balcony. From the top of the aisle, Kenji watched the disguised idol slide into one of their empty seats. He breathed a sigh of relief.

Beyond Flame, he could see Jimmy Harajuku's head, front and center. Why had the promoter gone to so much trouble to make sure there was a replica of his illegal gun at the concert?

Kenji sent a text to Yumi.

*Who has the air gun?*

She texted back.

*Stylist. But it'll be on prop table so Nana can grab it before the VDDs go on. How fast can you get backstage if Jimmy switches the toy for the real thing?*

•

Yumi sent her text back to Kenji and frowned, trying to figure out what Jimmy was up to. Why might he want Nana to have a real gun in her hands when she fired it at his seat from the stage?

She studied the crowd in the balcony. A lot of them were media VIPs, comped as a reward for hyping the concert on short notice. Yumi recognized a former TV drama star who now ran his own talent agency, making money off of up-and-coming actors the same way his promoter had made money off of him. And sitting to his left, right behind Jimmy, wasn't that—?

With a jolt, Yumi recognized one of the most famous faces in the pop industry. He'd been the front man of a band that soared to stardom in the '80s, then he'd springboarded into hosting a hit variety show that boosted the careers of the young bands he represented on his own label. One of them was Cologne, a girl group that began chasing Baby8 up the charts from the day they debuted. In the past month, their latest single had surged past Jimmy's idols to number one, and three industry magazines had proclaimed the up-and-coming promoter the new king of J-pop.

Did Jimmy know he was here?

"Hey, that's mine!"

Yumi looked over at the prop table in time to see Baby8's lead singer snatch a sparkly peach-colored electric bubble wand from the hand of one of the lesser members. The victim slunk back to pick up another wand from the ones left on the prop table.

Then the lights in the auditorium beyond the scrim

dimmed, and the crowd began cheering and clapping. The Baby8 members split up and streamed onto the stage from both sides, turning on their smiles as they entered the spotlight, shooting arcs of iridescent bubbles as they launched into dancing and lip-syncing to their hit single "Champagne Dreams."

Baby8 was followed by all of Jimmy's idol bands, each new act triggering a beehive of backstage activity as one group's equipment was switched out for the next. The lights came up in the auditorium briefly before the VuDu Dolls, so techs could sweep up the piles of silver confetti blown on stage during LoliPop's last song.

Through the scrim, Yumi checked the balcony seats again. Flame was now sitting in one of the comp seats. And there was Kenji, standing at the back of the balcony, keeping an eye on both Flame and Jimmy.

The pink-jacketed promoter was sitting exactly where he had been during the run-through that morning. He bent over to tie his shoe, and suddenly Yumi knew.

All he'd have to do is duck down at the right time, and a bullet fired from center stage at Jimmy's seat would take out his rival promoter. And it was almost time for the VuDu Dolls to take the stage.

She poked her head out of her niche and watched a tech wearing one of the coveted Love's Eternal Flame windbreakers set a shopping bag on the prop table and start laying out props for the VuDu Dolls.

It was Ninjaboy. Of course, she shouldn't be surprised that Jimmy had chosen the sneaky little blackmailer to help him do his dirty work. The fancy jacket must be his reward for switching the guns, no questions asked.

The table filled up with extra drumsticks and guitar picks to throw to the audience afterwards, plus glittery sunglasses to put on with the white suits when they took their curtain call. But why was he setting all the prop guns out on the table?

They only needed one.

Yumi pulled out her phone to text Kenji. No, wait, she'd better check to make sure the real Beretta was there before calling him away from his post. What differences had Kenji pointed out when he compared the photos of the air gun and the real one? She closed her eyes and pictured it. The trigger guard on the toy wasn't rounded in front, and it had extra diagonal lines on the barrel.

The lights in the auditorium dimmed. Sweepers were streaming backstage with their bags of silver confetti, and the VuDu Dolls plus Blade were walking toward the prop table, kitted out in their artfully slashed black leather "refugee" outfits over pure-white suits.

Nana selected one of the guns from the table and moved away from the scrum, settling it into the multi-buckled holster.

"Wait!" Yumi cried, emerging from her niche.

The vocalist turned.

"Hey!" Nana protested as Yumi reached down and snatched the gun.

It wasn't the Beretta. It was the air gun Nana had been using during the video shoot yesterday.

Yumi stared at it, puzzled. "Why aren't you using the new one Chiho brought this morning?"

"I dunno. Right before the concert, Jimmy changed his mind. He told me to use the gun that's in the video." Nana said, taking back the air gun and replacing it in the holster.

"We're on," the drummer said, sweeping Nana toward the stage.

Yumi ducked back into her niche, her mind racing. What was going on? Why did Jimmy make Chiho go all the way to Ueno to buy a Beretta air gun for the concert, then decide not to use it?

The audience surged to its feet with a roar as the VuDu Dolls sauntered onto the stage. Blade appeared last and the screaming doubled as he swept up his red guitar and slung the strap over his shoulder, launching into a virtuoso version of the solo at the beginning of "Don't Need You." Spotlights crisscrossed the audience, illuminating the fists pumping in unison as the rock anthem shook the I-beams.

Yumi remembered she owed Kenji a text.

*Gun on stage is a toy. It's not the Beretta.*

But where was the Beretta? Nana didn't have it. And Jimmy didn't have it, either. She looked over at the prop table. It was deserted now, bare except for two air guns. Two? Hadn't there been three? Yumi ran to the table. Neither of the props sitting there now was the Beretta. She spun around. Where was Ninjaboy?

Except for the theater's full-time professional crew, the only people backstage were Jimmy's techs. Yumi's gaze skipped from the three roadies in Top Talent windbreakers, leaning against the bank of speakers, to the stage manager muttering into his headset. A black-clad stagehand crawled behind the bank of speakers between Yumi and the stage wearing a tool belt. Shiro and Chiho were watching the show from stage right.

The band was playing an extra stanza with added lyrics that gave a nod to the earthquake victims. Then they crescendoed to the finale and segued seamlessly into "Kiss Me, Kill Me." Through the scrim, Yumi watched Blade axe across the stage as Nana pulled out the air gun.

"Kiss me. Or kill me," she sang, as a spotlight picked out Jimmy's pink jacket.

Then the stagehand with the tool belt stood and as Nana belted out the final line, a loud crack drowned out the words.

The flaming scrim rippled. A red rose bloomed on Jimmy's pink jacket. The last chord died just as the screaming began.

•

Suddenly the wall of flames projected on the scrim behind the band distorted with a sound that Kenji had only heard at the shooting range. The VuDu Dolls singer's face went slack with shock, staring up at the balcony. Then she looked at the gun in her hand and dropped it to the stage like it had burned her. A curtain of fire leaped up in front of the band, hiding the entire stage from view.

*What just happened?*

"Call an ambulance!"

Oki's voice. From the front row of the balcony.

The detective was pushing his way along the row toward the gap where Jimmy Harajuku had been watching the concert just a moment before. The promoter was slumped forward, a red stain darkening the back of his pink jacket.

The vocalist of the VuDu Dolls just shot Jimmy Harajuku.

*But that wasn't possible.* Yumi's text said that the gun on stage was a toy. Had she made a deadly mistake? Or had the shot come from somewhere else?

The curtain of fire on stage shut off on cue, just as Yumi had said it would, but instead of taking their bows in shiny white suits, the members of the VuDu Dolls were face down on the stage, immobilized by backstage security police.

But the shot hadn't come from Nana's gun. He was sure of it. He's seen the scrim distort, milliseconds before he heard the shot. The gunman had fired from backstage.

Kenji spun around and raced down the stairs, battling his way down to the first floor, then into the aisle against a flood of fleeing fans. The house lights switched on, police converging from all over the venue. But Kenji had no interest in the drama that was playing out on stage. He shouldered his way through the Staff Only door and ran backstage.

Looking at the scrim, he saw a pinpoint sparkle where a hole had been punched in the fabric.

Where was Yumi? Had she seen anything?

*Where was Yumi?*

•

Scared speechless, Yumi watched the silhouette of the stagehand calmly lower the weapon and push it into the drill holster on his belt, then begin to turn toward her. She dropped to the floor behind the prop table and scooted underneath. A pair of black-clad legs approached, stopped briefly while something thunked onto the table right above her head, then continued walking toward the stairs that led to the dressing rooms.

Shaking, she pulled her phone from her pocket to call Kenji, then realized that by the time he arrived, the gunman would have disappeared into the warren of rooms below. Unless she kept him in sight, he'd blend in with the rest of the backstage crew in his staff jacket and black knit cap. He'd walk away, his identity unknown, if she didn't follow him and get a good look at his face, or even better, snap a picture with her phone.

She scrambled out from under the prop table and ran after the dark figure, but halfway down the stairs encountered an oncoming wave of artists, stylists, and staff streaming out of the dressing rooms to see what all the excitement was about.

Fighting her way against the tide, she finally turned the corner into the hallway below and spotted the stagehand's black knit cap bobbing in the crowd ahead, making his unhurried way against the flow, heading nonchalantly toward freedom. She tried to close the gap, but it was impossible in the crowd of rubberneckers.

At least he couldn't move any faster than she could. She used the opportunity to get word to Kenji. Glancing between her phone and the knit cap ahead to make sure he didn't peel off into a dressing room, she keyed in a text.

*I saw everything. Following shooter. Downstairs.*

*Hurry.*

Send.

She looked up. No black knit cap. Damn. Where had he gone? The crowd between her and the exit had thinned. Had he escaped? She ran to the side door and yanked it open.

•

As if the *kami-sama* had heard his unspoken prayer, Kenji's phone vibrated with a text message.

*I saw everything. Following shooter. Downstairs. Hurry.*

Then the gods turned against him as both stairwells began disgorging the curious. Holding his badge ahead of him like a shield, he shouted, "Stand aside! Police!" as he waded into the scrum. The confirmation that whatever was going on upstairs involved police made some of the curious squeeze themselves against the walls so he could pass, but others surged into the gaps, afraid they were missing all the action.

Kenji made it to the foot of the stairs and craned his neck at the packed hallway beyond. No sign of Yumi or anybody else trying to make their way to the exit. Were they already around the corner? Or had they gone into one of the dressing rooms?

His phone vibrated again. Aya.

*Yumi Hata is with me. Says shooter is stagehand who came out and got into waiting limo. Permission to pursue?*

Kenji texted back.

*Go.*

Then he dispensed with every police regulation that required officers to treat the public with respect and used his elbows ruthlessly to carve a path through the crowd.

Leaving a trail of indignant celebrities in his wake, Kenji ran the last few meters to the exit and emerged into the narrow side alley in time to see a shiny black car accelerating away from the curb on the wide street that ran in front of the venue.

Flashing his badge, he identified himself to a limo driver who was standing next to his car farther down the block, staring after the shocking sight of noncelebrities commandeering a star's ride.

"You want to follow, too?" the driver asked Kenji, holding open the passenger side door with a white-gloved hand after seeing his badge.

Kenji slid in and the driver ran around to jump behind the wheel. He fired up the engine and eased into traffic. Kenji spotted two black limos in the line ahead, stopped at the next light.

•

"I don't know why I didn't scream," Yumi said, after explaining why they had to catch up to the car ahead at all costs. "It's like I didn't understand what I was seeing, and then it was too late."

"Hang on a second," said the officer whose nametag identified her as Assistant Detective Kurosawa. "I need to call Detective Nakamura and fill him in on what you just told me." She scrolled to his number. Kenji must have picked up immediately because Kurosawa twisted around to look through the back window.

"Yeah, I see you." She whipped back around to peer through the windshield at their quarry, three cars ahead. "We're following a black Lexus LS600, but I can't see the license plate."

Yumi's eyes were glued to the limo ahead with the shooter inside, thinking about what Kurosawa-*san* had said about the flu-masked stagehand who'd strolled out the exit door a few minutes ahead of her and stepped into the limousine that met him at the curb, as if it had been called.

Ninjaboy didn't have his own limo. Whose car was it? Had one of the Top Talent artists taken out Jimmy Harajuku? Had someone Jimmy abused gone down to a dressing room after performing and exchanged an idol costume for assassin-wear?

Ahead, their quarry got in the turn lane. The light changed. He made a U-turn.

"Don't let him get away!" Yumi urged their driver.

"Yes ma'am," he replied, squealing a one-eighty just as the light changed.

At the next light, the car ahead got in line to turn again. What? Another U-turn?

Is the shooter planning to go back into the arena? *Maybe he wasn't done yet.*

Yumi grabbed Assistant Detective Kurosawa's sleeve and pointed as their quarry signaled to pull into line behind the other limos lined up down the block from Zepp Tokyo, but she was already on it.

"He's pulling over," the assistant detective reported to Kenji. "I'll intercept him and hold him until you get here."

She ended the call.

"Let me out, then get back in the car," she said to Yumi, tension hardening her voice. She tapped the driver on the shoulder. "Stop the car and let me out, then follow that car. We'll need to search it later. Just follow. Do not—I repeat, do not—get out and approach whoever is in it."

"Yes ma'am."

"Out," she said to Yumi. Ahead, their target stopped and the back door opened. "Now."

Yumi scrambled out of the car and stood aside as Kurosawa boosted herself out, eyes riveted on the man now exiting the limo ahead.

Pink jacket. Pointy face beneath a red-buttoned

facemask.

*What?* Wasn't Jimmy Harajuku . . . *dead?*

The very much alive promoter closed the limo door and walked down the block toward the entrance, which was now a maelstrom of fleeing fans, police, and arriving media, all swirling around an ambulance that had backed up onto the sidewalk with its red lights flashing and back doors hanging open.

The limo Jimmy had just exited turned its wheels, preparing to pull away from the curb as soon as traffic permitted.

Assistant Detective Kurosawa stood there indecisively for a moment, thinking, then grabbed Yumi's sleeve. "Wait here for Detective Nakamura and don't let that guy in the pink jacket out of your sight. I'm going to follow that car. The shooter might still be inside."

Yumi nodded, then turned to watch Jimmy Harajuku. A female reporter whose camera crew was filming shot of her against the chaos stopped talking into her microphone the second she saw Jimmy coming toward her. Shock slapped across her face and she began to run toward the supposedly dead promoter, looking over her shoulder into the camera as her crew trotted behind her to intercept the biggest scoop of their careers.

•

Kenji's limo eased into line. What had just happened? Why had the car they were chasing made two U-turns and ended up back where it started? He watched as Yumi and Aya climbed out of the black sedan ahead.

"Thank you," he said to the driver, throwing open the door. "I'll get out here."

He ran down the block toward Yumi as Aya jumped back in the car and it pulled out into traffic.

"What's going on?"

"A guy who looked like a stagehand got into that car, then a guy who looked like Jimmy Harajuku got out!"

Jimmy Harajuku? Kenji looked toward Zepp Tokyo and saw a reporter shoving a microphone at a man in a pink jacket and red-buttoned flu mask. Other news teams were detaching themselves from the scrum around the entrance, converging on the newcomer like starving lions scenting fresh meat.

Kenji called Aya. She reported that she was two cars behind the one that might still have the gunman inside. He told her to follow, but not attempt anything herself. He'd arrange for backup. Then he called Oki, outlining what had just happened outside, asking if someone from Wangan Station or the elite murder squad could establish contact with Aya, and have backup there when the car she was following got to wherever it was going. He warned Oki that the assassin or the gun or both might be in the car she was pursuing.

Now Jimmy was pushing the microphone away and watching the crowd at the entrance make way for three white-coated attendants to rush their gurney out, a body buckled securely atop. They expertly slid it into the waiting vehicle.

Jimmy grabbed the sleeve of one of the paramedics as one back door slammed shut. The emergency worker shook him off and climbed into the back with the victim, pulling the other door shut behind him.

It shot off with a wail of sirens and the pink-jacketed promoter looked around, bewildered, as the reporters caught up with him and multiple mikes were shoved in his face.

"I can't tell you anything until I find out what happened here!" he cried in response to the clamor of questions. "All I know is that I asked my nephew to take my seat while I dealt with a professional emergency, so people wouldn't think that I wasn't supporting the earthquake victims. I'll never forgive myself if he took a bullet meant for me. I have to go the hospital now. Please excuse me. Please!"

Kenji shouldered his way into the clamoring circle,

leading with his badge. "I'm afraid you'll have to delay your hospital visit, Mr. Harajuku. I'm going to have to ask you to come with me."

•

Protesting all the way, Jimmy Harajuku accompanied Kenji through the Zepp Tokyo entrance.

"They're with me," Kenji told the officer stationed at the door as he shot a questioning look at Jimmy and Yumi. Apparently the doorkeeper hadn't seen the shooting, because he didn't seem to realize that the flu-mask-wearing man Kenji was badging through the door was supposedly strapped to a gurney and headed to the hospital, bleeding from what might be a fatal gunshot wound.

But as they entered the auditorium, all conversation stopped. Inspector Kobayashi detached himself from the crowd onstage and met them halfway up the aisle. He'd assumed command of the investigation as the ranking major crimes officer.

Jimmy demanded to be taken to his nephew's side immediately, telling Kobayashi that they'd be wasting precious time questioning him because he hadn't even been in the building when Ninjaboy was shot.

Kenji caught Kobayashi's eye over Jimmy's shoulder and shook his head. Kobayashi returned his attention to Jimmy and regarded him thoughtfully, then called for a pair of his assistant inspectors to usher Jimmy down to one of the deserted dressing rooms to wait for a few minutes until he could attend to him personally.

Jimmy reluctantly departed after a parting threat that he'd be calling his friend the Superintendent General if he were kept from his nephew's side for much longer.

Kobayashi now noticed Yumi standing behind Kenji and asked, "Who's she? And why is she here?"

"She saw the shooting."

"So did three thousand other fangirls."

"I saw it from backstage," Yumi said. "The gunman was right in front of me. I was hiding under the prop table when he dropped the weapon there on his way out. Is it still there?"

Kobayashi dispatched one of his assistant inspectors to check, then asked, "Can you identify the killer?"

Yumi looked at Kenji. "Sort of."

"'Sort of' as in 'yes,' or 'sort of' as in 'no'?"

"'Sort of' as in, between Assistant Detective Kurosawa and I, we've been following him since he shot the guy sitting in Jimmy's seat and got into a limo. But the guy who got into the car looked like a stagehand, and the guy who got out looks like Jimmy Harajuku."

"Where's Kurosawa?"

"Chasing the car he was riding in," Kenji replied. "In case the shooter is still in it. I'll call her now."

His call went to voicemail. Why wasn't she picking up? Kenji felt a prickle of foreboding, suddenly questioning his decision to allow her to pursue Jimmy's car alone. He left a message for her to call him immediately with an update.

"Wait here," Kobayashi said, returning to the foot of the stage to collect a couple of his subordinates to act as note-takers and witnesses. Then he called up to the Crime Scene Investigation team collecting evidence in the balcony, asking if they could spare a couple of bodies. He returned to Kenji and Yumi with his assistant inspectors in tow, just as the crime techs joined them.

"Now," he said, turning to Yumi. "Walk us through what you saw."

•

Kobayashi's assistant inspector called from backstage. He was standing guard over the prop table, on which sat three black guns. Two air guns, one real Beretta. By the time Yumi, Kenji and Kobayashi's entourage arrived, crime scene techs were swarming the table.

Kenji tried Aya again. Voicemail. He lowered his phone, the seeds of worry growing. Then it buzzed in his hand.

"I got him," Aya said, barely able to speak, she was breathing so hard.

"Who?"

"The man in the car." She paused to catch her breath. "He stopped. To throw something away. At a Family Mart." *Huff, huff.* "He pulled over. And threw a shopping bag. In the Burnable Trash bin."

"What was in the bag?"

"I don't know. It's still in the bin."

"Where's the suspect?"

"I'm sitting on him."

She paused as the faint sirens in the background grew louder, then stopped. "A Wangan Station patrol car just arrived. What should we do with him?" Then she remembered to add, "Uh, sir."

Kenji covered the mouthpiece and turned to Inspector Kobayashi "Assistant Detective Kurosawa and a local patrol team have the driver of Jimmy's car, who stopped to throw away a bag at a convenience store. Where do you want them to take him?"

"Tell her to grab that bag and bring him here."

While Kobayashi asked one of his assistants to tell the Wangan Station section chief to order his officers to bring the suspect to Zepp Tokyo instead of booking him at the station, Kenji relayed the information to Aya.

Ten minutes later, a patrol car pulled into the side alley, followed by Jimmy's limo with Aya at the wheel. The Wangan officers marched the suspect through the side door to the dressing room Kobayashi had readied for the driver's interrogation.

Aya got out of Jimmy's car with a family-size MOS Burger bag.

"Dinner?" Kenji asked.

"Only if you're craving a stagehand's windbreaker, a used flu mask, and a pair of gloves."

•

"He's trying to frame me! Why is Mr. Harajuku trying to frame me? What did I ever do to him?"

Kenji sat next to the murder squad note-taker as Inspector Kobayashi questioned the stagehand who had been driving Jimmy's car.

He turned out to be a longtime Top Talent roadie with a couple of misdemeanor arrests for drunk and disorderly. The square-built stagehand readily admitted that the Love's Eternal Flame windbreaker inside the MOS Burger bag was his. In fact, he was indignant that Jimmy had told him to throw it away and demanded it be returned to him "when all this gets straightened out." But he insisted he'd never seen the gun before and never wore gloves while he was working because it was dangerous to operate tools with them on.

He grew more and more outraged as he told them how Jimmy had pulled him aside right before the concert—after all the heavy lifting was done, but before the stagehands got to enjoy their better-than-front-row view—and sent him down the block to the limo to switch jobs with Ninjaboy.

"Mr. Harajuku even made me switch jackets with that sneaky little bastard, which is why I stopped to write my name inside the collar first."

"So what happened after you traded jackets with Jimmy's nephew?"

"I sat in the fucking car, except when I had to take a leak," he said bitterly. "And that smug little bastard got to swan in and watch the whole show from backstage without doing a lick of work. I had to freeze my butt off out here until the concert was nearly over and Mr. Harajuku called me to meet him near the artists' entrance. When he came out I didn't recognize him at first because he was wearing my windbreaker and a regular white mask, not that special weird kind he always has on. He got in the back and ripped the dry cleaning bag from one of the pink jackets he keeps back there. Everybody thinks he always wears the same one, but—go figure—he must have a bunch of them in case one gets dirty. He's one strange guy."

"What then?"

"He told me to make a U-turn at the next light. I thought he'd give me directions to where he wanted to go from there, but then he made me U-turn again and let him out at the passenger curb! Can you believe that? I mean, what the fuck? Before he got out, he handed me that MOS Burger bag and told me to toss it at a convenience store before coming back. So I found a Family Mart, but when I got out to throw away the bag, Commando Woman came out of nowhere and took me down."

A crime scene tech appeared with a tool case.

"We need to swab your hands for gunshot residue," explained the inspector.

"Swab away," the stagehand said. "When you don't find any, can I take my windbreaker and go home?"

The tech asked him to shove his sleeves up to his elbows, did her wiping and testing of his hands, arms, and shirtsleeves, then shook her head and said to Kobayashi, "Negative."

The inspector excused himself, beckoning Kenji and the tech outside the door.

"What about the gloves, jacket and mask from the MOS Burger bag?" he asked the tech.

"Reeking of gunpowder."

"Go next door and swab Jimmy Harajuku, same routine. Maybe we'll get lucky. Nakamura, observe and report back."

•

"I can't tell you. It'll ruin her career." Jimmy Harajuku insisted.

By the end of the next hour, Kenji could tell Kobayashi's patience was wearing thin. The gunshot residue swab had been inconclusive – which made sense, if Jimmy had traded the gloves he wore to shoot his nephew for the clean pair he was wearing when they arrested him. But Jimmy Harajuku was refusing to give up the name of the person who could verify that he'd been nowhere near Zepp Tokyo when his nephew had been shot.

The promoter had explained that right before the concert began, he'd received a call from the minder of one of his other idol groups, claiming she had an emergency situation on her hands. He'd asked his nephew to stand in for him until he'd dealt with it, explaining that the media were ruthlessly observant, and they'd interpret his empty seat as a lack of support for the earthquake victims. Even worse, there was a good chance that at least one news vulture would start poking his beak where it didn't belong, trying to discover why he hadn't been in his seat, and the scandal he'd run out to defuse would explode anyway. Dealing with the situation had taken longer than he'd anticipated, so he hadn't made it back to Zepp Tokyo until the concert was over.

But he couldn't give the inspector the girl's name. The police department leaked like a sieve, Jimmy explained, and if he told them who it was, his star's life would be ruined. They'd just have to take his word for it. He offered to write up a statement and sign it, if that would help.

"That's very generous of you, I'm sure, Mr. Harajuku," Kobayashi said, folding his hands on the table. "But you seem to be a little unclear on the concept. Let me spell it out for you. I have no interest in whatever messy little situation your baby celebrity got herself into. All I care about is arresting the person who tried to kill your nephew." His voice hardened. "So unless you'd like to volunteer for that role and be taken to

Wangan Station in handcuffs, I suggest you give me the name, address, and phone number of whoever you were with between six and nine this evening."

Jimmy shook his head and sighed. "You're putting me in a difficult situation, Inspector. I'll give you the information you want if you can guarantee it doesn't leave this room. Let me call my lawyer and ask him bring some nondisclosure—"

Kobayashi slammed his hands on the table. "You can call your lawyer and ask him to defend you on murder charges if you don't give me the information I need right now so I can get on with this investigation!"

"All right, all right." Jimmy raised his hands in surrender. "It was Sakura. Sakura Shiba, one of the members of 22 Lolitas. Last night the band's chaperone caught her with one of the boys from Burnable Trash, in clear violation of her contract. I told her I'd be deciding between demoting her to one of my trainee groups or terminating her altogether. At five thirty today, the chaperone caught her shaving off all her hair in the bathroom. She confessed she'd talked one of the other girls into helping make a video of her apologizing to her fans and begging not to be cut from 22 Lolitas. The chaperone called me, and of course I had to immediately see to damage control."

"Damage control?"

Jimmy looked at him like he was from Mars. "It would be a publicity disaster if one of my stars uploaded a video like that to the Internet! Besides needlessly hurting the thousands of fans who look to my girls for inspiration, it would be beyond embarrassing to have the public think someone in my organization couldn't do better than copy that pathetic AKB48 singer's video confession. It would take us years to live it down."

Kobayashi shoved his notebook and a pen across the table. "Full name, address, and phone number."

Jimmy consulted his phone and scribbled the

information on the pad. He returned it to the inspector, saying, "Of course, you won't be able to reach her for a while."

"What?"

"The only way to deal with a publicity bomb like this is to hide it away in a safe place until it's no longer dangerous. I sent Sakura and her chaperone to my cabin in Tateshima for a few weeks, where there aren't any distractions like cell-phone coverage or Internet. I can send you a map, if you'd like to drive up there and talk to her."

Kobayashi stared at him, then he smiled and stowed his pen and notepad in his jacket pocket. "I think we'll do that. But not until morning; the roads might be treacherous at night."

Jimmy nodded his agreement at the wisdom of that course and buttoned his jacket, preparing to go.

"Assistant Inspector Kato, cuff Mr. Harajuku and take him to Wangan Station for booking."

"What?" Jimmy was out of his seat like a rocket, but one of the First Investigative Division's officers stepped up and pulled his wrists behind him, snapping on the police detention ties.

"We'll be releasing you when we've had a chance to check out your story," Kobayashi explained smoothly. "If it turns out to be the truth, that is."

"My lawyer!" Jimmy was demanding as he was led away to a waiting patrol car. "Uncuff me immediately so I can call my lawyer!"

•

"Yumi? Yumi, wake up."

What? She pried open her eyes. Kenji's face was hovering over her.

She pushed herself up to a sitting position, blinking. Ow. Her neck had a crick in it from using a pile of discarded idol costumes as a pillow. All round her, LoliPop's dressing room lights blazed, illuminating the mess they'd left behind.

"What happened?" she asked groggily. "I hear Assistant Detective Kurosawa caught Jimmy's driver. Was it him or Jimmy who shot Ninjaboy?"

"Unless you mistook a hundred-eighty-five centimeter, eighty-kilo stagehand for a guy who's half his size, the driver didn't shoot Jimmy's nephew." Kenji replied. "But Jimmy Harajuku is one of the slipperiest liars I've ever seen."

He sat down next to her and told her how the promoter had set up the stagehand to be framed, then constructed an elaborate alibi for himself.

"Why did he shoot his nephew?"

"We don't know yet. Inspector Kobayashi wants you to come over to the other room so he can ask you about Jimmy's movements over the past few days."

Yumi hesitated, then asked, "Jimmy's nephew . . . is he . . . ?"

"He's lucky, is what he is. Jimmy's a good shot, but he must not have realized that shooting to kill means aiming for the head, not the heart. The bullet went right through the nephew's shoulder and he lost a lot of blood, but he should be able to talk to us in the next few days."

Yumi nodded. "And what about . . . Flame?"

Kenji sighed. "Disappeared. They found that Polaroid of Nana pushed down between the back seats of Jimmy's limo, so he must have cut his deal with Jimmy before the concert. But Jimmy's claiming he's never seen the picture before and Nana denies it's her.

"The bad news is, without Flame to tie the picture to Head Priest Yano's death, that case is dead in the water. The good news is if the nephew gives Kobayashi some case-clinching evidence, the prosecutor will want to throw the book at Jimmy for the attempted murder of his nephew with an illegal firearm instead of Head Priest Yano's murder anyway. It's a much stronger case."

Kenji rubbed his tired face, then stood and offered Yumi his hand. She took it and he pulled her up, then they were in each other's arms.

But they were both so tired, all they could do was hold each other close, swaying a little, feeling each other's hearts beating. As footsteps approached in the hallway outside, Yumi let go and stepped back. She had unfinished business to take care of first.

Monday, December 30

•

*8:00 A.M.*

Inspector Kobayashi and Kenji pulled two chairs over to the side of Ninjaboy's hospital bed. The murder squad inspector had asked that Kenji and Aya be loaned to his team while they worked around the clock to find hard evidence against Jimmy Harajuku. The forty-eight hours they were allowed to hold him without charges would be up tonight at 10:07. This morning, Ninjaboy's doctors had finally agreed that his condition was stable enough to allow a short interview.

"It was my uncle who tried to kill me?" Ninjaboy yelped from the bed that had been cranked up so he could face his questioners.

His look of innocent surprise failed to be Oscar-worthy. In the day and a half since the shooting, Kobayashi's team had discovered that the victim was quite the up-and-coming criminal himself.

Jimmy's idols had refused to talk about members of their own groups, but they had whispered plenty about their rivals for Jimmy's time and promo power. Several dozen young women who'd agreed when they were twelve never to taint the innocent image their fans adored, had plenty to hide from their promoter. At least seven of them had been paying Ninjaboy a king's ransom not to destroy their chances at stardom.

"Do you have any idea why he might have wanted you

out of the way?" Kobayashi asked.

"No sir, all I did was drive him around and do whatever he told me to."

"Except show him the pictures you took of the Baby8 singer coming out of a love hotel in Shibuya with her boyfriend, and the LoliPop dancer's pharmaceutical inventory, and the other assorted secrets you've been making about half a million yen a month on since you started working for him"

"What? How did you know that? Did you go in my room? You can't go in my room!"

"We can, now that you've admitted you're hiding evidence of blackmail." Kobayashi turned to Kenji. "Detective Nakamura, can you call the prosecutor's office and have someone meet you at Jimmy Harajuku's penthouse with a warrant?"

Ninjaboy's already pale face became even paler as Kenji rose and started for the door. "Hey, stop! That's not fair! Why are you picking on me? I'm the victim! My uncle tried to shoot me!"

"That's right. He did," Kobayashi said, signaling to Kenji to wait. "And maybe if you tell me what it was you were blackmailing him with, I'll decide that it would look much better on my record to send an important celebrity to jail for attempted murder than arrest his nephew for blackmail. I might forget all about those pictures in my excitement to put away the guy who will probably try to shoot you again if he's not in jail." He watched alarm break out all over Ninjaboy's face. "So tell me. Why did your uncle try to kill you? What did you have on him?"

"Pants," Ninjaboy blurted. "A pair of pants. And some Polaroids."

"Where are they?"

"The photos are somewhere in his room. Or in his bathroom."

"How do you know if you didn't see them?"

"I did. I just don't know where he hid them. The day before the earthquake, Jimmy came home from his tour with Baby8 and I told him I'd tracked down the VuDu Dolls guitarist. That night, he made me show him the shrine where Flame was working and told me to drop him off at the comic book café where she was hiding out. He went in, then came back out and told me I could go back to his Shibuya building, that he'd call me in the morning to come pick up him and Flame before the recording session."

"And . . . ?" Kenji asked, sliding into the chair Kobayashi had pulled up next to his so Kenji could take over the questioning.

"He called around ten. But when I started looking for him a couple of blocks away from the shrine, I almost drove right past him because I didn't realize he'd be alone and not wearing his pink jacket. I asked him where Flame was and he told me she'd be coming to Odaiba in a cab as soon as she told the priest at the shrine she was quitting. He didn't want to wait for her, he said, because he had to get back to the studio to prep for the 'Kiss Me, Kill Me' recording session. But once he got in the car, he was acting . . . weird."

"What kind of 'weird'?"

"I dunno, he couldn't sit still. He was excited, like he was on drugs or having an adrenaline rush or something. I sneaked a couple of looks at him in the rearview mirror, and I saw him take a stack of Polaroids out of his jacket pocket and look through them. There was something about the way he did it that made me think they might be, uh, valuable."

Ninjaboy flicked a glance at Inspector Kobayashi. "I asked him if he wanted to go straight to the studio and he said no, he had to stop at the penthouse first. I told him I had to take a leak and followed him in. He went straight to his room. I heard the toilet flush, then he came a back a few minutes later, wearing clean pants and a fresh pink jacket.

"We went to the studio and Flame didn't show, so he brought in a session guitarist to play Flame's part. Then the earthquake happened. While we were at the Disaster Park, he called together everybody who'd been in the studio that day, everybody who knew that Flame wasn't at the recording session."

"Who was there?"

Ninjaboy thought for a moment, then counted on his fingers as he rattled off, "Jimmy, two engineers, the other three VuDu Dolls, and this guy Taku who played Flame's guitar part."

"And what did Jimmy tell you?"

"He said that he had some bad news. That he'd just found out that Flame had died when the cab she was in had been swept away by the tsunami. Everyone freaked out. But I remembered that the pants he was wearing when I picked him up were dirty, that something dark had splashed on the front. I wondered if he . . . if he'd hurt her. Or . . . you know, *killed* her.

"So when we finally got back to the penthouse, I waited until he was on the phone, telling some reporter the story that Flame had died in the tsunami. I went to his room. I didn't find the pictures, but I found the pants balled up and stuck in the back of his closet. I took them to my room and shut the door and looked at them. I couldn't be sure, but the dark stains looked like blood."

"So you put the squeeze on him?"

"No! I was freaked out. Between the earthquake and not knowing what had really happened to Flame, I was scared shitless. It wasn't until a few days later, when the lights were back on and everybody was getting back to normal that I figured out how to, uh, use the pants."

He swallowed nervously and continued, "The night before the concert, I sent him a photo of the pants from my phone, with the message, *Are these yours, uncle?* He pulled me aside while everybody was having dinner and we went down to the studio to talk. He didn't admit anything, but I told him that when I asked my mom to get me a job with him, I thought he'd be training me to take over his business someday. I didn't think I'd still be his *driver*, a year later. That if he wasn't going to teach me the business and start giving me a few perks—like letting me hang out with those sweet young idols—I wanted him to give me some cash to start my own biz."

"How much?"

"Ten mil."

"And what did he say to that?"

"Said he'd think about it. I told him to take his time, that I'd give him the pants back when he either gave me a contract making me his partner, or a bankbook with my name on it. And that night I shoved a dresser up against my door before I went to sleep. By then I was pretty sure he'd killed Flame and I'd heard that session guitarist was dead, too. So even though I was family, I knew I could be next.

"I didn't get much sleep that night, and the next day it was a typical day-of-concert madhouse right up until it started. Then he came out to the limo and told me he'd decided to make me his partner, that his lawyer would meet us back at the penthouse after the concert to sign the papers. That instead of making me sit there at the curb and miss the concert, he'd start teaching me the ropes right away. He asked me to sit in his seat and pretend to be him while he dealt with a little problem with one of his girls. I was stoked. I figured that was a sign I was in, that he'd figured out how useful it would be to have a partner like me. I didn't think he was setting me up to shoot me."

"Where are the pants now?"

"Still in my room. In the closet. Folded and hanging underneath a pair of my pants. Unless--" Ninjaboy gave Kobayashi a worried look. "You arrested my uncle right after the concert, right? He's been in jail since then?"

Kobayashi's phone buzzed in his pocket.

"Kobayashi *desu*." He listened, then shot to his feet, his face tense. "When?" Listened again. "We can't let him get into that penthouse. The first thing he's going to do is destroy some evidence we just found out about. Grab as many bodies as Wangan Station can spare. Take some crime scene tape and set up a periphery around the entrance to his building and don't forget to block the elevator from the garage, if there is one. Do it now. Move."

He ended the call and made another one. Snapping to attention even though the person on the other end of the line couldn't see him, he said, "Good afternoon, sir. We just got a big break on the Zepp Tokyo shooting, but it's a little complicated. I need a search warrant on Jimmy Harajuku's apartment, and I need it now. I just heard that he pulled some strings and they're going to cut him loose at ten this morning instead of giving us the whole forty-eight hours of custody. The first thing he's going to do is try to destroy the evidence that will help us close this case." He listened. "Okay. Great. I'll stall him until then."

He listened some more, then his mouth quirked into a crooked smile. "Oh, I don't think you really want to know that, sir."

•

"What about the garage elevator, sir?" Kenji asked Inspector Kobayashi as the taxi swung into the roundabout in front of Jimmy's building.

"I'm going to put you in charge of blocking that one. Let people who are already in the building leave if they come down, but if Jimmy or anybody else shows up trying to get in, tell them that my guys in the lobby are cleaning up a toxic spill, that it's in the elevator too, and they can't go in until we say it's safe."

Kenji nodded as the cab stopped at the entrance. Do Not Cross tape was already fluttering convincingly across big glass doors leading to the lobby. Kobayashi's assistant inspector had stationed himself outside, and through the windows to the lobby, Kenji could see other figures moving back and forth inside with mops, wearing what looked like gas masks.

Kobayashi's face broke into a grin. "Gas masks. Nice touch. Wonder where they found those."

Kobayashi paid the driver and told Kenji to walk around to the garage entrance. "I'll send one of the locals down with the tape and tell him to stay as your backup."

A few minutes later, the garage elevator door pinged. The doors opened and Aya stepped out, holding a roll of yellow police tape.

"I volunteered," she said. "Sir."

"Okay, let's get that tape up," Kenji said, happier to see her than he wanted to let on. If Jimmy did turn up, it was good to know his backup could do the job.

They strung the tape and radioed to Kobayashi that they were in position. Kenji filled Aya in on what they'd learned from Ninjaboy, and she told him that the word around Wangan Station was that Detective Sato had been lobbying for Jimmy to be let out on his own recognizance since he'd been booked yesterday. Between Sato and Jimmy's lawyer, they'd shaved twelve hours off his detention time.

The radio crackled. Kobayashi. "Suspect arriving in cab."

Kenji turned to Aya. "I want you around the corner of the elevator shaft, out of sight. He's arriving by cab instead of being delivered in a patrol car, so he could have stopped anywhere and picked up something to arm himself with. If he tries anything, I want him to be surprised that there are two of us."

She nodded and slipped around the corner as the radio crackled again. "Suspect refused entrance, heading around the building toward the garage, on foot."

Kenji acknowledged.

A few minutes later, a familiar slight silhouette ducked under the gate and strode toward the elevators. Jimmy Harajuku was carrying a shopping bag from a toy store in Ueno.

Kenji tensed, ready for whatever the promoter was carrying to help him get to the damning evidence before the police did.

"*Sumimasen.* I live in this building. I need to get into my apartment," he said to Kenji.

"I'm sorry, but there's a toxic—"

"That's what the guy out front said, but I've got a bit of an emergency on my hands, and I've decided that this urgent matter is worth the risk to my health."

He moved to go around Kenji, but Kenji stepped in front of him.

"I'm sorry sir, but it's a matter of public health, and I'm afraid I can't—"

"Stand aside, I said!" Jimmy snapped, trying to dodge past. But Kenji's judo skills were good enough to anticipate his movements and block him, finally grabbing him by the shoulders and firmly backing him away from the Do Not Cross tape.

"I'm afraid I really can't let you into the building, Harajuku-*san*."

Kenji saw his mistake instantly. Jimmy heard his name and realized that the police presence in his building was much more personal than a health hazard.

He reached into the bag and Aya rocketed from her hiding place like a homing missile.

But she stopped short as Jimmy's hand emerged holding a gun, and pointed it at her. He backed away so he could cover both Aya and Kenji.

"Game over. Now let me into the elevator. Don't try and stop me, unless you want to spend a long time in the hospital."

Jimmy shifted the gunsights from Kenji to Aya and back to Kenji again.

He began to edge toward the elevator, keeping the gun pointed steadily at Kenji. "I'm going upstairs now."

With two strides, Kenji closed the distance and grabbed the gun by the barrel, twisting it and wrenching it from Jimmy's hands. The promoter turned and ran, but Aya chased and took him down. Kenji tossed the gun away, and as it skittered across the hard concrete floor of the garage, he pulled Jimmy's hands behind his back to cuff him.

Aya turned to Kenji, eyes wide. "You're crazy!" she said. "If he'd pulled the trigger . . . !"

Kenji smiled and stood up to retrieve the gun. Sliding his finger through the trigger guard so he wouldn't disturb Jimmy's prints on the grip, he held it up for Aya to see.

"If he'd pulled the trigger, we'd both have known this was a toy."

Tuesday, December 31

•

3:00 p.m.

"*Moshiwake gozaimasen.*"

The formal words of apology Yumi had hoped to hear from Ichiro were coming from his father's mouth as the three members of the Mitsuyama family bowed deeply over the gleaming lacquer table. The Mitsuyamas had chosen Hamada-ya, the Michelin three-star restaurant where family events and discreet business negotiations were often conducted. The private room, discreet kimono-clad servers, and obscure Ningyo-cho neighborhood ensured that nobody in the Mitsuyamas' social circle would spot them and wonder why they were meeting the Hata family in the middle of a workday.

Since Yumi had returned from Odaiba, an exhausting number of *nemawashi* exchanges had taken place between her family and Ichiro's, dissolving the engagement with the polite words reserved for the most delicate of negotiations. Nobody wanted to be surprised when they sat down at the table and said the phrases that would formally dismantle what they had put together half a year before.

Yumi's fears about her father's job had required an especially delicately worded message, suggesting that she was sure that even though she and Ichiro would not be getting married, she hoped that the Mitsuyama family's commitment to scholarship and learning would make them want to guarantee that Dr. Hata's professorship would continue to be supported until he voluntarily retired. Much to her surprise, the Mitsuyamas had been so relieved that she wasn't demanding an annuity, or an apartment or anything so financially painful that they'd be hard-pressed to provide it, they'd agreed without a murmur.

But Ichiro had ducked every attempt she'd made to talk to him alone. All she wanted to do was clear the air between them before they formally faced each other and went their separate ways, but he hadn't returned even one of her calls, texts or e-mails. Did she mean so little to him that he couldn't even bother to say he was sorry? Or was he so ashamed of what he'd done, he couldn't bear to face her? Yumi had flipped between hurt and anger, night after night, as she stared up at the crack in her ceiling that looked like a crooked heart.

Would Ichiro marry Ami after all the dust had settled? Or would his parents insist that he make amends for putting them through this socially and financially costly disaster by renouncing her forever?

Yumi and her parents returned the Mitsuyama family's bows and murmured the polite words of response. Ichiro's father then launched into the particulars, cloaking the reparations in vague euphemisms.

"In this most regrettable situation, it would be even more regrettable if the Hata family suffered any financial loss with regard to the canceled wedding expenses," Ichiro's father said, agreeing to cover all the nonrefundable deposits. He made eye contact with Yumi's father, who had typically been totally out of the loop when it came to the *nemawashi*, but had been coached to bow and accept each apology as offered.

Mr. Mitsuyama continued, "And our humble family continues to hope for Dr. Hata's ever-increasing success in his academic pursuits, until the day comes when he decides to retire with all honor."

Yumi watched nervously as her father bowed, hesitating

before he said the formal words of acceptance. At mention of his work his face had brightened and she knew how tempted he was to exclaim that he never intended to retire, that he loved his work—especially now that he was a full professor!—and that perhaps the Mitsuyamas would be interested in something he recently discovered in the loading documents of one of the Black Ships . . . ?

Much to Yumi's relief, he managed to restrain himself and was now murmuring the formal words of dignified acceptance instead.

As the process drew to a close, Yumi felt weary relief and a rare moment of appreciation for Japanese customs. Usually she chafed against the social pressure to conduct every aspect of life mindful of *tatemae*—showing the proper face, rather than one's true feelings—but she had to admit, having a formal method for dealing with difficult situations was a lot less painful all around.

But as they all straightened from their bows, her eyes met Ichiro's and she saw a sadness there that unexpectedly made tears well up in her own.

They rose and filed out of the private room, the two families parting for the last time in the stone-flagged entryway. The Hatas made their way out through the serene courtyard garden and turned toward the train station, the cold winter wind pushing dark clouds across the sky and blowing Yumi's hair across her cheeks. She adjusted her muffler as her parents began to hurry toward the station, hoping to be inside before the rain started.

"Yumi-*san*! Wait!"

She turned. Ichiro was standing on the sidewalk, looking at her with a face full of sorrow as the Mitsuyamas' driver helped his mother into the back seat of their car. Her now-ex fiancé took a step toward her and Yumi said to her parents, "Go on ahead."

Ichiro glanced around and spotted a small coffee shop on

the next block, but they didn't meet each other's eyes or say another word until they were sitting in a booth near the back. They ordered tea and wrapped their hands around their cups, desperate for a little warmth after the coldness of what they'd done in that room at Hamada-ya.

Then Ichiro bowed his head. "Yumi, I'm so sorry. I never meant to hurt you. I don't expect you to ever forgive me, but I wanted you to know I'm sorry. My father wouldn't let me talk to you until . . . until it was all over. *Moshiwake gozaimasen,*" he choked. "*Moshiwake gozaimasen.*"

The sadness she'd felt at the restaurant closed her throat and Yumi couldn't say a word as the tears that had been building up inside her overflowed. She reached across the table and found Ichiro's hand. They sat there for a long while, letting that single connection say what words couldn't.

Finally, Yumi gently withdrew her hand and asked, "So . . . will they let you marry her now?"

Ichiro sighed. "I don't know. My mother understands, I think, but my father . . ." He took a sip of his tea and stared down into the cup, as if it could tell him the future. Then he looked her in the eye and said, "Whatever happens, I hope that you find somebody who makes you happy, who can appreciate how lucky they are to have you."

Yumi gave him an appreciative bow. She already had. In a few hours, she'd be with Kenji.

And suddenly it hit her. She was free.

•

Yumi's beer was down to the final sip by the time Kenji finished telling her what they'd learned from Ninjaboy at the hospital and how Jimmy had tried to bully his way past them into his apartment.

They were sitting at a table in a little underground Shimokitazawa bar called the Apollo. A Thelonious Monk recording was playing in the background until the live music started at 8:00. Blue light gleamed off the whiskey bottles and beer taps as the owner pulled a fresh one for a customer at the bar, nodding in time to "Ruby, My Dear."

"We finally stormed in," Kenji said, "but only to keep Jimmy busy until the warrant arrived, so he couldn't destroy the pair of pants he was wearing when he hit Head Priest Yano over the head with Flame's Oricon Award."

"So, if the blood matches Yano's," Yumi said, "is that enough to prosecute him for killing the head priest?"

Kenji frowned. "Maybe. But we need more."

"Would this help?" Yumi passed her phone to Kenji.

He looked at the screen and exclaimed, "Where did you get this?"

"It arrived this morning. From someone calling himself Phoenix."

"Wait, isn't that . . . ?" He glanced at the Apollo's artist schedule on the flyer sitting on the bar. "Phoenix" was written under "New Year's Eve" in flamboyant gothic lettering. As if on cue, a beautiful young man in a Hanshin Tiger's baseball cap appeared from the back room toting a guitar by the neck, and plugged it into the amp set up in front of the tables in the small bar.

Kenji half rose from his seat and Yumi pulled him back down.

"He's not going anywhere until after midnight," she assured him.

"How did you know?"

She nodded at the phone in his hand. "Scroll down."

Below the e-mailed photo of Jimmy Harajuku fleeing the Tabata Shrine dressed in priestly summer robes and carrying a translucent trash bag with the Oricon Award visible inside were the words, "Apollo, Shimokitazawa, 12/31, 20:00."

"I talked to him this morning, to tell him we were coming tonight," Yumi explained. "He invited me to the Tabata Shrine for *hatsumode* tomorrow, and said he'd be helping his uncle Makoto serve the *amazake*. Makoto is letting him live at the head priest's house until he gets his career off the ground again. I guess Makoto's pretty grateful that Flame wants to follow in his father's musical footsteps, not his religious ones. Oh, and Makoto said to thank you again for stopping by to give him the news that his brother's killer had been arrested."

A woman joined Flame, adjusting the height of the mike while he tuned his guitar. Now it was Yumi's turn to be surprised. The singer's hair was dyed black and cut in a short spiky style, but Yumi had seen her without her elaborate doll makeup before.

Nana.

They started with a song Yumi hadn't heard before, but as Nana grasped the mike stand and closed her eyes, singing about being reborn again and again and finally getting it right, she realized she knew the story of Flame and Nana without being told. So it was no surprise when they appeared hand in hand at Yumi and Kenji's table an hour later, after they'd left the Apollo's patrons buzzing and uploading pictures.

"*Gomenasai*," Flame apologized, bowing to Kenji. He pulled over a chair for Nana and one for himself. "I tried to wait for you after the concert to keep my half of our deal, but there was a group of fans staring at me, and I knew they were gathering their courage to ask. So I had to disappear. Did you get the photo I sent to Yumi-*san*?"

Kenji nodded.

"Do you still need me to, you know . . . sign a statement or whatever?"

"Yes, but I'm afraid it'll be a long time before your father's murder comes to trial, now that the First Investigative Division has the gun that killed Taku Shinoda, on top of the attempted murder of his nephew. They'll use the pants he was wearing that day at the Tabata Shrine to hold him until test results on the other evidence comes in, but I'm sorry to say that he won't come to trial for your father's death anytime soon."

"As long as he spends a good long time in jail for something, I'll be happy," Flame said.

Nana took his hand and squeezed it sympathetically, then her face become troubled as she turned to Kenji and asked, "What about the . . . pictures?"

Kenji shook his head. "He must have destroyed the ones he stole from Yano-*kannushi*; they're not in his Odaiba penthouse. The only Polaroid left is the one of you that Flame gave back to Jimmy before the concert."

Nana tensed.

"But that picture will never see the light of day, even if there's a trial. Without Flame's testimony—or yours—it doesn't tie Jimmy to Head Priest Yano's murder. Now that we have the pants and the photo of him leaving the shrine, we don't really need it."

Nana smiled with relief and bowed her gratitude. The Apollo owner appeared and asked if they were ready to play the set that would ring in the new year.

Flame and Nana stood.

"Will you stay?" Flame asked.

Kenji checked the time, then looked at Yumi.

"Wish we could," Kenji said. "But we've got a *hatsumode* promise to keep."

They paid and climbed the stairs to the gleaming street. Unfurling his new seventy-centimeter umbrella, he offered Yumi his arm so she could huddle close as they dashed through the rain to make it back to Komagome before the bells rang at midnight.

They rode as far as Shibuya in silence, Yumi's head on Kenji's shoulder, then boarded the Yamanote Line along with a crush of passengers eager to arrive at their favorite shrine or temple to start the new year right.

Smashed up against Kenji, Yumi looked up into his face

and asked, "Are you disappointed that the prosecutor might not get around to charging Jimmy with Yano-*san*'s death for a long time?"

Kenji's smiled down at her and said, "I would be if Inspector Kobayashi wasn't so generous about sharing credit for getting him on the nephew shooting. He took me aside and told me not to slack off studying for the Assistant Inspector's Exam in May, because there was a spot waiting for me on his murder squad team if I passed it."

"Really? It's what you want, isn't it?"

Kenji nodded as her arms stole around him. He pulled her close and smiled.

As they stepped onto the platform at Komagome, he felt Yumi grab his jacket so they wouldn't be separated in the throng flowing toward the Komagome Shrine. From afar, the red lacquer and gold leaf of the sanctuary gleamed in the light of the traditional New Year's bonfire. As they joined the line waiting to make the first prayer of the New Year, Yumi's hand slipped into Kenji's pocket and found his. They waited on the walkway leading to the shrine steps as bells began to toll at distant temples, 108 strikes ringing into the night. The sky was now clearing and dotted with stars, the moon reflecting on streets still shining from the rain. The last bell faded as midnight arrived, and all up and down the line people began to wish each other happy new year.

Kenji found himself overcome with gratitude and unable to speak. He badly wanted to kiss Yumi, but that would be unseemly in the midst of their neighbors, so he contented himself with pulling her into his arms. He closed his eyes savoring the sweetness of the moment, until a discreet clearing of the throat by Mrs. Matsumoto, who was standing behind them, reminded him that it was almost their turn at the offering box.

Mumbling an embarrassed "*sumimasen*" to the smiling coffee shop owner when he saw the gap that had opened up in front of them, Kenji pulled Yumi up the steps and reached into his pocket for a pair of ¥100 coins. He handed one to her, and they stepped up to the big box with slats on top. Throwing in their coins, they bowed twice and clapped their hands in unison.

*Thank you for granting my wish,* Kenji prayed guiltily, hoping the *kami-sama* had disregarded his less-grateful thoughts on the day of the earthquake.

*Thank you for good health.*

*Please give me good luck in the year ahead.*

*And on the Assistant Inspector's Exam,* he added for good measure.

He followed Yumi down the steps to the line for the hot sweet sake that was being ladled out by shrine maidens in robes topped with puffy Uniqlo jackets. They downed their *amazake* in the flickering shadows thrown by the bonfire, then Kenji took Yumi's hand and they strolled toward home. When they got to the corner where a right turn led to her house and a left turn led to his, she didn't even hesitate before turning left with him.

The Ikedas' dog barked at them once from behind the fence, and he noted with approval that the construction crew had made good progress on the neighbor's house. Kenji paused to fish in his pocket for his key. His father was over in Tabata, manning the police box so his subordinates could spend New Year's with their young families.

They stepped inside and barely had their slippers on before Kenji scooped Yumi into his arms and the desire that had been crackling between them all evening burst into flame. He laughed as her cold hands found their way under his shirt to his warm back, then his lips met hers.

In his pocket, his phone vibrated. He tossed it onto the *tatami* floor and swept Yumi into his arms, carrying her to his room. He laid her softly on his futon, then lay down beside her, pulling the chilly covers over them and holding her close.

Soon, they became a little island of warmth, glowing in the cold winter night, her skin against his all the tinder they needed to feed the embers that had smoldered since that first night in the alleyway behind the Goth club in Shibuya.

•

By the time the full moon showed its face in a corner of the window, Yumi was sleeping like an angel, her hair fanned on the pillow. Kenji kissed her gently on the cheek and got up to fetch some water. Pulling on his bath *yukata* as he made his way to the kitchen, he kicked something lying on the floor and sent it skittering. His phone.

Squinting as he turned on the light, he got down on his hands and knees and discovered it under the kitchen table.

Someone had called. His father. Wishing him a happy new year?

Kenji filled a glass with water and drank deeply, then returned the call, knowing a belated new year's greeting would be welcomed even in the wee hours of the morning, as Sergeant Nakamura kept the police box lights burning until First Sunrise.

His father picked up.

"Happy New Year, Dad," Kenji said.

"Happy . . . New Year." His father's voice was strange.

"Are you okay? Dad?"

Silence.

"Dad, what happened?"

"You know that accident your mother had when you were in high school?"

How could he forget? It had killed her.

"Yes," Kenji answered, a bad feeling blooming as the silence stretched.

"Tonight I found out . . . it wasn't an accident."

## About The Author

**Jonelle Patrick** is the author of four *Only In Tokyo* mysteries. She's a graduate of Stanford University and the Sendagaya Japanese Institute in Tokyo.

She's also a member of the International Thriller Writers, the Mystery Writers of America, and Sisters In Crime.

Jonelle lives in Tokyo and San Francisco.

*Follow Jonelle at:*

Her website (jonellepatrick.com),

Her *Only In Japan* blog (jonellepatrick.me),

*The Tokyo Guide I Wish I'd Had* (jonellepatrick.com)

Facebook (JonellePatrickAuthor).

Twitter: @jonellepatrick

## Acknowledgments

Heartfelt thanks to my intrepid readers, Lisa Hirsch, Darlis Wood, and Ruth Girill – you not only saved Yumi and Kenji from implausible violence and literary faux pas, you did it on short deadline, with generosity of spirit, grace and tact.

And I couldn't have immersed myself in the world of Japanese music, costumes so fabulous they defy description, and the constant surprise of things not always being what they seem, without the friendship of Sarah, Yukiro, Tara, Masashi, Michelle, Lily, Mathieu, Midnight Mess Maya, Nekoi Psydoll and the incomparable La Carmina. Thank you for inviting me to come along on your never-ending wild ride!

A big thank you to Ayumi Shirao, for fearlessly accompanying me into uncharted music industry territory, even when things took unexpected turns.

For introducing me to the talented and carefree spirits of Yoyogi Park, thank you to awesome slackliner and climber, Atsuhiko Kida. For teaching me about *rakugo* and showing me how it's done, a deep bow to Hiroyuki Ootomo. For a little glimpse into the incredible life of a music industry stylist, thanks go to Miho Yoshida. For telling me about his first-hand experience helping rescue pets after the Tōhoku tsunami, *arigatō* to Satoshi Takamura. And to Shuhei Takei, Rie Fukazawa, Takahisa Matsuyama, Takuya Watanabe, and all the slackline *nakama*, thank you for the countless things you helped me understand. I stirred your friendship into this book, and that's what made it come alive.

As always, boundless gratitude to my editing team, Sandy Harding, Elizabeth Bistrow, and Carolyn Hiley. Your expertise in catching all the loose ends left maddeningly untied made this book better in every way. You are the best, and a pleasure to work with, always.

To my agent, April Eberhardt, thank you always for your unfailing support and friendship.

To Marcia Pillon, Katherine Catmull, Paula Span and Pamela McCorduck, my love forever for injections of friendship when I needed it most.

And for encouraging me to range far afield, supporting me while I study Japanese on distant shores, and not letting your eyes glaze over when I start talking about Japan *again*, thank you to my family, near and far. Special thanks to Matsuno Patrick, whose generosity made it possible for me to write this book.

Read on for a sneak peek at the next

Only In Tokyo Mystery:

## PAINTED DOLL

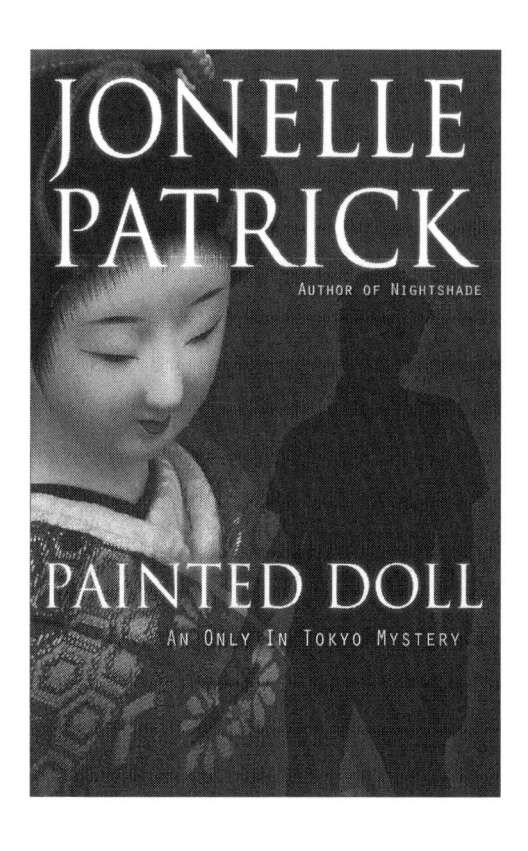

# Painted Doll

### Thursday, December 4

•

A pillow of white capped her gravestone, the first snow of winter.

He frowned at the dead flowers. Brown heads forever bowed, the dried chrysanthemum stalks shivered in the wind. Didn't her family care enough to keep them fresh? He lifted the withered stems from their stone vases and set them aside, then drew a stick of incense from his pocket. His hands were cold. It took him two tries with the lighter before a thread of smoke curled toward the leaden sky. He poked it through the icy crust on the altar.

Uncapping the bottle of water he'd bought at the vending machine down the street, he emptied it over her gravestone. The snow dissolved, leaving the pale granite beneath bare and gleaming. Setting the empty bottle carefully on the ground, he drew a pack of cigarettes from his pocket and stripped off the wrapper. Placing one between his lips, he held the flame to the tip, closed his eyes, tasted the unfiltered tobacco that reminded him of that day. Taking it from his mouth, he laid it next to the smoldering incense, watching as the twin streams of smoke mingled and twisted toward heaven.

Sinking to his knees, he folded his hands, wincing at the twinge that was new since the last time he'd knelt on this patch of cold ground.

Nine years, he thought. Nine death anniversaries. Tomorrow would be the tenth. He always came early, so he wouldn't cross paths with the remnants of her family. He always came on the day he'd actually killed her.

## Wednesday, January 1

•

Kenji Nakamura stepped off the train onto the Tabata Station platform and felt an icy finger of winter slip through a gap in his hastily wound muffler. The platform at this stop was deserted, even though it was New Year's Eve. Actually, he thought, New Year's Day. Midnight was long gone.

Beyond the sheltering roof, snow now plummeted down in earnest. He stopped to unwind the old gray scarf that had been his mother's last gift before she died. Gritting his teeth against the chill, he shook it out and put it on more carefully, stuffing the ends inside his coat and buttoning it up a notch. The button came off in his hand. He frowned, dropping it into his pocket. He needed a new winter coat, but shopping was such a chore—the largest size of the Japanese brands was too short for him, the foreign styles cut too wide.

The platform's warning bell rang and the train pulled away, riffling Kenji's hair and leaving a maelstrom of snowflakes spinning crazily in its wake. He shoved his hands into his pockets and began trudging toward the exit at the end of the long platform. How could it turn so cold, so fast? Six hours ago, he and Yumi had shared an umbrella, not letting a little rain dampen their giddiness that she was free at last. Her engagement to the man she'd met through an arranged marriage *o-miai* had officially ended yesterday.

Now they could be together, the way he'd dreamed of since the first day he saw her, the day his third grade teacher stood her up in front of the class and introduced the new girl from America. He *should* be with her right now. He should never have returned that missed call.

He was lucky that this was the one time a year that trains ran all night. Or, rather, *un*lucky—if there had been no easy way to get to his father before morning, he would still be snug in his warm futon, with Yumi by his side, maybe even finishing what they'd. . . . Kenji felt his face grow hot, remembering how he'd failed to open the box of condoms he'd bought that afternoon and tuck one under his pillow, just in case tonight turned out to be The First Time. When the moment arrived, he was afraid that even if Yumi didn't think badly of him for being prepared, she might misinterpret the reason he'd unthinkingly done the math and chosen the economy-sized pack.

Well, after last night, he was sure there would be other nights. They didn't have to rush things. He smiled, remembering how she had tucked herself in even closer to him after she fell asleep.

Stepping onto the escalator, he let it bear him up toward the south exit, then beeped his way through the turnstile without slowing. Feathery patches of snow began to spot his coat as soon as he left the protection of the overhang. Angling himself against the wind, he set out for the police box manned by his father on this loneliest of nights.

Even the most far-flung families reunited for the holidays, but ever since Kenji's mother had died ten years ago, his father had volunteered for duty every New Year's Eve, on the night nobody wanted to be at work.

*It wasn't an accident.*

That's what his father had said on the phone tonight. How could he suddenly know—after all these years, in the middle of the night—that Kenji's mother's death hadn't been an accident?

So, what was it? It hadn't been suicide. The investigation had ruled that out. And it couldn't have been a crime. Kenji knew about crime. As a police detective, crime was his business. But crimes were something that happened to other people, people who put themselves in harm's way, people who invited bad luck upon themselves. Crimes didn't happen to policemen's wives. Crimes didn't happen to policemen's *mothers*.

Crossing the street by the pachinko parlor, head down, clumps of falling snow pelted his face and melted as soon as they hit. An icy trickle ran through his hair and down his neck. He should have grabbed his dad's old felt hat before he left. He trudged up the hill, squinting into the wind. Two more blocks.

Why had his dad dropped this on him *now*? His mother had died ten years ago. In a train accident. *A not-accident.*

Sergeant Nakamura had been working the graveyard shift that night, too. He'd come home the next morning to find his wife's slippers lined up neatly at the edge of the *tatami* and an empty space in the shoe cupboard where her winter boots usually sat. There was no note, so he hadn't worried. No note meant she'd be back soon, that she'd gone out to do something that wasn't worth an explanation. That she'd be back before the family woke up and realized she was gone.

Kenji's father had gone to bed thinking nothing was amiss, but when he awoke in the early afternoon, he'd found both sons sitting in the kitchen, strangely silent and more than a little hungry. Two half-finished bowls of rice sat on the table, every grain still rock-hard in the center. Even though Kenji and his older brother were in high school, they still hadn't known how much water to put in the rice cooker.

The refrigerator was filled to bursting, but they hadn't dared touch the plastic-wrapped plates that their mother had made for her upcoming high school get-together, the ones papered in sticky notes scribbled with "DO NOT EAT!"

Sergeant Nakamura had phoned his sister first. His wife had gone out early, he said, but wasn't back yet. Had Sachiko stopped by to see Ayako and her family, by any chance? No, sorry, they hadn't seen her, but tell her thanks for recommending the new acupuncturist. Uncle's headaches were much better.

Next, his dad began calling the rest of the relatives, then friends, then everyone he could think of. By the time he slowly hung up the phone for the last time, worry had replaced the irritation that she hadn't returned in time to make breakfast for the boys.

Kenji's brother suggested a friend might have called with an emergency. Mom would have gone out any time, day or night, for a friend. They all nodded, then looked at each other. Who *were* her friends? None of them had ever stopped to wonder what Sachiko Nakamura did, in between the cooking and cleaning and washing that kept their lives running smoothly.

Her friends' numbers would be on her phone, wouldn't they? Kenji asked. They searched for it, but it was gone, along with her purse.

They didn't know what to do next. None of them could remember her saying anything about helping a neighbor or getting in line early for a sale. Of course, that didn't really mean anything —every day she told them plenty of things that went in one ear and out the other.

*I'm running out to the store to buy some fish for dinner.*

*I think I'll get you some new socks on the shopping street. They're having a sale.*

*I'll be a little late, because I'm picking up Mrs. Kimura's prescription for her.*

And then the phone rang. A female accident victim had been found near the tracks of the Toyoko Line. Kenji's father went to the hospital alone, to identify the body that had been spotted by a hungover high school student on his way to weekend basketball practice. The local police were conducting an investigation. Two days later, they'd pronounced it an accident.

*It wasn't an accident.*

Kenji turned the corner at the top of the hill and saw the police box ahead, its wide front window glowing like a beacon for lost children and victims of minor crimes. Every neighborhood had a *koban* like this, manned by officers who knew everyone on their patch by name, thanks to the mandatory visits they made twice a year to update the particulars of every household. The police box officers were as much a part of everyday life as the mailman, consulted not only if you wanted to report a crime, but also if you needed directions to the new café, had lost your cat, had found a dropped glove on the street.

As a boy, Kenji had always stopped to look at the wanted posters on the bulletin board outside, wondering what bungles had caused a fugitive to be missing joints on both pinky fingers, or why a suspected murderer had only three remaining teeth. But tonight he didn't even glance at the sketches as he strode past, slowing only as he approached the door of the narrow stucco-clad building with the Tokyo Metropolitan Police's bronze star over the door.

Through the window, he could see his father seated behind a wide metal desk, official notices tacked to the wall beside him. A well-thumbed book of local maps sat neatly squared on the corner of the desk. The gold buttons on his uniform gleamed, and his hat was firmly settled on his graying brush-cut hair.

But tonight Sergeant Nakamura wasn't sitting ramrod straight, he was hunched over a red clay teacup, staring into its depths. It was one of the pair his father and mother had brought home from their honeymoon.

He looked up as Kenji pushed through the door. He wasn't alone.

"Happy New Year, Ken-*kun*." A man with sad eyes bowed from the doorway to the back room.

Kenji returned the bow, recognizing his father's longtime poker crony, who had just retired in November.

"Happy New Year to you, too, Officer Toyama."

It was the first time Kenji had seen the ex-policeman out of uniform. In his plaid flannel shirt and fleece sweatpants, he looked . . . smaller. Had Toyama-*san* shrunk? Kenji remembered him from boyhood, an imposing figure who always had a riddle for the boss's son and would fish a piece of candy from his pocket if Kenji guessed right.

"What are you doing here in the middle of the night, Toyama-*san*?" Kenji asked, pulling the door shut behind him.

"He came with me," said a voice Kenji hadn't heard since high school. A younger version of Officer Toyama appeared behind his father.

"Sho-*sempai*! Happy New Year."

Mr. Toyama's son returned the greeting with the same lopsided grin he'd worn when their high school baseball team won the division championship. Sho had been Kenji's mentor, his *sempai*—a senior pitcher when Kenji was a first-year rookie. Sho was shorter, but made up for it by being built like a brick wall. As expected, Toyama Junior had followed in his father's footsteps and gone straight to the police academy after graduation.

"You still working out of Saitama Station?" Kenji asked.

"No, they transferred me to Shinjuku two months ago." He grimaced. "Just in time for the quake."

Ten days ago, a 7.9 temblor had given Tokyo a severe shaking. Every division was still working around the clock to deal with the criminals who had been caught with their pants down in the chaos that followed.

"And actually, that's why I'm here," Sho explained. "I was one of the locals assigned to help bag and tag a scene for the First Investigative Division after a warehouse in East Shinjuku collapsed."

"Why were the big boys involved in an earthquake accident?" Kenji asked. The First Investigative Division was only called in to take over when an incident turned into a major crime: extortion, robbery, rape, murder.

Sho snorted. "It turned out that the janitorial service headquartered in the building was storing more than mops and wax there. A bunch of illegal Chinese girls were locked in a back room, and one was in the wrong place at the wrong time when a stack of crates fell. The scumbags moved her body outside, trying to make it look like an accident, and a patrol officer caught them dumping her purse and passport into a storm drain. When we searched what was left of the building, we discovered the traffickers had stripped the girls of everything they owned, and locked their stuff in a storeroom marked 'Toxic, Keep Out,' along with a couple of crates of Chinese handguns. At the very back, we found . . . *that*."

He nodded toward a small suitcase sitting beside the front door. Cobwebby and coated with dust, it had once been dark blue. "Inspector Mori got pretty excited when he opened it up. He made me take it to the crime lab right away. Said it was tied to a case he'd worked on ten years ago."

Ten years ago. The same year Kenji's mother died?

"What kind of case?" Kenji asked, suddenly uneasy.

"Don't know, except that it's an unsolved."

So it couldn't be his mother's death. That had been ruled an accident. *It wasn't an accident.*

Kenji turned to his dad. "But what does this piece of luggage have to do with Mom?"

His father's frown grew deeper.

Sho answered for him. "Inspector Mori wasn't actually interested in the suitcase—it was the stuff packed inside he wanted. But they found a receipt for three bus tour tickets in one of the side pockets, along with a luggage tag that had your mom's name on it. He figured the bag belonged to her, asked me to return it to you when the lab boys were done with it."

Kenji raised his eyebrows at his father.

"It's hers," Sergeant Nakamura admitted. "She bought it right before she went on that damn trip to the Ise Shrine with her old high school friends."

"And . . . ?"

His dad scowled. "Mori wants me to come in, ask me a bunch of questions that I won't know the answers to. He's going to try to make this into something it's not."

"Hey, now," Mr. Toyama chided. "Just because Mori-*san* wants you to come in and talk to him about that suitcase doesn't mean Sachiko's death was anything but an accident. Sho said it was only the stuff inside he was interested in. Who knows how some illegal Chinese girl ended up with that bag? Maybe your sister gave it away after the funeral, and didn't realize there was anything still in it that belonged to your wife."

Sergeant Nakamura shook his head, unconvinced.

Kenji crossed the small room to stand before his dad's desk. "There's only one way to find out," he said. "When you go see Inspector Mori, I'm going with you."

•

Kenji's father shot to his feet, scooping up his empty cup, said something about getting more tea. But when he got to the back room, he dropped his cup on the counter by the hot water pot and detoured to the toilet instead, pulling the door shut with a bang. Flipping the lock, he spun around and braced himself on the sink, hung his head, breathing hard.

*Get a grip, Nakamura.* His old judo teacher's voice echoed in his head. *Breathe. Breathe. In*, two, three, four, *hold it*, two, three, four, *out*, two, three, four. *Again. Again. Slower. Again.* He straightened and raised his chin, making the tears drain back inside. *Manly sniff. Clear. Swallow.* Good. He frowned into the mirror, assured himself he didn't look like someone who would ever weep like a woman, and gave thanks for the *sensei* who had taught him to control his weaknesses.

He'd hated the old bastard for how he'd done it, of course, but it had been worth it. He'd never have become the man he was without the old taskmaster, certainly never would have made it through the police academy. And if he'd never made it through the Academy, he never would have married Sachiko. That first day at the *koban*, while he was filling out her missing bicycle theft report as slowly as possible so he had time to think of a way to see her again, she'd told him that her father had been a sergeant at the police box on the other side of the train station. That her uncle was a beat cop in Chiba.

For a long time, he'd figured that was why a tall, sparkly girl like Sachiko had chosen a quiet, square guy like him—she came from a family of cops. It wasn't until they were arguing over how to handle the bullying Kenji's brother Takeo was getting in first grade, that he realized how determined Sachi was to raise a family that was nothing like the one she grew up in. That was the first, in a long line of compromises: She had allowed him to find Takeo a judo teacher, and he'd allowed her to have a quiet word with the bullies' moms and find someone to help Takeo with his stutter. Something had worked, because both the bullying and the stuttering had stopped, and they still got New Years postcards from the bullies' families.

Twisting the cold water faucet, he splashed water on his face, rubbing it dry with the towel he'd brought from home, freshly laundered for the new year. Sachi had always insisted they start the year right: house clean, debts paid, apologies made. She'd always tried to do the right thing. And so had he. Until the day she died, he'd tried his damndest to be everything she wanted him to be.

Fear clamped his chest again. Sho said Mori had found clothes, makeup and a metallic blue Nikon CoolPix camera inside that suitcase. He didn't know that was the same kind Sachi had owned, the one he'd looked for after her death.

*Breathe, dammit, breathe.* He slumped over the sink. *Fucking Mori.* He had to stop Kenji from coming to that meeting. Couldn't let his son hear the questions the inspector would ask, the same questions he'd been asked ten years ago. The questions he'd pretended he didn't know the answers to.

•

*Boom. Boom. Boom. Boom.*

Yumi drifted up from sleep. Pulled the pillow over her head. Who was beating a drum at this hour of the. . . ? Oh. This wasn't her room. Kenji's house was a lot closer to the Komagome Shrine than hers. *Kenji.* Rolling over, she turned to peek at the face she'd never seen defenseless in sleep before, but her happiness evaporated when she saw his side of the futon was empty. Where was he? Did he get up early to see the First Sunrise of the New Year? Without her?

She listened. The house was quiet. Feeling around for her phone, she clicked it on. 5:54.

Maybe he'd gotten up to make tea. First Tea of the New Year. First tea *together*. She climbed to her feet, wrapping the comforter around her shoulders like a royal robe. Switching on the light, she looked around for her slippers, found them. Smiled. They didn't match: last night he'd given her one blue plaid, one brown. The First Mismatched Slippers of the New Year.

Scuffing them on, she reached for the doorknob, then hesitated. Had her mascara run while she was sleeping? Yumi swiped beneath each eye with a finger, just in case. She didn't usually wear makeup to bed, but last night after washing her face, she'd put a little back on.

Then she realized what time it was. 5:54. Didn't Kenji's father get off work at six? How long did it take to get to Komagome from Tabata? What if he came through the front door and caught her barefoot, wrapped in Kenji's bedclothes, wearing only her underwear and his son's old baseball jersey?

She looked at the unappealing pile of cold clothes she'd abandoned on the *tatami* last night. Taking a deep breath, she dropped the comforter and scrambled for her tights and skirt. Goosebumps prickled against the chilly t-shirt as she pulled it over her head. Poking her arms into her hoodie, she zipped it up, stuck her hands in the pockets and jumped up and down a few times. Even her bedroom at home was warmer than *this*.

Slipping into the hall, she spied the door to the bathroom standing open and ducked inside. Peering into the mirror over the chipped enamel sink, she experienced the First Regret of the New Year. She should never have cut her hair. Tugging at the short ends near her face, she sighed. It would grow. Eventually. Leaning in, she examined the mascara that had survived the night and decided it would do.

Hustling down the dark hall toward the kitchen, flipping on lights as she went, she hugged herself, hoping Kenji had turned on the old kerosene heater and started tea brewing. But as she rounded the corner, her steps slowed. The kitchen was dark. No heater, no tea, no Kenji. She stopped, confused. Had he gone out? Had he left her here *alone*?

She found the light switch and flicked it on, illuminating the old-fashioned green linoleum floor, the scarred countertops, the blackened gas burner sitting on the counter. Crossing to the low table surrounded by faded floor cushions, she looked for a note. Nothing but a police exam cram guide, splayed face down where Kenji had left off studying.

Last night, he'd told her about the test that would catapult him into an assistant inspector's uniform in the First Investigative Division if he passed it next May. A promotion to the elite murder squad would mean he'd be set for life. Once he'd stepped onto the career escalator that would steadily raise him into the lofty heights of police administration, he'd be able to afford a car, a house, a family.

A *wife*. They'd avoided the word "marriage" because this thing between them was still too new. But she knew how Kenji felt about her. And she no longer had to hide how she felt about him.

At the moment, though, she wasn't feeling so great about his choice of career. Had he been called out on a case? In the middle of the night? On New Year's Eve? Why couldn't criminals take a day off, like everyone else?

Picking up the study guide, she thumbed through it. *Proper search procedure. Hostage situations. Guidelines for use of deadly force.* She quickly set it back on the table, not wanting to be reminded that knowing how to shoot meant that others could be shooting back, and someday he might go to work and never come home.

Turning off the lights, she retraced her steps. Stood in the entry, unsure what to do, but not wanting Kenji's father to come through the front door and find her there alone. That would be . . . awkward. Then she remembered there had been unread messages on her phone when she checked the time. She went to fetch it from Kenji's room.

Sure enough, the one sent at 2:41 a.m. was from him: *got a call, will try to get back before you wake up*

Well, he hadn't.

5:17 a.m., Kenji again: *sorry, still tied up here, not sure when I'll be back. call you later?*

Disappointment closed her throat, as the day that had stretched ahead with such promise shriveled and died. Instead of wandering hand-in-hand among the festival booths at the Komagome Shrine, laughing as they tried to scoop up goldfish with paper nets, sharing sticks of grilled squid and *yakitori* chicken, she'd be stuck with her parents in their drafty old house, eating cold New Year's food, and being dragged along to exchange dutiful New Year's greetings with her father's university colleagues. If Kenji had been assigned to investigate something serious, he'd be on duty until further notice.

Yumi glumly unhooked her coat from the rack. Shrugging into it and winding her muffler around her neck twice, she pulled on one glove, then stopped to see who the other text was from.

12:37 a.m. Her mother. *Where are you? Come home immediately. We have some things to discuss.*

Ugh. It looked like she was about to have the First Fight of the New Year.

Hoping Kenji wouldn't mind if she borrowed one of the umbrellas propped by his front door, she slipped out, angling it against the storm. It was still dark. She trudged through the familiar streets, silent except for muffled crunches as her boots poked holes in the fresh snow. She fumbled a tissue from her pocket and wiped a drip from the end of her nose, skirting a jumble of bikes pushed over by the wind. Her footsteps slowed as she turned the corner toward home.

Snowflakes swarmed down like insects through the cone of light cast by the streetlamp in front of the Hata family's house, settling in the rickety planter beside the front door. The chrysanthemums her mother had been so proud of in November had withered in the sudden cold snap, the stalks now bent under their heavy caps of white.

The Hatas' old wooden house huddled between two modest apartment buildings, one clad in grimy stucco, the other in beige tile. The neighborhood had survived the World War II firebombing, but not the temptation to modernize afterwards. Those who could afford it tore down the drafty old wood-and-paper structures their families had lived in for generations and put up multi-story boxes with aluminum windows and a separate floor for the in-laws.

But Yumi's grandparents hadn't been among them. The Hata family home was still made of unpainted cedar, stained so dark by years of weather that the wood grain was barely visible anymore. The roof was tiled in dark gray, each crack and dip now outlined in white. Her grandparents had replaced the paper in their *shoji* screen windows with pebbled glass, and stapled thick electrical cords ending in a single boxy outlet to the baseboards of every room, but nothing short of tearing the place down and rebuilding would keep the old house warm in winter and cool in summer.

When Yumi and her parents had moved back from America so her father could take a lecturer's position at Tokyo Women's University, they'd planned to renovate. But as her dad was passed over time and again for promotion, the plans to tear down the old place and rebuild a home that Yumi's mother could be proud of slowly curled up and died. Over the years, they'd replaced the two burners sitting on the kitchen counter with a real stove and traded the weathered front door for one made of stamped metal and frosted glass. Her mother considered it an improvement, but Yumi secretly thought it looked like lipstick on a washerwoman.

She paused outside, dreading hearing what *things* her mother thought they needed to *discuss*. But luck was with her—the windows were still dark. Maybe she'd be able to sneak into her room, shut the door, and sleep past the time her parents left to make the obligatory New Year's visits.

Pulling off one glove with her teeth, she pawed through her purse in search of her key and stepped up to fit it into the lock. *Thwap*. She winced at the sound, slid the door open just wide enough to slip inside, listened. Silence. Easing the door shut behind her, she stood for a moment to let her eyes adjust to the dark, then unwound her muffler, plucked off her hat, and hung her coat by the door.

All she had to do now was get past the squeaky patch in the hall, avoid tripping over the recycling bag in the kitchen, and remember to lift the door to her bedroom as she slid it open, so it wouldn't catch. Slipping out of her boots, she crept down the hall, located the recycling with a cautious toe, then aimed at the door on the far side that led to her bedroom.

"It's about time."

Yumi groaned. Her mother. Sitting at the kitchen table. In the dark.

Mrs. Hata climbed stiffly to her feet and flipped on the lights, wincing at the sudden brightness. A cup of cold tea and a half-finished Sudoku puzzle sat on the table. Hair lopsided from dozing during her vigil, Yumi's mother squinted at her watch, then glared at her daughter.

"Sorry," Yumi muttered.

"What do you mean, 'Sorry'? Why didn't you answer my calls?"

"I'm twenty-six years old," Yumi reminded her.

"And you're *unmarried* and you live at *home*, which means you at least owe us the courtesy of letting us know where you are."

"Sorry," Yumi repeated, feeling even less sorry than before.

Silence.

"I didn't want to wake you up, coming in at two in the morning after we visited the shrines, so I crashed at . . . a friend's house."

"I certainly hope that 'friend' wasn't Kenji Nakamura."

Holy crap! How did she know?

"I ran into Haruko Matsumoto on the way home last night," said Mrs. Hata. "She mentioned she'd seen the two of you at the Komagome Shrine, around midnight. What in heaven's name do you think you were you doing? You're supposed to be engaged to Ichiro Mitsuyama!"

"But I'm not!"

"As of yesterday. Which nobody knows. Yet."

Yumi felt a twinge of shame. She hadn't thought about how being seen with Kenji would look to everyone who didn't know the wedding was off, and the news had yet to be broadcast on the neighborhood grapevine.

Tokyo might be the most populous city in the world, but living in Komagome was like living in a small town. Most of the businesses on the shopping street had been handed down for generations, and most of the residents had grown up together. And their parents had grown up together. And their *grandparents* had grown up together. Gossip from fifty years ago was still repeated as if it had happened yesterday.

"Sorry," Yumi muttered again.

"If you had an ounce of common sense," her mother scolded, "you'd realize that people would jump to the wrong conclusion if they saw you in line at the shrine on New Year's Eve with someone who's not your fiancé." Her eyes narrowed. "Or was it the *right* conclusion? What's going on, Yumi? Were you carrying on with that Nakamura boy while you were engaged to Ichiro?"

"No!"

But Yumi's face burned. She'd never *technically* cheated on the man she'd been cornered into marrying after his family arranged for her father to become a tenured professor at Toba University, but she hadn't been able to entirely resist the attraction that had blazed up six months ago when she and Kenji had crossed paths again for the first time since high school.

"I don't think you realize how important it is to let people know about this business in the right way." Mrs. Hata's aggrieved tone told Yumi she had yet to forgive her daughter for turning her back on the match of the century. "If people hear you were already out with someone new on the very same day your engagement was broken, they'll assume you were the one who deserved to be dumped."

•

The sun poked a tentative beam through the trees surrounding the Komagome Shrine, and Kenji breathed a sigh of relief, watching his father laugh for the first time since the blue suitcase had reentered their lives. Toyama Senior had talked them into cutting through the shrine grounds on their way home, where they ran into another poker buddy, busy setting up the grilled squid stand he manned every New Year's Day. Two hours later, the tide in a party-size bottle of saké had been lowered, and they were still there, wearing dark blue festival coats and reddened holiday faces.

Behind them, the shrine's red and gold eaves spread like benevolent wings, soaring over the parishioners as they stamped their feet in the snow, waiting to toss their coins into the slatted wooden offering box. Bright banners snapped in the breeze all around, touting everything from fried octopus balls to roasted sweet potatoes. Fragrant smoke filled the air as the first chicken, squid and skewered sweetfish began to sizzle over charcoal fires. The squid stand enjoyed a choice spot among the vendors lining the main path to the shrine, and a long line of locals arriving to make the new year's first offering had been tempted into detouring for a tasty skewer to munch as they waited to climb the steps to the offering box.

But Kenji and Sho had made their First Shrine Visit the night before, so instead of waiting in line, they were listening to Mr. Toyama reminisce about epic poker games past, when his wife arrived, towed by a foxy-looking shiba dog.

"There you are!" she said, fixing a baleful eye on her husband and son. "How long does it take to deliver a suitcase, anyway?"

Toyama winced. "Sorry. We got to talking and—"

"—and then Ken-*kun* came, so we had to catch up—" Sho added.

"—and then they stopped by to give me a hand," supplied their friend, the squid-griller, beaming with holiday cheer.

"Looks like they've been giving you a hand with that bottle of *dai-ginjo* too," Mrs. Toyama observed dryly, spotting the half-empty saké bottle.

The dog whined and gave her a reproving look.

"I know, sweets," she said, slipping it a treat. Turning to Sho, she said, "Kaiju still has to leave his calling cards at his favorite bushes, but Haru-*chan* asked me to bring her a rice ball for breakfast. Are you going home soon? Could you stop by the Family Mart on your way back?"

"Sure." Sho heaved a party's-over sigh.

Kenji turned to him and said, "That reminds me: congratulations. I hear you're having a baby."

"Yeah, Haru's due any day now. What about you? You married yet?"

"Not yet, but . . . . " Kenji grinned. *Yumi. Last night.*

"Anyone I know?"

Kenji hesitated. It was still too early to tell anyone. But he smiled, remembering the way her hair fell over her cheek as she slept, how her...*oh shit*. What time was it? He checked. How could it already be 9:20? He'd meant to message her long before now. The suitcase had pushed everything else from his mind. He pulled out his phone. *good morning & happy new year! meet me at the shrine? i'm at the squid stand.* Send.

"Hey, by the way," Sho said, "did you hear about that girl you had such a crush on in high school? Yumi Hata? Haru told me she's engaged to some super rich guy, family owns the Mitsuyama department stores. Every girl in the neighborhood is wondering how she got so lucky. I mean, she wasn't even popular in high school." He laughed. "Except with you."

"Actually," Kenji said, a smile spreading across his face as he pocketed his phone, "I hear that wedding is off."

•

Yumi awoke with a start as the phone still clutched in her hand pinged. She must have dozed off after the First Fight.

Text from Kenji. Yes! The First Date of the New Year was back on. She squinted at the time. 9:21.

*See you soon*, she typed, then flung off the covers and made her way across the cramped room, scooping up last night's dirty clothes and dumping them in her laundry basket. Sliding open what used to be the futon closet, she shivered, rummaging for the pants that would go with her new...*kawhumph*. The clothes bar slipped from the wire loops that had been temporarily rigged fifteen years ago and every piece of clothing she owned collapsed in a heap on the floor.

Crap. Why did this always happen at the worst time? It would take half an hour to unhook all the hangers, stick the bar back where it belonged, and re-hang all her clothes. Forget it, she'd do it later. Pawing through the heap, she found the pants she wanted and pulled them from the tangle, then rescued a squashed shopping bag with the sweater she'd been saving for her date with Kenji.

Plucking fresh socks and underwear from her clean laundry basket, she ran to the bathroom for a quick wash.

Fifteen minutes later, she waited until she heard her father cross the kitchen floor, rinse his teacup and head back down the hall, then slung her bag onto her shoulder, and tiptoed to the front door. Pulling a slouchy knit hat down around her ears and grabbing her coat, she muttered a barely audible "*itte kimasu*" and was out before anyone had a chance to reply.

A biting wind was pushing the clouds around the sky and the temperature was dropping. Yumi squinted against the snowy glare, buttoning her coat and pulling on her gloves.

The snow had capped everything—from the corner vending machine to the stone bollards in front of the station—with round white beanies. Yumi slowed to join the throng funneling through the shrine's pi-shaped *torii* gate.

She had already given the gods their due last night when she visited the shrine with Kenji, so she didn't stop to join the four-deep line of people waiting to make their First Offering of the New Year. A shorter line stood before the jumbo bin that was built specially for New Year's trash, and she was sorry she'd forgotten to bring last year's good-health amulet to burn with the sacred garbage. A shiny laminated sign was tacked to the front of the bin, forbidding people to throw in stuffed animals, good luck Daruma figures and baby dolls. The priests were probably tired of being exposed to the toxic fumes that roiled up as plastic parts went up in smoke, but Yumi couldn't really blame people for wanting to honorably cremate childhood toys that had acquired a soul after years of being loved.

She detoured to the shrine store to buy a wooden prayer plaque screened with this year's zodiac animal. Taking her *ema* to the nearby counter, she flipped it over and penned a wish that she and Kenji would be happy together in the coming year. She took it to the rack already stacked ten deep with her neighbors' hopes and dreams, looking for a peg that wasn't quite full yet.

Making her way back through the crowd toward the food booths, she spotted Kenji behind the counter of the squid stand, smiling and handing two skewers to someone who looked vaguely familiar. Was that their middle school math teacher? Mr. Ito used to be young and crush-worthy! When had his hair turned *gray*?

Kenji looked up and saw her coming. He grinned and waved. Excusing himself, he whipped off his head cloth and shed his festival coat.

"Hey," he said, shouldering through the crowd and handing her one of the squid skewers he'd grabbed on his way out.

"Hey."

"I'm really sorry about last night," he began. "I mean, not *all* of last night." His face reddened. "Just the part where I left while you were still asleep. Were you still there when you got my messages?"

"No, I went home around six for a shower, some clean clothes and the First Lecture of the New Year."

"The what?"

"My mom heard we were together at the shrine last night, and now she's worried that everyone will think I'm a brazen hussy because they don't know the wedding is off."

Kenji groaned. "On no. I hadn't thought about that. I'm really sorry. I—"

"Don't be. It's stupid. I mean, what is this, the Edo era? Why should we care what people think?"

Kenji was silent. He looked away, suddenly uncomfortable.

"You do care," she said. Her heart sank.

"I'm sorry, Yu-chan. It's just . . . I don't just live here, I'm stationed here. It's not that I don't—" He looked around. "Look, can we talk about this somewhere that's not so crowded?"

She fell in behind him as they aimed for the shrine garden, threading their way through the scrum of festivalgoers. Arcs of split bamboo leapt in and out of the snow, fencing the stone path that led to the gate. It creaked as Kenji pushed it open.

While Kenji brushed the snow from a bench under the bare plum trees, Yumi looked around, thinking how different the familiar garden looked when it was blanketed in white. The moss and low bushes had become undulating hills, with sparkling crests and blue-shadowed hollows. Overhead, crisscrossing plum branches framed fast-moving clouds. In a few weeks, they'd be robed in frilly pink, but today the flower buds knobbing the twigs were still gray and hard as knots.

Kenji sat, pulling her down next to him. Keeping hold of her hands, he said, "You know how I feel about you. How I've always felt about you. But . . . . "

"I understand," she said with a sigh. "It's Ichiro's family, isn't it?"

Her ex's father had friends in all the right places, and the ones in the loftier heights of the Police Administration had turned a blind eye last spring when Mitsuyama Senior had forbidden Yumi to testify in one of Kenji's cases. If any of them heard gossip that Kenji was responsible for breaking up the Mitsuyama heir's engagement, it wouldn't matter how mistaken they were, they still might block him from rising any further up the elite career escalator.

"Look," she said, trying to smile. "It's not the end of the world. While we're waiting for word to get around—or Ichiro to run off with his American girlfriend, whichever comes first—we can still see each other, can't we? We just have to do it in some part of town where the Great and Good fear to tread."

"Like...?"

"I dunno, Sugamo? Takadanobaba?"

Kenji cracked a smile, recognizing the name of the area known for street markets that sold lucky red long johns to the over-sixty set, and the neighborhood that boasted the highest concentration of outlandish makeup and beauty schools in Tokyo.

"I'm sure there are plenty of places that the Mitsuyamas have yet to conquer," he said. Sobering, he added, "I'm really sorry it has to be like this, Yu-chan. I—"

"Shh!" she stopped him, laying a finger on his lips. "Save the apologies for something you really *should* be sorry for. Like running out on me in the middle of the night, so I had to face the First Phone Alarm of the New Year alone." She withdrew her hands and tucked them into her jacket pockets. "What happened? Did you get called out on a case?"

"Yeah. Sort of." He fell silent.

"Ken-kun?"

"It was my dad who called. About my mom."

"Your mom?"

"Yeah. He thinks her accident . . . wasn't an accident."

"What?"

Kenji explained about the blue suitcase that had been found in the aftermath of the big quake, a suitcase that had belonged to his mother.

"How did your mom's luggage end up in a basement full of Chinese immigrants?" she asked.

"That's what I'd like to know. My father said she bought the bag for a bus tour to the Ise Shrine, but I'd never seen it before." He shook his head. "Something about this is really upsetting him. I'm going with him when he talks to Inspector Mori tomorrow, to find out what I can."

"But why did he tell you your mother's death wasn't an accident?"

"I don't know that either. I asked him, but he never really answered. The guy who found it told me that the stuff packed inside was tied to an unsolved case from ten years ago, but I don't know why my dad thinks it has anything to do with my mom. I mean, the bag was hers, but the things inside weren't. What's worrying me is that he said Inspector Mori was going to 'try and make this into something it's not.' Sounds like there's some history there, something he's not telling me. Which is why I want to go with him tomorrow and hear what Mori has to say."

Yumi nodded. She wanted to know more about his mother, but cold was seeping through her clothes. And she was getting hungry.

"Want to get in line for the First Octopus Balls of the New Year, before the line gets too long?" she asked, as a gust of wind blew the ends of her hair across her eyes.

"Sure." Kenji pulled her to her feet and she followed him out of the garden, the gate latching closed behind them.

The crowd had swelled while they'd been talking, and the shrine grounds were now a roiling river of merry locals. All round them, people were hailing neighbors they hadn't seen since at least yesterday, stopping to bow and exchange new year's greeting, but as Kenji steered them upstream toward the *takoyaki* stand, a different kind of cry rang out over the hubbub.

"Doctor! We need a doctor! Is anyone here a doctor?"

Heads turned toward a flurry of activity, centered at the squid stand. Kenji craned his neck, then abruptly changed course and began pushing his way through the crowd. Yumi followed as best she could in his wake.

"What's going on?" he called to Mr. Toyama, who was standing behind the grill, stabbing at the keypad of his phone.

"It's your dad! He just . . . collapsed!" Putting the phone to his ear, Toyama shouted, "Hello? *Moshi-moshi?* We need an ambulance! Right away!"

•

Kenji's father lay motionless on the ground, his face ashen. He twitched, opening his eyes. Disoriented, he tried to sit up, but Kenji knelt next to him. "Dad, don't."

The elder Nakamura lay back and looked at his son as if he didn't recognize him. "What? Where—?"

"Just lie still, Dad. The ambulance will be here in a minute."

A faint siren grew louder, then stopped nearby. The crowd parted to allow two white-coated medics to push a gurney through. In a moment they were behind the counter, one kneeling to flip open the latches on the mobile diagnostics case, one moving to Kenji's father's side to begin examining him.

"Stop! What are you doing?" Sergeant Nakamura raised himself on an elbow, trying to sit up. "Get away from me! I'm fine!"

Struggling to his feet, Kenji's father backed away, refusing to let the EMTs near him. "Who called the white coats? I don't need them!" he protested, shakily brushing bits of dried leaves from his festival coat. He glared at the onlookers, who turned away, embarrassed they'd been caught staring.

Kenji stepped up and said, "Dad, just let them check your blood pressure and—"

"I'm fine!" he snapped.

But Mr. Toyama had fetched a chair and Sergeant Nakamura grudgingly allowed himself to be lowered into it as the emergency crew strapped on a blood pressure cuff.

"A man ought to be able to have a few cups of saké after pulling a night shift without calling in the cavalry," he grumbled.

Kenji tried to drape his own coat over his dad's festival jacket, but Sergeant Nakamura shook him off, protesting that he wasn't an old woman and didn't need to be treated like one.

But the paramedic's face was grim as he pulled Kenji aside, showing him the numbers he'd jotted in his work log.

"Dad," Kenji said, kneeling next to the chair. "Why don't you go with them to the hospital anyway, so they can give you a thorough check-up and make sure everything's okay. The paramedic says they want to give you some saline because your blood pressure is dangerously low, and your heart rate is—"

"Of course it is!" his father barked. "Yours would be too after—"

His gaze faltered and his face pinched into the grim mask Kenji hadn't seen since the terrible days after his mother died.

*It wasn't an accident.*

Kenji turned to the paramedics and thanked them, apologizing that they'd been called out for nothing. He promised them he'd get his dad home and make sure he took it easy the rest of the day. They left the elder Nakamura with stern instructions to rest, drink plenty of water, and avoid alcohol.

Kenji glanced toward Yumi, who was hovering on the other side of the counter, a worried look on her face. He ought to go over there, tell her what was happening, but there were too many people watching, including a couple of Traffic Division officers who'd like nothing better than some fresh gossip to chew over with their grilled squid.

He pulled out his phone and keyed in a message. *sorry, i have to take my dad home. can i call you later?*

A moment later, he saw her reach into her purse and bring out her phone, then type in a reply. *i understand. do you want me to come along? i could help.*

Kenji glanced at his dad. Sergeant Nakamura's gaze was turned inward, his mouth creased in a deep frown.

*thanks,* Kenji wrote. *but I think i'd better handle this myself. i'll call you later.*

He watched her read his response, saw the disappointment on her face. But all her reply said was, *sure. call me.*

•

The sun had arced across the sky and was on its way down again as Kenji turned his back to the eye-watering breeze that was blowing a glittering plume of snow from the eaves of Sanjo-in Temple. He hunched into his coat, wishing his father would hurry back from the hut where the grave-visiting supplies were kept. He balanced the two skinny bunches of cellophane-wrapped chrysanthemums on a corner of the cemetery's utility sink and shoved his gloved hands into his jacket pockets.

Sergeant Nakamura had gone straight to bed once they got home that morning, ordering Kenji to wake him before 3:00 so they could go to the family New Year's gathering together. But Kenji wasn't convinced that the annual nephew wrestling and saké drinking was such a good idea, so he'd let 3:00 come and go. His father had been so irritated when he woke up at 3:30 that he'd charged around like a bull, angry that they were going to be late. Kenji hadn't dared suggest further changes to the day's plans, so here they were, making their usual visit to the family grave on the coldest New Year's Day he could remember.

His father returned with a wooden bucket and dipper. Kenji took the bucket emblazoned with the Nakamura family crest from him and filled it, as his father picked up the flowers and stalked off into the graveyard. Kenji followed him around the back of the main temple, slipping a little on the snow that was hardening to ice as shadows reclaimed the walkways.

The sun slanted low through the trees as they followed a wide avenue already trampled by dozens of feet since last night's storm. This was an ancient graveyard, in an old part of Tokyo, and only the newest plots had gravestones with spaces for individual names. Family names and crests were all that marked the final resting place of most of the souls spending eternity at Sanjo-in. Monuments lined the path like miniature skyscrapers, each unique. Some were topped by polished slabs of granite carved with the family name, others were marked by obelisks. Many had fresh flowers in the vases flanking the headstone, and fresh ashes in the carved stone incense altars that crouched below.

It was easy to tell which graves had been visited today— freshly washed, they were wet and bare, naked-looking next to monuments still cloaked in white. As they made their way to the Nakamura family plot, Kenji saw personalized offerings that told of a mother remembered, an uncle mourned. A favorite cup, filled with tea; a can of beer, to be enjoyed in the hangover-free afterlife; sometimes a pack of cigarettes with one left smoldering beside it.

Right again, then left, the scuffle of footprints narrowing to a path, then a single pair. Those stopped before a rough-hewn slab carved with the crossed-arrow Miura crest. A parting ray of sunlight glinted off a small bottle of saké, the cap cracked open. Whoever had visited the Miura family grave had bought flowers at the same shop as Kenji's father—

Kenji recognized the lace-patterned cellophane and the chrysanthemum mix sold by the flower shop near the station.

His father's steps slowed as he approached the stone marked with the Nakamura plum blossom crest. A black cat crouching on the plinth tensed as they approached, then flowed off its perch, pausing to give them a final yellow-eyed stare before disappearing into the bushes.

The tall lotus-topped slab that rose behind the incense altar sported a white cap, and little commas of snow had blown into the deeply carved characters that read "Nakamura." Made of pale granite, the marker had been smoothed by a century of wind and rain. It was scrubbed clean every August before the holiday when spirits returned to visit, but patches of pale gray and black lichen had begun to spot the base again, and were creeping up to claim the incense altar.

Kenji pulled a small trash bag from his pocket, then noticed that someone had already removed the dried chrysanthemum stalks he'd expected to find in the flower holders. Who had visited his mother's grave since they were last here? Had Takeo been here, and not told them?

Kenji's older brother didn't come often, and never at New Year's. He was technically no longer a Nakamura. After high school, he'd landed a job at a venerable sushi restaurant out in Jiyugaoka, and married the owner's daughter. His wife's family had no sons, so the Watanabes had formally adopted him. As Takeo Watanabe, he would someday inherit the restaurant that had been in the family for seven generations. His first duty as eldest son was now to his new family, not the one that had been broken wide open when his mother died.

*If you'd like to continue reading* **Painted Doll**...

*Download the ebook from:*

amazon.com

barnesandnoble.com

itunes.apple.com

kobobooks.com

*Or order the paperback from:*

amazon.com

More books by Jonelle Patrick

NIGHTSHADE

FALLEN ANGEL

IDOLMAKER

PAINTED DOLL

Printed in Great Britain
by Amazon